Ms. Marvel MC Naught
2505 263rd Street Ct E
Spanaway, WA 98387-9613

P9-DYE-149

DREAMERS

DREAMERS

ANGELA ELWELL HUNT

BETHANY HOUSE PUBLISHERS
MINNEAPOLIS, MINNESOTA 55438

Dreamers
Copyright © 1996
Angela Elwell Hunt

Cover design and illustration by Peter Glöege

All rights reserved. No part of this publication may be reproduced, stored in a retrieval system, or transmitted in any form or by any means electronic, mechanical, photocopying, recording, or otherwise without the prior written permission of the publisher and copyright owners.

Published by Bethany House Publishers
A Ministry of Bethany Fellowship, Inc.
11300 Hampshire Avenue South
Minneapolis, Minnesota 55438

Unless otherwise credited, scripture quotations are from the New American Standard Bible, © The Lockman Foundation 1960, 1962, 1963, 1968, 1971, 1972, 1973, 1975, 1977.

Ramla's prayer, Ramla's healing incantation, the love poem, the poem Sagira recites for Potiphar, the poem Sagira has Joseph read, and Narmer's death dirge were all adapted from chants contained in *The Wisdom of Ancient Egypt*, translated by Joseph Kaster (Barnes and Noble: New York, 1968).

Printed in the United States of America.

ISBN 1–55661–607–4

For Gary

But I, being poor, have only my dreams;
I have spread my dreams under your feet;
Tread softly because you tread on my dreams.

The Fiddler of Dooney, William Butler Yeats

Contents

TUYA   11

POTIPHAR   75

SAGIRA   145

JOSEPH   217

MENKHEPRURE, PHARAOH TUTHMOSIS IV   277

AMENHOTEP III   339

Angela Elwell Hunt is the award-winning and bestselling author of over fifty books and a thousand magazine articles. Among her books are three historical fiction series for adults, two series for teenagers, and bestsellers like *The Tale of Three Trees*. She and her husband have two children and make their home in Florida.

Author's Note

Though the ethics and practices of the ancient Egyptians were certainly more civilized than those of many subsequent cultures, the arrangement of Egyptian royal marriages may bewilder the modern reader. The kings of Egypt's earliest dynasties married aristocratic women to augment their claims to the throne; polygamy, therefore, was an accepted part of royal life. The more wives a king had, the stronger was his position.

Unlike most of the world, where inheritances passed from father to son, Egyptian property descended from mother to daughter. A husband retained property and position as long as his wife lived. Upon her death, her daughter and her daughter's husband inherited the wife's property. Each pharaoh, therefore, safeguarded the throne for himself and his sons by marrying the family heiress no matter how closely she was related to him. The age of the heiress-bride did not matter—she might be an aged woman or an infant. The marriage was not necessarily consummated.

Normally the son of a king married his sister and made her the Great Wife, the highest-ranking queen. He then took other wives to ensure legitimate heirs. The marriage of a king to his sister or daughter was not considered improper for either moral or genetic reasons. The ranking heir to the throne, the Crown Prince, was often the child of a lesser queen, so the family avoided the possible negative genetic effects of what we would consider incestuous marriages. In later dynasties, Egyptian kings also married foreign princesses to keep peace in the buffer states between Egypt and neighboring kingdoms.

The pharaohs and queens mentioned in this book live in the annals of Egyptian history. Joseph, Potiphar, and Potiphar's wife endure in the pages of Holy Scripture. At one point, the two records must intersect.

This, then, is the story of the Hebrew and the Egyptians who dreamed.

TUYA

And they said to one another, "Here comes this dreamer! Now then, come and let us kill him and throw him into one of the pits; and we will say, 'A wild beast devoured him.' Then let us see what will become of his dreams!"

Genesis 37:19–20

~~~~ Prologue ~~~~

Dothan

THE COLLISION OF BONES AND ROCK STOPPED HIS fall. He did not immediately lose consciousness but gasped in the depths of the narrow cistern, his limbs and tongue and vision paralyzed by shock and a wave of unspeakable horror. Murder had gleamed in their eyes. Did they truly hate him so much?

Pinpricks of pain ripped along every nerve of his body, and after a moment of senseless suppression, Joseph released the scream clawing in his throat. The sound echoed through the rock-walled cistern and grew into a chorus of agonized cries. From somewhere above him, his brothers heard. And laughed.

Familiar voices, crackling sharply in hostility, came spiraling down from the mouth of the cavern. "Hear that? The dreamer is not hurt badly enough. We should have found a deeper pit."

"The brat is not so high and mighty now. Yet just last month he had visions of authority and power!"

"They were but the dreams of a seventeen-year-old, for all youths think themselves invincible and immortal. Even you, Dan, were of such a mind when you were his age."

"Dan never had the gall to predict that even our father would bow down to him. Yet our father scrapes before the boy already, he gives Joseph everything—"

"We should kill him, I tell you. If he survives, this talebearer will run to our father. He will take even our birthrights, for he is the pampered favorite—"

"Judah is right, our father sides with the would-be king in every argument. Have you noticed how the old man smiles at him? My stomach churns when I think of it. My own son is older, stronger, and better-favored, and yet—"

"I despise his pride, as do you." Reuben's stately voice hushed the others and echoed in the pit. Listening below, the boy bit his lip in an effort to quiet his involuntary moaning as Reuben continued: "I, too, have reason to hate him. I should receive the firstborn's inheritance, but I know our father will honor this stripling with the largest share of his goods. But we are of the same flesh. I cannot kill him and neither can you."

"Then we will have someone else do it," Dan replied, his voice brimming with eagerness. "If you are hesitant, Reuben, I will hire someone to spill his precious blood over this cursed coat—"

"We will say a lion caught him," Levi inserted. "Our father will believe it, and we will forever be rid of the troublemaker."

Reuben's stentorian voice hushed the others. "Would you have our father die of grief?" he asked, his words bringing a measure of comfort to the boy in the pit. "We will not kill him. We shall leave him here and let him ponder his own fate. Let him who aspires to rise a king pass the night in the depths of the earth."

The brothers mumbled and murmured, but most of them moved away. "I would still like to spill his guts," Asher grumbled, his voice overriding the fading sounds of the others. "Look at him whimpering there! If he rises from this pit, our father will never forgive us for his injuries! But if we cut out his tongue, Reuben, he will never boast again."

"We will shed no blood before dinner," Reuben answered. "Come, Asher, our meal is waiting."

Joseph remained still until he was certain the last of his brothers had gone; then he struggled to focus his blurred vision on the walls around him. Reuben would not let them kill him. Reuben was respected; he would be obeyed, but for how long? Murderous intent might bring any of the brothers back during the night with a dagger thirsting for blood.

He had to escape. He pulled his heavy head from the rock and steeled himself to ignore the white-hot pain that shot along his limbs as he fumbled against the stone beneath him. His left arm would not cooperate, and when he glanced down at his side he saw why: above his elbow, where there had once been smooth skin and healthy muscle, a white shard of jagged bone protruded from an oozing red wound.

A hoarse cry escaped his lips as unconsciousness claimed him.

One

Thebes, Egypt

A HIGH-PITCHED GIGGLE BROKE THE STILLNESS OF the garden. From between the branches of the bush where she hid, Tuya saw her mistress Sagira pause in mid-step on the garden path.

"Tuya, I command you to speak," she called, peering carefully around the slender trunk of an acacia tree. "You must make more noise, or how am I to find you?"

Tuya deliberately rustled the ivy that covered the garden wall behind her, but the noise was slight and Sagira did not turn toward the sound. Finally Tuya took a deep breath and spoke up: "Life, prosperity, and health to you, my lady!"

"Aha!" Sagira turned and sprinted toward Tuya's hiding place as the slave girl darted from the bush. "I have found you!"

"But you have not caught me!" Tuya cried, arching away from Sagira's grasping hands.

The two girls ran laughing through the garden until Sagira tripped over a rock at the edge of the garden pond. Pinwheeling, she struggled to keep her balance, then surrendered to the pull of the earth and fell with a splash into the shallow water.

Tuya's heart leapt to her throat, but after a moment Sagira sat up and howled with the unrestrained glee of a twelve-year-old. Tuya laughed too, then stopped abruptly. The Lady Kahent might be watching. Would she have Tuya whipped for this mishap?

Sagira pulled dark ribbons of wet hair from her face and stood up in the knee-deep water.

"I am sorry, mistress, truly I am," Tuya said, glancing toward the house.

Sagira took a deep, happy breath. "It was not your fault, Tuya," she said, moving to the edge of the pool. Her thin linen sheath clung to her wet body and accented her budding figure. A trace of mud lay across her delicate face and her dark eyes sparkled with mischief. "Would you like me to pull you in? The water is wonderfully cool."

"No, my lady." Tuya glanced toward the house again. "I should not like to muss my dress. Your mother would not approve."

"Then I command you to keep still," Sagira said. The floating lotus plants jostled each other as she climbed out of the pool. "Our little game is not done."

Tuya obediently stood like a post, her arms hanging rigid until her mistress dripped in front of her. "There!" Sagira said, clapping wet hands upon the slave's bare shoulders. "I caught you! I win again, Tuya!"

"Yes, my lady," Tuya said, tactfully choosing not to mention Sagira's unfair advantage.

"I must," Sagira said, grinning wickedly as she flung water from her hands into Tuya's face. "After all, it is only fitting that Pharaoh's niece should win in everything she undertakes."

Tuya said nothing, but smiled in reply as Sagira whirled in front of the long, reflecting pool.

"Do you think me beautiful, Tuya?" Sagira asked, studying her image reflected in the water.

Tuya lowered her eyes as she pondered her answer. Should she speak as a friend and tease Sagira about the small gap between her front teeth? Or should she reply as a dutiful servant and assure her mistress that no girl in the two kingdoms could rival her beauty and charm?

It was not an easy decision, for Tuya had lately been reminded of the solid line between friendship and servanthood. She had been only six years old when presented as a gift for Sagira's third birthday, and as children they had shared everything together. But though she often felt like Sagira's older sister, when her mistress's red moon had begun to flow, Sagira's mother had urged her daughter to put aside her baby name and assume a mantle of dignity. Her new name, "Sagira," or "little one," referred to her diminutive size.

Tuya had never been called anything but Tuya, for slaves were not permitted the luxury of adult names, and of late, Sagira's mother, the Lady Kahent, had been quick to emphasize the great gulf that existed between masters and their slaves. Certain attitudes and actions were proper and others were not. Twice Tuya had been whipped for overstepping the bounds of propriety, but Sagira seemed not to have noticed the newfound care with which Tuya formulated her answers, attitudes, and comments.

Diplomacy won out. "You are beautiful, mistress," Tuya whispered obediently, lowering her head in a proper attitude of deference. "Lucky is the man who will be your husband."

"And you, Tuya? Do you never dream of marriage?" Sagira cocked her head and gave her friend an engaging smile. "Do you wonder what it is like to kiss a man? To sleep with him as my mother sleeps with my father?"

Tuya felt her cheeks burning. "I do not dare think of those things," she said, stealing a quick glance toward the wide doors that opened out into the courtyard. "I am your servant. I will go where you go and serve you always."

"Tuya." Sagira's tone was heavy with reproach, for she had seen her servant's frightened glance toward the house. She took Tuya's hand and pulled her into the privacy of an arbor. "There, you can speak freely now," she said, a slow smile crossing her face. "You need not fear my mother."

"I do not—"

"Do not pretend with me, Tuya. I know about the whippings. Even though you acted as though nothing had happened, I saw the mark of the lash upon your shoulders and asked Tanutamon about them. He said my mother ordered both whippings."

"I am sure I deserved them," Tuya said, her stomach tightening as her ears strained for sounds of eavesdroppers beyond the trees. Would even this conversation be reported to Lady Kahent?

Sagira's eyes lit with understanding. "You did *not* deserve it. The first time was because you were wearing my jewels, but you did not tell my mother that I asked you to model them for me. And the second time was because we were laughing together—"

"I was too familiar. A slave should not be on such close terms—"

"You are my friend, Tuya. We have laughed and cried together since I was a baby. Can we stop being friends now?"

Tuya felt a ringing impulse of hope. Sagira seemed earnest, and her mother could not see into the thickly green arbor. Perhaps she could safely open her heart.

"I do not know how to behave anymore," she confessed, slowly lifting her eyes from the ground. "Your mother says that now you are grown, I must be your servant and not your friend. And although you may confide in me, I must not speak what is on my heart, for no one cares what a slave thinks."

Sagira flushed to the roots of her hair. "She did not say such a thing!"

Tuya pressed her lips together and kept silent.

"My mother is the best mistress any slave could have," Sagira said, turning on Tuya with a flash of defensive spirit. She crossed her arms and sat on a low bench in the arbor. "Our slaves have greater freedom than those in any other house I have seen. My father is as rich in graciousness as he is in treasure."

"You are right, my lady," Tuya said, cautiously perching on the bench next to Sagira.

Sagira sniffed in satisfaction. "Well, then, you do not

need to worry about anything. And I have a surprise for you. When I am married, I shall take you out of this house and give you your freedom. Then you can marry as well, and we shall live next to each other and talk every day as we do now."

"Truly?" Hope rose from Tuya's heart like a suddenly startled bird.

"Truly." Sagira's eyes glowed as she contemplated her future generosity. "And then you shall tell me all about your husband just as you told me about what to expect with the flowering of my red moon. And when you have a baby"—Sagira looked down and twisted her hands—"you shall tell me if it is truly as terrible as it seems."

"It cannot be too terrible," Tuya said, realizing that Sagira spoke now out of fear. She softened her voice. "I am sure that bearing the child of a man you love must be a great joy. And the priests say that offerings to the goddess Taweret will keep evil away from a woman giving birth."

They sat in silence for a moment, pondering the mysterious rites of womanhood, which they were just beginning to understand. Overhead, a hawk scrolled the hot updrafts, precise and unconcerned, a part of the sky. Tuya envied his freedom.

"Do you ever think about love, Tuya?" Sagira said, running her hands through her wet hair.

"Love, mistress?"

"Yes. How and when it begins. My mother says love comes after marriage, but I have heard scandalous things from some of the other servants. They say one of the serving girls fell in love with a shepherd boy. For the love of this shepherd she openly defied Tanutamon, so he sold her that morning for her rebellion."

"I am sure," Tuya said, a creeping uneasiness rising from the bottom of her heart, "that the captain of your father's slaves is wise. Rebellion cannot be tolerated."

Sagira tilted her head and gave Tuya a searching look.

"You would not do that, would you, Tuya? Fall in love with some boy and leave me?"

"I do not think that kind of love is meant for one like me," Tuya answered slowly. "I love you, mistress. I want to follow wherever you go. I have not left your side in nine years and am not likely to leave it now."

"Nor would I have you leave it," Sagira answered, suddenly serious. She reached out and clasped Tuya's hands. "By all the gods, Tuya, when I think of marrying and leaving my father's house, my heart goes into shock. Only because I know you will be with me can I think about going at all."

"There is no need to worry," Tuya said, her heart warming at the light of dependence in her young mistress's eyes. "Your mother and father are in no hurry to find a husband for you. You are no commoner, Sagira. Pharaoh himself must be consulted."

Sagira sighed in relief, and the mocking smile returned to her face. "Then we will marry at the same time and you will be my friend always," she said, planting a brief kiss upon Tuya's cheek. She dropped Tuya's hands and stood to stretch. "Oh, this wet dress grows cold! Come, find me a dry garment and bind my hair. We will play the hiding game in my chamber until my mother tells us it is time to eat."

Tuya smiled and hurried to match the eager step of her mistress.

The girls' happy voices danced ahead of them into the house. Reclining upon a pillow-laden couch in the villa's reception room, Kahent heard their carefree chatter. "Our daughter is growing up," she whispered, her dark, liquid voice intended for her husband's ears alone.

Intent upon studying the scrolls upon his lap, Donkor only grunted.

"It is time, I believe," Kahent persisted, sitting up, "to approach Pharaoh about finding Sagira a suitable husband.

Surely the king knows his sister has a daughter of noble blood.''

"Pharaoh knows what?'' Donkor answered, looking up.

Kahent sighed, careful not to let her frustration show. "Our king knows we have a daughter. Now he must be told that she is of marriageable age. Her red moon has flowed twice now.''

"She is too young.'' Donkor waved his hand carelessly and returned his attention to his scrolls.

Kahent was not deterred. She had borne her husband's indifference for years. Perhaps if he had been more attentive, or she more beautiful, they would have had more than one child. But Donkor cared more for his treasures than for the people who lived in his house. After resigning herself to her husband's cold heart, Kahent had invested her love and life in her daughter.

She stood and leaned back against one of the tall columns in the room, steeling herself for a confrontation. "Sagira is young,'' she said, not daring to contradict him, "so we have time to find the best man for her.'' She lifted her chin so the beads in the heavy wig she wore clicked together as they fell back against her smooth shoulders. "This endeavor will not require your effort, my husband, only your permission. Grant me your blessing to speak to my brother about our daughter. It is for your honor that I must do this.''

"What?'' Donkor's brow furrowed as he looked up from his scroll, and Kahent knew that he had only half heard her words. "A husband? Pharaoh will see to it when I publish the news of our daughter's maturity.''

"We must proceed slowly,'' Kahent said, with a cautionary lift of her finger. "We should find a suitable man before we reveal our intentions; then we may drop the suggestion upon Pharaoh's ear. Our daughter's husband must be close to Pharaoh, for the line of kings flows through my veins and through Sagira's. If something should happen to

Pharaoh or to his sons—" She finished with an expressive shrug.

Donkor gave her a smile of reluctant admiration. "I have seen eyes like yours in the faces of my enemies," he said, lifting his scroll again. "I would not like to have your determination set against me."

"Why should you?" she asked, glad that he had looked at her with the pleasant light of amusement in his eyes. "There is one other thing, Donkor. I must be rid of the servant girl Tuya."

"Tuya?" The scroll dropped again. "But Sagira would be lost without her. It is impossible to imagine one without the other—"

"Have you looked at Tuya lately, my husband?" Kahent found it impossible to keep an edge from her voice. "The slave has become quite attractive. If Tuya follows our daughter into her marital home, Tuya will capture the groom's attention, not Sagira."

"Sagira is lovely," Donkor said, scoffing. "I cannot believe that you, her mother, would belittle her so—"

"I do not dispute Sagira's loveliness," Kahent answered, sinking gracefully into a gilded settee. She reached for one of the figs piled upon a golden platter on a nearby stand. "But I want to give her every possible advantage. Sagira is attractive, but a woman must believe herself beautiful to become so. And I fear that Sagira will compare herself to Tuya, whom the gods have unfairly blessed."

"So how do you intend to separate the girls?" Donkor's voice had flattened and Kahent knew that she had already lost his attention to the papyrus scroll in his lap.

"I will make an offering to the goddess Bastet," Kahent murmured, bringing the fig to her lips. "She will find the best way."

Two

THE GLARE OF THE DESERT SUN BLINDED POTIPHAR for a moment. He raised his hand to shade his eyes and nodded in silent satisfaction as the bodies were laid before him: twenty-six rebels dead, their blood staining the sand; thirty-three others now in the bonds of defeat. He would present them to his royal master, Pharaoh Amenhotep II, and further prove that he had earned the name *Potiphar*, captain of the guard, the appointed one of Pharaoh.

He signaled for his men to leave the dead as a warning to any others who might invade Pharaoh's peaceful delta. Let their mongrel bodies be consumed by worms and rats; their immortal souls did not deserve to travel through the afterlife.

"Potiphar!"

The cry from a warrior on a cliff above them wrested his eyes from the dead.

"Horus, the falcon god, salutes you!"

The warrior lifted his hand to the sky where a hawk circled lazily above the blood-soaked sands. Potiphar smiled in reply. "So be it," he said, turning from the grisly scene toward his awaiting chariot. He murmured under his breath as he walked, "But it is not Horus's approval I seek."

He had entered royal service during the latter part of the reign of Tuthmosis III, the pharaoh whose first battle had been to unseat his stepmother from the throne of the Upper and Lower Kingdoms. A common man with an uncommon love for battle, Potiphar joined the king's army for the campaign that culminated at the fortress of Megiddo, Armageddon. Overflowing with youthful enthusiasm, drive, and shrewd intuitions, Potiphar discovered that the color of war affected him like a fever. In a moment of reckless abandon, he approached the king's generals and suggested that the Egyptian army cross Mount Carmel to surprise the enemy from behind.

Tuthmosis appreciated the subtlety of the strategy. The Asiatics expected the Egyptians to approach in a direct attack from the southern plains, so when the Egyptian cavalry appeared suddenly on the northern horizon, the panicked Asiatics fled into their fortress. Leaving Potiphar to maintain the siege of the stronghold, Tuthmosis raided the lands of neighboring kings and chieftains, then returned to the starving fortress to claim his victory. Pharaoh completed his conquest by harvesting the crops of the land. The Asiatics, who had to eat, bowed before the Egyptian king in submission.

The king's victory at Megiddo secured Potiphar's place under the royal eye. Under Tuthmosis III, Potiphar led armies that conquered lands from the fifth cataract of the Nile to the Euphrates River. Tuthmosis, like Potiphar, relished the thrill of war. His standing army included hundreds of ferocious Nubian warriors whose ancestors had won battles for previous pharaohs.

Iron-willed and hard as stone, Potiphar thought himself invincible until he was taken prisoner on one northward expedition with the Nubians. After his capture, he spat in his captors' faces, fully expecting to die. The king of Kadesh, a wily and able adversary, wielded his sword and extracted from Potiphar what many would have considered to be the ultimate sacrifice a man could make for his king.

But after days of blinding white pain, Potiphar did not die. A contingent of Egyptian troops stormed the enemy king's camp and rescued their general, bringing the wounded Potiphar back to stand before Tuthmosis. The fading warrior-king, in the fifty-fifth year of his reign, proclaimed before his court that Potiphar was a friend of Pharaoh and would henceforth serve at home as captain of the king's bodyguard. Potiphar was awarded a villa, a staff of slaves, and a secure position. But before Potiphar's body could heal, the great king died.

From his bed of convalescence, Potiphar watched with some trepidation as the Crown Prince assumed the throne. Twenty-year-old Amenhotep II loved the sea and had spent most of his princely preparation at the Egyptian naval base at Per-nefer, near Memphis. Potiphar wondered how the new king would feel about assuming his father's court at Thebes, but assume it he must. The Pharaoh of Egypt could not afford to appear weak or indecisive. With the mighty general Tuthmosis III dead, the Asiatic city-states and their allies would undoubtedly attempt to throw off the Egyptian yoke. They would put the military prowess of the young new king to the test.

In the months that followed, neither Potiphar nor the far-flung cities found the new king lacking. Excelling in battle, archery, and horsemanship, Amenhotep delighted in hand-to-hand combat. With Potiphar at his side, he led his troops into battle, howling in royal rage, and often the mere sight of his ferocious visage dismayed enemy troops into immediate surrender.

Now in the thirteenth year of his reign, Amenhotep had accomplished his military goals. The far-flung provinces dutifully sent tribute to their king and toiled to keep peace in the land. Military maneuvers now involved only infrequent skirmishes in rebellious territories, and Potiphar rarely rode with the army. He found it difficult to admit, but at forty-four, he was tired of the wind in his face and the desert sand in his teeth. But he continued to venture onto the battlefield in the hope that a spectacular victory would bring him the one prize he lacked—the Gold of Praise to encircle his neck.

The Gold of Praise—the most obvious and visible symbol of Pharaoh's favor—was a solid gold chain awarded to the man who had proved himself a friend of Pharaoh. Though Tuthmosis had proclaimed Potiphar his friend, that noble king had died before presenting his wounded general with the Gold of Praise.

Potiphar had earned it. If the gods were just, he would yet wear it around his neck in this life.

Three

A BITTER WIND HOWLED AROUND THE CARAVAN, and Joseph found himself wincing with every step across the desert sand. A stout rope of hemp bound his wrists tightly together, and the end of the rope connected him to the saddle of a sour-faced camel belonging to a caravan of Ishmaelites from Gilead. With each step of the Ishmaelites' beast, the rope tightened and tugged on Joseph's broken arm.

Every step, every breath brought excruciating pain. He had fainted when they first wrenched his arm to tie him with the other prisoners bound for Egypt, and one of the traders tossed a bucketful of foul water in his face to wake him. Now Joseph stumbled through the desert in a stupor of agony and grief. In lucid moments he wondered why his life had taken such a vicious and unpredictable turn.

His father, the one constant, loving figure in his life since his mother's death, would feel this loss even more keenly than the grief of losing his beloved Rachel. "At least I have you," his father had often said, his gnarled hand patting Joseph's as they walked together. "As long as I have you, Rachel lives on in your eyes."

How could his brothers do this to their father? To him? Why did they hate him so?

Nothing in his past warranted such treatment. A loving and obedient son to his father Jacob, he had been the favored firstborn of Jacob's preferred wife, Rachel. His brothers were less than doting, probably because they were envious of the close relationship he shared with their father. When Rachel died while giving birth to Benjamin, Jacob took Joseph aside and spilled his heart, opening a window through which Joseph glimpsed a love as strong as God and a grief as deep as death. For the first time, Jacob spoke of his personal history, explaining to Joseph how each of his other ten brothers came to be born. The sons of Leah were conceived in compassion, the sons of Bilhah from duty, the sons of Zilpah from guilt. Only with Rachel, Jacob told his beloved Joseph, were sons conceived and given life in love.

Perhaps it was this knowledge that gave birth to his dreams. One night not long after his mother's death, Joseph had dreamed that he and his brothers were binding sheaves of grain in the field. Suddenly Joseph's sheaf jerked itself out of his hands as if it possessed a life of its own. Dancing away from the rope with which he would have tied it, the tall sheaf moved to the center of the cleared field and stood upright. Within minutes, the sheaves of his brothers were similarly animated, but those sheaves circled around Joseph's, then bent into human form and prostrated themselves on the ground before the golden sheaf in the center of the circle.

His brothers had not found the dream at all entertaining. "Do you intend to reign over us?" Judah sneered the next morning when Joseph told them of the strange vision. "Will you actually rule us?" Only Reuben's diplomatic intervention had prevented a fight between the brothers.

The next night Joseph had a similar dream. In this dream he sat upon a star, and the sun and moon and eleven stars came near and bowed to him. When he described the dream the next morning, even his father laughed in derision. "What is this?" Jacob asked, his face darkening to a deep shade of red as he sat before the breakfast fire. "Will your departed mother and I join your brothers and actually bow down before you? Surely you think too much of yourself, Joseph, and of these dreams. Forget them, my son, and remember when pride comes, disgrace follows."

His father's words proved strangely prophetic. Joseph had found a quiet pleasure in those dreams while he dwelled securely in his father's favor. But now, in the harsh light of reality and the bitterness of pain, those mocking fantasies seemed as false as vows made in wine. He had dared to dream that God would honor him as primary inheritor of the blessings and promises of Abraham, but those hopes, too, were surely foolish. Disgrace and despair walked with him across the desert.

From the chatter of the Ishmaelites, Joseph knew he was on his way to the "black land," Egypt. He had heard much of the place, for his great-grandfather Abraham had found trouble among its people. Plagued by fear and blessed with a beautiful wife, Abraham lied to the Egyptians and told them that Sarai was his sister, not his wife. Unaware that he was taking another man's wife, Pharaoh took Sarai into the royal harem and suffered the plagues of God for his sin. When the truth was finally revealed, Pharaoh asked Abraham to take his wife, his livestock, all that he had, and leave the country. The king's army had escorted Abraham from the land to insure that nothing of him remained behind.

But now Abraham's great-grandson was returning to Egypt as a bloody and broken slave, reeking of camels and filth. Was this God's divine punishment for Abraham's sin? Were the Egyptians now to have their vengeance upon one of his descendants?

Joseph lifted his head in stubborn pride as the rope bit into his wrists and pulled him forward. Whatever happened, he would not repeat Abraham's sin. He would not lie. But to preserve his life, neither would he admit to anyone that he was of the house and lineage of the one they had known as Abram.

⟿ Four ⟾

KAHENT WOKE BEFORE THE SUN'S RISING AND dressed in her finest garment, a narrow sheath of white linen that fell in intricate pleats from her shoulders to the floor. She selected her favorite beaded necklaces, bracelets, and belt, then sat at her table to paint her face. Dipping an exquisitely carved copper applicator into her kohl container, she outlined her eyes and then dabbed her fingers into a secret compartment inside the carved ivory duck on her dressing table. With a deft movement, she swiped a mixture of ground malachite and animal fat across her eyelids, effectively giving them a golden green glow. Green, she reflected, was the color of fertility. It was fitting that she remind the goddess that fertility was the root and purpose of the petition Kahent would bring today.

When her face had been properly painted, Kahent's maid lifted a heavy wig from its stand and placed it on her mistress's head. Like all Egyptian noblewomen, Kahent wore her hair clipped short, a necessity because no woman of standing went out in public without her wig. The wig was massive, as wide as Kahent's shoulders and several layers thick. A lush fringe of bangs accented the dark lines around her eyes, and the beads which had been woven into the ends of the strands of sheep's wool clicked together with a pleasing sound.

Moving quietly, Kahent slipped her feet into her papyrus sandals, then lifted a bag of silver from her husband's treasure chest. Offerings of fruit and meat would not be enough for today. She planned on asking the goddess Bastet for a serious boon, and a noteworthy offering would certainly be required.

Her maids stood back when she was ready, and Kahent pointed wordlessly to the one who would accompany her to the temple. The others blinked in relief, and the chosen maid lifted the earthen lamp from its stand and moved toward the outer courtyard where a special bundle waited. Kahent had chosen the goddess Bastet as her patron god, and since cats were sacred to that goddess, more than thirty cats lived within the walls of this household. When they died, Kahent paid handsomely to have the animals mummified and wrapped in linen bandages. A storeroom near the temple of the house was stocked with cat-shaped coffins in which the mummified cats rested in their eternal journey.

The sleepy servant lifted one of the papyrus coffins into her arms and laid it across her mistress's open palms. Reverently, Kahent carried the burden through the gate and led the way through the streets of Thebes to the temple dedicated to the goddess Bastet.

———

After entering the rectangular enclosure surrounding the temple, Kahent left her maid in the outer courtyard and carried the small coffin into Per-Hair, the House of Rejoicing. In front of its towers stood twin statues, two cats carefully carved of green marble. Dark crevices loomed where the eyes should have been, and golden rings hung from the nostrils. A silver pectoral with the sacred eye of Horus decorated the chests of both animals, signifying the cat was protected from evil by Horus himself.

Kahent always felt a sudden chill whenever she saw an amulet depicting the wadjet eye. According to the legends of the gods, the eye of Horus was torn out by Seth, a god of evil, in the struggle for the throne of Egypt. Once in a temple play which Donkor forced her to attend, an actor portraying Seth had actually plucked the eye from an unfortunate prisoner chosen to depict Horus. After the bloodletting, Kahent had left her husband's side and fled the theater, knowing full well that the ancient legend would require the prisoner also be dismembered before the play's end.

There were no bloody legends associated with Bastet. She was the daughter of Re, the sun-god, and represented the benign power of the sun to ripen crops. After kneeling before the two regal statues, Kahent proceeded to the sacred burial grounds and placed her cat coffin in an empty space. She bowed her head to the ground and murmured words of allegiance, then walked slowly back to the Per-Hair and passed through the entryway.

The morning sun had begun to beat upon the earth in relentless waves of energy, but inside the House of Rejoicing the air was pleasant and cool. Moving through a long, columned hall adorned with wall-carvings of the king and queen, she came to the chamber known as Gem-Bastet—the Finding of Bastet. Ahead of her stretched a long, narrow court crowned by an altar atop a flight of steps. Beyond the altar a causeway ran toward yet another pair of lofty columns. Kahent passed through them into a second court, then into a third, and finally into the smallest sanctuary. She was one of the privileged few, she knew. By reading her dress and jewels, the temple priests and priestesses allowed her to pass, knowing that the offering in the bag at her waist would permit entry into the holiest of holies.

The floor rose at a gentle angle under Kahent's feet as the roof gradually lowered, and soon her feet brought her to the innermost sanctuary of the goddess. The goddess sat upon a platform behind the altar; her priestesses hovered near with towels and basins of water to wash and dress the goddess for the day. A pile of discarded nightclothes lay in a heap upon the floor, and a slave stood nearby bearing a platter of fruit and meat for the goddess's breakfast.

Kahent fell to her knees and bent her head to touch the floor three times. She was as devout in her practice of religion as Donkor was indifferent in his, yet still the goddess had apparently blessed them. Kahent and her husband and daughter were strong and not afflicted with the many diseases which struck less wealthy people. In gratitude and reverence, Kahent remained upon the floor. She would wait until the goddess had breakfasted before presenting her petition.

The priestesses adorned the goddess with robes and jewels, then placed the food on the altar. Bastet's attendants waited for several moments in silence as the tall statue stared down upon the platter, her emerald eyes twinkling in the shafting rays of sunlight from the high clerestory windows. At a signal from a shaven-headed priestess, the food was whisked away, the goddess clothed in a fresh collar, and a priest solemnly announced that Bastet would receive visitors and deliver oracles.

Kahent was the only petitioner in the sanctuary. She took a deep breath and clasped her hands to her breast. "Oh, most divine Bastet," she began, kneeling before the imposing statue. "Behold your servant who came into being from your goodness! I have a daughter of marriageable age who needs a worthy husband!"

Her words echoed in the stillness of the chamber, yet nothing moved. Kahent waited, breathing in the bittersweet aromas of the burning incense, the tiled floor hard under her knees. The few priests who moved in the shadows beyond the goddess paid her no heed, as if wealthy women came every day to implore their goddess for such favors.

No answer came to her, nothing at all. She shifted uneasily, not sure how to proceed, then a flat, inflectionless voice cut through the silence. "Bastet will hear you."

A young, thin woman stepped out of the shadows, the pale skin of her shaved head gleaming in the torchlight. "The majesty of Bastet says to you, 'Listen to my servant Ramla who will work my magic. Tell her what you will and she will relay my divine message.' "

Kahent studied the girl. Tall and slender, she wore the

simple white robe of a priestess with a golden collar about her neck, a symbol of the goddess's ownership. The girl could have been anywhere from fifteen to thirty, so unlined was her handsomely sculpted face. Kahent made a mental note of approval, but as her eyes traveled downward one sight gave her pause: the girl's right hand was terribly malformed. Only three fingers grew where five should have been. How could this be? Most malformed children were thrown to the crocodiles of the Nile.

" 'Do not let the sight of my servant disturb you,' " the priestess went on, her voice powerfully urgent. Her eyes hardened and Kahent knew the girl had seen the revulsion in her glance. " 'She has been given graces and power to atone for her physical losses. Ramla will serve you well.' "

With these closing words, the slender girl bent at the waist and bowed before Kahent.

"So be it," Kahent said, frowning. She paused but a moment, then dropped the bag of silver at the girl's feet. "My petition is a matter of the heart. My daughter, who must marry well, has spent nearly every day of her life with a slave who far surpasses her in beauty. I want to rid my daughter of this girl, but do not know how to proceed without arousing her to anger or breaking her heart."

Straightening into the ramrod posture of a royal guard, the priestess closed her eyes and tilted her head as if she were listening to a far-off voice. After a moment, her face cracked into a smile and she nodded drowsily.

"Yes, Bastet," she murmured, opening her eyes. She shared the smile with Kahent. "Love cannot easily be killed, but it can be distracted," she said, casually tossing the bag of silver onto the altar. She walked to Kahent's side and took the lady's arm, gracefully lifting her to her feet. "Take me to your home, lady, and give me a day with your daughter. Bastet has directed me to make the proper spells and incantations. I can divine the future and will not leave your daughter's side until all be well."

Stunned by the magnanimous gesture, Kahent allowed

Ramla to lead her from the sanctuary.

———

"You sent for me, Mother?" Sagira asked, coming into the reception room. She was about to complain about the interruption of her playtime, but the sight of the stranger with her mother left her speechless. The young woman who sat in one of the gilded chairs had an unearthly air about her, and from her shaved head and the collar of gold about her neck, Sagira knew the stranger had to be a priestess from one of the temples.

"Sagira, this is Ramla," her mother said, gesturing to her visitor with a graceful hand. "She is a priestess at the Temple of Bastet."

Feeling awkward and gauche before such an important person, Sagira barely managed to nod in acknowledgment.

"I do not live at the temple all the time," Ramla said, giving Sagira a warm smile. "Only one month out of four. Tomorrow I begin my time of absence, and your gracious mother has said that I may spend three months as part of your household."

"We need the blessings of the goddess," Sagira's mother said, studying Sagira with careful eyes. "Do you not agree, my daughter?"

"Yes," Sagira stammered, managing a crooked smile. For what reason did they need the special favor of the gods?

"I am especially looking forward to getting to know you," Ramla said, rising from her chair. In that moment Sagira saw the woman's misshapen hand and she knew from her mother's disapproving gasp that she had not managed to disguise her reaction of disgust.

But Ramla did not seem to care. "Pay no attention to things that can be seen with the eyes," she said, reaching for Sagira's hand with her whole one. "I can teach you how to discern with your heart. The gods have compensated for my missing fingers with other gifts, and I can teach you secrets you have never known. I can read the future for you, Sagira."

"Truly?" Fear fell from her like a discarded cloak and wonder slipped into its place.

"Yes." Ramla's voice was low and soothing, and her hand slipped up to stroke Sagira's hair. "Kneel before me, child, while I work a spell of divination."

Sagira caught her breath as she fell to her knees. Her mother had often participated in such religious rituals, but until now Sagira had been considered too much a child to have a priestess divine her future. That her mother would now allow such a practice spoke more of Sagira's maturity than the flowering of her red moon.

As Sagira's mother hurried to fetch the family's silver bowl, Sagira smoothed her face of all traces of curiosity and eagerness and tried to copy the look of earnest interest that her mother wore. A moment later Lady Kahent returned with the bowl of blackened silver. The bottom of the inner bowl had been engraved with the figure of the jackal-headed Anubis, the opener of roads for the dead.

Ramla accepted the bowl and placed it on a stand, then filled it with Nile water from a pitcher. As she murmured fervent prayers and incantations, she poured a small amount of fine oil into the bowl from another clay vial. As the oil swirled and eddied over the surface of the water, Ramla closed her eyes and lifted her hands.

Hail to you, O Re-Harakhte, Father of the gods!
Hail to you, O ye seven Hathors,
Who are adorned with strings of red thread!
Hail to you, Anubis, Lord of heaven and earth!
Cause Bastet to appear before me,
Like an ox after grass,
Like a mother after her children,
Send her to me so that I may ask the future of Sagira,
Born of Donkor and Kahent!

The sweet incense in the room seemed suddenly overpowering, and a cold lump grew in Sagira's stomach as she looked up at the priestess. Beads of perspiration glistened at the woman's temple; her features twisted into a maddening grimace. Chilly tendrils of apprehension wound through Sagira's body as the priestess opened her black eyes and seemed to stare straight through her. Strange words flew from the seer's mouth, and suddenly her eyes darted down to the bowl where oil swirled upon the waters.

"I see, Sagira, that you are surrounded by people who love you," Ramla said in an awed, husky whisper. A slight smile twisted one corner of her face. "You are much loved. You will marry a man of great importance, according to your parents' wishes, and Pharaoh will pronounce his blessing on the union."

"Children?" Lady Kahent called from a corner of the room. "Will she have children?"

Drops of perspiration shone like gold on the young woman's forehead. "You will be remembered through all time," the priestess droned, her eyes as dark as caverns. "As long as men walk upon the earth, they will speak of you. Your memory will be immortal—"

"Me?" Sagira blurted out, disbelieving.

Ramla began to tremble and her hands flew to the sides of the bowl as she steadied herself. "Not your name," she whispered hoarsely. "Your . . . role. You will leave an imprint upon the sands of time that cannot be erased."

At these words the seer's dark eyes rolled up into her head, and she slumped to the floor, her limbs thrashing in a violent seizure. Sagira put her hands to her face and began to shriek, but Kahent flew to Ramla's side and held the woman's flailing arms. "For you she has borne this," she said, looking up at her daughter with something like awe in her eyes. "What a destiny! You will be remembered, daughter, longer than Pharaoh, for more years than those who built the ancient pyramids."

Pressing her hand over her mouth, Sagira stopped her frantic crying. The body of the priestess stilled, but the young woman did not move. Kahent left Ramla on the floor and reached for Sagira with her arms outstretched.

"My little one," she crooned, enfolding her daughter in an embrace. "How often did I dream that you would bring glory to this house! And now I find that your glory will eclipse that of all other women!"

"She didn't say that," Sagira mumbled, her mind whirling with fear and confusion. "She only said I would be remembered. And not my name, but my role." She raised her head to look at her mother. "What can that mean?"

Kahent pressed her lips together and helped Sagira rise from the floor. She said nothing as she led her daughter to the couch; then she motioned for Sagira to sit beside her.

"It can only mean one thing," she said, a smile dimpling her cheek. "And you must never speak of this to anyone, for to do so would be treason."

"Treason?" Sagira felt a shiver pass down her spine.

"Yes." Kahent pressed her finger to her lips as she thoughtfully weighed her words. "As you know, daughter, the royal blood of the two kingdoms passes down from woman to woman. Amenhotep, my brother, is Pharaoh because he married the heiress Merit-Amon, the daughter of Tuthmosis."

"But you are also a daughter of Tuthmosis," Sagira pointed out.

"Yes, but my mother was a lesser wife."

"What does this have to do with me?" Sagira asked, disturbed by the wildly expectant look in her mother's eyes.

"I am also a daughter of Tuthmosis," Kahent answered, her voice a thin whisper in the room. "If the gods will that Pharaoh's house, all his sons and daughters, should be destroyed, I will be the heiress. And when I die you will be the heiress, Sagira. Whomever you marry will be Pharaoh, and your sons and daughters will continue the dynasty."

The words swirled around Sagira like a mist, and she clutched the arm of her chair, stunned by the revelation. "Your *role*," Kahent whispered, the breath from her lips stirring the hair at Sagira's ear. "You will be the mother of pharaohs. The mother of a new dynasty, the greatest in all Egypt. You and your children will leave an imprint upon the sands of time that *cannot be erased.*"

Kahent's head fell upon Sagira's shoulder in a bout of joyous weeping, but Sagira sat still, thinking. She had been relieved enough to hear that she would marry well. This prophecy of immortal influence was too much to comprehend.

———————

Tuya noticed a difference in her mistress almost immediately. In the days following Sagira's introduction to the strange priestess of Bastet, she seemed withdrawn and tense, but she would not give an explanation for her altered mood. In the mornings as Tuya arranged her mistress's toilet, Sagira was snappish and irritable, quick to complain about Tuya's heavy hand or chattering tongue. The long hours of play in the courtyard disappeared entirely as Sagira began to spend more time alone with Ramla. Once when Tuya casually asked what Ramla and Sagira talked about, her young mistress turned on her in fury and said if Tuya did not mind her manners she would have Tanutamon administer yet another whipping.

Two weeks after Ramla had come to live in the household, Tuya made her way to the kitchen. Taharka, the chief butler in Donkor's house, had always been a friend and gave both girls sweet treats from his lunch box whenever they managed to sneak into his workroom. On this day he was tasting a new wine especially selected for a party Donkor intended to give for several noble guests, and he had little time to spare for a lonely slave girl abandoned by her mistress.

"Taharka, may I speak with you?"

"Not now, my pretty one," Taharka said, frowning as he looked at her sad face. "The master has invited guests to eat, drink, and make merry through the night. Spiced wine and beer, the wine jars, and even the alabaster vases have to be made ready."

"May I help?"

Taharka paused, then smiled as though in pity for her. "You are bored?"

"I would love to help. Surely there is something I can do."

Taharka nodded. "All right. You can see to the perfumed cones. The animal fat must be set out in the sun to liquefy, then mixed with the precious oils of perfume. When they are mixed, bring them into the coolness of the house and pour the liquid into the molds."

"I can do that," Tuya replied, moving toward the large copper pots of animal fat. The cones of perfumed fat were a treat enjoyed only by the nobility, for perfume was precious. As each guest arrived a perfumed cone was placed upon his head. As the afternoon and the party wore on, the cones would slowly melt and run down the heavy wigs and drip down the sweltering skin of the overheated guests.

Tuya lifted one of the pots and staggered toward the doorway, but halted when Taharka let out an ear-splitting scream. She dropped the pot, startled, and whirled to see him standing at a table, his hand purpling before her eyes. A scorpion scuttled across the table.

"I am bit!" the butler screamed, his eyes wide in fright and pain. "Oh, daughter of Seth, why am I bit tonight?"

Obeying a primitive instinct, Tuya scooped up a handful of ashes from the fire pit, mixed them with some of the animal fat, and placed the cool mixture over the rapidly swelling spot on Taharka's hand. Stunned by the pain, the butler slipped to the floor and leaned against the wall, still holding his wounded hand out in front of him.

As if in response to his call, Ramla and Sagira appeared in the doorway.

"What happened to Taharka?" Sagira snapped, her eyes meeting Tuya's as if she were somehow to blame.

"A scorpion," Tuya said. She lowered her eyes so Sagira

would not see the sense of betrayal Tuya was sure she had revealed there.

Ramla stepped dramatically into the room and lifted her hands. "I am a priestess of Bastet and have come to lay bare the poison which is in the limbs of Taharka, Donkor's cup-bearer. As Bastet lives, so shall live Taharka!"

Taharka clenched his jaw against the pain as Ramla began to sway in front of him. "You, poison, shall not take your stand in his forehead; Hekayit, Lady of the Forehead, is against you! You shall not take your stand in his eyes; Horus Mekhenty-irty, Lord of the Eyes, is against you! You shall not take your stand in his ears; Geb, Lord of the Ear, is against you!"

Tuya watched Sagira's face as Ramla continued the roll call of the various gods. Her mistress's eyes shone toward the interloper with devotion and admiration.

"You shall not take your stand in his nose; Khenem-tchau of Hesret, Lady of the Nose, is against you! You shall not take your stand in his lips; Anubis, Lord of the Lips, is against you! You shall not take your stand in his tongue; Sefekh-aahui, Lady of the Tongue, is against you! You shall not take your stand in his neck; Wadjety, Lady of the Neck, is against you!"

Taharka groaned as Ramla called out for the gods of the arm, back, side, liver, lung, spleen, intestines, ribs, and flesh to stand against the scorpion bite. A crowd of servants began to gather as Ramla continued to chant, calling upon the gods of the buttocks, perineum, thighs, knees, shins, soles, and toenails.

Finally, as sweat dripped from her brows, Ramla stood still and raised her voice in a terrible shriek. "You, poison, shall not take your stand anywhere in him! You shall not find refreshment there! Go down to the ground! I have in-canted against you, I have spat upon you, I have drunk you! As Horus lives, so does Taharka. Go down to the ground! I know you, I know your name! Come from the right hand, poison, come from the left hand! Come in saliva, come in

vomit, come in urine! Come hither at my utterance according as I say! Grant a path to Taharka! As the sun shall rise
and as the Nile shall flow, so shall Taharka be better than
he was!"

She ended in a hoarse shriek and threw her arms upward toward the heavens. As if on cue, Taharka leaned
sideways and vomited onto the packed earthen floor. Tuya
frowned and lifted the poultice she had used to cover the
scorpion bite. The wound was still red and slightly swollen, but seemed less violent than it had before.

The assembled crowd cheered Ramla, and Sagira
slipped her arm around the priestess's waist and helped the
exhausted woman from the room. Two slaves from the
kitchen lifted Taharka to his feet, and after a moment Tuya
found herself in the workroom with a handful of other servants while guests were arriving at the entryway.

"Hurry," Tuya commanded, gesturing toward the pots
of animal fat and the trays of fruit. "The party begins and
our master will not care that Taharka has met with a scorpion. This food must be ready, so help me!"

Knowing that Tanutamon's lash awaited anyone who
displeased Donkor, the slaves did as they were told.

Kahent sighed in satisfaction as her slave poured a
pitcher of cool water over her tired back. She lay on a slab
of polished granite in the bathroom of the house, and her
maid had just massaged the worries of a hectic week into
oblivion. Not that her worries were major ones. In the three
weeks since the priestess Ramla had come to dwell with
them, Sagira had spent less and less time with Tuya. It
would not be difficult now to manufacture an excuse to remove the girl from Sagira's quarters. And when Sagira had
been weaned from her dependence on Tuya, the serious
search for a husband could begin.

"Excuse the interruption, my lady." Another of the
maids appeared in the doorway that led to the ladies' sit-

ting room. "Your daughter and Ramla wait to see you."

"I will see them at once," Kahent said, sitting up. Her handmaid threw a light gown over Kahent's upraised arms, and she stood and slipped into it, then went with open arms to embrace her daughter.

"Sagira, what brings you to me in the middle of the day?" she asked, resting her hands upon her daughter's shoulders as she lightly kissed the girl's cheeks. Behind Sagira, Ramla stood in practiced detachment, her arms crossed, her eyes fixed upon Kahent's face.

"I have been thinking," Sagira said, her lower lip edging forward in a familiar pout. "If I am truly to be the mother of kings, perhaps it is best if I am not attended by such a familiar slave. Tuya knows too much about me to be properly respectful. Ramla has suggested that I should send her away."

Kahent blinked in honest surprise. She had not dared to dream that Ramla's influence would work so quickly. "You would be rid of Tuya?" she whispered.

"Yes." Sagira crossed her arms. "She is jealous and spiteful, and I don't trust her anymore. For months now Tuya has been looking at me with a strange gleam in her eye. I don't like it. She frightens me."

"Perhaps one of the dark gods has invaded her heart," Ramla suggested in a cool voice.

"Exactly!" Sagira slammed her clenched fist into her palm. "That is what I am afraid of, Mother. You gave her to me once, but now I would like to be rid of her."

"Perhaps she could work with the butler," Kahent suggested, deliberately wreathing her face in an innocent smile. "Taharka seems to think much of her."

"No!" Sagira snapped. "I will not have her anywhere near. I want her out of the house as soon as possible. She does not understand my destiny. She sees herself as my equal and that she can never be."

Joy flooded Kahent's heart. "As you say, Sagira," she said, placing her hands on her daughter's shoulders again.

"And because she is yours, whatever silver comes from her sale shall go to you."

"I shall give it all to Ramla as an offering for the goddess," Sagira said, turning to the priestess. "Without her I would never have learned of my future."

"Thank the goddess we discovered it," Ramla said, leaning forward in a gentle bow.

Kahent closed her eyes in relief. "Bastet be praised."

———

The sun bark of the god Re had moved only a short distance across the sky when Ramla came alone into the women's room of the villa. Surprised by the visit, Kahent put aside the scroll she had been reading and waited expectantly for the priestess to speak.

"Your daughter is resting," Ramla announced, gazing at Kahent with dark eyes that seemed to probe the recesses of her soul. "And your petition has been heard."

"I trust it has," Kahent said, sitting up from the couch on which she had been reclining. "I owe you a great debt."

"Your daughter's offering will suffice," Ramla answered. "That, and the opportunity to watch the future unfold. I did not fabricate or elaborate on my vision, Lady Kahent. Sagira will leave a mark upon the world." She stood in silence for a moment and Kahent toyed with the fabric of her dress, dimly aware that she was fidgeting. What was she supposed to do? Did the priestess expect special favors for the good news she had brought?

"Please sit," Kahent said finally, gesturing to an empty chair. Ramla moved stiffly to the chair and sat down without breaking the stiff line of her back. She perched on the edge, a collection of straight lines and severe angles.

"You and Sagira have become friends," Kahent said, casting about for some avenue of conversation. "I am sorry you must leave soon. I fear Sagira will be lost without either your company or Tuya's."

"She will never be lost," the priestess answered. "We

have already made arrangements. I will serve my month for
the goddess, then live with your daughter for three
months." Her pale lips curved into a mirthless smile. "I am
your daughter's spiritual counselor, and she has decided
that we shall always be together."

Kahent frowned, then forced a laugh. "You want to remain always with Sagira? But she is still a child and you
are a woman of intelligence and maturity. Surely there are
others who will value your unique gifts—"

"May I speak frankly?" A dark brow shot up, creating a
startlingly oblique line across the young woman's face.

"Yes."

"I am old enough, lady, to know where favor and fortune
lie. A woman cannot find them within the temples of
Egypt's gods." She shrugged. "But I know Sagira's future
and I know she will need a friend. You asked me to pull her
away from the slave girl, but your daughter is weak; she
cannot stand alone. She needs love, a companion, and she
has found both in me."

"I am grateful, of course," Kahent answered, her stomach tightening at the thought of having the priestess in her
home for nine months of the year. "But you know that Sagira will be married soon—"

"I will go then to the house of her husband," Ramla answered, tilting her head slightly. "You should be grateful
for my help, Lady Kahent. Without my special gift, you
would never have known of the gods' plan for Sagira's future." The corner of her lip curved in a half-smile. "But you
will not want Pharaoh to know of these things."

"Of course not," Kahent snapped. Suddenly she could
feel sweat beading under her heavy wig. It was treason even
to think of taking the throne from the one who ruled as the
incarnate god! If Pharaoh heard rumors that those in Donkor's house were grooming themselves to become the next
rulers of Egypt—

"Do not fear, lady," Ramla said, an artificially sweet ripple in her voice. "As long as I am your daughter's spiritual

counselor, I will say nothing of her destiny. With the patience of the gods I will wait for her sun to rise."

Kahent recognized the implied threat in the words and pressed her finger to her lips as the priestess rose and left the room.

———

"Why, my pretty one, are you alone so often these days?" Taharka asked, rolling a heavy barrel into his workroom. His short, graying hair gleamed silver in the bright rays of the sun.

Tuya kicked a shard of broken pottery out of her way and shrugged. "Sagira is busy," she muttered, not looking up. "She is always busy. She talks to that priestess for hours, and she has made it clear I am not supposed to overhear their conversations."

"It is only an infatuation," Taharka promised, standing the barrel upright. "Girls do that, you know. Remember the time you and Sagira swore you would eat only pigeon and nothing else? You drove me crazy with your picky ideas, and Lady Kahent was out of her mind with worry that Sagira would not grow properly."

Tuya laughed. "I had forgotten. But this is different, Taharka. Sagira has changed somehow. She is not playing a game this time. In fact, I have never seen her so serious. Sometimes I think she went to sleep and a stranger woke up in her body."

"Tuya!" A hoarse voice bellowed through the kitchen, and Tuya automatically wiped her hands across her skirt as the master of the slaves came into the room. As broad as he was tall, Tanutamon was a man to be feared, especially when ill winds blew through the household of Donkor. He never called for Tuya unless the Lady Kahent had commanded that she be whipped.

A chilly dew formed on her skin, but Tuya stepped forward to meet him. "What is it, master?" Reflexively, she dipped her head toward him in submission.

"Come with me," Tanutamon said, gesturing toward the door.

What had she done? Tuya threw a questioning glance toward Taharka, but he waved her through the doorway with a hurried gesture that said *go, and don't ask questions!* Tuya followed the master of the slaves through the winding halls of the house until they reached the gatekeeper's lodge at the entrance to the villa. The gatekeeper rose slowly from his stool as Tanutamon approached, and then backed away.

Tuya held her breath, dreading whatever was to follow. There was no whipping post in the lodge—what new punishment was this?

In answer, Tanutamon pulled a length of chain and four shackles from a corner of the gatehouse. "Your hands," he said, his voice strangely flat.

Bracing herself for an assault, Tuya lifted her arms. Had Lady Kahent heard about the cup of wine she accidentally spilled in Taharka's workroom? Had Sagira complained about Tuya's sad countenance?

Tanutamon's rough hands caught her hands. With a deft gesture he snapped the shackles upon her wrists and then secured them by running a length of chain through the loops.

"Am I to be whipped?" Tuya whispered, afraid to lift her voice. "Have I done something wrong? What has the mistress said, Tanutamon?"

The giant did not answer but knelt to clasp the other pair of shackles around her ankles. The cold metal chilled the warmth of her skin and fell heavily against the fragile bones in her feet as he ran chain through the loops.

"Tanutamon," she asked again, hearing with dismay the sound of tears in her voice. "Tanutamon, if I have done nothing wrong, what is this? And if I have done something, tell me what it is so I may avoid trouble in the future—"

"You have done nothing wrong," the master of the slaves answered gruffly. "Your mistress wishes to sell you. It is her right and her request."

"Sell me?" For a moment the words did not register in Tuya's mind. She had been a part of this family since her childhood. She and Sagira had bounced upon Lady Kahent's knee, eaten their meals together, splashed in the same pool, shared gossip and dreams. It should have been easier to stop the yearly inundation of the Nile than to separate her from this family! Yet the shackles hung heavily upon her wrists and ankles, and even now Tanutamon was adjusting the length of chain so he could lead her through the gate.

"Where are you taking me?" she cried, the world blurring around her as tears distorted her vision. "What happens when a slave is sold? I am sorry, Tanutamon, but I know nothing of these things—"

"You must trust me," Tanutamon said, not looking at her. "You are a good girl, Tuya, and if I were the master, I would not allow this thing. But I will do as I am told, as will you. You should be grateful that you have been pampered for so many years. I will do what I can for you. I have friends in high places."

She wanted to ask other questions, but horror rose up like a lump in her throat and blocked her speech. Hanging her head, she shuffled obediently forward as the gatekeeper opened the gate, and Tanutamon led the way from the marvelous house of Donkor, kinsman of the king.

⌒ Five ⌒

TUYA SHOOK LIKE A FRIGHTENED CHILD AS TANU-
tamon led her through the dusty streets of Thebes. She saw
nothing but the chains that bound her and heard nothing
but her own frantic gulps of air and the pounding of her
heart. When she awkwardly lifted her hands to steady her
throbbing head, she realized that her cheeks were wet with
tears.

How could her young mistress have sent her away? The
answer was readily apparent—Ramla had somehow poisoned Sagira against her most beloved friend. But how
could Sagira have allowed herself to be misled? Tuya had
always given Sagira the affection she craved, while Ramla
was about as warm as a corpse. But Ramla was fascinating
and foreign, while Tuya had always sought to be helpful
rather than interesting. . . .

Pain washed through her heart as a wave of sorrow
swept over her. Perhaps Ramla had nothing to do with Sagira's change of heart. Sagira was ready for marriage, hadn't
she said so? And she undoubtedly thought of Tuya as a
playmate, not a noble lady's handmaid. She had outgrown
her usefulness and was now being consigned to the trash
heap like a discarded toy.

She stumbled through the streets, grappling with her
thoughts, and nearly ran into Tanutamon when he stopped
outside a tall brick wall. A narrow gated entry guarded
whatever grand house lay inside. Tuya wiped her nose with
the back of her hand as a fresh wave of grief threatened to
engulf her, and she bit her lip to substitute one pain for another.

"Tanutamon of Donkor's house wishes to see Kratas, the keeper of Pharaoh's slaves," Tanutamon announced in a stately voice. Pharaoh's slaves! Tuya struggled to breathe as bands of apprehension tightened around her chest.

"Tanutamon—" she whispered, but the burly man cut her off with a harsh glance. He waited until the gatekeeper stepped away, then turned and flashed into sudden fury.

"Keep quiet!" he blazed down at her. "Slaves should be seen and not heard, or have you not learned that yet? You were pampered and spoiled in Donkor's house, and it is possible your beauty will cause you to be pampered here as well. But if you speak or protest or cry, you will be sold in a common auction to the highest bidder—do you want that?"

Scared speechless, Tuya shook her head.

"Then say nothing and do nothing unless you are told."

"Tanutamon may enter." The gatekeeper unlocked the gate and Tuya followed her master into a long corridor intricately painted with scenes from daily life in Pharaoh's house. She immediately recognized the sharp, clear features of Amenhotep II and his royal consort, Queen Merit-Amon.

"Ah, my friend Tanutamon." A tall, regally dressed black man appeared from a doorway in the corridor, and Tuya lifted her eyes to look at him. He was not Egyptian but bore the features of the people from the southern reaches of the Nile. A small round paunch hung over the waistband of his kilt, and deep lines of worry creased his dark face.

"It is good to see you, Kratas," Tanutamon said, bowing. "May you remain in the favor of Amon-Re, King of the gods, of Ptah, of Thoth, and of all the gods and goddesses who are in Thebes."

"The same to you, my friend," Kratas answered. "And how may I help you today?"

Tanutamon pivoted slightly and pointed at Tuya. "My younger mistress has outgrown her childhood maid and wishes to sell her." He rolled his eyes, effectively sending the disloyal message that he disagreed with his mistress's judgment. "Because I am obedient, I thought to take her to the marketplace, but surely such a young woman should be offered first to his majesty Pharaoh. Surely there is room in his harem for another young beauty?"

"She is—unspoiled?" Kratas's eyes swept over Tuya's slender figure, and she felt herself blushing.

"Yes, she has been carefully guarded. She is of age, at least fifteen years, and has excellent manners. Donkor, as you know, is a man of breeding and noble reputation. I can assure you that any slave from his house will bring honor to the house of Pharaoh."

Kratas stepped toward Tuya and ran his hand over her arm. She flinched, resenting his familiarity.

"She is shy," Kratas said, his mouth tipping into a faint smile. "Pharaoh likes the shy ones. Not for him, a brazen prostitute."

"So you will buy her?"

"One hundred deben weight of silver, with an extra ten for you," Kratas said, snapping his fingers toward a boy who waited in the shadows of a broad pillar.

"It is agreed," Tanutamon said, smiling with warm spontaneity. "You are most generous, Kratas."

The boy ran to his master, a gilded chest in his hands, and Kratas withdrew a handful of silver coins and began to count them. "I am not being overly generous," he said, pausing as he emptied a handful of silver into Tanutamon's broad palm. "I am sure she is worth much more."

———

Kratas paused outside the women's room where he kept recent additions to Pharaoh's assemblage of slaves. The new girl, Tuya, sat silently on a stool inside while other women sponged her body and washed her hair. Tanutamon was right to bring the girl to Pharaoh's house. She possessed an alluring uniqueness, a sweet shyness of spirit that was refreshingly different from the practiced, pouty beauties of Pharaoh's harem. Perhaps, in time, she would harden and grow into a stupid, bovine woman, but Kratas was certain Pharaoh would now find this youthful flower to his liking. If not for the knife which had made him a eunuch, Kratas would have bought her himself.

He leaned against the wall and rubbed his chin, thinking. The girl was taller than most and held herself like a queen. She had not shaved her head as did so many wig-loving slaves of rich women, but had kept her long, thick hair which framed her face and elongated her swanlike neck. Her facial features were coffin-shaped and elegant, her nose slender and fine, and the nostrils delicate. Her eyes shone like a stream of gold in the fading light of the room, deep, watchful eyes that missed nothing.

A chuckle of self-satisfaction escaped him. In one week, if the girl proved willing, he could turn her into a queen to rival Merit-Amon, or even the king's favorite wife, Teo. With the right garments, a proper wig, cosmetics and jewels . . .

Kratas clapped his hands for his servant and frowned in annoyance when the boy did not appear. Slaves were a defeated, worthless lot. He would give his right arm to buy one who was dependable and trustworthy, but he could more easily count the waves of the Nile than find such a creature.

Six

OUTSIDE THE THRONE ROOM OF AMENHOTEP II, Potiphar nervously cleared his throat. His men, Pharaoh's bodyguard, were already inside at their positions alongside the throne dais. Usually he stood in front of them, facing all who dared approach the king, but word had come in the night that Pharaoh insisted on greeting Potiphar formally after the battle in the desert.

He shifted uneasily on his feet. The enemy had been defeated, but not without cost to Egypt's armies. At least a score of Egyptian warriors had perished, and three were missing and assumed dead or captured by the rebels. Potiphar was not sure if this formal audience had been granted to publicly praise him, or to punish him.

Behind Potiphar a corps of men waited, their arms heavily laden with an assortment of swords, helmets, spears, and cunningly worked arrows. These represented the spoils of war Potiphar had managed to gather after the skirmish, but they were a paltry symbol of the true success of the battle. Rebels had dared to rise and challenge Pharaoh's authority, and he had again proven himself to be every bit as cunning and fierce as his father. The rebellious outer settlements should not rise again in this king's lifetime.

"Potiphar, Captain of the Guard, Pharaoh calls for you!"

Two slaves pulled open the great double doors, and Potiphar took a deep breath and moved into the long, sunlit throne room. Murals depicting the king's military exploits had been brilliantly painted on the walls of the room, and in front of these paintings, to Potiphar's left and right, the king's courtiers and members of the royal family witnessed the day's business. A group of musicians in a far corner played softly upon harps and lyres. The green tile floor, gleaming in the sunlight like the Nile itself, stretched before Potiphar in a seemingly endless vista. Conscious of hundreds of eyes upon him, he began the walk toward the throne.

With military discipline he kept his eyes facing forward toward the king and his wives. Potiphar jerked his chin upward in brief acknowledgment to his guards, who stood alert and ready around the royal family, their shields, spears, and body armor properly in place. To the right of the king's throne stood his eldest son and heir, seven-year-old Webensennu, and behind the eldest son stood the younger four-year-old Abayomi. The queen, seated to the left of the king, was surrounded by a group of fashionably dressed ladies of the royal harem. Her majesty's pet dwarf waddled in front of her chair, scowling at Potiphar as if he took too long to transverse the royal throne room.

Potiphar bowed his head toward the queen, and the dark eyes under the gold tiara and weighty wig blinked slowly in response. To keep from glancing in fear to Pharaoh, Potiphar forced himself to read the bold engraving upon the queen's gilded chair: "Mother of Upper and Lower Egypt, Follower of Horus, Guide of the Ruler, Favorite Lady."

Finally Potiphar allowed himself to look upon the person and face of his sovereign and only god. Amenhotep had dressed in complete royal regalia for this meeting, a sign that could portend either evil or good. Upon his head Pharaoh wore the red-and-white double crown, signifying the union between Upper and Lower Egypt. At the front of the headdress gleamed a golden model of the cobra goddess Wadjet, who could deal out instant death by spitting flames at any enemy who dared threaten the king. A long, white robe disguised the king's wiry, athletic body, and the wide pectoral at his breast covered the battle scars he had won years before while fighting with Potiphar against the

Asiatic city-states. Over everything, beating against Pharaoh's heart, hung the heavy necklace known as the Gold of Praise. Pharaoh wore it because he was king. A few select men wore it because they had earned Pharaoh's admiration.

Potiphar allowed his eyes to dart toward the battle paintings for a moment to remind Pharaoh that they had been through much together. *I remember, my king*, Potiphar thought, turning from the images. Amenhotep's dark eyes met his and held them fast as he extended the crook and flail.

"Come forward, Potiphar," Pharaoh intoned, the tip of his false beard wagging like the finger of a scolding tutor.

Potiphar's feet obeyed.

"I am the embodiment of the god Horus," Amenhotep went on, speaking slowly for the scribes who transcribed every word. "I am Golden Horus, the king of Upper and Lower Egypt. I am the son of the sun-god Re. I am your father, Potiphar, and I wish to honor you this day."

Potiphar closed his eyes, afraid he gazed too hungrily upon the heavy chain of gold around Pharaoh's neck. By the king's favor he had a house and cattle and sheep and goats and slaves. He had more than he knew how to manage, but the Gold of Praise had always eluded him.

"What can I give you, my son Potiphar, that you do not already have? I have long pondered this question. I and my fellow gods have already blessed you with life and health."

"It is enough, O Pharaoh," Potiphar answered. He fell to his knees and pressed his forehead to the ground. "It is enough that you, a god, have consented to rule over us. I am honored beyond any man because you allow me to serve as the captain of your guard."

"And yet I think it is not enough," Pharaoh answered. Potiphar rose from the floor, in grave danger of losing his self-control as he stared at his king. The royal hand was fingering the Gold of Praise, the most visible sign of the king's honor that any man could wish to wear. . . .

"My wife, the mother of all Egypt, has given me the answer," Pharaoh said, his paint-lengthened eyes narrowing in some secret amusement. "What you need, noble Potiphar, is a woman's touch to steady the lion's heart that roars in your breast. You need a wife."

Potiphar stared at Amenhotep in a paralysis of astonishment. Gold and favor he had expected, but a wife? He had no interest in women, and his independent spirit rebelled at the thought of an equal partner to share his house and wealth.

"I have not thought of taking a wife," Potiphar stammered, finding his tongue. An idea leapt into his mind, and he ran with it, pouring forth golden words to soothe Pharaoh's prideful ear. "A wife, my king, might impede my service to you. You are a god, you can divide your limitless time and power between your duties and your pleasures, but I am a man of restricted capacities. I would rather surrender my life than one iota of my devotion to you."

"It is well-spoken," Pharaoh said, nodding sagely. He raised the ancient crook, the symbol of the shepherd's staff by which Pharaoh guided his people. "But you will not deny me this gift, Potiphar. I will give you a woman and you may marry her or not, as you please. As the sun-god embarked this morning, the keeper of the royal harem reported that a most ravishing young girl had been brought to the palace for my pleasure. I give her to you, noble Potiphar, as a token of my divine approval."

"A thousand thanks, my king," Potiphar said, not daring to protest again. "I will honor and cherish this beneficent tribute."

"I know you will," Pharaoh replied, crossing the crook across his chest. "Go now, and walk in the favor of Amon-Re and your king."

The return of the crook to the king's chest meant the interview was over. The musicians began to play as Potiphar stood and walked backward from the throne room. He would have to find the girl in the harem and take her to his house immediately, or some wagging palace tongue would tell the king that his favor had not been readily appreciated. Though Potiphar felt secure in Pharaoh's favor, never was it wise to assume anything in the royal court of Amenhotep II.

———

Since only emasculated slaves and the king were allowed into the chambers that housed the royal harem, Kratas escorted Potiphar's prize from the royal apartments to the wide room where foreign slaves were sorted and evaluated. Despite his disinterest, Potiphar smiled in appreciation at the sight of the slender girl walking by the eunuch's side. Tall and willowy, her skin was the color of burnished honey and surely as sweet. She wore a simple linen sheath which accented her naturally elegant posture, and her face, when she finally lifted it to meet his, was as elegantly chiseled as were the goddess statues in the finest temples.

"I must thank you as well as Pharaoh," Potiphar told Kratas, his eyes sweeping over the girl again. "She will be a beautiful addition to my household."

The eunuch bowed. "Is your house fully staffed, my Lord Potiphar? We have just purchased several slaves from traveling Midianites. The Asiatics will not do for Pharaoh—he wants only Nubian slaves."

"I do not know, Kratas." Relieved for an excuse to turn from the fear-widened eyes of the girl, Potiphar glanced around the room. Several bearded men, uncouth and ravelled in appearance, sat or lay on the floor in a molten mess of humanity. Their eyes were burned out, haunted, soured with bitterness. Most wore defeat like a banner across their faces, but one youth caught his eye. Though stained with dust and fatigue, the teenager's face seemed lighted from within. Some god had chiseled indomitable pride into that handsome face, along with intelligence and hard-bitten strength. This lad, if harnessed correctly, would pull more than his share of the work load.

"That one," Potiphar said, pointing to the boy. "How much for him?

"Him?" Kratas frowned. "You do not want him. His arm has been broken, and his body burns with fever from the devils of the desert. He will die before two suns have set."

"I do not think he is ready to die," Potiphar countered. "How much?"

The eunuch scratched his head and eyed Potiphar thoughtfully. "Fifty deben weight of silver."

"You have just said he is worthless. Ten deben weight."

"I paid forty for him. Do you want your king to suffer a loss?"

"Within two days the crocodiles will have him. Take twenty and be content with your profit."

Kratas frowned again, but nodded. "So be it, Lord Potiphar. But I only do you this favor because our divine Pharaoh holds you in high regard."

"Whatever you say," Potiphar answered, pulling his purse from his kilt.

———

Through a haze of exhaustion and pain, Joseph realized that he had been sold to the loud-voiced man who had come for the pretty girl. Silver changed hands and one of the guards yanked Joseph to his feet. Colors exploded in his brain as the rope chewed on his splintered arm. The long journey through Egypt had not afforded his body a chance to heal, and fever coursed through his veins like the quick, hot touch of the devil.

The girl's wrists were bound as well, and a broad-shouldered slave took the ropes and led Joseph and the girl out of the chamber. They followed the loud man as he walked through the palace courtyard and along the streets of Thebes. People babbled in an unfamiliar tongue all around Joseph, and though he had managed to pick up a few words while on the journey southward, his thoughts drifted into a fuzzy haze where nothing made sense. He was tired and

beaten; every step taxed the small store of energy he possessed. His body cried out for rest, water, and peace.

He was dimly aware of the hot sun, the whining wind,
and the rushing Nile at his right hand; then the sound of
the water retreated into the gray fog surrounding him. He
slumped to the ground, surrendering to the cloud of pain
which had enveloped him since Dothan.

He thought he slept for a long time, perhaps days. When
he opened his eyes again, he was lying on a narrow bed in
a darkened chamber. A rushlight burned in a corner of the
room, and in the flickering light he could see that the walls
around him were covered with a patina of dirt. The air felt
as if it had been breathed too many times, and reflexively,
he gasped for breath. He had passed his life in tents and
open fields; the confining atmosphere of the small space
was unbearable.

At the sound of his gasp, a dark shape on the floor
stirred. Joseph blinked in surprise when a blanket lifted
and a pale face peered forth. A spirit! He stared in astonishment as the spirit spoke, but Joseph could not understand the words.

"Have I died?" he whispered, struggling to rise. For a
moment he dared to hope that he was dying on his own
mattress at home in his father's tents, that the memories of
the past few days were only a disturbing nightmare. But
then the creature murmured something and sat up, pressing
her hand to his chest and gently forcing him back onto the
bed. He realized then that his guardian was no ghost, but a
flesh-and-blood creation. Slowly, the memory of his last
conscious day returned, and he knew that the girl beside
him was the slave who had journeyed with him to this
place.

"You are—?" he asked in Hebrew, pointing to her.

The girl lifted her eyebrows; then the light of understanding brightened her dark eyes. "Tuya," she whispered,

resting her delicate hand upon her chest. She pointed to him. "Paneah."

"No," he answered, shaking his head. An inexplicable surge of anger rose within his breast. Had his brothers stolen even his name? "I am Joseph."

"Yusef?" She shook her head and pointed toward the doorway. "Potiphar." Her hand fell upon his head. "Paneah."

Joseph sighed and let his head fall back upon the bed's curious headrest. Anger and denial were of no use. He had a new name, a new position—because of his brothers' treachery, he who was once the favored son was now a slave. What had God done with his dreams of power and authority? Who would bow to him in this foreign place? Cattle? Jackals?

As the girl settled down to sit beside him, Joseph closed his eyes in exasperation and frustrated grief. At least a measure of his strength had returned. His arm no longer throbbed, and the fever-fog which had clouded his thoughts seemed to have lifted. He lay still, helpless in his ignorance and weakness, lost in the lonely silence of the night.

He would never see his father again. Nor his brothers, nor the two bright-eyed daughters of the camel trader he had laughingly promised to marry. Like a woman with a baby in her womb, grief blossomed suddenly in his chest, crushing his lungs, stealing the air he needed to breathe. Like a drowning man he gasped aloud, trying to lift his head, reaching out for the family he would never see again—

The girl rushed forward and caught his hands, then stroked his brow as she murmured gentle sounds. As if she sensed his thoughts, the girl began to hum a gentle melody, and the room warmed to the sound.

Someone had tended him—probably this girl. Turning from his self-pity, Joseph lifted his head to look at the fine shape of her mouth and the slender column of her throat.

Her dark eyes caught his and a blush colored her cheeks, but she did not look away. A smile tugged at his lips and she returned it, her face shimmering like sunbeams on the surface of the ribbon of running river the Egyptians considered the center of their universe.

Perhaps, Joseph thought, closing his eyes against his grief and despair, God had shown great mercy by bringing him to a girl who could be a well of understanding and hope, an oasis in this heathen wilderness.

After her arrival at Potiphar's house, Tuya was spared from her new master's attention because the sick slave needed a nurse, and no one else in the household seemed willing or able to care for him. And during the first few days that she nursed Paneah, Tuya discovered that although Potiphar owned a vast villa with many rooms and many servants, the poorly organized estate barely functioned. Because he spent most of his time on military expeditions or in the presence of Pharaoh, Potiphar had neither the time nor the inclination to oversee his own property.

But Tuya's first concern was for her patient. On the day he was placed in her care, the young man from Canaan was flushed with fever beneath the stubble of his beard. Under the dirty bandage around his arm Tuya found an oozing wound from which bare bone protruded. While the young man was unconscious, she sent for a surgeon to set the bone and pour wine over the broken skin. After manipulating the bone and wrapping the arm in clean bandages, the surgeon assured her he had done all he could do. Now the young man's fate rested in the hands of the gods.

Tuya sat by the side of her fellow slave and worried. She had tended to this young man's physical body, but what if the gods wanted appeasement before he would be healed? She knew she could never make an offering to Bastet. Though that goddess had been the favorite in Donkor's house, Ramla's cool betrayal had hardened Tuya's heart against the cat goddess. And so she begged one of the kitchen slaves for a stone statue of Montu, the war god and guardian of the arm.

The statue depicted a man with a hawk's head surrounded by the golden disk of the sun. Tuya took the statuette to the sick room, where she placed it in a shaft of sunlight and began a healing chant: "As for the arm of Paneah, it is the arm of Montu, on whose head were placed the three hundred and seventy-seven Divine Cobras. They spew forth flame to make you quit the arm of Paneah, like that of Montu. If you do not quit the temple of Paneah, I will burn your soul, I will consume your corpse! I will be deaf to any desire of yours. If some other god is with you, I will overturn your dwelling place; I will shadow your tomb so you will not be allowed to receive incense, so you will not be allowed to receive water with the beneficent spirits, and so you will not be allowed to associate with the Followers of Horus.

"If you will not hear my words, I will cut off the head of a cow taken from the forecourt of Hathor! I will cut off the head of a sacred hippopotamus in the forecourt of Set! I will cause Sebek to sit enshrouded in the skin of a crocodile, and I will cause Anubis to sit enshrouded in the skin of a dog! Then indeed shall you come forth from the temple of Paneah!"

Every morning Tuya threatened the statue of Montu with her fierce refrain, and every morning the young man on the bed seemed stronger. He ate gruel from her bowl before the first week had ended, sipping the broth from the wooden spoon without speaking much, his dark eyes flickering with a reserve Tuya could not understand. Why did he not seem more grateful? He was a slave, as she was, and slaves were not often blessed with the tender care he was receiving. He could have been sent immediately to work in the fields; few masters would care if a slave costing only twenty deben weight of silver dropped dead over a furrow.

As he slept, Tuya studied him closely. Though his illness had left him wafer-thin, finely defined muscles slid beneath his skin's golden tan. A head taller than most Egyptians, his dark hair flowed in gentle waves to his shoulders and was perfectly matched by the beard which had filled in the clean purity of his profile. His hands, with long, sensitive fingers, were well kept, and Tuya was struck by the lack of calluses on his palms. Perhaps she was wrong in assuming that he had been born to slavery as had she.

After a few days he began to speak and gesture with his good arm. In the weeks that followed he proved to be a willing pupil as Tuya schooled him in the basics of the Egyptian tongue. He had a sharp and clear mind; rarely did she have to explain anything more than once.

"Who is that you pray to?" he asked one morning when she had finished bowing to the statue in the sunlight.

Tuya rose from the floor and reverently put the statue away. Montu had met all her requests; he deserved to be handled with respect.

"Only the king has access to the gods; only he can pray. I was chanting before Montu, an ancient war god. He has healed your arm."

Horror flashed in the young man's eyes. "Please do not think such a thing! It is an abomination for my people to bow before any stone object. We worship the invisible God, the one and only Creator of heaven and earth."

Tuya crossed her legs and sank to a papyrus mat on the floor. Only one god! Despite his quick intellect, how simple and unsophisticated he was! She tilted her head and looked at him. "Does this god have a name?"

"The God of Abraham, Isaac, and my father, Jacob, spoke to them as El Shaddai," he answered, lifting his chin in unconscious pride. "God Almighty, the unseen God."

Tuya shook her head. "Amon is the invisible god," she explained in the voice she would have used to teach a stubborn and ignorant child. "He is Amon-Re, King of the gods, the chief god of our king's empire. He is the creator, the one who rose from chaos and created maat, the principle that guides our actions. He created all things that move in the waters and upon the dry land, and he took a form like ours, becoming the first pharaoh. After a long life, he ascended to the heavens and left the other gods in charge of the earth." She could not resist smiling. "There are many other gods, Paneah. Our land grows gods as freely as it grows grain."

"My God is not Amon-Re," the young man answered, giving her a quick, denying glance. "And my name is not Paneah. It is Joseph."

Tuya lowered her voice. "You will bear the name our master gave in the hope that you will survive. The name is a gift, for 'Paneah' means 'he lives.' This 'Yusef' is foreign to our ears, and the master will not like it."

The young man did not answer but regarded her silently for a moment. Then a shy smile tweaked the corner of his mouth. "If my master will not call me Joseph, then you must. I give my true name to you and you alone, for you are the only one in this land who has shown kindness to me."

His eyes touched her with warmth, and Tuya struggled with the inner confusion his smile always elicited. "All right, Yusef," she said finally, managing the foreign pronunciation as best she could. "But I will not speak that name in front of the master. I will do nothing to offend him, for a slave who offends will be sold . . ."

His heavy eyelids closed. Outside the small chamber, darkness glided across the sky with the silken slowness of an infinitely languid tide. Shadows lengthened in the room, and Tuya shifted uncomfortably as she looked out the doorway at the fading sky. The hour of sunset had been her favorite time of day in Donkor's house, the time when she and Sagira relaxed and settled down to sleep. Now darkness brought nothing but phantoms of the past and a throat that ached with sorrow.

"Was it so terrible?" Joseph asked, his voice quiet and low in the darkening room.

Tuya started; she had assumed he was asleep. "What?"

"Whatever it is that fills your eyes with sadness."

His gaze held her tight. Tuya had an odd feeling that he had forgotten himself and cared only for her. No one had ever made her feel that way before. Shivering, she recalled her overwhelming feeling of helplessness, her fear of facing Pharaoh as a concubine, her still uncertain future. "Why does the past matter?" she finally answered, whispering in the near darkness. "Surely you have faced terrible things, too. Your hands tell a story, Yusef, and they say you were not born a slave."

His nod was barely perceptible. "I was betrayed and abandoned by my ten brothers," he said, a somber note in his voice. "I once dreamed of greatness, and now I am a slave upon an invalid's bed."

For a brief moment Tuya caught a glimpse of some internal struggle, but he did not weep or grow angry. His expression cleared.

"All I have seen teaches me to trust El Shaddai for all that I have not seen."

Bitter tears stung her eyes. "I was abandoned by one who called herself my sister," she whispered, tearing her eyes from his face. She stared into the darkness, reliving those terrible hours of grief. "During the one night I spent in Pharaoh's house, I dreamed that I stood upon a round disk while the sun-god threw his arms around me. In that moment I felt protected, safe, and loved."

She looked up at Joseph again. "I do not believe in dreams because we always wake up to face a new fear. And there is no escape because a slave cannot know what lies ahead."

"God knows," Joseph answered, his hand reaching out for hers. Stung by the unexpected gesture, Tuya withdrew her arm, and then relented and placed her fingers in his strong grip. She did not want to become attached to this youth, for Potiphar might sell him for a quick profit once his health was restored.

But for now, Tuya felt blessed to have a friend.

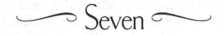

Seven

TUYA AND JOSEPH HAD ENTERED POTIPHAR'S
household at the beginning of the inundation, the four winter months of the year. Within two weeks the fever had left
Joseph's body, but since he could not work in the house or
the fields with a broken arm, Tuya began to teach him the
written language of the Egyptians. She had learned the
seven hundred signs of the hieroglyphic language along
with Sagira, and though her rendering of the pictorial elements was not as perfect or as elegant as those of a professional scribe, Joseph had no trouble understanding the
meaning of her scratchings.

As the Nile receded and the fertile silt-laden land reap-
peared, Joseph's mind became occupied with learning.
Tuya found that Potiphar did not care what his slaves did;
his concerns were all for Pharaoh, the prison, and his
guards. So each morning after bringing Joseph his breakfast
of bread and parched corn, she spread before him several
shards of broken pottery and a basket filled with flakes of
limestone. A papyrus reed made a fine pen, and Joseph often detained her for an hour, asking questions as he practiced his writing and honed his understanding. His brain
was like a sponge, always absorbing, always demanding
more, and she realized he would master in a few months
what the royal scribes took years to learn.

"What is the sign for captive?" Joseph asked one day,
looking up from the shards he had covered with scrawlings.

Tuya peered over his shoulder. "It is the sign of a kneeling man that you have drawn, but the hands extend behind

him and are bound," she said. "The sign can also mean 'enemy' or 'rebel.'"

"Another question," Joseph said, chewing idly on the end of his pen. "What is the sign for Pharaoh? And how may I show it with other signs?"

"You would not dare," Tuya said, taking a step back. "Pharaoh's name is sacred; to write it is almost a sacrilege. If it is absolutely necessary to write his name, you must enclose it in a circle, the sign of the sun."

Joseph turned back to his writing, deep in concentration, and Tuya hurried out the door with the breakfast tray. Distracted by her thoughts, she nearly stepped into a pile of dung in the courtyard. She gritted her teeth, annoyed that someone had left the cattle pen open. She would have to speak to the stockyard boys.

Donkor's prosperous household and Potiphar's estate were like a tree and its reflection upon the Nile, Tuya decided. The former thrived in prosperity; the latter, being insubstantial, only appeared to flourish. Though Potiphar's estate was large and well-situated, his slaves were a disjointed mass of workers, a hive without a queen. After a week of trying to function in total disorganization, Tuya called the servants together, announced that she had come from a nobleman's house, and assigned her fellow slaves to various stations. She gave orders to the kitchen slaves every morning, saw to it that the bathrooms, cattle yards, and stables were cleaned out, and ordered the waters of the pool to be changed and stocked with fish. Used to the lazy life of fat cats, the slaves obeyed, but grumbled the entire time.

Tuya could not believe that Pharaoh's captain could live in such a disorderly house. Despite his lionlike reputation as a warrior, his slaves neither feared nor respected him, for he appeared to show no care for his home or for his lands. Discipline did not exist in the household, for as long as Potiphar had an edible meal and a bed to lie upon, he made no demands. He threw no parties, commemorated no feasts or festivals. The captain of the guard found his amusements elsewhere and spent most of his time in the palace.

Tuya took her problems to Joseph and found that although he had never lived in an Egyptian house, he had strong opinions as to how people should be handled. He had a gift for administration, and his diplomatic suggestions of how to handle the balking slaves helped Tuya establish the changes she wanted to make.

When Joseph was strong enough to move about, Tuya took him on a tour of the villa. Potiphar's house resembled every other Theban nobleman's except for two things: first, it contained the jail for Pharaoh's prisoners, and second, it was uncommonly shabby and charmless. Surrounded by a high, crumbling wall of mud-dried brick, the house stood in the midst of an extensive plot of valuable riverfront land. A towered gateway led into the estate, and the prison warden's lodge rose immediately at the visitor's left. The prison, a collection of solid buildings of stone and iron, lay off to the east, far away from the main house. Tuya assured Joseph that they would have no responsibility for the prison. Potiphar kept a slovenly house, but his guards ran a tight and secure dungeon. Their lives depended upon it.

To the right of the entry, a small path lined with drooping, anemic-looking trees led to the family temple. "When I first came here it was obvious from the dilapidated look of this place that our master is not a religious man," Tuya whispered to Joseph. "No incense burned in the censers, no offerings had been spread out, and the gods themselves were covered in dust. No wonder they have not blessed Potiphar's household! I myself cleaned the statues and appointed one of the slave children to bring food, water, and incense each morning and night."

Joseph said nothing as she led him from the temple. The narrow dirt path in front of them pointed a curving finger toward the west and led to a flight of steps and a pair of peeling columns. Beyond them was an inner courtyard and a doorway framed in stone. Its lintel had been carved with Potiphar's name and position, but the paint had weathered out of the fading letters. At the end of the portico was the vestibule, which led to the north loggia, a large reception room which had been poorly furnished and barely decorated. The west loggia, used by most families as a sitting room in winter, stood totally unfurnished and smelled of dust, as did the guest rooms. The master's bedroom was as spartan as a battlefield tent, and the bathroom offered neither a slab for bathing or a basin for washing hands. Throughout the house, sprained doors hung open and walls shed their coats of fading paint. The stables, servants' quarters, kitchen, and stockyard were located on the southern and eastern sides of the house so the prevailing wind would carry away the odors of dung fires, cooking food, horse sweat, and the slaves' sour beer; but the servants of Potiphar had allowed sewage, garbage, and manure to accumulate for so long that the sirocco winds accumulated in a single blast could not have diffused the stench.

Potiphar's horses were in fine fettle, for he loved to ride and often engaged in chariot-racing, but the few cattle in the stockyard were scrawny and blotched with various skin diseases. Joseph paid special attention to the cattle, probing their skins with deft fingers and examining their eyes and noses with great care. "I know how to cure this condition," he said, catching up to Tuya as she moved through the stockyard. "With the right grains and a poultice or two, these cattle can be made well."

From the stockyard, an open, roofless corridor led to the well, and beyond the wall surrounding the well lay the master's formal gardens. Tuya showed Joseph the small door that led to the gardens. The pool's water, which had been stagnant and laden with green scum, now glimmered in the sun while lotus plants dotted its surface. "This is beautiful," Joseph said, admiring the pool.

"The blue lotus is my favorite," Tuya said, unwillingly remembering the lotus blossoms of Sagira's pool.

"Not just the flowers," Joseph answered. "Everything. You have done well."

"Not I alone," Tuya answered, taking his good arm as she led him back to the servants' quarters. A thin sheen of perspiration shone on Joseph's forehead, and she knew even this brief walk had tired him greatly. "Without your support, I would never have had the courage to speak to the other servants."

If any of the older slaves bore resentment toward Tuya, they dared not show it after Potiphar praised her administration. He called her into his presence one evening as he sat at dinner in the central hall. From the high windows near the ceiling, the pink rays of sunset tinged the room.

"You were presented to me because of your beauty," Potiphar said after she knelt at his feet. "But now I find that you are more than merely ornamental."

Bent into submission, Tuya felt her stomach tighten. Donkor had never summoned her into his presence, and the few occasions she had faced Kahent had ended in punishment or rebuke. What did Potiphar have in mind?

"Rise, girl, and speak freely," her master mumbled through a mouthful of food.

Slowly, Tuya stood, lifting her head at the last moment. Potiphar sat before her, his hands busy with his food, his eyes bright and alert as an eagle's. She gathered her courage. "What would you have me say, master?"

"How does a harem girl know so much about running a house?"

"If it please you, my lord, I was not reared for the harem. Before entering Pharaoh's house, I was a companion to Sagira, daughter of Donkor, a kinsman of the king."

Potiphar bit into the pigeon the cook had prepared according to Tuya's direction. "And does Donkor know that you now live with me?"

Tuya shook her head. "I have no way of knowing, my lord. I was sold when his daughter no longer wanted—*had need of*—a companion."

"I see." Potiphar lifted his goblet and took a deep drink, then sighed lustily and smacked his lips. "Well, Tuya, I have no harem and no need of a concubine. But I like what you have done, and you may continue to oversee the house."

Relief washed over her, but Tuya did not leave. In three months, Potiphar had spoken to her only this once, and if all went well in his house he might never speak to her again. If she wanted to speak to him of Joseph, she would have to do it now. For despite her intentions to remain aloof from the young man's dancing eyes, she could not bear the thought of waking one day to find him gone.

"If it please you, my lord—"

"What?" The master lifted a brow as if surprised to find her still there.

"If you want your estate to truly prosper, you would do well to heed the advice of Paneah, the injured slave you bought from Pharaoh's court. His arm is mended now, and he has cured your cattle of a mange that would have spread through the herd. He has great vision and is a capable overseer. Let me supervise the kitchens, but place everything else in Paneah's hands. By Pharaoh's life, I swear he will not fail you."

"By all the gods, I knew he was bright," Potiphar said, slamming his cup down upon his dinner tray. "Bring him to me at once."

Tuya hurried away, her heart as light as her step. Joseph would turn the estate into the pride and treasure of Thebes. And soon he would be as important to Potiphar as he had become to her.

POTIPHAR

And it came about that from the time [Potiphar] made [Joseph] overseer in his house, and over all that he owned, the Lord blessed the Egyptian's house on account of Joseph; thus the Lord's blessing was upon all that he owned, in the house and in the field.

Genesis 39:5

Eight

A YEAR PASSED. THE WATERS OF THE LIFE-GIVING Nile changed from the heavy gray of the inundation to the shimmering green of verdigris growing on copper. Potiphar's slaves tilled the soil of his lands during the *proyet*, the months of the land's emergence, and harvested during *shemu*, the four months of drought. Far to the south, monsoon winds swept inland from the great ocean and dumped torrential rains on the highlands of the continent, feeding the tributary known as the Blue Nile. Through steep mountain gorges, tracts of marshland, and fetid jungles, the swollen river roiled northward and merged with the White Nile. Beyond the point of their confluence lay six cataracts; the northernmost cataract, a rock-studded gorge through which the flood waters tumbled in a mad rush, marked the southern boundary of Egypt.

Unaware of the natural forces at work, during the summer solstice the priests made their offerings to Egypt's gods and waited for the annual arrival of the bounteous flood. Pharaoh prayed to the god Hapi, begging him to pour the holy waters into the river known since ancient times as Hep-ur, or "sweet water." According to legend and Egyptian belief, Hapi sat upon a mountain and from two bottomless pitchers poured the Nile upon the land. One pitcher brought forth the sweet bright green river of harvest time; from the other pitcher flowed the inundation's gray, silt-laden waters that would flood and fertilize the thirsty Egyptian fields. Pharaoh and the priests did not doubt the gray waters would come, but they prayed that the god would dispense his gift with mercy and wisdom. Too much water, and villages would be swept away; too little, and Egypt would starve.

When Sirius, the dogstar, arrived in the vast and endless plain of evening, the priests announced the waters were near. As they had predicted, the flood came rushing northward a few days later. Over the centuries, natural mound-like levees had built up along the Nile, and on the Night of the Cutting of the Dam, the people of Thebes mounted these natural walls along the riverfront and waited for Pharaoh's signal. Once the dam was "cut," or broken, the precious waters would flood a series of man-made channels and carry their life-giving nourishment to the fields.

Scowling at the noise of celebration, Potiphar climbed one of the towers built into the walls of his villa. To the west, he could see the vista of silver water and shimmering skyline where the earthen dams at the border of his property bristled with life as the sun dropped toward the horizon. Soon small glowing orbs of torchlight moved through the fire-tinted darkness. A twinge of nostalgia struck him. In every year until this one, he had been at Pharaoh's side for this ceremony. He would have been upon the royal barge this year, too, but a royal courtier called Narmer had convinced Pharaoh that Potiphar needed time to rest.

The high squeal of the priests' trumpets rent the air. Though he could not see clearly in the darkness, Potiphar knew that long boats of bundled papyrus reeds were breaking through the banks to allow the river to spill her bounty into the land. He smiled. Aside from Narmer's tiresome presence, he had no reason to complain. Whatever gods there were had been good to him in the past year. Under Paneah's direction, his cattle had begun to produce and his fields to grow. His slaves, previously a motley crew who had once managed his house in spite of themselves, had become a disciplined corps, each content to labor in his or her assigned task.

While Joseph oversaw the stockyard, fields, and running of the estate, the girl Tuya had become a valuable housekeeper. Under her direction, Potiphar's new cup-bearer had become almost as skilled as Taharka, the talented slave who had been purchased to grow, ferment, and offer Pharaoh's own wines. Potiphar was not sure what sort of magic Tuya had worked, but he now slept on perfumed, softened linen sheets and wore pressed and pleated kilts. Even Pharaoh had noticed the change. "How polished and well-fed you look, Potiphar," he had remarked only a few days before. "Age certainly seems to agree with you."

"I only reflect your bounty, divine Pharaoh," Potiphar had replied, bowing. "The light of your favor has caused the Nile to bring forth a good crop. Your people will not hunger this year."

Paneah had worked wonders in the fields outside the walls of Potiphar's villa. What had once been a sprawling field of haphazard planting was now a neat arrangement of small squares, each divided by mud walls a few inches high. Between the squares a runnel conveyed water from a shaduf at the river's edge. Each square could be watered separately by blocking the runnel with a mud wall, thus insuring that thirsty crops received plenty of water while the drier crops were not overwhelmed.

After the floodwaters had receded in the spring, Paneah urged the serfs to walk slowly and drop seed in neat rows across Potiphar's muddy fields. Teams of long-horned African cows plowed the seed under, their hooves burying the seed deep within the life-giving earth. To insure the seed lay snug beneath the silty soil, Paneah had the stockmen drive a herd of goats through the fields. Potiphar had been home long enough to watch the merry affair. A scampering young boy lured the stubborn goats through the fields with a handful of grain while the adult herdsmen chased the goats with whips of twisted rope.

Paneah directed Potiphar's slaves with a steadfast and sure hand through each stage of agriculture: plowing, sowing, treading in the seed, reaping, treading out the grain, winnowing, loading it on donkeys, and depositing the harvest in granaries. The result was a crop that filled Potiphar's coffers to overflowing. In the past he had relied on his wages as an officer in Pharaoh's army to supply his haphazard household, but after a year of Paneah's leadership, he was pleasantly surprised to realize that his household might be able to support itself. *Perhaps*, he thought as he walked upon the wall of his villa, *I may yet become a rich man!*

Quiet laughter interrupted his musings. Someone walked through the garden below, and Potiphar's hand automatically crept toward the dagger sheathed at his side. Nervously rubbing his tongue against the back of his teeth, he peered down through the shadows of the trees but saw only Paneah and Tuya walking along the edge of the lotus pool.

Potiphar released his dagger. His training as a bodyguard and warrior kept him too much on edge. Perhaps Narmer had been right to suggest that Potiphar learn to relax in his own home. What better place could there be? The house that used to remind him of his own inefficiency and shortcomings had become a place of refuge, an oasis away from the quicksand of Pharaoh's court. Paneah had made the villa efficient; Tuya had filled it with the sweet sounds of singing. He took a deep breath, forcing himself to ease his rigid posture.

"You did not!" Tuya's voice was a teasing caress in the warmth of the night. "You would not do such a thing!"

Surrendering to the human urge to eavesdrop, Potiphar stepped back into the shadows upon the wall.

"I did," Paneah said, facing the young girl at his side. Her face turned upward toward his in the moonlight. From his hiding place Potiphar could see love shining from Tuya's eyes like a meteor streaming in the night.

The nearness of that lovely face seemed to take Paneah's breath for a moment; then he caught the girl's hands in his and held them close to his breast. "I did," he repeated, looking at her as if he could drink her in. "I did ask the shepherds to name a lamb for you. So when I go out to the fields, I will think of you instead of—"

He looked away for a moment, and Potiphar noticed the way her body curved toward him. "The old dreams again?" she whispered.

"The old memories," he said, turning his dark eyes back to her glowing countenance. "My brothers. I think of them every time I walk under the sun, every time I see a herd of sheep or cattle. I pray that God will rid my heart of my sorrowful bitterness—"

Tuya's fingertips stopped his words. "Speak not of it anymore," she said, lifting her face to meet his. "Anger is a poison that destroys the soul. It will destroy our happiness, too, Joseph, if you dwell on these things."

"I would not destroy your happiness for even the throne of Egypt," the young man answered, his words running together in a velvet sound. He bent to brush his lips over the girl's forehead, and Potiphar felt the bitter gall of envy burn the back of his throat as he studied the sweet scene before him. How could two slaves without power, position, or possessions find such happiness while he, Pharaoh's Potiphar, wandered upon the wall of his villa with nothing to fill his lonely heart? It was only natural that such a handsome youth and beautiful girl should find each other, for they were young, and the appetites of love were fierce in youth. . . .

But he had always been more stirred by bloodlust than lust alone.

He stood motionless in the dark until the couple parted to walk to their separate chambers; then the master clasped his hands behind his back and took the stairs down to his empty room.

———

Anticipation of evenings in the garden with Joseph dulled the cutting edge of Tuya's loneliness. The young man stepped into the void left by Sagira and more than filled the empty spaces in her life. He was handsome enough to set even the oldest kitchen slave's tongue to wagging when he appeared in the doorway, but for Tuya, Joseph's attraction went far beyond physical appearance alone. In him she found a depth of understanding and insight sorely lacking in the Egyptians around her. Her people were simple, cheerful, and quick to learn, but most of the Nile's children were practical and unimaginative. Not given to deep speculation or thought, they were unable to evolve or express the abstract ideas that Joseph delighted in debating.

Joseph differed from the typical Egyptian in other ways, too. While the average resident of Thebes was highly superstitious and quick to placate any god he may have offended, Joseph often spoke with deep and abiding respect for El Shaddai, the God to whom he prayed every morning. And yet his devotion could not have been based upon blind faith, for though most Egyptians accepted everything the priests said without question, Joseph wanted to know the reasons behind every law or precedent Tuya mentioned.

He seemed to take particular pleasure in teasing Tuya about the myriad of Egyptian gods. "You say Pharaoh is one of the gods," he teased her one afternoon, "and yet they say our divine Pharaoh has a headache today. How can a god suffer pain? And when Pharaoh's life is done, how can a god-king die?"

"He is both god and man," Tuya explained, trying not to lose patience with him. "When a Pharaoh dies, the divine spirit is removed and placed within the heir. After death, the chosen heir becomes god and Pharaoh, and the dead and buried god becomes King of the dead, the ruler of the underworld. He becomes the great and terrible judge to whom the dead must answer for their deeds on earth."

"I would rather serve a God who cannot die," Joseph answered, lazy laughter in his eyes. "A God who is the same today as he was yesterday, and will still be the same tomorrow."

"You are a dreamer," Tuya chided.

She was about to remind him that dreams were foolish nonsense, but the light in his eyes suddenly dimmed. "Yes, I am," he replied, and his expression filled with such pain that she resolved never to speak of dreams again.

She knew he had come from a large family in the land of Canaan. From his speech she had gleaned he was a Hebrew, but he had taken great pains in the last year to become fluent in the Egyptian language. With his quick ear and agile tongue, no trace remained of his Canaanite accent or heritage. He had shaved his beard in the Egyptian fashion and wore his hair covered by a cloth of ribbed black silk. Tuya had ordered his smelly tunic burned on his first day in Potiphar's house, and now he wore the traditional white linen kilt of a slave, ornamented with an enameled collar and bronze arm bands. There remained nothing of the Hebrews about him but his memories, and Joseph clung to them with the tenacity of a terrier, but he kept his pain and past to himself. Occasionally his eyes darkened and he spoke bitterly of the brothers he had mentioned before, but he would not dwell on the subject or speak further when Tuya pressed him.

Like the Egyptians, Joseph was gentle, devoted to his friends and his God, and easily pleased. He had the courageous confidence of a lion, a quiet air of authority, and even when seated he looked taller than any other slave in the house. She could feel the power of his presence in a crowd of people, and her heart thudded like a drum whenever he happened to pass by. Without stopping to analyze her feelings, Tuya allowed her attraction for him to blossom into love. But she could not understand why he seemed to resist caring for her in the same way.

His eyes had followed her in the garden, and she knew by the way he smiled at her that he felt something for her when they were together. She could tell from his admiring gaze as they worked that he appreciated her skill at managing the household fully as much as he esteemed her beauty. Interest had radiated from the dark depths of his eyes from that first day when she began to nurse him, and their friendship had grown and deepened on a number of levels. But whenever the conversation turned to personal topics, or whenever Tuya felt Joseph was close to opening his heart, an invisible wall sprang up between them, and he withdrew from her as surely as if he had moved across the garden.

Tonight Joseph was intent upon the scroll in his lap. The air of the garden vibrated softly with the insect hum of the trees, and Tuya sat on the tiled walkway near him and traced her fingers over the still waters of the reflecting pool. The lotus blossoms on the water moved gently in the quiet of the night shadows, a romantic picture, but Joseph's thoughts were far away.

"The language is fascinating," Joseph murmured, running his hand over the papyrus spread between his knees. "Such beauty in these hieroglyphics! You were a good teacher, Tuya, and I a poor student. If I could only learn to write this well—"

"You will have no more time for learning here in Potiphar's house," Tuya said, looking over her shoulder at him. "Those who go to scribes' school labor from dawn until dusk for a dozen or more years. Their signs must be perfect, and the teaching priests believe that a boy's ears are on his back." Joseph looked up with an inquisitive glance, and Tuya smiled as she explained. "They are great lovers of the whip," she said, leaning toward him. "But you, Joseph, know nothing of this. Potiphar does not often beat his servants."

"Only because Potiphar does not care for his household," Joseph answered, returning his attention to the scroll. "I am sure he would not hesitate to use his whip upon his soldiers."

Leather suddenly slapped against the cool stone of the patio, and Tuya jerked upright. Potiphar stood before them, his eyes gleaming like lighted coals in the dim light. What had he heard? She and Joseph might feel the whip yet.

"Greetings, master," she blurted out, throwing her arms toward him as she touched her forehead to the floor. She closed her eyes and hoped that Joseph would have the good sense to follow her example.

"Good evening," Potiphar replied. Tuya blinked in surprise. His voice was composed and casual, much like that of a man out for a walk in his garden. Had he heard nothing of their conversation?

"You may lift your heads," the master called, and Tuya did so cautiously, half expecting to feel the sting of his hand across her cheek.

But Potiphar stood before them with his hands joined loosely at his waist. Their master's weather-beaten face was calm, but something flickered far back in his dark eyes.

"Paneah . . ." he began, looking at Joseph.

"Yes, master?"

"Why does Tuya call you by another name?"

Joseph hesitated only for the flash of an instant. "It is not because I dislike the name you gave me. I have come to appreciate the name Paneah. The life in which I was known by the other name is far behind me."

Potiphar lifted an eyebrow. "And yet this girl calls you by the other name." In one disobedient glance Tuya allowed her eyes to leave her master's face and dart toward Joseph.

"She is my bridge," Joseph answered, a wry smile curling on his lips. "She brought me from the old life safely into the new. If she had not nursed me—"

"It was you, master, who rescued him from the slave market," Tuya added hastily, eager to return the conversation to a more proper vein. "Paneah owes his life solely to you."

Potiphar nodded in approval, but Joseph interrupted.

"No. My life is owed to God."

Tuya cringed inwardly. Apparently Joseph had not been enslaved long enough to learn proper humility.

Potiphar did not take offense. "They say we owe everything to the gods," he said, offhandedly waving in the direction of the river. He returned his hands to his waist and
clasped them, squinting in amusement toward Joseph.
"Which god do you credit for your health and intelligence,
Paneah? Which god gave you those good looks? Hathor?
Amon? Osiris, perhaps?"

"The Egyptians do not know El Shaddai," Joseph answered, giving the master a look of mock superiority. "He
is the God above all others, the Almighty God who sees and
knows all."

A little spasm of panic shot across Tuya's belly. Had Joseph not learned that a man was only as great as his gods?
With one mention of his Almighty God, Joseph had claimed
to be greater than all in Egypt, even Pharaoh himself.

But Potiphar only rolled his eyes in amused disbelief.
He nodded as if considering Joseph's reply, and Tuya
thought a smile played briefly on his lips. "Believe in whatever you like, Paneah, for you have done well," he said finally. "Though I am sure your success has less to do with
divine blessing than with your sharp intellect."

"I appreciate your kindness, but I must disagree,"
Joseph answered. "I have found that faith is a higher faculty
than reason. Though, of course, faith is only as strong as the
object in which it is placed."

Potiphar pushed his bottom lip forward in thought.
"You know I do not worship any gods. Are you saying that
I am weak?"

Tuya felt the blood drain from her face. What had Joseph
done?

"Each man must test his own faith and his own gods,"
Joseph answered, ever the diplomat. "You, master Potiphar, must find strength great enough to sustain you
through life. Where you will find this strength, I cannot
say."

The moon, sailing across a sky of deepest sapphire, cast
a sudden bar of silver across Potiphar's face. His granite

eyes were locked on Joseph, but after a moment he lifted his head and folded his arms as tight as a gate. "You are clever," he said, the corner of his mouth lifting in a grudging smile. "For surely you know that I have the strength I need, Paneah, right here." His clenched fist knocked upon his chest. "And because I appreciate cleverness, one day I shall reward you. Perhaps my reward shall have something to do with the affection you have for this girl."

The master's bony finger suddenly pointed to Tuya, and she felt her frantic smile jell into an expression of shock. She had tried to hide her feelings for Joseph, for with one word Potiphar could send her away forever. . . .

"Who can say?" Potiphar continued, folding his arms again. "If you both serve me well, in time I will allow you to take her as your wife. If you regulate my household to run itself, in six years or so I may even grant your manumission." An understanding, arrogant grin spread across his features. "The collar of slavery does not suit you, Paneah. 'Twould be shameful for you to wear it too long."

With that parting promise, Potiphar turned and disappeared into the house.

Tuya turned to Joseph in stunned surprise. "Freedom!" she whispered, hardly daring to hope. "And marriage!"

Speechless, Joseph only nodded.

Joseph clasped his hands behind him as he walked down the narrow corridor to the room he shared with the other male slaves. Potiphar's offer of emancipation and marriage had taken him completely by surprise, and his emotions bobbed and spun like a piece of flotsam caught in the Nile flood. After six more years of service he would be twenty-four, a young man still, and capable of building an estate of his own as surely as he had brought Potiphar's house from the brink of ruin. Was this the avenue by which his dream would be fulfilled?

He stopped in the darkness and closed his eyes, searching his memory. The sun and moon and stars had bowed before him in the dream—could they not represent the merchants of Thebes? He could be a wealthy man before he reached thirty years of age.

Perhaps. He gave himself a stern mental shake and moved on toward his room. He did not want to leap ahead of the God who had blessed everything he touched and everyone who touched him. Tuya, without whose guidance he could never have begun to understand the Egyptian way of thinking, had blossomed under his attention. Devoted, dependable, and sympathetic, she had worked hard to insure his success with the other slaves. Her rich, fawnlike beauty warmed his heart every time he looked her way. He could marry her without hesitation if not for—

The past. She did not know that hidden part of him, the history he concealed beneath his industrious activity and casual conversation. She thought him an ordinary son from a large family, a foreigner with only fragile connections to the past, but he was the favored son of Jacob, Rachel's firstborn, the son who had stood to inherit the major portion of Jacob's flocks and treasures and goods. Despite the fact that he was younger than his brothers, the blessing and birthright of the eldest son would have been his, for Jacob had loved his beautiful mother most.

As the snores of the other slaves punctuated the darkness of the room, Joseph slipped down onto his papyrus mat and settled his thoughts about him. He had not told Tuya the entire story of his past because the act of submerging himself into memory hurt too much. During his illness he had scarcely felt the pain of his shattered arm because his few coherent thoughts centered around his father's grief and his brothers' betrayal. Had his unfaithful brothers told their father that fabricated story about Joseph's death in a struggle with a wild beast? Had not a single one of them listened to the convicting voice of El Shaddai and confessed the truth?

And another, darker fear hovered always at the edges of

his mind: did they intend to kill or kidnap his mother's other son in the same way? His brother Benjamin was yet a boy, but with Joseph gone, Jacob would cling to Rachel's remaining son like a shadow. Benjamin had undoubtedly been forced into Joseph's place as the favored son, and that gentle boy would never suspect that the older brothers he admired were capable of murder and betrayal. . . .

A sudden rise of panic threatened to choke Joseph where he lay; his throat worked as he struggled to stifle the cry that wanted to burst from his lungs. He had nursed his wounds for too long. He should escape and join a caravan heading north; he should return to his father and expose his brothers for the misbegotten malefactors that they were—

Trust me. The voice fell upon Joseph's consciousness even as he realized the stillness of the room had not been broken. The snorers slept on, undisturbed. Joseph shivered with a cold that was not from the air. He was not alone.

As I called Abraham from Ur, I have called you to this place. Forget the former things, do not dwell on the past. I am making a new path for you! Now it springs up before you, do you not perceive it? I am making a way in the desert and streams in the wasteland to give drink to my people that they may proclaim my praise.

Joseph sat up and blinked at the shadows in the room. The hair on his forearms lifted. Abu, the goatherd, and Bebu, the chief baker, tossed and turned in sleep as they did every night. Joseph's heart thumped against his rib cage. If he had not heard the voice of a man, then it was God who had spoken to him—but why?

"Will you speak again?" he whispered, feeling his way.

No answer came in the night; he heard nothing but the scattered breathing of his fellow slaves. After a long moment, Joseph lay down again and made an effort to calm his pounding heart. Eventually he withdrew into a dreamless sleep.

———————

Tuya readied her brightest smile for Joseph the next morning, but the smile died on her lips as he approached her at the well. Hollows lay beneath his eyes, dark, bluish gray circles. He looked as if he had not slept all night.

"Are you ill, Joseph?" she whispered, hurrying to his side.

"I am fine," he said, regarding her with a polite smile that did not reach his eyes.

"You wear the face of a man who has been troubled by dreams."

"Would that I had been. I slept little last night."

Tuya felt the thin, cold blade of foreboding slice into her heart. Joseph had been fine before their meeting with the master, and he had gone to bed immediately afterward. What, apart from Potiphar's suggestion of freedom and marriage, could have kept him awake all night? Since no slave would refuse liberty, Joseph's distress could only have come from the idea of marrying her.

"Did our master's words upset you?" she croaked, barely able to force the words past her unwilling lips.

"I cannot talk about it now. Let us begin our work, Tuya." His face emptied of expression as he spoke, and an icy silence fell between them. The sudden heaviness in Tuya's chest felt like a millstone. She dropped her water buckets and sat down upon a bench, utterly wretched.

"Can we not talk now?" she whispered, staring at nothing.

"No." His voice was as gentle as his words were disturbing. "I am not ready to talk about it yet." A host of emotions struggled beneath the surface of his handsome face. "There are some things that cannot be shared before they ripen into clear thoughts."

"Even with one who loves you?" Tuya whispered, lifting her eyes to his.

There. Right or wrong, she had said it. No slave dared to love another, for a life of slavery was too transitory and fleeting, but she had just admitted to Joseph that she loved him. Her feelings for him had grown in the past year, running far deeper than affection and stronger than the pleasure of their tender embraces.

"Tuya—" he began, his voice thick.

"I love you, Joseph," she cried, slipping from the bench to fall at his feet. "I would follow you to the end of Egypt if the master were to sell you. If Anubis came tonight and opened the road of the underworld for you, I would follow into death's darkness and find you in the gardens of paradise—"

"Quiet, Tuya!" Joseph knelt beside her, gripping her arms in his strong hands. All shadows of restraint fled from his face; his eyes blazed with fire. "You must not love like that! Such fierce longing can bring only sorrow and pain." His face paled as emotion clotted his voice.

"So you *have* loved," she whispered dully, wilting in his grasp like a thirsty lotus blossom. "At last the gods have put a figure on the barrier that keeps your heart from me. Who is she, Joseph? A Canaanite girl?"

"No," he answered, releasing her. He stood and regarded her with sad, tired eyes. "There is no girl. My father loved me with the love you speak of. And now he thinks me dead, while I, who would have been his heir, am a slave in a heathen land."

His father! Her feminine perception instantly understood. Joseph's heart had been wounded by the grief of separation, not by a lost love.

"Oh, beloved," Tuya said, rising to her feet. "Do you not realize we all know what you are feeling? Every slave has a story like yours, for we lost our families when we lost our freedom. I have never known a mother or a father, but I have grown accustomed to my place. And you, Joseph, remember how our master trusts you! He could not be more proud of you if you were his son. He believes you are blessed by the gods!"

"Potiphar believes in no one but himself," Joseph answered, folding his arms. "But last night when I considered running away, God spoke to my heart and assured me that I am to remain in Egypt. Perhaps He knows that my father could accept my death more easily than He could accept me"—Joseph swept his hand over his body to indicate the bronze collar at his neck and the linen skirt of a slave— "like this."

A lump formed in Tuya's throat at the thought of Joseph leaving, but she swallowed hastily and clutched at the hope that Joseph's God approved of their love.

"Surely your God is wise," she answered, leaning close. "Surely He can be trusted. You have trusted Him thus far—"

"I have had no choice," Joseph answered, looking past her toward the great blue bowl of sky. "He is the nameless longing, the voice who called Abraham out of Ur. He set a dream in my heart and has called me away from the bosom of my father. Now He bids me trust Him."

"Trust Him, then," Tuya said, clasping his hands in hers. Not caring who might see, she leaned her head forward to Joseph's chest and heard the beating of his heart. "Trust your God, Joseph. As Potiphar trusts in your common sense, and I trust in the strong arm of Montu, trust in your God and all will be well."

Nine

POTIPHAR BRISTLED AS NARMER ENTERED HIS BED-chamber and extended a scroll directly from the hand of the king's scribe. "Why does Pharaoh send a message instead of calling for me?" Potiphar asked, sliding his weary legs out from beneath the linen sheet that covered him. "Even at this late hour I have often been summoned to the royal presence."

The young courtier's air proclaimed his unutterable boredom, but no amount of studied nonchalance could conceal the jealousy in his eyes or the disdain in his posture. There was something awkward and milk-fed about him, like a calf, but he never failed to shine in Pharaoh's presence.

Narmer lifted a shoulder, attempting an inoffensive shrug. "The king thought it best to send his wishes with me," he said, clearly indicating that he stood inside the king's favor and confidence. "Perhaps you should not keep your king waiting longer, Potiphar."

Scowling, Potiphar broke the seal on the scroll and read the message penned there:

> In life, prosperity, health, and in favor of Amon-Re, King of the gods, and of the Ka of King Amenhotep II. Greetings, Potiphar, most trusted guard of Pharaoh. The empire carved out by my father, Tuthmosis III, may his name be ever praised, has experienced turmoil in the eastern nomes along the river known as Euphrates. I am ready to vent my displeasure on these rebel chieftains, and await your presence for this venture. Come

at once, and do not delay. Narmer waits to bring you to me.

The scroll had been sealed with Pharaoh's official scarab, and Potiphar knew that he could not waste a moment of the king's patience. "I will make ready to go at once," he murmured, not looking up. "You will wait outside in my reception rooms. I will send a girl to wash your feet."

"I would not stop to wash my feet while our king is waiting," Narmer said, holding up a defensive hand.

"Nevertheless, you shall, for I am not ready," Potiphar answered, standing. With shameless efficiency he propelled Narmer toward the doorway. Tuya was walking not far away in the corridor, so he clapped his hands. "Tuya! Take our king's messenger to the central hall and wash his hands and feet."

"I am not, Lord Potiphar, a mere messenger," Narmer said, fury lurking beneath his smile.

"You brought me a message; you are a messenger," Potiphar answered with an easy smile. "Our divine Pharaoh will not mind that you are a moment out of his presence. And I will have you back at the palace before your youthful face can sprout its next blemish."

Narmer flushed and clenched his fists, but Potiphar stalked away, indignation seething beneath his calm exterior. The trouble lay in his spending too much time at home. Of late his villa had become a refuge from the pitfalls of the palace, but while Potiphar was away, a new cat had come to toy with the royal favor. Narmer smelled of ambition as strong as cheap scent, and Amenhotep was wily enough to goad his old friend and fellow soldier with a fresh and competitive face.

This Narmer would not be high and mighty for long. _I may be an old cat_, Potiphar thought, stepping into a fresh kilt and fastening a belt at his waist, _but I have learned tricks from the wisest souls in this world and the one beyond._

Abruptly, he bellowed for Paneah.

———

Joseph's head was still filled with the haze of sleep when he entered Potiphar's chamber and automatically stooped to help his master dress.

"I must go away," Potiphar said as Joseph strapped on his sandals, "and I leave the entire household in your care. I cannot say how long this whim of Pharaoh's will last, for something has aroused the bloodlust in him. We are traveling to the eastern dominions and back, a journey of some months."

The sleepy haze vanished like fog before the sun. "Through the lands of Canaan?" Joseph asked, not looking up. Did he dare suggest that he accompany Potiphar? The traveling army might cross the lands of Jacob, might even encounter the family itself. Joseph could return to his father in the company of the foremost military general of the world's greatest king. He could repay his brothers' treachery with righteous vengeance; in one bold move he could reveal to Jacob that ten of his sons were fiends, and the one thought dead, still alive and strong.

"Of course we will pass through Canaan," Potiphar snapped, fumbling with the leopard-skin belt that held his dagger. "The Mitanni tribes are in trouble again, probably feuding with the Hittites."

Joseph finished fastening the sandals and reached up to hook the enclosure of the dagger belt. "You might have use for a servant on the journey."

The master's brows knitted in a frown. "I have ten thousand soldiers at my bidding, Paneah," he said, his voice surprisingly gentle. "What I need—what I have never had till now—is a home waiting when I return. I place you in charge of everything you find here. Speak with my full authority and act as my steward."

Narmer stepped impatiently into the room as Potiphar finished speaking. With a superior smirk he lifted a jeweled hand and pointed to Joseph: "Dare you leave your house in the care of a slave? You will have nothing when we return, for even this boy will run away." He snickered. "Can it be that Potiphar's renowned wisdom is fading?"

"My gift of discernment is still strong," Potiphar answered, not bothering to look at the younger man as he made a last-minute check of his person. "I would trust Paneah with my life."

He turned again to Joseph and lowered his voice, his eagle eye staring down his heavy nose. "I trust you, Paneah, with all I have. Do not prove my intuition wrong."

Joseph straightened his back. "I will not, my lord."

Potiphar nodded, then scowled out the doorway.

Rebellious would-be-kings from the northeastern provinces of Carchemish and Tegarama had amassed a sizeable force, but their troops were no match for the swift battalions of Pharaoh's golden warriors. The well-organized Egyptian army, comprised of both infantry and chariot troops, flew across the desert like a whirlwind, churning up sand and wind and debris. The chariots, each manned by two soldiers and two horses, were made of the lightest wood available and designed so that wounded horses could be unstrapped and the chariot hauled by prisoners of war if necessary. Behind the chariots came the infantry—foot soldiers carrying spears, shields, and battle-axes to wipe the field clean of any enemy troops that might have survived the first onslaught.

Potiphar rode next to Amenhotep's own chariot. The king's charioteer, a grizzled veteran of other foreign wars, kept the horses steady as the king bellowed and sent his arrows flying in a whistling cloud toward the enemy. Potiphar preferred the battle-axe to the bow. His axe, a curved golden blade resting in a silver-shafted handle, had been blessed by Pharaoh himself and had never failed to leave a battle without tasting blood.

Enemy arrows dropped so thickly that the ground bristled with them like quills in a goose's wing, but Amenhotep's courage did not fail. Delighting in combat and red-faced as the setting sun, he sent his arrows flying into waves of the approaching rebels. A rogue arrow from some quarter glanced off the king's face, and blood from the wound in his forehead painted his visage into a glistening devil mask that did more to discourage his foes than the overwhelming Egyptian weaponry. Whether from fear or intimidation, the enemy began to fall back, and Potiphar felt inwardly relieved that this battle would not be a long one.

When at last the rebels threw down their weapons and surrendered, scores of men lay motionless on the ground, the life gone out of them like a suddenly extinguished light. Potiphar drove his weary horses to Pharaoh's chariot and bowed his head. "A good victory, my king," he said, taking pains to keep his voice strong and pleasant. "Are we ready to turn the army for home?"

"By all the gods, no!" Amenhotep roared, his eyes still shining with the thrill of the chase. "I will follow in my father's footsteps and subdue these troublesome kings again. We will march from this place to the River Euphrates, and there I will raise my own stela of victory to record my accomplishments and military successes. We will return to the Nile with a host of captive kings to sacrifice to Egypt's gods, and the tale will go forth from this place so none of these will dare rise up against Egypt again!"

Potiphar was slightly surprised that the king's bloodlust remained at fever pitch, but he bowed and forced a smile. "I will tell the men," he said, slapping the reins of his horses. "Rest well, my king. May the morrow bring forth yet another victory."

Ten

"JOSEPH!" TUYA CALLED FROM THE GATE OF POTI-phar's villa. Slanting sunlight shimmered off the glowing green foliage of the trees; the day was too pretty to waste. "Will you never finish? The festival is beginning!"

"The cattle and sheep do not know today is a feast day," Joseph grumbled, hurrying out of the stockyard. He left his box of papyrus records with the gatekeeper and paused to give the man detailed instructions about the duties of the other household slaves. The Feast of Opet was a national festival during which no one worked, but Joseph was determined that neither Potiphar's fields nor his livestock would feel a lack of attention during the holiday.

"All right," Joseph said, stepping out of the gatehouse. He gave Tuya a smile as bright as the sun. "Your escort awaits you, my lady."

A deep sense of happiness flooded Tuya's soul as she took Joseph's arm, and a blush of pleasure rose to her cheeks. With Potiphar gone, there was virtually no one to remind them that they were not lord and lady of the house. For nearly a full year Joseph had run the estate with a firm hand, monitoring the servants who ran the fields and the stockyard and managing to keep Pharaoh's tax collectors at bay while he stockpiled Potiphar's crops and treasures. When and if the master returned from his military foray, he would find himself a vastly wealthy man.

Tuya took a deep breath of the dry air and enjoyed the warmth of the sun upon her face. The rising sun had swallowed up the wind, and the dazzling blur of the sun-god's boat stood proud and fixed in the white-blue sky. Heat covered the city like a blanket, but Tuya felt deliciously cool in the exquisite white linen dress she had sewn for herself. As fine as any lady's gown, the loose garment was tied at the shoulders with delicate tassels. A pair of red leather slippers adorned her feet, and she felt especially pampered because scented yellow saffron oil perfumed her arms and neck. The precious perfume had been a gift from Joseph, and she had protested its extravagance when he slipped the vial into her hand.

"Potiphar's name will be praised when people see that even his slaves conduct themselves like royalty," Joseph murmured, giving her a heart-stopping smile. "And when they see you, my beautiful Tuya, Potiphar's reputation will ascend to the heavens."

And so she had relented, hoping that the sweet scent of the perfume would draw Joseph to her the way a flower attracts a bee. Like any man who loves work, he found it difficult to relax, but Tuya took his hand and led him through the streets, explaining the meaning of the festival ceremonies and the altars and stelae which had been set up to commemorate the occasion.

"The festival begins when the shrine of the god Amon is carried from the dark chamber of his temple at Karnak into the sunlight," Tuya explained, pulling Joseph through a jostling crowd of drunken merrymakers who vied for a spot along the riverbank.

"Why does the god wish to leave his temple?" Joseph asked, indulgently following her.

"Well," Tuya said, blushing, "he goes each year to visit his harem at the Temple of Southern Opet."

"Ah," Joseph laughed, his eyes twinkling with mischief. "And what pleasure can a harem give a god of stone?"

"Quiet!" Tuya whispered, afraid someone would overhear his blasphemy. "Who knows what the gods do? Men cannot see into the underworld. We cannot divine things of the spirit."

"Perhaps we can," Joseph answered, but Tuya wasn't in the mood for one of his religious discussions. Craning her neck, she pointed toward the river. "Here they come! Closer, Joseph, stand here. You have never seen anything like this!"

He did not answer but moved closer and rested a hand upon her shoulder as they swayed in the throng along the riverbank. The anticipatory roar of the crowd reached them first, then Tuya could hear the whine of the priests' horns and the pounding of the drum. Finally the god's cedarwood barge came into view. Upon the flat platform a host of bald priests in long white robes stood guard over an object swathed in white linen and supported by a gleaming gilded altar. Many in the crowd fell to their knees as the barge passed, and petitions to the great god Amon began to fill the air.

"Merciful Amon, hear my cry!"

"Restore unto me the money I have lost!"

"Amon, hear the plea of a childless woman!"

"Amon-Re, grant our king safety and return him to the land!"

The barge did not travel under its own power but was pulled by teams of horses on both riverbanks. The pious pilgrims closest to the banks scattered as the horses approached, but many of the most fervent dashed beneath the ropes as if they meant to swim out and personally present their petitions to the god. The sudden appearance of leather-skinned crocodiles in the water kept even the most religious celebrants on shore, however, and within a few moments the god's barge had passed.

"Now the real excitement comes," Tuya promised, looking up at Joseph. Behind the sacred god came the gold-plated barge of Pharaoh, commanded today in the king's absence by Queen Merit-Amon. Upon this barge the queen and the high priest of Amon made continual offerings of food and incense to the god, while on the riverbank opposite them paraded a great host, which included befeathered

Nubian drummers, a band of lute-playing musicians, scantily clad acrobats, blind harpists, and Egypt's finest wrestlers. A company of soldiers in the gilded chariots of Pharaoh's royal guard followed, their standards lowered to indicate their captain was away.

"Potiphar's men," Tuya said, a feeling of pride stirring in her breast as she watched the royal guard. "They are anxious for his return."

"Are you?" Joseph asked in a low voice, his hand moving to her waist.

"No," she answered, then turned about to face him. "I mean, yes. He is a good master, but it has been so nice—"

"You do not have to explain," Joseph answered, smiling in the calm strength that came from knowing her so well. "I, too, have found myself imagining what it would be like if the house, the horses, the fields, the servants . . ." His gaze focused on her lips. ". . . were mine."

The crowd surged around them and moved to follow the procession, but Joseph and Tuya stood as if rooted to the riverbank. "You could pretend until the master returns," Tuya whispered, gathering her slippery courage. "No one will know, Joseph, that you are not the master, and I am not . . . your wife."

She could almost feel his thoughts, and she knew that he wanted her. They had worked and laughed and worried together for nearly two years, and their souls were as close as two could be without joining their bodies in the mystical union that the gods had ordained for husbands and wives. She had labored to bring him back from the edge of the underworld, and he had rescued her from unendurable loneliness. Why should they not enjoy each other? No one would care if two slaves did not wait for marriage; no one would bother two subcitizens who found delight in each other. . . .

"Ah, Tuya," he whispered, looking at her with something deeper than mere masculine interest. Her heart shuddered expectantly. The crowd continued to jostle them, and a company of drunken merchants began to argue over the price of some trinket. "Come," Joseph said, pulling her away. "This is not the place for us."

A trembling thrill raced through her as Joseph linked her fingers with his and pulled her away from the crowd of revelers.

Yes. No. Yes. No. With every step Joseph's heart turned from one conviction to the other. Why should he not take this girl who loved him? Over the months he had come to trust Tuya, and in the security of her humble devotion he had finally found the courage to confide the secrets of his past, his hopes, even his strange dreams. Surely the feeling between them was as strong as that which had existed between his father and Rachel! And Potiphar had practically promised to grant them permission to be married. It was not a question of *if*, but *when*. And why not now, when the bloom of youth still graced them both and the fragrance of love filled the air?

He had become a man of Egypt—he dressed like an Egyptian, spoke like an Egyptian, wrote the language of the Egyptians. The Egyptians would see nothing wrong with his taking Tuya into his arms and mingling his flesh with her own. Egypt had a dozen gods and rituals dedicated to the celebration of fertility, and the act he was considering would be little more than a ritual of worship in the eyes of the pagan priests. The other slaves did not curb their passions. Many of the men who slept in the slaves' quarters consistently baited him with rude comments, doubting his masculinity because he had not already surrendered to Tuya's considerable beauty.

His body yearned to possess her. His heart slammed into his ribs every time he thought about pressing his lips to hers, and the sight of her passing through a corridor was enough to send a wave of warmth along his pulse. He was nineteen years old, strong in limb and desire, and alone in a place where the pursuit of pleasure was a common pastime for kings and slaves alike. Tuya was willing, he knew. Only her great love for him had preserved her patience thus far.

The crowd buzzed around him, but his ears centered on the sound of the quiet puff of her eager footsteps in the dust. He realized that she had no doubts about his reason for seeking a private place—she was certain the time had come.

Had it? Yes. No. Perhaps.

Unbidden, the voice and image of Jacob came to him in a surge of memory. "For seven years I worked and waited for your mother without taking her into my tent." His father spoke slowly, still staring at the mound of rocks where they had just buried Rachel. "And the years passed like hours, so great was my love for her." Jacob let out a short laugh touched with embarrassment. "Although her beauty drove me to kiss her the first time I saw her, I did not sleep with your mother until her father gave her to me in marriage. Remember this, my son—a patient man is better than a warrior. A man who controls his desires is stronger than one who rules a city."

Joseph stopped in the middle of the street, knowing what his decision must be. "Oh, Tuya," he whispered, turning to her. He caught his hands in her hair. What words could he use to make her understand?

"Joseph," she murmured as she lifted her lips and flowed toward him.

"What are ye waitin' for?" an aged crone called from the side of the street. Startled, Joseph looked up to see a toothless hag regarding him with bright eyes. "Kiss her, boy, and get on with it!"

Joseph flushed as a rush of warmth washed over him, and he yanked Tuya forward, desperate to be rid of the eyes of the crowd.

The fierce sunlight cast deep shadows upon the street, and Tuya willingly followed Joseph into the shadows of an acacia grove. Away from the teeming life of the multitude along the river, the world seemed now to consist of only two. How fitting it was that he should lead her here, for trees were the confidantes of lovers. . . .

"Tuya," Joseph said again, and she turned to face him, offering her heart and her embrace.

"Joseph," she whispered drowsily, wrapped in a warm bunting of her own feelings.

"We cannot do this." His hands tightened upon her arms, but Tuya did not feel the pressure, so startled was she by the dart that had pierced her heart.

She shivered in the chill shock. "You do not want me—"

"This is wrong. You belong to Potiphar, and he has placed his trust in me. To do this would be a sin against God and a crime against my master."

"Potiphar will not know! He is far away, perhaps dead—"

"God will know. I will know, and you will know that I have committed this wrong."

"Is it wrong to share love?" Tuya cried, her mind reeling with his denial of their desires. "You cannot tell me you do not want me."

"I do want you," he whispered in an aching, husky voice she scarcely recognized. "God knows how much. But I cannot sin against Him. Our love will have to wait."

"Wait?" Her heart sank with swift disappointment. "For how long, Joseph? Until tomorrow? Next year? When will this God of yours approve? Perhaps you are only waiting for some nice Canaanite girl to enter the household!"

"No, Tuya," he whispered, dropping his hands from her arms. Without the warmth of his touch, she felt suddenly alone and vulnerable. "I love you with all my heart and soul," he said, his eyes raking her face as if he could will her to believe his words. "But here," he tapped the space of flesh over his heart, "I know we must wait."

She choked at the sight of his hand upon the place where she had pressed her head to hear the reassuring beat of his heart. In an instant, her capacity for sorrow reached its limit, and her emotions veered crazily from grief to fury. "You have mocked me with your talk of love!" she snapped, turning to run away.

"No." His strong arm caught her and pulled her back. "I honor you too much to mock you." His head came to rest beside her own as he held her. "I honor you too much to commit this wrong. We will do what is right, and when our master returns, he will see that his faith in us was justified."

Tuya turned her face away from his as she struggled to gather her thoughts. He did not truly love her. The trees, the gray and blue-green shadows of the grove reminded her of the garden where once, during another lifetime, she had offered her love to Sagira. That love, too, had been spurned.

"I have often thought," she whispered brokenly, watching the slender fingers of golden sunlight probe through the foliage, "that I was not meant to find love. Love is for other people, not for slaves like me."

"Tuya, you must not say that," Joseph said, pulling her chin up with his hand. A wounded look lay behind his dark eyes. "Love will find you, it will find us, in God's time. We will have to wait and trust Him."

"Trust Him," Tuya echoed. She lifted her hand and gently ran her fingertips over the lovely face she could never deserve to call her own. "You are right, Joseph. We must honor the master; we must not lose our heads." A measure of composure returned, and she gathered the rags of her dignity about her and lifted her chin. "So be it," she said, giving him a brittle smile even though she longed to throw herself upon the ground and weep in frustration. "We will wait for Potiphar, my Joseph."

She pulled herself away from his grasp and had taken three steps when his voice made her pause. "I love you,

Tuya," he called, his voice heavy with pain and longing.

She was certain he spoke only out of kindness, but she could not be angry with him. Her wounded pride would heal, but not without the balm of friendship from the only person she dared to trust.

"I love you, Joseph," she answered, glancing over her shoulder. She held out her hand, waiting, and breathed a sigh of quiet relief when he took it and led her from the acacia grove.

⟶ Eleven ⟵

POTIPHAR BIT BACK AN OATH WHEN HE LEARNED
that Narmer, the king's obsequious courtier, had been
named a standard-bearer and placed in charge of two hundred fifty men. In addition to the elite royal guards that Potiphar commanded, other troops were organized into various corps. And at the head of one of those corps, Narmer
now strutted like a haughty ostrich.

Amenhotep II and his troops had been in the east for
fourteen months. During their trek through the numerous
buffer states, either Pharaoh's warriors put down rebellions
or his courtiers visited the camps of kings to secure extant
peace treaties. For his help in subduing the warlike Hittites, the king of the Mitanni tribe, a short, plump polyp of
a warrior, demanded and received assurance that one of his
daughters would wed the next Pharaoh of Egypt. Tribes
from many kingdoms sent tributes to Pharaoh, and those
who did not were engaged in battle and forcibly van-
quished. Kings were captured and defeated men pressed
into service. Pharaoh's army soon grew to cover the land
like a swarm of locusts.

At last Pharaoh stood on the banks of the Euphrates
where his father and grandfather had erected stelae to commemorate their victories. Amenhotep raised his own pillar
to record his meritorious accomplishments. After the
proper sacrifices, chants, and prayers, the king ordered his
army to return to Egypt.

The captive kings were bound and marched overland in
front of the advancing army. When Pharaoh boarded the
royal barge at the naval port of Peru-nefer, the captive

chiefs were hung upside down on the prow of his boat to be displayed before the throngs of adoring, triumphant Egyptians. Potiphar knew the chiefs would eventually die at Pharaoh's own hand as he beheaded them in a religious ceremony.

The army was at last on its way home. The late afternoon sun streaked the water crimson as Potiphar stood at the stern of the king's boat. "Sweet breath of the Nile, lead me southward," he whispered, absently staring at the line of boats following Pharaoh's. Their oars flashed like the wings of a dragonfly, churning up the river with furious motion. Along the side of the ship a run of living water sang; along the side of the river, Pharaoh's adoring people cried and wept and fainted from sheer joy. Their god, the divine Pharaoh, had returned.

Potiphar concentrated on the steady slush and suck of the water and the rhythmic beat of the drums giving the rowers their stroke. He was too old to enjoy the adulation of the crowd; he had cut too many throats to continue relishing the blood sport of war. War was for foolish young men and idle kings. If this god-king had at last had his fill of it, perhaps the country could rest in peace.

The blue-green ripples of water glistened in the sun as the barge cut through the summer Nile. Potiphar clasped his hands behind his back and wondered if Paneah would prove worthy of the trust he had placed in him.

——————

From his first glimpse of the walls of his villa, Potiphar wondered if he had come to the wrong estate. The tall, crumbling walls had been repaired and heightened; sweet gardens of flowers grew outside the entrance gate. The gatekeeper, a new slave whom Potiphar had never seen, bowed and was about to discreetly ring a bell when Potiphar stopped him. "No," he said, his scarred hand falling upon the youth's tanned one. "I would like to see the house alone."

The slave nodded stiffly, his heavy cheeks falling in worried folds over his slave's collar, and Potiphar moved past the gate onto the curving path. A new wall had been erected to partition the grounds of the prison from the villa, and Potiphar noted with satisfaction that the sights, smells, and sounds of the prison would no longer intrude upon the house. The guard on duty at the prison gate saluted sharply at Potiphar's approach, but Potiphar only nodded and turned his back on the somber structure. Paneah would have done nothing there. The prison undoubtedly remained as it had always been, a bitter, foul place for bitter, foul prisoners.

The house rose from the sterility of the sunbaked ground like an oasis in the desert, its little temple gleaming like new silver in the savage sunlight. The crumbling statues of Anubis and Osiris had been removed, and nothing remained inside the chamber but a clean altar and a bowl of burning incense. Potiphar found that the spareness of the place suited him. He had never pledged allegiance to any personal deity, so why should he play the hypocrite and pretend at piety in the temple of his own home?

Bemused, Potiphar left the temple and continued toward the house. The sand beneath his sandals had been sprinkled to control the dust, and his courtyard smelled of nothing but clean, bone-dry air. For the first time in his memory, he could not smell the stockyard. Through an opening in a wall ahead and to his right he could see women carrying baskets of grain, and beyond them, three tall, cone-shaped granaries to hold stores of grain and wheat. There had been but one granary when he left.

"I feel like a stranger visiting the house of a prince," he said aloud; then he laughed at the absurdity of his words. Briskly climbing the steps to the house, he saw that the doorway had been repainted, and his name on the lintel outlined in bold, black letters. A servant prostrated himself at Potiphar's approach, and the master stepped over the slave's body and waved the man away.

He swept through the north loggia and into his reception room, then stepped back, amazed at the sight that greeted him. This central hall, the heart of every nobleman's residence, had always been a hollow, vacant symbol of Potiphar's empty, single-purpose life. Unpainted and unadorned, in past years the room had represented the truth that Potiphar enjoyed no important guests, no life, no pleasure apart from his service to Pharaoh.

But now the room glowed with a vitality and life of its own. The bare ceiling had been painted the soft blue of a morning sky and accented with gold at the place where the ceiling joined its supporting pillars. The windows, high on the softly painted walls, were open so that air stirred in a sweet morning breeze, and the four pillars were covered in red paint bold enough to satisfy even Pharaoh's elaborate tastes. Against one wall a low brick dais had been built for Potiphar to sit upon, and next to the dais a brazier glowed with burning charcoal to chase away the chill of morning. On the other side of the room, a handsomely carved limestone slab with a raised edge waited for the dusty hands and feet of Potiphar's guests. A pitcher of the purest white marble stood ready to cleanse away the irritating sand of the desert.

Handsome panels of red and yellow moldings gleamed from above the doorways, and niches had been carved into the walls opposite the doorways to balance the openings in the room. At the northern end of the hall, a staircase led up to the roof. From peering up through the opening, Potiphar could see that a light shelter had been built to provide shade from the sun.

A pair of sandaled feet appeared on the staircase, and Potiphar stepped out of sight and waited. A tall, imposing man came into view, a scroll in his hand and a frown upon his handsome face.

"Do I know you?" Potiphar asked, pursing his lips suspiciously.

The frown broke into a familiar smile, and the man instantly lowered himself to the floor at Potiphar's feet. "Master! I am Paneah, your servant."

"Paneah?" Potiphar stooped and tapped the young man's shoulder. "Lift your head so I may see you better. I did not realize the desert sun had blinded me so completely."

"There is nothing wrong with your eyes," Paneah answered loyally, lifting his face.

Potiphar crossed his arms and stared at the stranger before him. By all the gods, how a year had changed him! The awkwardness of adolescence had completely vanished from the lad's limbs and left him slim, but powerfully built. He had always been well favored, Potiphar recalled, but the man before him now was the precise definition of handsome, with a striking face, a broad pair of shoulders, and an easy, open manner. His eyes snapped with intelligence and good will, his smile was more a spontaneous expression of pleasure than a mechanical civility.

"I can only hope I have not changed as drastically," Potiphar answered, finally finding his tongue. "The house is a different place, and my youthful steward is now a man."

"You honored me greatly by placing me in charge of your household," Paneah said, standing to his feet. "I hope you have found everything to your liking."

"Well—" Potiphar raised his arms, looking around, then let them fall at his side. "I can find nothing to dislike, Paneah, unless you have spent all your energy on this room and no others."

"Never fear, master, all your affairs are in order," Paneah said, laughing. "If you would like a tour of the villa—"

"Of course, lead the way and show me what you have done," he answered, thrusting his hands behind his back. "I only hope you have not depleted my treasure room so completely that I will have to sell you to feed my sheep."

"Your treasures are intact and increased," Paneah answered, leading the way from the reception room. "The cattle produced well this year; every cow brought forth a calf. The sheep, too, were fertile, and the harvest of your lands has been so bountiful that I purchased additional slaves to bring in the harvest. I have trained them all in other jobs as well, so you will have no fear of waste during the winter months—"

"I do not fear anything, Paneah," Potiphar said, slapping the slave's back as he fell into step beside the young man. "And with you in charge of my house, I will not worry about anything but Pharaoh."

———

One week after his return home, Potiphar joined the other royal troops at the palace for Pharaoh's massive awards ceremony. Feasting and rituals would take place throughout the day, beginning with the sacrifice of the enemy kings at dawn and concluding with the transportation of Pharaoh's gods along the Nile at sunset.

After the bloody sacrifice at the temple, Pharaoh's nobles, warriors, and courtiers moved to the throne room in Pharaoh's palace. The gigantic hall was as crowded as Potiphar had ever seen it, and he gripped the handle of the dagger in his belt as the crowd churned and surged behind the row of guards at the open doors. One by one, the royal scribes read off the names of those who had been with the king on his military expedition, and those men, great and small, came forward to acknowledge Pharaoh's gratitude and accept his praise. Foot soldiers who had done well in combat received tiny golden flies for "stinging" the enemy; to others, Pharaoh presented golden daggers, carved and painted shields, and handsomely carved bronze arrowheads. To the archers, Pharaoh gave painted leather forearm protectors, and to captains like Narmer, the king awarded permission to kiss his royal foot, not just the ground at his feet.

The crowd around Potiphar buzzed when the royal scribe looked his way. Every standard-bearer, petty officer, and foot soldier had been rewarded, only the captain of the king's elite guards waited to receive his prize. For the first time since the presentations had begun, Pharaoh stood from his throne.

"Potiphar! Your king and god summons you!"

Potiphar stepped forward from the line of guards at the king's right hand and prostrated himself on the floor before Amenhotep. He had lain in this position before, hoping for the golden chain that hung around the king's neck, but this time he had certainly earned the prize. The Gold of Praise was an exalted and high honor few men could wear, but he had served not only this pharaoh, but Pharaoh's divine father. . . .

"Potiphar, how can a king reward his most trusted servant?"

"The warmth of your favor is enough, my king," Potiphar called, lifting his head from the floor just enough for his words to be heard.

"No, it is not enough. I must do something more for you, my friend, and have thought many days on this matter. Horus himself has shown me what I can do. Rise, Potiphar, and accept the gratitude and devotion of your king."

Potiphar pressed hard upon the floor, feeling his age as he pushed up to his feet. *He could thank me properly by staying home for the rest of my days*, he thought, bending his head in submission as he walked toward the king's throne. *Another eastern expedition is likely to mean the end of me. . . .*

"I have thought, faithful friend, about what you do not have," Pharaoh said, his voice low. Surprised at the king's conversational tone, Potiphar lifted his eyes to meet Amenhotep's. "And I am prepared to give you this day what you lack. You have received every honor Egypt can give her servants and every right a Pharaoh can bestow. You kiss the royal foot, even the leg; you travel by my side and stand beside my throne. A hundred golden flies decorate the animal skins you wear for a mantle, and yet you do not possess one reward I can give."

Potiphar's disobedient eyes slipped to the Gold of Praise about Pharaoh's neck as the crowd drew an expectant breath.

"Once I gave you a beautiful woman; now I will give you a noble one. Donkor, my kinsman, has a daughter of fourteen years. She was born in the royal line of pharaohs, and today she will be your wife."

The saving grace of long habit prodded Potiphar to fall at Pharaoh's feet in the proper pose of gratitude. Reflexively, he murmured his thanks, but his brain roiled with the king's words. A wife! Pharaoh did not know, he could not know! Potiphar was a forty-six-year-old soldier, not the sort of man to be a husband, and yet Pharaoh wanted to give him a royal wife who would demand to be coddled, petted, teased, and spoiled. . . .

An audible hush suddenly fell upon the droning gossips who had sprung to life at Pharaoh's words, and the soft swish of fabric over marble reached Potiphar's ears. "Rise, Potiphar, and meet your bride," Pharaoh called, and Potiphar's arms trembled as he pushed himself up and turned to face the child who would share his future and his house.

Clothed in a diaphanous sheath of reddish gold, a vision of a young goddess stood before him. Her pleated dress was bordered with rich fringe, and the gauzy fabric of the garment allowed him to see the handsome shape of plump legs, a solid stomach, and strong arms. Distracted, he looked up into the young eyes that peered from beneath a heavy wig. "I am Sagira, my lord," a voice whispered. "Daughter of Donkor and kinsman to the king."

His first thought was that the wreath of lotus blossom circling her head put forth an unusually heady scent; then he realized that the lady also carried a floral bouquet. She had come to the palace dressed for a wedding.

Pharaoh must have guessed at Potiphar's discomfiture, for an abrupt burst of laughter escaped him. "Potiphar, my old friend," he said, speaking with as much warmth as he dared before a jealous court. "Did you think you could escape matrimony forever? Your duty lies in raising sons as brave and devoted as you are. Take this girl as your wife, here and now, and do not fail your king."

"I would not fail you," Potiphar answered, his stomach tightening. The crowd broke into pleased applause.

In his younger days, he would have seen such a trap coming long before it snared him.

Sagira felt the burn of a blush upon her cheek. Despite his posture of gratitude, she could read in his eyes that her husband was not happy about this marriage. He should have been overjoyed, for many fathers had sought to have her for their sons. But unwilling to marry Sagira without Pharaoh's permission, her parents had waited anxiously for the king's return from the East. In a private meeting arranged by one of the king's courtiers, Donkor and Kahent approached Pharaoh and mentioned their desire to find a suitable husband for their noble daughter. Flushed from the thrill of his military campaign, Pharaoh had been enthusiastic to honor a warrior and declared that the resolute and courageous Potiphar would prove an admirable husband for Sagira. He needed to honor the grizzled champion of a hundred wars, and marriage to the daughter of his sister was a brilliant solution.

Potiphar, Kahent later confided to Sagira, was strong enough to serve as Pharaoh should Ramla's prophecy be borne out in his lifetime. And if he proved to be less than a good husband, he was old enough to die and give Sagira a lifetime in which she could marry again.

Her fate could have been worse, Sagira knew. Despite his age, Potiphar was known as a fair and dutiful man, and his household had prospered even in the year of his absence. She had asked her father to drive his chariot past Potiphar's villa, and she found it to be one of the most handsome in Thebes. As the villa's mistress, she would bring grace and elegance to the place. In time, this old goat would be grateful for Pharaoh's favor.

Lifting her eyes from her husband-to-be, she pivoted gracefully and walked down the open aisle spreading before the throne of all Egypt. Promptly on cue, the priests from the temple of Bastet, her patron goddess, brought forward the marriage canopy that had been woven from river rushes. Sagira met her father under the canopy, then turned and waited for her groom.

A silence settled upon the throne room, an absence of sound that had about it an almost physical density. Potiphar stood without moving, his mouth gaping like a fish taken from the safety of the river, and for a desperate moment Sagira thought he would refuse the king's gift.

Suddenly Pharaoh's voice filled the strangely thickened air. "Potiphar," he called, a thin note of warning in his voice, "surely you will want to thank the man who has served you in this venture. As I searched for a way to honor you, Narmer came from Donkor and put your bride's name into my thoughts."

Sagira saw Potiphar jerk his heard toward the spot where the courtier stood like a cocky rooster preening his feathers. Dressed in fine linen and animal skins, Narmer stepped forward at the mention of his name and fell onto his knees before Pharaoh.

"And what should I give you, beloved and faithful Narmer?" Pharaoh asked, glancing down. "You who have provided so many answers to my questions?"

"Nothing I could ask for will replace your affection in my heart," Narmer said, his eyes humbly fastened to the floor. "But if I could wear the Gold of Praise about my neck, I would forever be reminded that Pharaoh holds me in esteem."

Amenhotep laughed and lay aside the crook and flail. "So be it," he cried, lifting the heavy chain from his neck. He held it aloft for all to see. "Narmer will wear his king's favor upon his shoulders. He has received the divine praise of Pharaoh for having had a part in bringing Potiphar his noble bride!"

A decidedly ugly and angry look settled upon Potiphar's features as he turned from the strutting figure of Narmer and faced the bridal canopy. Sagira took note of the expression, for Potiphar's reputation as a warrior was well-known, and he could undoubtedly be violent if pressed. For the sake of her safety, she would be careful never to rouse her husband's anger.

———

The wedding was but another celebration on the program of Pharaoh's grand festival, and Potiphar was irritated by his role in it. In time he might have considered taking an older, quiet woman to be his wife, for often he longed for a companion to share the home he had come to enjoy. But he did not care to have a youthful bride thrust upon him. The daughter of Donkor was lovely, in the dark fashion of most Egyptian girls, but she lacked Tuya's devoted smile and the long-limbed gracefulness of the women he had observed in the northeastern provinces. At fourteen, she was probably still much a child, but her face was composed when she turned to face him.

He should have studied his bride-to-be as the priests began the incantations of the ceremony, but he was distracted by the entourage with her. Behind her stood a bald priestess in a spotless white robe, a sour-faced, somber creature who regarded Potiphar with distrust and loathing in her eyes. Donkor stood at his daughter's right hand, a royal relative whose enormous belly advertised his prosperity far better than words. Behind this trio Narmer paced confidently, his hands behind his back, a curved smile upon his thin lips, and the Gold of Praise glittering about his neck.

Why did I not just ask for it? Potiphar chided himself. *Instead of prattling about Pharaoh's favor and indulging in false humility, why did I not come out and tell the king what*

and why he owes me? Then I would have the Gold of Praise,
and some young fool like Narmer would have this girl.

But the gods worked in mysterious ways, and Egypt's
divine Pharaoh was the most unpredictable of them. On
any other day, had a man dared to ask for the chain about
Pharaoh's neck, he would be crocodile meat before the sun
set. Narmer was a fool, but Potiphar could not disparage his
boldness.

The high priest of Bastet, a bald, sallow-faced man, gestured for Potiphar to extend his hands and feet. Potiphar
obeyed, as did Sagira, and with fresh water from the Nile,
the priest washed the limbs of both bride and groom to sym-
bolize the purity of their union. After the washing, a servant offered up a corn loaf, and Potiphar fumbled with
memories of the few weddings he had attended. He was
supposed to feed his bride as a pledge of support, but his
hands felt awkward and big as he broke the corn loaf and
placed a crumb of its crust between the red lips of the girl
beside him.

The priest uttered another incantation, and the priestess
behind Sagira waved a stalk of sweet-smelling incense. Another servant handed Potiphar a jug of wine. He would
gladly have drunk the wine in a mad guzzle—better to be
roaring drunk than endure this humiliation—but the eyes
of Pharaoh were upon him. He placed the jug on the ground
according to tradition, then drew his sword from its sheath
and smashed the jug with a single blow. With that action,
the marriage was complete.

The crowd swelled in cries of praise and approval, and
Potiphar lifted the hand of his bride and presented her to
the people. Sagira, daughter of Donkor, kinsman to the
king, had officially become Potiphar's wife.

Twelve

"HE HAS TAKEN A WIFE?" TUYA ASKED.

Speechless with surprise, Joseph could only stare at the messenger who nodded and wiped perspiration from his forehead with the edge of his tunic. "Yes, this very hour. The master and his bride are feasting at Pharaoh's palace; soon they will return here. You must make everything ready."

A nervous fluttering rose in Joseph's stomach as he turned to Tuya. "I do not know what to do," he whispered. "How do the Egyptians marry? In my time here, I have never seen anything to tell me—"

"How we marry is not important," Tuya teased, sweeping the messenger's dusty footprints from the polished floor of the entryway with a palm frond. "What matters now is how they spend their wedding night. And that, Joseph, is the same in any culture."

Joseph could only stammer as Tuya moved past him toward the master's chamber.

"Fresh linens on the bed, fresh water in the basin and pitcher," she called over her shoulder. "Hot coals in the brazier. Flowers in the basin, and a garland of blossoms for the room, I think."

"But how can our master be married?" Joseph asked. He took three sprinting steps toward Tuya and caught her arm, turning her toward him. "Surely he will not marry unless he is in love, but he has said nothing of it—"

"Joseph, are you truly so simple?" Her fingers gently pulled a stray strand of hair from his eyes. "Sometimes I think you are not truly the wise and capable Paneah, but a simple shepherd boy from the desert. Our master may not love this woman now, but he will one day. The divine Pharaoh has arranged the marriage, and so it will be."

"Does no one ever protest Pharaoh's wishes?" Joseph asked, still holding her. "My father was forced to marry a woman he did not choose, but he protested and then married my mother. If he had been allowed to marry the one he loved from the beginning, much strife could have been avoided."

"Who are we to question the will of a god?" Tuya quipped, tapping him lightly on the chest. Joseph clung to her for a moment, relishing the scent and feel of her in his arms, then she laughed and pulled away. "Let me go, or our new mistress will be screaming for us to be whipped before she even knows our names. I must tend to the bridal chamber, Joseph, and you must see to the rest of the house. Warn the butler and the baker; tell Mert-sekert to bring a supply of linen, for the lady will want to see what we can offer her wardrobe. There is no time to waste."

Sighing, Joseph let her go.

Darkness had settled its black cloak over the villa by the time Potiphar and his wife arrived. Tuya watched from behind an arbor in the courtyard as the master helped his bride out of the chariot and into the house. It was impossible to tell what the woman looked like, for her wig was like that of any noble lady, and her figure was obscured by the wine-colored robe that proclaimed her a virgin bride.

Tuya heard Joseph's confident greeting in the entryway and knew that he was welcoming their new mistress. Potiphar answered in a low murmur and escorted his bride into the house. After a moment Joseph slipped out of the front entry and into the courtyard.

"Did you see her?" Tuya hissed from behind the arbor. "Did you get a good look? What is she like? Is she very beautiful?"

"Quiet!" Joseph whispered, walking calmly over the pathway. A single torch burned by the entrance gate, and he barred the gate and snuffed the torch, effectively plunging the courtyard into darkness. After a moment, Tuya's eyes adjusted to the dim light of the moon and she crept from behind the arbor.

"Tell me everything," Tuya said, pulling Joseph into the privacy of the shadows. A bench waited in the arbor, and she pulled Joseph down, twining her fingers with his.

"Is she beautiful?"

"She is—fair. Very young."

"Younger than me?"

"Probably. But I am not skilled at guessing a woman's age."

"You are too diplomatic. Is she plump or thin?"

"Shorter than you, and therefore she seems—thicker. But very lovely, with dark eyes and hair."

"How could you tell anything under that mammoth wig?"

"Her eyebrows." Joseph turned and gave her a grin. "Her brows were black as the night."

"Do not speak so favorably of other women when you are with me," Tuya complained, squeezing his hand.

"What other women? I saw only Potiphar, and you out here hiding behind the bushes."

"I was not hiding, I was waiting," Tuya murmured. "I had a thought to share with you."

"Only a thought?" Joseph asked, draping an arm lightly about her shoulders.

"One," she said, pulling back to give him her brightest smile. The moonlight illumined his face, and she saw amusement lurking in his eyes.

"Do you remember when our master suggested we might be married if we serve him well?"

"I remember," he said, picking up her free hand. "He mentioned six years. We have five remaining."

"Does that not seem like a long time?"

An inexplicable, lazy smile swept over his face. "No. My father worked seven years for Leah, and another seven years for Rachel. He told me often that the fourteen years flew by like days, so great was his love for my mother."

"Has your time here flown by, my Joseph?"

He cradled her hand in his own as his eyes grew thoughtful. "In the beginning, no. I wondered what God had done by bringing me here. And then I would not allow myself to love you for fear I would be taken away again. But now," his smile warmed her, "now the days fly by, and I wait and pray and hope that God will be merciful."

"I offer petitions to Montu," Tuya said, lifting her chin. She strengthened her voice so he would know how serious she was. "I think our master's marriage may be a great boon for us. If Potiphar, who never thought to marry, finds joy with his bride, perhaps he will wish the same joy for us. He looks with favor on us, Joseph, do you not agree? There is no reason we could not marry and still serve him five more years before he grants our freedom."

The grooves beside his mouth deepened into a full smile. "You truly believe our master will discover the happiness we have found?"

"In time, certainly," Tuya went on, studying his face. "Don't you think it could happen? If we offer sacrifices to the gods—"

"My God delights in obedience, not sacrifice," Joseph answered, his hands closing about her wrists. "My beautiful girl, there is so much I do not understand. I cannot speak for God, or assume to understand why He moves as He does. I do not know why He called me out of my father's tents. I do not know what He has planned for my tomorrows. And I do not know why He has rooted your image in my heart."

She was about to tell him that reasons did not matter, but his finger fell across her lips. "I do know that your touch is enough to drive me to distraction," he whispered, his voice husky in the darkness. "But my father taught me

that a righteous man does not touch a woman until she becomes his bride. So until our master allows us to join in
marriage, your wise Paneah should keep a careful distance."

To challenge his resolve she lifted her face to meet his,
but Joseph only smiled and stood, still holding her hands.
"Good-night," he whispered, dropping her hands into her
lap.

"Joseph," she called, frustrated.

"Good-night, my love," came the echo through the night
shadows.

~~⚬ Thirteen ⚬~~

THE LATE MORNING AIR WAS WARM AND BURNISHED
with sunlight as Tuya walked to the series of storage and
workrooms that served as the kitchen. Her new mistress
would probably be sleeping late, but would welcome a bath
and a bowl of fruit to break her fast. Tuya had seen no slave
accompanying her mistress, so if the lady did not own a
personal maid, Tuya was prepared to offer herself.

"Have you met the new bride?" she asked Abu, who
stood in the doorway busily stuffing grapes into his mouth.

The goatherd shook his head and muttered around a
mouthful of food. "Our master left early this morning to attend to his duties at the palace. Paneah is in the house now,
trying to find a suitable chamber for the lady's companion."

"A companion?" Tuya asked, frowning. "Will her maid
sleep in the house?"

"She is not bringing a maid," Abu answered. "She
comes to us with her own priestess. The lady decreed this
morning that Potiphar's temple is to be dedicated to Bastet." Abu looked around as if spies for the goddess could
overhear him. "They are bringing a horde of cat mummies
this afternoon. The lady says they are to be kept in the temple, and no one is to argue about it."

A sense of foreboding descended over Tuya with a
shiver, but she thanked Abu and carried a bowl of fruit to
the house. There were hundreds of priestesses in Thebes,
and thousands of men and women who claimed Bastet as
their patron goddess. Abu's words meant nothing.

She climbed the steps to the outer portico and met

Joseph. "Is our lady awake?" she said, sharing the smile she reserved for him alone.

He returned the smile, and for a moment she thought he would have kissed her in greeting, but there were others about. "She is awake," he said simply, checking a sheet of parchment in his hand. "And she has a list of needs and wants that I am to see to at once. Our master is out for the day, but we are to make our lady happy."

"I will see what I can do," Tuya offered, moving past him into the central hall. The room was empty, spacious, and quiet in its grandeur, but noises came from the master's chamber at the end of the hall. The women's sitting room stood empty, as usual, but would now have to be furnished. Tuya made a mental note of mentioning this room to Joseph—suitable furnishings could be found immediately, of course, but if the lady wanted something spectacular she would have to give the carpenters and artisans time to work.

A wailing sound came from the master's chamber, and Tuya paused on the threshold, uncertain how to proceed. Peering around the edge of the doorway she saw a short-cropped head swathed in sheets, a huddled mass in the center of Potiphar's bed.

The shrouded figure silenced her weeping, and dark eyes fastened upon Tuya. The slave carefully lowered the bowl of fruit to the floor, then prostrated herself. "I am here to serve you, mistress," she said, hoping the lady had not seen her spying glance.

The sheets rustled, a bare foot smacked the floor. Footsteps padded over the tile until ten pampered and painted toes moved into Tuya's range of vision.

"Rise, slave, and let me have a look at you," a young voice commanded.

Steeling herself for the confrontation, Tuya slowly stood up, lifting her head at the last moment. The bride gasped before she did, but Tuya had heard Abu's warning.

"Good morning, Lady Sagira," Tuya said, her heart skipping a beat. It would be easy to turn and walk away, leaving Sagira as alone and frightened as Tuya had once been. But Sagira had stared out from beneath the bed sheets like a frightened animal looking out from the brush. She gave her mistress a polite and practiced smile, then folded her hands and lowered her head, waiting to see how this joke of the gods would play out.

She stepped back, stung, when Sagira rushed forward and embraced her.

————

Sagira did not know whether to laugh or cry at the sight of Tuya standing before her. Part of her wanted to flee in embarrassment, but another part wanted to embrace her childhood friend. Finally she did both. She hugged Tuya tightly for the sake of their former friendship, then retreated under the bedcovers, cowering like a frightened child. She did not have to act the part of a regal bride and noble lady before Tuya.

"Mistress, what is wrong?" Tuya called, coming over to the edge of the bed. She bent and lifted a corner of the sheet. "You can come out. No one will hurt you."

"Oh, Tuya, it was awful!" Sagira cried, the horror of the memory sweeping over her again. "Never in my life have I imagined that marriage would be like the night I have just passed."

Tuya pressed her lips together and lifted an eyebrow. "Did your mother or the priestess not prepare you?"

"I was prepared for a night of love," Sagira sniffed, wiping her nose with the back of her hand. "I was prepared for anything and everything that could have happened except—"

"Except what?" Tuya's expression was honestly bewildered.

"Nothing!" Sagira cried, fresh tears stinging her eyes. "Potiphar lay down and fell asleep. I sat beside him, waiting, until I knew he would not wake, then I paced this chamber all night, trying to decide what I should do."

Tuya sat on the edge of the bed, a look of confusion on her gentle face, and Sagira threw herself into the older girl's arms as she had a thousand times when they were younger. It felt good to fall into Tuya's comforting lap. The slave girl had always been unflappable. Whenever Sagira did wrong as a child, Tuya took the blame or made everything all right. And now the gods had returned Tuya, and Tuya knew Potiphar. She would know how to correct Sagira's problems.

"Our master Potiphar did not plan on being married yesterday," Tuya was saying. Sagira sniffed and tried to concentrate on the girl's words. "He had just returned from the military expedition. He is a man of age, and he was tired. He probably wanted to rest."

"He does not think I am pretty," Sagira said, fumbling for Tuya's skirt to wipe her nose. "I read that much in his eyes as we were married. I do not know what kind of woman he likes, but I am not his—" Abruptly, she shrank back and glared at Tuya. "Are you his concubine?"

"No, no, my lady," Tuya said, flushing scarlet as she pulled away. "Never. The master has kept me busy with work of the house and has never invited me to his bed."

"Do you swear this by the goddess Bastet?"

"By whatever god you like, my lady. You can ask the other servants. Our master sleeps alone."

Sagira lay down and propped her head on her hand. "He has never had a wife?"

"No, my lady."

"Or a concubine?"

"None I know of."

"He is not—" Sagira raised an eyebrow.

"No," Tuya said, blushing. "He is not like that."

Sagira idly ran her finger over the linen sheets. "Tired or not, if he is a man, he can be stirred to action. Ramla has told me what I must do. The prophecy demands that I bear a son—"

Tuya frowned and seemed to stiffen at the mention of

Ramla's name. "The prophecy, my lady?"

Sagira pressed her lips together. She had said too much, especially in the house of the captain of Pharaoh's bodyguard. Even a hint that Pharaoh's lineage might not be established for eternity would be tantamount to treason. "It is nothing of importance," she said, waving the matter away. "I want a child. Does not every woman?"

Ramla's sharp voice interrupted the reunion. "By the crust between Seth's toes!" the priestess called from the doorway. "I thought we had rid ourselves of this slave once before."

"Ramla, do not scold," Sagira said, sitting up. She twinkled responsively at the priestess. "Tuya assures me that my husband was tired last night. I am not to blame for his diffidence."

The priestess lifted an elegantly narrow brow. "I am not surprised."

"He went to sleep," Sagira said, standing up and taking the sheet with her. "But he will not sleep tonight. Prepare my bath, Tuya, and then spread the fruit on a mat for me. I am hungry."

"You should eat first," Tuya said, reaching for one of the papyrus mats rolled in a corner of the room.

Sagira paused to look at the gleaming grapes, pomegranates, and dates in the bowl. Tuya had taken pains to gather the ripest, most delicious-looking fruit.

Sagira reached for a bunch of grapes, but Ramla stepped forward and slapped her hand. "I cannot believe you would listen to the suggestion of a slave," she snapped, fire in her eyes. "You are the mistress here, you are a child no longer. Such softness was allowable in a young girl, but you are a woman of means now. You do not confide in slaves, you do not obey them, you do not heed their wishes. Do you understand?"

Sagira shrank back as if the goddess herself had chastised her. Ramla had often been coyly disapproving, but never had she let loose with an outburst like this one.

"Tuya is an old friend and means me no harm—"

"Tuya is a slave who once thought herself your equal. Have you forgotten the words I have taught you? The instruction of King Amen-em-Hat warns those who will rule that they should be on their guard against subordinates: 'Trust not a brother, know not a friend, make not for yourself intimates, for in these things is no satisfaction.' Remember the prophecy, Sagira! Live like a queen, discipline your heart!"

Sagira shrank back from Ramla's words, but in an unusual display of courage, Tuya turned to face the priestess. "I mean no harm to my mistress," she said, her voice more firm than Sagira had ever heard it. "I have always loved her. I would not harm her or my master Potiphar for the world."

Ramla lifted her hands to the sky in an eloquent gesture. "Bastet, preserve us! Must I endure a pair of fools?"

Torn between the longing for the past and her hopes for the future, Sagira buried her head in her hands. "Where is the master of the slaves in this house?" she said, spitting the words between her clenched fingers. "I would speak to him at once!"

"There is only one master below Potiphar," Tuya answered, her voice coolly distant. "Paneah is the steward and keeper of the house."

"Bring him to me at once!" Sagira muttered, not lifting her eyes. "No! Send him. You need not return."

She waited until Tuya's footsteps died away before lifting her eyes to meet Ramla's.

"Sometimes, my little Sagira, you are nothing but a child," the priestess said, crossing to an elegant chair in the corner of the room. She seated herself and inclined her head like a queen granting favors. "Tuya is a great beauty, can you not see it?"

"She is a slave," Sagira whispered. "I am a lady."

"Your mother sent Tuya away because she knew the slave's beauty would overpower yours," Ramla went on, her dark eyes glowing with malevolence. "She thought you would never win a husband if you stood in your maid's shadow. And yet today you embraced your enemy, not seeing that your husband will never look at you with desire or give you the child you need as long as she remains here."

"Potiphar has not touched her—"

"So she says. Would she tell you if he had? But even if she speaks the truth, how do you know he does not dream of her?" Ramla laughed quietly, a delicate, three-noted giggle as out of character as her misshapen hand was out of place. "A wise woman never allows competition near."

The oily tone in Ramla's voice, so different from Tuya's honest answers and soft responses, brought bile to the back of Sagira's throat. "Then why," she whispered, fighting an impulse to gag, "do you stay with me, Ramla?"

The priestess tented the fingers of her good hand against the deformed digits of the other. "I have seen the future, and it fascinates me," she whispered. "You, Sagira, will be immortalized in this world as well as in the eternal one. Men will speak of you for as long as the Nile flows." Her eyes narrowed. "I hope to follow in your shadow."

———

Joseph found the two women eating fruit in Potiphar's bedchamber. The bride, who looked more like a child than a woman in the dazzling light of early afternoon, regarded him with a frankly admiring glance. The other woman, a tall, slender creature with the shaven head of a priestess, did not lift her eyes to acknowledge him.

"I am Paneah," he said, bowing to the stranger. "I assume you are our mistress's priestess. A chamber not far from this one has been reserved for you."

"I will need it only three months out of four," the woman answered, nodding slightly to acknowledge his concern. "When I am away, I must attend to my duties at the temple."

Joseph turned to his mistress. She paused with her hand in the fruit bowl, watching him. "I met you this morning, did I not?'' she asked, turning so that a bare leg peeked from beneath the bed sheet she had wrapped around herself.

Joseph nodded. "Yes, mistress. You gave me a list of your desires, and we are hurrying to find the things you need.''

"There is another thing I need," the girl said, plucking a grape from the bunch in her hand. She regarded the grape for a moment, then popped it into her mouth in a practiced gesture. "There is one slave here who does not please me." She gave the priestess a one-sided smile. "I want you to sell her immediately."

Joseph felt his smile stiffening. His staff had been trained to be quick, efficient, and subtle. How could any of them have displeased this girl?

"Which slave?" he asked, looking up. "Perhaps there has been a misunderstanding."

"No misunderstanding," the mistress answered. "The slave called Tuya is offensive to me. My priestess has suggested that the gods would be pleased if Tuya were given as an offering to the temple of Bastet. See to it at once, Paneah.''

Joseph blinked in astonishment. "Tuya?''

"Yes." The lady Sagira cast him a bright smile. "I want her gone by day's end, or you will find yourself sleeping tonight in the slave market, Paneah."

Unthinking discipline took over his limbs; Joseph nodded and withdrew. His feet carried him from the lady's chamber into the courtyard. Once he was safely away from his mistress's eyes he held his head in his hands and rocked slowly back and forth, trying to regain his sense of balance. He had hoped God would have mercy, but his soul had just been torn asunder again. For the second time in a short life, someone dear to his heart would suffer the deepest throes of grief on his account.

Staggering with the realization, Joseph made his way to his workroom where he fell on his knees and begged God for an answer.

Mercifully, the answer came with Potiphar's arrival. The master entered the courtyard just as Joseph called Tuya out from the kitchen, about to break the terrible news. Potiphar took one look at the stricken look on Joseph's face and asked what troubled him.

"My mistress, your wife," Joseph said, taking pains to keep his voice under control, "has ordered me to take Tuya to the temple of Bastet before the sun sets today."

"By all the gods, why?" Potiphar roared, his voice snapping through the courtyard like a whip. "What has the girl done?"

"Nothing, my lord," Tuya whimpered. She turned horror-filled eyes on Joseph. "Upon my honor, I did nothing."

"I asked our mistress myself, and she admits Tuya has done nothing wrong," Joseph told Potiphar. "Apparently my mistress's priestess thought Tuya would make a favorable offering to the gods. I was ordered to take Tuya or surrender myself to be sold at the slave market." He lifted his chin. "And although it would pain me to leave you, sir, I would endure such a fate if necessary."

Potiphar took a quick breath of utter astonishment. "You shall do no such thing!" he roared, turning toward the house. For a moment he glared at the walls as if he could see the lady within; then he softened his glance and laid a hand on Joseph's shoulder. "You are like a son to me, Paneah, and I would sooner lose a wife than you. Trust me—neither you nor Tuya will be forced out of this household as long as you continue to serve me as you have in the past."

With his hand on the dagger in his belt, Potiphar climbed the steps to his house and went in to confront his wife.

Ramla hovered near when Potiphar entered the women's reception room, and Sagira thought even the iron-willed priestess cowered slightly before the warrior's fierce gaze. "What are you thinking, girl?" he roared, the muscles of his face tightening into a mask of rage. "I leave you for the space of a few hours and find that you have already begun to destroy my household!"

Sagira thrust her chin upward. "The slave Tuya is no stranger to me. I have known her for years, and know that she is not a suitable ladies' maid—"

"Then find another girl to be your maid," Potiphar snapped, planting his feet as though he intended to fight. "I have twenty slave girls in this house. Surely one of them can learn how to paint your face! If not one of them, then let this one do it!"

He indicated Ramla with a disdainful flip of his hand, and Sagira saw the priestess's bosom heave in indignation.

"Ramla is my counselor," Sagira answered, smoothly arranging her skirt. "She is not a slave. She will not do a slave's work."

"Tuya and Paneah have been in my household for over two years," Potiphar answered, his voice steadier. "And you will not dismiss them on a mere whim."

Sagira saw the seriousness in his eyes and decided not to argue the matter. She gave him a suddenly obedient smile. "As you say, my lord and husband."

"And now you will dismiss this one from the room," Potiphar said, jerking his chin toward Ramla, "for I wish to have a private word with you."

For a fleeting instant Sagira considered arguing that Ramla should stay, but perhaps it was time she learned to live with the man she had married. She needed a son, and would never have one if she made this man her enemy. "Leave us, Ramla," she said, hoping her voice was sufficiently regal to impress her worldly-wise husband.

Ramla gave Potiphar a killing look as she moved out of the room, but soon her footsteps faded. Sagira threw Potiphar her brightest smile, like bait for a starving fish, but apparently the old dogfish was not hungry.

"I am glad to have a chance to talk alone with you," Potiphar said, lowering himself into a chair across from her. Obviously uncomfortable, he took a long, slow swallow. His Adam's apple slid up and down the wall of his throat as if it were made of words he could not bring forth.

Perhaps he needed her help. "What would you like to tell me?" she asked, crossing her legs so her posture was less formal and forbidding. "I am pleased to be your wife, Potiphar. I have heard many stories of your bravery and your prosperity."

He shrugged at her words, then drew the back of his hand across his brow. "I am a man of war, my lady," he finally said, resting his hands upon his knees. "I do not know how to be a husband. Pharaoh's favor was a complete surprise to me, and I must apologize that you were not better received."

"I was well received by all but one," she answered, uncrossing her arms. Leaning forward, she looked up into his strained face. For the sake of the prophecy, she would win this man's heart. "You, Potiphar, did not properly welcome your bride last night."

A shudder visibly shook him. He rose from his chair and turned to face the wall. "I will honor you as my wife," he said, thrusting his hands behind his back. "But I have no desire to embrace you. You are but a child, and yet a stranger to me."

"Surely you want children. Every man wants children." She stood and moved toward him until their shadows mingled on the wall. At this slight contact, Potiphar flinched and turned his head away.

"I never thought to have children. I am content to serve my king."

"Every man needs an heir," she said, putting her cool hand upon his arm. The muscles were firm under her palm, his waist trim, his legs sturdy beneath the linen kilt he wore. Though three times her age, Potiphar was handsome still, a striking figure, a husband of whom she could be proud.

His skin seemed to contract beneath her touch, but he did not move away. "I thought I would leave my estate to Paneah," he said, his throat working. "He has managed it so well—"

"You should not leave your estate to a slave when you can have a son of your own." Carefully, tenderly, she lifted his hand and placed hers under it. His eyes widened at her boldness and he examined her as he might have studied an intricate painting in the temple. "I am your wife, Potiphar, and I could love you if you would let me," she murmured, her voice a silken whisper in the quiet of the chamber.

She ran her free hand over the bronzed skin of his chest and felt the ripples of scars beneath her fingers. Three, no, four rough and red welts lay under her hand; how many times had he been injured? She felt the whisper of his quickened breath upon her cheek. Surely he would come into her arms in a moment . . .

She pressed her lips to his shoulder, awaiting his shuddering sigh of surrender, but Potiphar abruptly thrust her away. "I am sorry, my lady," he said, his face and neck flooded crimson. "But duty calls me from the house. If you need anything, call Paneah. I may be gone a few days."

Before she could open her mouth to protest, Potiphar whirled and left her alone.

———

The next morning, Tuya tiptoed through the corridor outside the master's chamber, hoping that Potiphar and Sagira had found happiness in each other's arms. But a clattering crash from the chamber drew her upright, and she heard Sagira's scream: "I do not care what his duties are! He cannot leave me like this!"

Tuya peered into the room. Ramla sat on the edge of Sagira's bed, her arms folded defensively with an "I-told-you-so" look on her face. Both women frowned to see Tuya in the doorway, and Tuya's adrenaline level began to rise when she sensed the hostility in the room. These were, she told herself, the two women who had tried to send her away. Perhaps she should not have come into the house.

"Is there anything you need, Lady Sagira?" Tuya asked.

"Have you forgotten how to bow to your mistress?" Ramla barked.

Tuya obediently dropped to the floor and pressed her forehead to the cool tile. "Mistress," she repeated, "is there anything you need?"

"No," Sagira snapped, her voice a sharp stiletto in the quiet of morning. "Wait—I will need a maid. Send Paneah to me so that I can describe the sort of maid I want."

Tuya nodded and stood to leave.

"Has your mistress dismissed you?" The priestess's iron voice drizzled disapproval.

Tuya fell to the floor again.

"You may leave," Sagira said, her tone flat. "But send Paneah at once. Do not keep me waiting."

⟶ Fourteen ⟵

POTIPHAR STAYED AWAY FOR A FULL TEN-DAY WEEK, then sent a message instructing Paneah to prepare a comfortable, separate chamber for Sagira and her maid. The instruction was not unusual, for most noble ladies lived in separate quarters from their husbands, but the entire household knew without being told that Potiphar did not intend to take the time to become thoroughly acquainted with his bride. Sagira knew it, too, and fumed with frustration and embarrassment.

Again and again, he came and left, treating Sagira with the polite interest he might have displayed toward an esteemed visitor. Often he brought her a trinket of jewelry or the latest court gossip, which he shared over a breakfast tray, but he never returned to the house until night had fallen, and Sagira had tucked herself away in the privacy of her room. Often in the morning she heard his easy laughter in the stockyard as he checked the horses with Paneah, and occasionally she heard him tease Tuya in an almost paternal tone. Yet for her, his wife, he had nothing but polite conversation and the most casual of greetings.

Sagira's temper rose to a flash point each time she thought of her husband's disinterest, and then she remembered the prophecy. She had to win his affection; there was no other choice. Her father had been a coolly indifferent figure in her life, and it galled her to think that her husband might prove to be as distant. But one way or another, she would bear a son. She had not studied the love lyrics of the ancient poets for nothing.

"Rehearse for me the song I will sing to Potiphar,"

Sagira called to Ramla one afternoon as the priestess settled into a chair by the reflecting pool in Potiphar's garden. Two servants had loaded a stand at Sagira's right hand with fruit, flowers, and wine; a harpist and fan bearer stirred the warm air in an effort to make their mistress's afternoon a little more pleasant. The sight of the lotus-filled pool stirred Sagira with memories of playful days gone by, and for a moment she wished that Tuya, not Ramla, sat with her at the water's edge. But Tuya kept a careful distance from both Sagira and Ramla.

Ramla opened a papyrus scroll and ran her finger along the colorful images as she read:

My god, my brother, my husband—
How sweet it is to go down to the lotus pond
    and do as you desire—
To plunge into the waters and bathe before you—
    to let you see my beauty in my tunic of sheerest
    royal linen,
All wet and clinging and perfumed with balsam!
I see my husband coming—
My heart is in joy, and my arms are opened wide to
    embrace him;
And my heart rejoices within me without ceasing—
Come to me, O my lord!
When I embrace you and your arms enlace me,
    ah, then I am drunk without beer!
O would that I were the ring upon your finger,
    so that you would cherish me as something
    that adds beauty to your life!

"Stop," Sagira commanded, emotion clotting her voice. Her husband did not cherish her, for she did not possess beauty enough to add to his life. Why should he long for a wife when he could feast his eyes and heart upon Tuya, whose beauty put all others to shame? Even the handsome Paneah possessed more beauty than Sagira did. No amount of perfume, cosmetics, or fine clothing could disguise the fact that she was by far the plainest thing in Potiphar's household. No wonder he despised her.

"You are pitiful," Ramla said, her icy voice intruding upon Sagira's thoughts. "Sitting in a gilded chair while you feel sorry for yourself."

"Be quiet," Sagira said, turning away from Ramla. "I do not need you to help me feel better."

"I will not flatter you now," Ramla said, rising from her chair. She moved toward Sagira like a hovering vulture. "There was a time for flattery, a time when your childish ego could not bear the truth. Your mother and I assured you of your beauty, your intelligence, your wit. Well, that time is over, Sagira, and yet you still yearn for childish coddling."

"I do not!" Sagira said, blazing up at the priestess. "I am a wife, mistress of this house—"

"You do nothing here. The slave Paneah runs this house, for Potiphar cannot trust you to do even that. Tuya pleases your husband more than you do, for I have heard them laughing together in the courtyard, and Paneah has become the son Potiphar wants. You are good for nothing, Sagira, and yet you sit here, loving your wounds. A born whiner, all you ask for is a little neglect—"

"Be quiet! You are wrong! I am going to do something about Potiphar!"

"Prove it."

Ramla tossed the challenge casually, then turned and sank gracefully into her chair. Looking away, Sagira bit her thumbnail. How could she do anything with a man as strong-willed as the captain of Pharaoh's guards? Potiphar did not trust her; he would not even allow her to dispose of a troublesome slave. But perhaps, if he saw her administrative and social talents on a small scale, he would appreciate her. Then he would spend time with her, just as he visited with Paneah for hours whenever he came home.

She clapped her hands and her handmaid came running. "Send the household scribe to me at once, and have a messenger ready to take a message to Potiphar at the palace," she said, tossing her head so that the weight of her wig fell back over her shoulders. "And send Paneah to me. Tell him to drop everything he is doing, for Potiphar is going to host a party."

"Do you truly think a party is going to win your husband's heart?" Ramla asked in a vaguely mocking tone.

"It is something I do well," Sagira answered, bounding out of her chair with the first burst of energy she had felt in weeks.

She was not sure how Paneah managed to convince him, but Potiphar agreed to host a party, the first he had ever given. All of the greatest nobles in Thebes received invitations to the villa, and not one of them declined the opportunity to visit Potiphar's fabled house.

The party fell on a quiet day after an entire week of wind, and Sagira rejoiced to see that the house looked its best. Fresh flowers adorned each room, the braziers burned with incense, the perfumed cones of fat sat in orderly rows on a tray by the front portico. After making certain that the house stood ready to receive its guests, she retreated to her chamber to make herself as beautiful as possible.

She had ordered new jewelry, for Potiphar's treasure chests contained nothing worth wearing, and her neck, wrists, fingers, and ears were adorned with the finest creations the jewelers of Thebes could provide. Cunningly wrought in gold, silver, and electrum, the ornaments dazzled her handmaid and even Ramla as Sagira preened before them in her dressing room.

"Be still and let us adorn your face as well," Ramla said, pressing Sagira down onto a stool before her dressing stand. The maid stood ready with kohl and ground red ochre to color Sagira's lips. Ramla studied Sagira's face for a moment, then motioned for the maid to begin. "You will be so beguiling that Potiphar will forget his demented notions of not needing a wife."

"He thinks me a child," Sagira said, pouting so the maid could freely apply the lip color. "Tonight he will see a grown woman before him."

"He will see only you," Ramla said, picking up the perfumed cone which would adorn the top of Sagira's wig. Ramla sniffed at the cone, nodded in approval, and wiped a trace of the fat between her fingers. "With perfumed and oiled skin, you will win him," she said, winking coyly. "Tonight you will have all the weapons of a woman at your disposal."

"And I shall win!" Sagira said, studying her reflection in her bronze mirror. "The old warrior will at last surrender!" Her golden reflection twinkled back at her with a confident smile.

———

Joseph crinkled his nose as he and Tuya stood apart from the merrymakers in a doorway off the central reception room. Before them, in various stages of drunken revelry, the most illustrious nobles of Pharaoh's court were eating, drinking, and singing. The guests had been drinking long and deep since their arrival at noon, and the sickly sweet odors of beer and perfume mingled and filled the hall. According to her mistress's command, Tuya had placed garlands and bouquets of the most fragrant flowers throughout the chamber, and to Joseph had fallen the task of securing enough brightly painted wine jars and cups, bowls, and vases of gold, silver, and alabaster to lend an air of opulent gaiety.

"I thought Potiphar's house was lovely before tonight," Tuya whispered, leaning toward Joseph's ear. "Tonight I find it gaudy. I prefer the ordinary arrangement of things."

Joseph nodded in wordless agreement as he surveyed the scene. Though he had long ceased to be surprised by the ostentatious Egyptians, his senses were overwhelmed by the abundance of fleshly pleasures available in the room. An orchestra of thinly clad girls played double reed pipes, lutes, lyres, and harps, while a dancing girl wearing a bronze belt and little else, beat out rhythms on a rectangular tambourine as she whirled in front of the drunken guests.

The mood of the gathering had been formal and decorous when Potiphar and Sagira greeted their guests at the outset, but the party had gathered momentum as the wine and beer flowed. Now it surged with raucous life in the tinkly rhythms of the slave girls, and those who chose to dance had progressed from slow, dignified posturings to wild gyrations. A dark slave brought by one of the nobles culminated her dance in a series of leaps, somersaults, back flips, and hand springs. The delighted partygoers applauded with heavy hands and loud cries for more.

An army of serving girls circulated among Potiphar's guests, plying the drunken nobles with a surfeit of food of every description. Some wove their way through the crowd refilling silver cups with spice-flavored beer and wine, while others supplied disheveled guests with fresh garlands of flowers or paused to tidy up kilts that had slipped out of their proper and modest positions.

Joseph thought he could measure the disintegration of the party by the speed with which the cones of perfumed fat had begun to drip and run down the persons of the formerly dignified guests. Only two participants at the party had kept their composure, Joseph noticed. Neither Sagira nor Ramla had partaken of more than one cup of wine. Ramla sat apart from the company, her dark eyes surveying the group as if she measured and weighed their hearts, and Sagira contented herself with wandering through the crowd and overseeing the needs of her guests. But as the sun set and darkness began to come on, Sagira surprised the entire gathering by standing on a stool and clapping for attention.

"Hear me, oh, guests of Potiphar, the appointed guard

of Pharaoh!" she called, her voice ringing over the gathering. A silence, thick as wool, wrapped itself around the revelers. Secure in the limelight, Sagira lifted her hands and turned toward her husband, who leaned drunkenly upon the arm of his chair.

"My husband!" she cried, clapping her hands together over her head. "I have composed a poem for you!"

"Let us hear it!" came the cry.

"A poem for Potiphar!" another voice called.

"Tell us!"

"Speak!"

Swaying like a palm tree in the desert, Sagira let the long cloak she had worn all night fall from her shoulders. She stood before her husband and the crowd in a sheer golden sheath as transparent as a clear sky. Joseph felt a blush burn his cheek. Embarrassed, he lowered his eyes from Sagira's slender figure and studied his master.

Hurriedly scampers my heart,

Sagira recited, swaying faster in the pulsing rhythm of the room,

When I recall my love of you—
It does not allow me to go about like other mortals—
It seems to have been uprooted from its place.
It does not let me put on my tunic or even take my
    fan—
I am not able to paint my eyes or anoint myself with
    perfume.
"Do not linger thus! Get back to yourself!"
I say when I think of you.
"Do not cause me silly pain, O my heart!"
Just sit cool and he will come to you, and everyone
    will see!
Let not people say of me,
"There is a girl fallen hopelessly in love!"

Stand firm when you think of him, O my heart!
Do not bound about so!

Wild applause met the finish of her poem, and Sagira sprang from the stool and prostrated herself at Potiphar's feet. Joseph could not hear if she said anything to the master, but amid the wild hooting Potiphar stood, lifted Sagira to her feet, then covered her lips with his in a rough kiss that set the crowd cheering. Sagira blushed and pulled away, suddenly modest and coy, and in response, the master swept his bride into his arms as the guests raised their cups and cheered his prowess. In the rhythm of the drunken throng's escalating roar, Potiphar winked and lurched from the dais where he had been sitting, while Sagira tightened her arms about his neck. In a moment the party's unsteady host and hostess had departed the hall for the privacy of the master's chamber.

Joseph and Tuya exchanged glances. It had taken a party and two hin of wine to accomplish it, but Sagira had finally won her husband.

SAGIRA

Now Joseph was handsome in form and appearance. And it came about after these events that his master's wife looked with desire at Joseph, and she said, "Lie with me."

Genesis 39:6b–7

⟝ Fifteen ⟞

SHADOWS WREATHED POTIPHAR'S CHAMBER AS THE sun rose, and Sagira moved silently away from the bed where her husband snored off the effects of the party. Grabbing up her gown, she retrieved her wig and sandals from the floor and slipped wordlessly through the corridor until she came to her own room. Ramla was still asleep, a thin covering thrown over her.

Sagira tossed her costly wig toward its stand and sank onto her bed, biting her knuckles. She wanted to scream, to beat someone, to cry and lament, and tear her clothing. Life was not fair! She had entered this marriage fully expecting a *normal*, happy union, but last night's reality hit her like a cold slap in the face. Potiphar should never have married her, but her parents, Pharaoh, and Narmer had not given him a choice in the matter. The entire world had conspired against the bride and groom to play an ironic joke, a terrible trick.

Ramla stirred, and Sagira dropped her hand from her mouth and sat upright, gathering what little dignity she had left. Last night she had behaved like a prostitute, flaunting herself before a drunken crowd and gyrating to silly, useless poetry to please a man who could never be a husband to her. Did everyone know the truth? How many nobles would mock her name this morning over their breakfasts? How would the gossips magnify her forward behavior? What would Pharaoh say when he heard? What would her mother think?

"Bastet have mercy," she murmured, dropping her head into her hands.

Ramla sat up in the gloom. "Are you happy now, little one? Shall I begin counting the days until your son is born?"

Drained of will and thought, Sagira shook her head.

"Well, perhaps I will wait," Ramla murmured. "And if a child does not come from this occasion, there will be other times when Potiphar will call for you. Now that the wall between you has been breached—"

"There will be no son," Sagira answered dully. "No daughter, no child. The mighty Potiphar has left his manhood behind on some battlefield."

"You lie," Ramla burst out, shocked.

"I do not," Sagira answered, clenching her jaw as she rejected the priestess's words. "I am not a fool."

"But Pharaoh would never—"

"Pharaoh does not know," Sagira answered slowly, shaking her head. "How could he? If this were the morning after our wedding, I would demand that the marriage be set aside. But how can I explain to Pharaoh that I did not discover this truth about my husband until now? Too many months have passed, Ramla. I would die of embarrassment if I had to expose the truth before Pharaoh's court—"

"You cannot have the marriage set aside," Ramla interrupted, settling her elbows on her bent knees and steepling her fingers. "You will lose Potiphar's property." Her eyes, clever as a cat's, narrowed in speculation. "You must say nothing of this to anyone, Sagira. Keep Potiphar's reputation intact. Be kind and respectful to him—he was so drunk he will probably recall nothing of last night. He will think you went to your chamber as usual."

"What of my son?" Sagira cried, running her hand through her short hair in a detached motion. "The prophecy! How am I to have a child with Potiphar? The gods have made a mistake, I was not meant to marry him—"

"Hush, now, be quiet," Ramla soothed her. "The gods cannot be wrong. There is a way out of this, there has to be." The priestess swung her thin legs out of her narrow cot and came to stand next to Sagira. Placing her elegantly cool hands on Sagira's hot shoulders, she said, "Sleep now, my lady, and let me consider this. I will consult the goddess, and she will tell me what we should do."

Relaxing in the older woman's authoritative tone, Sagira allowed herself to be pressed back onto her bed. Ramla dropped a linen cover over her, and Sagira closed her eyes to block out the haunting knowledge she'd gleaned in the last hours. How many others knew about Potiphar's war injuries? Did Paneah know? Had he told Tuya? She had felt their eyes upon her as she swayed before her husband in the ritual of seduction—were they laughing at her?

She turned onto her side and thumbed tears of anger and frustration from her eyes as Ramla began a sacred chant to the goddess Bastet.

For three days Sagira moved throughout the household in a false and brittle dignity. Underneath her artificial smile seethed an anger and indignation unlike anything she had ever felt, but everyone except Ramla seemed indifferent to it. When she could no longer endure the sickening sensation of her life plunging downward, Sagira decided to confront her husband.

Potiphar had come home after dark, as usual, probably hoping that she had already gone to sleep. She waited until the rushlight burned steadily in his room before creeping to his door. She was about to enter but heard Potiphar speak to someone, so she flattened herself against the wall of the corridor and coiled into the shadows. Paneah answered, his voice like steel wrapped in silk, and for a moment she forgot her resolve and concentrated on the sound of it. Now there was a man! How handsome the slave was and how youthful! But he did not like her, and she had made no attempt to win his approval since the awful day she had tried to send Tuya away.

She lingered until Paneah finished his report and left

the chamber. He walked out with his eyes glued to a papyrus scroll in his hand and did not look back. Relieved, she pushed aside the door and walked boldly to stand before her husband.

"Sagira! What is it?" he asked, honestly startled by her appearance. He had removed his sword and his wig; she could see the ginger freckles on his bald skull.

"Do not worry, Potiphar," she said, her eyes darting to the bed where he would soon take his rest. "I do not intend to stay. I came only to say that you have wronged me. We both know why you have neglected to treat me as a proper wife, and you should have told me the truth long before this."

His face flamed crimson, but he did not deny the truth. "I tried to tell you that I did not intend to marry," he said, his hands fumbling awkwardly with the clasp of a leopard-skin mantle across his shoulders. "But Pharaoh forced a bride upon me, and who can deny the divine Pharaoh?"

"Still, you should have been more honest with me. For months I thought you did not bring me into your arms because—" She paused and took a deep breath. It hurt to tell the truth, but she was urging him to be brutally honest, so she should be just as forthright. "I thought you did not love me because I am not beautiful."

The warrior's stone face cracked into humanity at her words. "Ah, Sagira, I never meant to hurt you," he said, his dark eyes pleading for understanding. "Perhaps I should have approached things differently. But I thought you would be relieved that I did not call you into my chambers. Why should a young girl yearn for an old, scarred, battle horse like me?"

Without his wig, he looked like a day-old hatchling, bald, wobbly, and nervous. Sagira thought she could almost feel sorry for him, but he had wronged her too deeply.

He shook his head in regret. "I did not consider that my indifference might hurt you. You seemed content with your friend, and I—"

"You did not want the court to know the extent of your scars," she whispered, looking down at the floor. "Does anyone know?"

"No. Tuthmosis knew and would probably have forced me to leave the army, but he died before doing anything about it. Amenhotep has no idea, and I am not going to tell him."

This last remark was delivered with a commander's conviction, yet Sagira sensed that it was also a plea. "Fear not, Potiphar," she said, giving him a slight smile. "I will not reveal your secret. To do so would tell the world that Pharaoh made a mistake."

"A god cannot make mistakes," Potiphar whispered, a note of fond indulgence in his voice. "How often I have reminded myself of that truth." He turned and motioned toward a chair. "Will you sit down, my dear? Perhaps we should have talked long ago. I find that this conversation has left me feeling quite—relieved."

Sagira nodded and took the seat he offered, while Potiphar squatted on the edge of his low bed. "Do not think you are not beautiful," he said, looking at her with wisdom in his eyes. "You are a true daughter of the Nile, a composite of all that is good in our people. I have seen your cleverness and your zest for living. I must confess that bringing you into my house has made me feel old."

Sagira had no answer but studied her husband carefully. She had never imagined he thought about anything but Pharaoh and his warriors. Had she truly affected him?

"Beauty counts for little at the end of a man's life," Potiphar went on. "Faithfulness is what I have come to treasure most. The faithfulness of Pharaoh, of the men in my command, and of my able Paneah, who has brought blessings upon my humble house. I do not ask you to shine as a beauty, Sagira. I only ask that you be faithful to a husband who will do you no wrong. And someday," he gestured toward the outer hall, "this will all be yours."

He rested his elbows on his knees and laughed softly.

"When a man has more yesterdays than tomorrows, he learns the value of forthrightness. I will always speak truly to you, Sagira, and ask that you speak plainly to me. Let there be no more secrets between us."

"Agreed," Sagira said, rising from her chair. She walked toward her husband and pressed her fingers to the battlefield of wrinkles on his cheek. "No more secrets," she echoed, then turned and left him alone to his sleep.

"What did he say?" Ramla demanded when Sagira reentered her chamber. "Was he angry? Did he deny the truth?"

"He denied nothing," Sagira answered, slipping her heavy wig from her head. She placed it on its stand, then sighed and reclined on her couch. "He was glad to be honest with me. He said if I am faithful to him, he will treat me well. And someday I will inherit all he possesses."

"When he dies," Ramla whispered, her eyes wide. A sudden smile broke her usually stern countenance. "So that is how the gods will work. When Potiphar dies, Sagira, you will remarry. *Then* you will bear a son to head the next dynasty!"

"No," Sagira answered, studying her nails. "I will have a son of my own choosing. I am tired of waiting for the gods to work their will. I will travel the road of my own life!"

The priestess blanched. "You speak blasphemy. Bastet will not listen to you."

"Bastet may do whatever she likes," Sagira answered, her voice tight with mutiny. "If Bastet does not approve, I will send my offerings to Hathor or Horus or the temple of Amon-Re. One of them will hear my petition. You have said, Ramla, that the prophecy cannot be changed. So any god can come to my aid, and one of them will!"

Ramla stiffened and took on a defensive air, but Sagira ignored her disapproving frown. In time she would change her opinion, for Sagira could easily cast off the priestess of

Bastet in favor of a representative from one of the other temples.

"Perhaps with the proper offerings Bastet can be persuaded to assist you," Ramla finally murmured. "But how will you choose a son? You cannot plant seed into your own womb—"

"I will have a son whose beauty makes up for my lack," Sagira said, swinging her legs onto the floor. She stood and paced slowly in the room. "I will bear a son whose presence will slap Potiphar in the face, just payment for the grief I have endured on his account. My son will be well suited to wear the double crown of Egypt—he will possess my cunning and his father's gifts of administration and knowledge. The royal blood of the Two Kingdoms will flow through his veins."

"Who?" Ramla asked, standing to block Sagira's path.

"Paneah," Sagira said, lifting her chin. "I will present Potiphar with the son of a slave, and he will not deny my son's legitimacy."

"He will have you put away for adultery!" Ramla hissed, clenching her fists. "The captain of the king's guard will not accept a child he knows is not his—"

"Yes, he will," Sagira answered, nodding in stubborn conviction. "All who attended our party think Potiphar the embodiment of virility. His pride will not allow him to disown the son I will place into his hands. He is firmly in my power, for I know his secret." Her mouth curved in a mirthless smile. "A slave's son will become Potiphar's heir and Egypt's king. The faithful and able Paneah will sire my son."

———

Gritting her teeth, Ramla walked alone in Potiphar's garden. The darkness among the trees was so complete it felt like liquid. Walking through the gate, Ramla felt as if she were descending into a black, bottomless lake.

She had a similar feeling each time she invoked the dark

powers that gave her the ability to see into the future. The first time she had attempted it, fear of the unknown knotted and writhed in her stomach, but soon that terrible sensation gave way to a brilliant burst of light as the heavens opened and revealed their secrets. Those secrets bound her to Sagira even now. She had known for years that Lady Kahent would come to call at the Temple of Bastet, and the first time her eyes fell upon Sagira she had known that in the swarthy little girl she would find her destiny.

If not for that certainty, she would have left Potiphar's house long ago. Sagira was spoiled, headstrong, and apt to be foolish, but Ramla could not deny what she had seen. The girl would make an impression upon the sands of time, and Ramla wanted nothing more than to be a part of it. As a baby, she had been deposited on the steps of Bastet's temple, a nameless, malformed creature whose mewing elicited pity from the hearts of the priests. With bitter pride as her strength, she had grown wise in the ways of the priesthood, and on a dark night like this she had opened her soul to the powers of the gods.

That power had led her to Sagira, and her unwavering faith in the vision of the future would force her to stay.

———

Sagira moved through the next few days like a waterfowl on the Nile—calm on the surface, but paddling furiously underneath. The seduction of Potiphar's slave must be carefully planned, for many obstacles lay in her path. First and foremost, the entire household knew of the deep love between Paneah and Tuya. Perfectly attuned to each other, the two slaves read glances and upraised brows across the room without speaking a word. Such a bond would not be easy to break.

Sagira's second problem involved Paneah's inscrutable detachment. He had learned far more quickly than Tuya how to avoid bridging the gap between master and slave, and he kept a careful physical and social distance between himself and his mistress. Winning his confidence would not be easy. Sagira knew that if she stepped toward him with anything akin to interest in her eyes, the young man would turn and leave the room without a moment's hesitation.

Other complications begged to be considered—the when and how and where of the act of conception, as well as what should be done about Potiphar when her belly began to swell with new life. Perhaps he could be pacified with a story about a god who assumed human form and visited her to beget the worthy and wounded Potiphar a son. After all, thousands of Egyptians believed a variation of that tale every time a son of Pharaoh was born. Without such a visitation from the gods, Pharaoh would not be a son of his father-god, Osiris.

Sagira smiled in contemplation of her success. Her son's birth alone would punish those who had hurt her, and he would be a destroyer of Egypt's enemies throughout his life. He would be the greatest Pharaoh the world had ever seen, and as his mother, she would live forever in the memories of men. *For as long as the world exists, men will speak of you . . .*

Such had the prophecy promised.

In order to win Paneah's participation, Sagira set out to understand him. Without calling him to her side, she studied him as he served meals; she peered down at him from the roof as he moved through the stockyard, the granaries, and the slaves' workrooms. And once she realized that he met with Tuya every night in the garden, Sagira secreted herself among the bushes to spy on the lovers.

On her first night of watch, she thought them a terribly boring couple. They behaved like old people who had been married for years. Tuya inquired about Paneah's day in the fields; Paneah asked about the bakers and butler and supplies of oil. Soon the topics of ordinary conversation passed, however, and the pair of slaves fell silent. The sky was black and icy with a wash of brilliant stars, a perfect night for lovers. When Paneah ran his hand over Tuya's glossy hair, Sagira leaned forward in interest, her hands pressing upon the moist black earth and her knees sliding over the slippery wet-paper texture of fallen leaves.

"I do not know what I would do without you, Tuya." Paneah's voice gentled as he spoke to the lovely girl sitting by his side, and Tuya's oval face glowed in breathtaking beauty as she sighed and called her loved one *Joseph.*

Joseph? Sagira frowned. The name was not Egyptian, but it seemed to suit Paneah and fell readily from Tuya's lips as if she had spoken it a thousand times. It must have been his name before Potiphar's house, or perhaps it was a boyhood name. *Joseph.* The word had an Asiatic sound, perhaps it was a name from one of the Canaanite tribes; she would ask Ramla to investigate.

Sagira turned her ear to listen more closely. The black earth was undoubtedly staining her fine linen dress, but Sagira did not care.

"I like the cornflowers and nightshade along the garden wall," Paneah was saying, his dark head inclining closer toward Tuya's. "But the lotuses . . . the fragrance is so sweet, especially when the flowers have been around your neck."

He ducked as if to sniff the flesh of her neck, and Tuya laughed gently and pushed him away. "The blue lotuses are my favorite, but I shall not wear a lotus garland ever again if you cannot control yourself," she said, teasing him with her eyes. "I shall wear plain ivy. It has no fragrance at all."

Tuya rose to her feet. "When the sun rises, my work begins, and I must have sleep."

"As must I," Paneah murmured. His hand came up and clasped hers. "We must say good-night, my love. Until tomorrow."

"Until tomorrow," Tuya answered, lowering herself until she sat on the ground facing him. Their foreheads met for a long moment of communion, then Paneah lifted his head and pressed his lips to the girl's forehead.

From behind the bush, Sagira held her breath, imagining his lips on hers.

"Four more years," Tuya murmured when they parted.

"They will fly like hours," Paneah answered, then Tuya stood and moved away, releasing his hand only when his arm would reach no further. Sagira waited until Paneah also left the garden, then she emerged from her hiding place and brushed the soil from her knees and hands.

Four years? What were they talking about? She frowned, then set her feet toward Potiphar's chamber where a thin stream of lamplight still glowed from beneath his doorway. He would know what Tuya meant. And being in her power, he would tell her.

Sagira fidgeted uncomfortably in the garden's heat. The fan Tuya moved back and forth did little but displace hot air, and the water in Sagira's goblet was blood warm, impossible to enjoy. The sun beat down upon the villa with the strokes of a coppersmith's hammer while the sky smoked with heat haze.

Ramla approached, back from her month at the temple, and Sagira sat up, eager to hear news from other parts of the city. "Welcome, my lady," Ramla said, as cool as ever in her spotless white gown and golden collar. "Bastet has smiled upon you."

"I am glad to hear it," Sagira remarked, her mouth curving in a half-smile. "Sit down, Ramla, and tell me everything you have heard this month. What is the latest gossip of Thebes?"

"Dismiss these slaves," Ramla ordered, abruptly tossing the back of her hand toward Tuya. "I find them distracting."

Sagira nodded toward Tuya and the servant girl who stood ready at the pitcher, and both slaves hurried into the house, eager to be out of the hot sun. When they had gone,

Ramla frowned and shook out the linen veil she used to protect the tender skin of her head. "By the wisdom of Bastet, why do you sit here when you could be inside? The sun has obviously baked your brains."

"I like the garden," Sagira said, smiling in pleasure at the memory of spying on Paneah. In the last few days she had given Tuya work to keep her busy into the night. Paneah had wandered in the garden alone, waiting, unaware that Sagira watched his every move. "Tell me," she said, leaning toward the priestess. "What have you learned about the name *Joseph?*"

Ramla sighed, but a satisfied smile curled upon her lips. "It is a Hebrew name," she said, "meaning *add to me.*"

"A Hebrew," Sagira said, marveling. "Our Paneah is a Hebrew."

"The Hebrews," Ramla went on, lifting a sculpted brow, "have a history with the ancient Pharaohs, and the story is recorded in the temple scrolls. The father of the Hebrews, Abram, came to dwell in Egypt years ago. He traveled with a beautiful woman he called his sister, Sarai. Her loveliness was so unusual that she was taken into Pharaoh's harem, and as a result, Abram's god closed up the wombs of Pharaoh's wives. Several of them bore dead babies, and others lost the fruit of their womb before the time of birth had come. Pharaoh's priests divined the truth—Sarai was not Abram's sister, but his wife."

"How terrible," Sagira said, relishing every word of the tale.

"When the priests of Amon-Re revealed the plague's cause to Pharaoh, he called Abram and expelled him, his wife, and all his possessions from Egypt's borders. A sizable military force escorted Abram and his people from the land of the Two Kingdoms. It is written that Pharaoh prayed he would never again see a Hebrew in the dominions of Egypt."

"And we have one in our own house," Sagira whispered, turning to stare at the reflecting pool.

"Do you not think this a bad omen?" Ramla asked, leaning forward. "You want to have a child with this Hebrew, and his god has the power to kill babies in the womb—"

"My Hebrew has but one god, and I have a plethora of them," Sagira said, turning to the other woman. "Are many not more powerful than one?"

Ramla lifted her eyes in a questioning glance, but Sagira only smiled and tucked her leg under her skirt. She had Bastet, and Amon-Re, and all the gods of Egypt to do battle for her. Above all, she had time to consider her challenge and study the object of her desire.

∽ Sixteen ∾

TIME PASSED. JOSEPH NOTICED WITH PLEASED SUR-
prise that the crop of his fourth year in Potiphar's house
surpassed all others and more than tripled the amount harvested in his first year. The healthy cattle lowing in Potiphar's stockyard pressed for larger quarters, and Potiphar's
fleet horses won so many chariot races that the noblemen
of Thebes clamored for the foals of the estate's stallions. Potiphar now paid more in taxes than any man in Thebes, and
this significant fact finally earned him the coveted Gold of
Praise.

His master wore the face and manner of a happy man,
and Joseph thought the household a contented one. Tuya
seemed satisfied to wait out the remaining years until they
should be freed and wed, and Sagira seemed to have settled
into her role as pampered mistress of the sprawling estate.
Ramla kept to her mistress's side or to herself in the small
temple at the villa. Though the strange priestess regarded
Joseph with wary, troubled eyes, she stayed clear of his approach and did not bother him.

While deprived of precious freedom, the slaves living
in Potiphar's household were a great deal more prosperous
than the poor of Pharaoh's kingdom. Well fed, clothed, and
housed by their affluent master, they did not have to work
past sundown or labor to pay taxes to the divine Pharaoh
who ruled over them. The last few years had brought major
changes for the better. Now even the most disgruntled slave
admitted that Paneah was a gift from the gods. He was a
compassionate but firm taskmaster who would freely listen
to their grievances and requests. Most of the slaves even

bore a grudging respect for Potiphar's wife. Though head-strong and spoiled, she had brought the household into the circle of nobility. The once dull and dusty villa now regularly rang with the cultured voices of visiting nobles and their wives. Potiphar's slaves felt themselves superior to the poor and quite the equivalent of the merchants who lined the dusty streets of Thebes.

Joseph had just finished settling a squabble between the cook and the baker one afternoon when Tuya came with word that Lady Sagira had asked to see him in the garden. "I will go at once," Joseph said, giving Tuya a conspiratorial wink. "She probably wants me to decorate for another of her parties."

"Shouldn't she have asked me to do that?" Tuya asked, casting him a strained smile. "What would you know about a lady's party?"

"I was speaking in jest," Joseph said, waving her away. "I am sure it is nothing important."

He found his mistress alone in the garden. Her back was to him as he approached, her thick wig heavy with golden beads that sparkled amid the darkness of her hair like stars in a midnight sky.

"Mistress? You sent for me?"

Her eyes were strangely veiled when she turned to look at him, but the smile on her face was genuine and warm, the smile between two equals, not slave and owner. "Thank you for coming, Paneah," she said graciously, her voice as golden and warm as the sun overhead. He was about to prostrate himself before her, but she motioned for him to remain on his feet. "Please, do not bow. When we are alone, just you and me, you need not observe foolish formalities."

"Yes, mistress," Joseph answered, nodding carefully. "How may I serve you?"

She gave him a beautifully bright, confident smile. "I know that you work magic upon everything you touch, Paneah. I wonder if you would give me a few suggestions about this garden? I have come to love this place and want to expand it beyond its present borders."

"Temporarily?" Paneah asked, thinking that perhaps she planned to impress her friends with a garden party.

"Permanently," she said, tilting her head as she looked up at him. The deft makeup around her eyes gave her the sleepy-eyed look of an elegant kitten. "I want to have it beautiful always so I can enjoy its charm whenever I want."

She stepped forward upon the tiled pathway and gestured for him to follow. "I love the serenity of a garden, don't you?" she asked, stopping to face him.

Joseph's mouth went dry. Masters did not often ask their slaves for personal opinions. Even Potiphar, who trusted Joseph to run nearly every detail of his life, did not trouble himself to ask for Joseph's views. "Well, yes, I like the garden," he said, feeling tongue-tied and dull. She would think him a total imbecile.

But Sagira only turned to walk farther down the path. "I like all flowers, but the lotus blossom is my favorite," she said, turning to smile at him again. "The fragrance is perfect—not too sweet, not too woodsy. Do you not agree?"

Stunned by yet another personal question, Joseph could only nod in agreement.

"So what do you think?" she asked, moving again along the walkway. "What plants can we add to bring more beauty to this place?"

She was two steps ahead of him before he found the words. "Mandrakes, iris, narcissus, and poppies for the ground; blue water lily and white lotuses for the pond," he said, grateful that at last she had asked a question that did not require a personal reply. He hurried to keep pace with her. "And we can bring in additional white lotus plants. They grow well in the pool."

"And they bloom at night," Sagira whispered, almost to herself.

"The blossoms remain open until nearly midday," he said, hurrying to defend the plants Tuya loved. "It is only the heat of the sun they cannot stand."

"Do not worry, Paneah, I shall not want them at midday. I like the garden at night and think I shall walk here often. And of course, I shall want all of the flowers to myself." She gave him a guilty smile as if she knew her request was slightly selfish. "Tell the servants not to touch them, will you please? Those I do not wear I shall offer to the goddess in the little temple."

"As you wish," Joseph answered, following.

Sagira stopped and bent down, reaching for a lotus blossom growing near the edge of the pool. Looking at Joseph, she smiled helplessly when her short arms could not reach the flower. Seeing her dilemma, he splashed into the water to retrieve the blossom, then bowed and presented it to her with a flourish.

"Thank you," she said, a blush coloring her cheek as she lifted the flower to her nostrils. Joseph waited with his hands folded, watching her eyes close in pleasure as she inhaled the exotic fragrance. "You must share this," she murmured, not moving the blossom from her face. "Bend down, Paneah, and let the lotus entice you."

He paused, uncertain how to proceed, and her dark eyes flew open. "Do you not like the scent of our lotus blossoms?"

"I like it very much."

"Then breathe in this one," she whispered, closing her eyes again. "It is sweeter than most, for it is offered by your mistress."

Awkwardly, Joseph bent at the waist. Feeling like an adolescent boy, he lowered his head toward the flower only inches from her lips. Once he was within a believable distance, he scarcely dared to breathe lest he offend her with his nearness.

The lids rose from her black velvet eyes. "Is it not wonderful?" she asked, her gaze holding him to the flower.

"Yes, mistress," he whispered, his voice flat in his ears.

With surprising grace and the unpredictability of a butterfly, her dainty hand suddenly rose to tap the bridge of his nose. Shocked into stillness, Joseph did not move.

"You are as beautiful as the lotus, my Paneah," she said, a dark, sultry tone in her voice. "A most striking and unique *Egyptian.*"

He suppressed the alarm that rose up in his mind as she emphasized the latter word. Why was she toying with him? Did she suspect that he was not of Egypt? But she did not seem to notice that his breathing had quickened, and she turned without further comment and tucked the lotus blossom into the neckline of her dress.

"See to the flowers, will you, Paneah?" she asked, turning for the house. "Have them installed as soon as possible. I do so love the garden."

Joseph sighed in relief when her small figure disappeared beyond the gate.

"I could not believe it, Tuya," Joseph said, nervously glancing over his shoulder as he sat and spoke with Tuya that night in the garden. "She made me uncomfortable!"

"What did she do, exactly?" Tuya asked, struggling to smother a smile. Joseph was as jumpy as a kitten.

He lowered his voice as if the papyrus reeds might hear him. "She asked me to smell a lotus blossom. And then she touched my face."

For an instant, a white-hot dart of jealousy burned through Tuya's heart, but she shook the feeling aside. Joseph loved her steadfastly. His discomfort was another proof of it.

"You are making too much of this," Tuya said, placing a comforting hand upon his arm. "Think, Joseph, of all our mistress has endured! I know her like no one else, and though she is spoiled and headstrong, above all, our Sagira is lonely." She turned her gaze upon the moon's reflection in the shallow pool. "I think she has grown tired of her priestess. She has spurned me and is too proud to call me back, but Sagira cannot live alone, Joseph. She needs company, the fellowship of friends, and I am afraid our master is not home often enough to give her the society she needs."

"She has parties every week," Joseph pointed out. "Surely you cannot want her to have more guests and feasts—"

"No, I have all the work I need," Tuya answered, softening her voice. "And Sagira does love parties, but what happens when the last guest is gone? She is left alone. She needs a friend, Joseph, and you are close to Potiphar. Perhaps she hopes to win her husband's attention through you. She is turning to you—"

"I would rather she turned to one of her maids."

"Maids and mistresses cannot be friends. I learned long ago that such things are not done."

"Potiphar and I are friends."

"Potiphar is an unusual master," Tuya answered. "And though he treats you as a confidant, does he invite you to eat with him? Does he take you with him to Pharaoh's court? No. You are his slave, and you will be kept in your place."

She sighed, for she knew these things instinctively, but Joseph had not been born a slave. His had been a privileged life, and in moments like these, his background showed.

"Please, Joseph, for my sake, be kind to Sagira," she whispered. "And then Potiphar will reward you for being a friend to his lonely wife. Perhaps our time of waiting will be shortened."

He shook his head and clasped his hands around his knees. "All right, Tuya, for you I will be her friend," he finally said, giving her a sidelong glance.

"You are wonderful," she said, nudging him gently with her shoulder. Something rustled in the bushes nearby, but when she turned to investigate, the garden shimmered still and quiet in the moonlight. "Did you hear something?" she whispered.

"Only the pounding of my heart," Joseph murmured, smiling drowsily in the stillness of the night.

Sagira idly ran her finger over the rim of the bowl she had placed on the altar at the villa's temple. Ramla had been gone for a full month, fulfilling her duties, and Sagira was anxious to speak with her. The priestess should have returned two days ago, but perhaps she had been delayed. . . .

A commotion at the gate distracted Sagira's attention, and she lifted her head and peered through the temple's doorway. A tall, veiled woman was greeting the gatekeeper, and Sagira recognized the disfigured hand on her traveling veil. Good! She turned back to the altar, determined that the priestess should not know how eagerly she had been awaited.

Sandaled footsteps slapped upon the pavement behind her, then Ramla prostrated herself before the statue of Bastet. Impatiently, Sagira pressed her lips together and allowed the priestess a moment of silence. Finally Ramla sat up and regarded her friend. "How are things in Potiphar's house?" she asked, coyly lifting an eyebrow. "What have you done in my absence?"

"Nothing," Sagira said, turning to Ramla with undisguised enthusiasm. "I nearly lost my self-control once, but then I realized that I need the gods to help me through this. If Paneah's Hebrew god is truly powerful, I dare not proceed without Bastet's protection."

"So you still plan to conceive a child with this Hebrew?"

"So you still disapprove of my plan?" Sagira snapped, turning her eyes to the stone idol. "Bastet has answered my petitions thus far. *She* must approve of me."

"Bastet sometimes allows her children to do things they ought not to do," Ramla answered, slipping the dusty veil from her shoulders. "Many hard lessons of life are learned this way." She paused, her dark eyes fixed upon the floor. "As a priestess, I would advise you to wait until Potiphar's death. Then you can remarry and bear a legitimate son. But as a woman—"

"Yes?" Sagira whispered, turning from the statue.

"As a woman, who would not desire Paneah?" Ramla's lean shoulder lifted in an elegant shrug. "My own heart has been stirred on occasion by the beauty of his countenance. He is truly a man among men. . . ."

"Keep your heart toward the goddess," Sagira answered, bracing herself on the altar as she rose from her knees. "Paneah is mine. But if you are still willing to help me, I need you."

"What can I do?" The priestess's mouth curved in a dry smile.

"Divine the future for me. I know the goddess will allow women to conceive only on certain days, and I would know the proper day for my son's conception. And I would know Paneah's future, to be certain he is the best one for my plan." She fixed the priestess in a determined gaze. "Consult the goddess, work your magic, and you will be handsomely rewarded."

Ramla's thin chest heaved slowly up and down as if she were weighing the cost, then she nodded and rose to her feet. "I will do it," she said. "But not for a reward. I do this to insure your success, my Sagira. If Paneah's future proves your plan, you will have my enduring support. But if the gods reveal a dark future, will you promise to give up this foolish notion?"

"Yes," Sagira nodded, eager to promise anything that would put her plan into motion. "Just call upon your powers, Ramla, and do it quickly!"

An hour later, Sagira helped Ramla to her bed. The priestess had worked her magic, uttered her predictions, and collapsed onto the floor in another of her strange seizures. Such pain was a dire price to pay for knowledge of the future, but Sagira would have been willing to sacrifice even Ramla's life for the final news.

The prophecy was both thrilling and disappointing. Well into her trance, Ramla had moaned and trembled and proclaimed that Paneah would be elevated to a position of power, and that every knee in Egypt would bow at his approach. Exhilarated, Sagira pressed for more news. "So when shall I confront him?" she urged, ready to shake the answers from the wide-eyed priestess. "When?"

"The eighteenth day of the second month of the third year," Ramla muttered. "The first day of the Feast of Opet."

"So long?" Sagira cried, upon hearing the date. "Three years from now?"

As Ramla nodded and collected her strength, Sagira paced through her chamber and chewed on her henna-tinted nails. "I cannot wait three years," she stormed. "I am eager to have a child now!"

"Perfection cannot be rushed," Ramla murmured weakly. "The gods know what they are doing. Besides, you will need time to prepare for this assignation."

"I have already begun preparation," Sagira replied hotly.

"Then slow your pace," Ramla warned. "You will need three years to bind him to your side. And three years to rid his heart of the slave girl's memory."

"Tuya?" Sagira stopped pacing as her throat tightened in despair. "But how can I get rid of her? I cannot sell her; Potiphar will not allow it."

"There are other ways," Ramla replied. "Paneah's love for Tuya is rooted in his heart. His love for you must spring from the flesh. Fleshly love is easily enticed. You must separate them, keep him from her arms so that he will be mad with longing for a tender embrace. Then, in time, you will feed him with your kisses, and command your will to be done." Her eyes narrowed. "Together we can do this. You work with the man. Leave the slave girl to me."

Even in her exhaustion, Ramla's eyes glowed with dark malevolence, and Sagira paused, momentarily distracted from her thoughts of Paneah. One sudden, cold, lucid thought sprang to the fore. "You truly hate Tuya, don't you?" she asked. "Why?"

"Why does a cat hate a dog?" Ramla answered cryptically. "Some beings are natural enemies." Without further discussion, she turned her back on Sagira and pretended to sleep.

Two days later, Joseph told Tuya that the mistress wanted her to accompany Ramla to Bubastis, the home of Bastet's main temple. An important center of trade and commerce, Bubastis lay far north in the Egyptian delta. At Sagira's request, Potiphar authorized an escort of ten warriors to safely guide his wife's patron priestess.

There was no time for Tuya to say goodbyes, for Sagira had not announced that Tuya would accompany Ramla until it was time to leave. Tuya had to gather Ramla's possessions and then load donkeys with their bundles of provisions. The ten guards, properly outfitted with bows and with quivers filled with shining bronze arrows, waited impatiently in the courtyard as Tuya flew throughout the house, leaving instructions to those who would step in to fill the vacancy she would leave. She had no opportunity for a private goodbye with Joseph, for Sagira kept him by her side, reminding him of the arrangements he had promised to make for her new garden.

Take care, and may God go with you, Joseph's smile seemed to say as he caught Tuya's eye in the courtyard. She gave him a timid, fleeting smile, then took her place beside the donkey in the midst of Potiphar's men. Tall and coolly dispassionate, Ramla mounted another donkey in front of Tuya and nodded to the guards. Sagira called a noisy goodbye from the portico; Potiphar lifted his hand in blessing and farewell.

I will not look back. Tuya kept her eyes fixed upon the scrawny tail of the donkey ahead of her as a nameless fear swept through her soul. *The days will fly like minutes, the years will fly like days. I will be back soon. This means nothing.*

As they passed out of the villa, she balled her hands into fists, fighting back the tears that swelled hot and heavy in her chest.

Seventeen

SAGIRA WATCHED THEM GO WITH A TRIUMPHANT smile. When no sign of the caravan remained on the dusty horizon, she turned and placed a hand on Paneah's arm. "Bring a pitcher of water and honey to my chamber," she said, taking pains to keep the eagerness in her heart from her voice. "This heat—and this day—have drained me."

Paneah bowed obediently, then turned toward the kitchen. Sagira gave Potiphar a bright smile, but his thoughts had already drifted toward his guards, for he gave her an absent wave and stalked away toward the ivy-covered wall that disguised the prison. Sagira shuddered, watching him go toward that awful place. She did not like to remember that criminals lurked in dank cells only yards away from her lovely house, but the captain of Pharaoh's bodyguard was also the overseer of Pharaoh's jail. The king certainly did not want criminals near the palace.

She turned and nimbly ran up the portico steps and hurried through the central hall. Her chambers had been cleaned and aired that morning, and sheer linen curtains billowed about her bed. Sagira touched a burning coal to a coil of sweet incense. She would not win Paneah in a day, but she would teach him not to jump at her touch. Any wild rabbit could be taught to eat from the hand with a little gentle persuasion.

She checked her face in her bronze mirror, adjusted the angle of her wig, and lay down upon her bed, artfully spreading her garments so that a modest length of her leg peeped through the slit in her gown. She moistened her lips with her tongue, peered at her fingernails, then froze like a nervous bride at the sound of footsteps in the hall.

A discreet little servant's cough signaled Paneah's arrival outside her door. "Now it begins," she whispered. "Come in," she called, her voice a mournful wail. The door opened and Paneah's handsome face peered in upon her. She forced herself to bite her lip until her chin quivered; she looked as woebegone as her pounding heart would permit.

"Mistress, is something wrong?" He hovered near the doorway, the cup and pitcher on a tray in his hand.

She squinted her eyes closed and pretended to wipe tears from her cheeks. "It is nothing, Paneah, that you would understand. Sometimes I think no one understands."

He paused. From eavesdropping on his conversations with Tuya, she knew him so well she could almost hear two voices arguing in his head. Part of him wanted to leave the tray and run; another wanted to obey the sweet urgings toward friendship that Tuya had given him in the garden.

"When I think no one understands," he answered slowly, "I remember that God always does. God is good, a stronghold in the day of trouble, and He is a friend to those who trust in Him."

His answer was safe and impersonal, but a man lived beneath that cool exterior. Sagira lifted wide eyes to meet his. "No god cares for me. Put down the tray, Paneah. You may go. But if you do, I will have no one." She lifted her voice in a plaintive wail and turned her face to the wall. "Ramla has left, and Tuya has gone, and Potiphar is busy with his jail! My mother will not see me because—well, you do not want to listen. Even the servants here care nothing for me."

"You are wrong, mistress," he answered, his voice careful and quiet in the room. "You are held in great—*affection*—by all who serve you. The master is busy, but he will be back, and Ramla and Tuya will return soon—"

"Each day here feels like a year," she whispered, hiding

her face behind her hands. "Every month an eternity. And I am alone, without a friend in the world. . . ."

Crying came easily, for her heightened emotions had left her fragile. She burst into tears, curling into a ball on the bed, and she heard Paneah step toward the door as if to call for help; then he moved to her side. "Please, mistress," he whispered, trying to quiet her. "Do not cry."

She did not stop weeping, but put out a hand in entreaty. Unable to resist the impulse to help another, his hand clasped hers. Her senses began to flutter in response to his touch, and for a moment she nearly forgot her careful plan. She held the hand of a future king of Egypt! Before her stood the man who would give her a child! Like a drowning woman, she pulled at him, unwilling to let him go.

"Oh, Paneah," she wept, genuine tears now flowing. "Can you know how it feels to be utterly forsaken?"

His eyes filled with words, yet he did not speak. But as her tears flowed he patted her in wordless sympathy. She was conscious of his nearness, his power and strength, but she did not break the silence or move until many moments had passed.

At last her tears stopped and his hand ceased its gentle patting of her arm. The tingling effects of his touch spread through her like wildfire, but she forced herself to calm her emotions, to think clearly. He was still skittish and very much in love with someone else.

"Oh," she said, forcing a laugh as she wiped her eyes, "I suppose you shall think me a silly, homesick child."

"No, mistress," he said, moving carefully away. He lowered his eyes to the floor in proper respect. "I know what it is to be abandoned."

"Perhaps you shall tell me your story sometime," she whispered. "We have much in common, you and I."

Smiling, he turned to go, and Sagira nodded. "Thank you, Paneah," she said, looking up fully into his dark eyes. "I feel—so *safe* with you."

"I am glad to serve you," he replied automatically, and as he left her chamber Sagira pressed her lips together to stifle her exultant smile. "Ah, Ramla, if you could have seen this," she whispered. "The wild rabbit is tamed!"

During the two months of Tuya's absence, Sagira called Paneah to her side as often as she could without seeming to pay him undue attention. Keeping the conversation light and her interest friendly, she inquired about the fields, the cattle and horses, and the servants. Finally, she linked her arm through his one morning and boldly announced that she had decided to become his shadow.

"What, mistress?" Paneah said, honest alarm in his eyes. "It is not proper that you should walk in some of the places where I must go—"

"Paneah," she chided, facing him. She glanced right and left to be sure they were alone, then gave him a shy smile. "I know that Potiphar has promised to give you freedom and his permission to marry our lovely Tuya. If you are going to leave us in a few years, should I not know how this household is run? After all, it is a woman's proper place to run the house, and I have been spoiled to have you take care of things for me. But since you will be leaving," she prodded his arm playfully, "don't you think I should know what you do and how you do it?"

For this he had no answer but a baffled nod, and Sagira smiled. "You must wait here while I go and change into something more appropriate for the fields. Then you shall lead the way, Paneah, and show me how and why Potiphar's house has become the wealthiest in all of Thebes."

She left before he had time to protest and hurried into her own chamber where she had already set aside a short tunic of white linen that showed her arms and legs to their best advantage. She tossed aside the heavy noblewoman's wig and donned a light hairpiece similar to the short, swinging hairstyle the slave girls wore. With quick, deft movements she pulled off her heavy gold bracelets and earrings, then pinched her cheeks and thrust her feet into tiny leather sandals. She felt like a girl, simple and light-headed, and she knew from the look in Paneah's eyes when she rejoined him that he found the change pleasant.

"You know," she said, leading the way from the house, "I have never had a brother, Paneah. How I wanted an elder brother! Someone like you who would understand me and teach me things. . . ."

"I will be happy to teach you, mistress," Paneah answered, his long stride easily catching hers. He gave her an open and admiring smile. "Anyone who wants to learn deserves a willing and faithful teacher."

Ramla served in Bastet's glorious temple through the months of Thoth and Paopi, while Tuya spent her days pacing in the priestess's spare living quarters. Why had Ramla needed a handmaid? Over one hundred slaves served at this temple, eager to fulfill the commands and needs of the priests and priestesses. Perhaps she had brought a maid to lend herself prestige, but Ramla had never seemed the type to care what other people thought of her. Whatever the woman's reasons, Tuya counted the days, anxious for her time of service to be at an end.

One night not long after they had completed their second month at the temple, Ramla entered the chamber and sat in her chair, staring moodily at the tangerine tints cast upon the wall by the setting sun. Tuya moved as silently as she could, unwilling to disturb Ramla's pensive mood. She had just picked up the priestess's night dress when Ramla's iron voice broke the silence.

"We will leave tomorrow. You will be happy to return to Thebes, won't you." The latter was a statement, not a question.

Tuya jumped at the sharp sound, but she took a deep breath and forced her pounding heart to remain steady. "Of course. Everyone loves to go home."

"Slaves have no home." Ramla paused and ran her long fingernail along the arm of the chair. "Neither do priests and priestesses."

Tuya let that observation pass without comment. She would not allow the poison in Ramla's bitter soul to infect her happiness at the prospect of going home to Joseph. Ignoring the other woman, she placed Ramla's nightdress upon the bed, but the priestess turned and faced her directly. "I have often thought it an ironic joke of the gods that we crossed paths again in Potiphar's house. I did not expect to ever see you again, and when Potiphar refused to send you to the temple, I divined that the will of the gods had brought us together."

Tuya listened with a vague sense of unreality. She had instinctively known that this woman hated her, but how could Ramla believe Tuya's presence was a divine jest?

"Why do you despise me?" she asked, daring to speak honestly in the solitude of the cavernous chamber.

The priestess leaned back in her chair and propped her head on her hand, her mouth curving in a dry, one-sided smile. "I am glad you speak what is on your mind. I will be frank, also."

She gazed at Tuya with chilling intentness for a long moment, then tented her fingers and centered herself in the chair. "In the beginning, I think I was jealous of the friendship you shared with Sagira. You were taken from your parents as a child, as was I, but you were placed into a loving family. You had a friend."

Her black eyes widened as she stared mindlessly over the tips of her fingers. "I was taken to the temple, the place I would have sent you if Potiphar had allowed it. The priests shaved my head and circumcised me to persuade me to remain a virgin consecrated to Bastet."

Tuya felt her heart turn to stone in her chest. Every feeling of antipathy she had borne toward Ramla shuddered and melted into pitiful concern. "I am sorry," she managed to whisper, scarcely daring to look at the woman who had suffered so much.

"I should have seen that you would come into my life again," Ramla said, an odd smirk crossing her striking face. "What a jest the gods have played on their resentful priestess! But I, too, have a sense of humor. Tell me, Tuya, do you want to know the future?"

"No," Tuya said, shaking her head. She turned to Ramla's box of possessions to begin packing for the journey back to Thebes. "Some things are better left unseen."

"Some things are better *foreseen*," Ramla contradicted, a strangely cold look in her eyes. She dropped her hands and stood to her feet in a single, fluid motion. "Tell me the future, Tuya. Do you think we will find things at Potiphar's house as we left them?"

Struggling to mask her rising fear, Tuya painted on a warm smile and shrugged. "The flood has come, so the land will be muddy and gray. But our Paneah will be busy preparing for the planting. . . ."

A glaze seemed to come down over the woman's black eyes, and she sneered. "*Our* Paneah? Do not think of him as yours, my dear, for despite what you may think, he is a slave belonging to your master and mistress."

Tuya paused. "Of course. I did not mean to imply—"

"I am not implying anything." Ramla moved back to her chair. "I know the future; I know the present. I know, for instance, that Paneah will give Sagira a son, it is her sworn ambition. Even now your mistress works to win your love's heart. You are here with me so you would be out of Sagira's way."

The lid of Ramla's trunk fell from Tuya's hand. She felt numb, as if her arms and legs and feelings had suddenly paralyzed.

Unrelenting, the priestess continued: "You know Sagira as well as I, and you know her determination. She is a woman of great strategy and cunning. She will lure your handsome Paneah into her arms before he can think to resist."

The horror of Ramla's announcement stole Tuya's breath, which came only in short, painful gasps. "Paneah will not!" she managed to stammer.

"Paneah is a slave, and he will do whatever he is commanded to do," Ramla went on, her eyes gleaming in the chamber's gloom as she studied the effect of her words. "He will give Sagira what she wants, or he will die. If he wants to be rewarded, he will perform his duties—*enthusiastically.*"

A sudden vise pressed upon Tuya's stomach. Overcome by nausea, she bent over and ran from the room.

Eighteen

"HAVE YOU REMEMBERED EVERYTHING, SAGIRA?" Joseph called. They were far outside the city, in the center of the Theban Hills. He had spent the greater part of two months showing Sagira, mistress of the household, how it all functioned. She had promised to show him, in turn, the wonders of the land he had never really seen.

"I brought everything," she said, struggling to carry the last basket. She had ordered the kitchen slaves to load the chariot with special provisions for this outing, and Joseph was impressed that she arranged everything herself. Together they had left the house shortly before sunrise while the rest of the house still slumbered.

"Let me get that," Joseph said, springing to assist her. The basket seemed enormous in her slender arms, and her eyes lit with gratitude when he lifted it and carried it to the papyrus mat she had spread upon the sand.

"Now that everything is unpacked," she said, hands on her hips, "look around you, Paneah! This is Egypt's glory! Some have called this place the Temple of the World."

Joseph stopped and lifted his eyes to the open horizon. The west bank of the Theban Hills was dominated by a huge semicircle of sheer cliffs that rose straight from the floor of the Nile Valley. Forming an extraordinary foil for the elaborate temples across the yawning chasm, the two-mile-long prominence of cliffs shimmered in the heat as if dancing to an elusive rhythm only audible to creatures of the desert. The sun burned bright and hot here, shrinking all distance until the landscape's elements seemed to stand one on top of another.

"Look there!" Sagira called, holding her light wig with one hand as she pointed in the direction of the wind. To the east lay the silvery Nile below a black bank of the fertile soil Joseph had come to love. Green cultivation glowed bright under ochre cliffs as red as Sagira's lips. The entire spectrum of colors brushed up against a blue sky that dazzled Joseph's wide eyes.

"I told you it was beautiful!" Sagira called above the wind.

Joseph nodded, too moved for words.

Far below, in the canyon beneath the cliffs, a whirlwind twirled and swayed with the grace of a Hittite dancing girl. He and Reuben had once seen such a whirlwind together, and Reuben had made a jest about one of Dan's wives who danced just that way. The funny-sad memory made him smile, yet he had to blink back unexpected tears.

The wind ruffled his hair, brushed his clean-shaven cheeks, and billowed his kilt about his knees. He had not felt the strength of such a wind since he traveled the open land with his brothers . . . with his father. Would they know him now if they saw him with this face, in this kilt? He would go to them if he could and offer his forgiveness . . . but were they ready to accept it?

"Is it not—why Paneah, what is wrong?" Sagira said, seeing the emotion in eyes. She clasped his arm when he turned to move away and would not let him go. "I am your friend, Paneah, you can tell me your deepest sorrow," she said, her eyes blazing up at him brighter than the sun. "As you care for me, let me care for you. Do not cry."

The soothing sound of her voice broke the dam of resistance in him. Embarrassed and ashamed at his weakness, he lowered his head into his hands, then allowed her to lead him to the mat, where he crumpled into a formless heap and released the bitter tears he had never been able to shed.

He did not know how long he cried, but he felt doubly the fool when he lifted his head from his hands. A man did not cry in front of a woman, and a slave certainly did not weep in his mistress's presence.

"I am sorry," he said, his voice gruff as he straightened himself to sit beside her. "I have behaved badly."

"Nonsense," Sagira said. "You were upset."

"What I did was not proper."

"There is no one here but you and me, and we shall judge what is proper," Sagira answered, her eyes bright and bemused. "I cried on your shoulder once, remember? I have only returned your kindness." She paused a moment and pressed nearer to him. "What was it that upset you, my Paneah? The sight of the tombs? We do not fear death, you know. We are afraid only of being caught unprepared for it."

"It was not the tombs." He shook his head. "The whirlwind reminded me of my brothers and my father. I try not to think about them, for the memory is painful, but yet today I would have leapt into that chariot and driven northward to find them if you—"

He meant to say that he belonged to Sagira and could not very well steal her chariot and leave her stranded in the desert, but she seemed to find a deeper meaning in his words, for she suddenly grasped his hands. He resisted the urge to pull away from her; to do so would offend her, and she had been kind. After all, in his weakness, he had reached out to *her*.

"You would not leave me, would you Paneah?" she whispered, laying a warm hand against his shoulder.

"No, mistress," he answered, shifting uncomfortably. He propped his elbows on his knees and gripped his hands.

"A moment ago you called me Sagira," she said, looking up at him. "I would have you call me that whenever we are alone. In fact," she lifted her arm in an imperial gesture, "I command it."

"As you wish, Sagira." Perhaps he had misread her. He could not resist a smile at her playfulness. She could be quite charming, and he took quiet pride in the fact that he alone had managed to befriend her.

"You are quick to please me," she murmured, her eyes watering in the wind.

"I am your slave."

"You are my friend."

"Yes," he answered, remembering the easygoing fellowship they had shared over the past two months. "I suppose if it is possible for a slave and mistress, we are friends."

"Of course it is possible." She pouted prettily. "Friends want to make each other happy, do they not?"

"Yes."

"And a slave aims to make his mistress happy, does he not?"

"Yes."

"Then it is no contradiction for us to be both." She moved across the mat until she sat facing him. "Kiss me, Paneah. The kiss of friendship."

He frowned, and she threw back her head and laughed for a long moment. "If you could have seen your face," she said when she caught her breath. "By the eye of Horus, Paneah, what did you think I meant? I am a married woman!"

He laughed, a little awkwardly. "I didn't know what to think."

"Have you never heard of the kiss of friendship? Potiphar kisses Pharaoh's leg every time he stands before him, and only very important people are allowed to kiss the royal leg. And here I offer you a chance to kiss my lips because you are a special friend, but you gaze at me as though I had suddenly sprouted the horns of Thoth!"

She leaned forward and deliberately gave him a childish pucker. Joseph bore the kiss with good humor and gripped his hands more tightly, eager to begin the journey back to the villa. Sagira was playful, and spoiled, and a trifle dangerous when she did not get her way. If she would only finish this little game so they could begin the drive back. . . .

"Sagira," he said, "the sun dips toward the west. This

heat will tire you unless we leave soon."

"In a moment." She did not even glance toward the sun, but kept her eyes riveted upon him. Suddenly she took a deep breath and lowered her eyes fully into his. "Kiss me as a man kisses the woman he loves, Paneah," she whispered, a small smile curling upon her lips.

"No!" The word sprang from him before he had time to think.

"Come now," she said, playful again. "We are friends, are we not? Do you not desire to please me?"

"I cannot do this—you are my master's wife!"

"He will never know."

"I will know!" He stood up in a panic, pushing her away with as much force as he dared use.

Standing, she gave him a steady look and a steadier smile. "Don't be so alarmed, Paneah. That was only a little test. I can tell Potiphar you passed with flying colors."

"A test?" Struggling to catch his breath, Joseph eyed her with suspicion.

"To discover the strength and resolve of your virtue. I shall tell Potiphar that you are as unexcitable as a eunuch."

She turned and stepped toward the chariot with the ease of a departing queen. Joseph crossed his arms and turned to face the open canyon of the Egyptian hills as he regained his composure. He was accustomed to her biting wit and quick temper, but her last remark was a slap in the face of his manhood. She had inferred that he was not a man at all, but had he accepted her offer, she would certainly have slapped him and had him thrown to the Nile crocodiles.

Joseph shook his head and sighed. Sagira was alternately hot and cold, loving and sharp, caring and diffident. Compared to soft and gentle Tuya, Sagira was a bundle of sharp angles and rough edges, but for some reason God had placed him in this house, with these people. "Help me, God of my fathers," he prayed.

Amon-Re's blurred and blood-red sun was setting beyond the western horizon when Ramla's entourage returned to Potiphar's house. Tuya was disappointed when
the crowd of welcoming servants did not include Joseph.
Where was he? At this hour he should have been in the
house attending his master, but Potiphar stood on the portico alone, his hand lifted in greeting.

Sagira was absent as well. As much as she tried to force
Ramla's cruel prediction from her mind, Tuya could not forget the last image she had of Sagira and Joseph standing
closely together. He would not do what Ramla predicted!
He would not even listen to such a suggestion!

The donkeys had been put away and the guards sent
home by the time a single chariot churned the dust outside
the gatehouse. Tuya ran to the portico, straining through
the gathering darkness to see who had arrived.

Sagira's light laughter broke the silence of the night.
"Paneah, let Enos put the remains of our meal away," she
called, apparently not caring who heard her. "You must be
tired after our long day."

The couple moved up the path toward the portico, and
Tuya stood in her place like a helpless rabbit caught in a
panther's hypnotic glare. When the mistress and her slave
entered the circle of torchlight, Sagira's mouth opened in
surprise. "Tuya! You have finally returned! I hope you had
a pleasant journey. I should find Ramla, but we have had
an exhausting day out among the hills."

She swept through the portico on the way to her chamber, and Joseph paused on a step below Tuya. "Welcome
home," he said, giving her a dusty smile, but Tuya could
not return it. Red ochre stained his lips and the side of his
face.

Gulping back a sob, she turned and sprinted toward the
women's quarters.

———

Tuya wept for an hour, then hiccuped until one of the

maids tossed a sandal at her from across the room. "Go outside if you cannot be quiet," the maid grumped, and Tuya
wrapped a thin shawl about her shoulders and slipped out
into the night. She might never be able to sleep again. Each
time she closed her eyes she saw Joseph locked in an embrace with Sagira. Ramla *could* foretell the future, and soon
a child would be born. Joseph had rejected *her* love, claim-
ing that he owed obedience to his God and to his father, and
yet to Sagira he had given himself as eagerly as a bride-
groom. . . .

From force of long habit, her feet carried her to the garden. Standing at the edge of the reflecting pool, she gazed
into the water and dismally wondered if it were possible to
drown in knee-deep water. She hiccuped again, then wiped
her nose on the back of her hand. "Oh, Joseph," she wailed,
forgetting herself in her misery. "Why did you do it?"

"Do what?" He stepped from the shadows of the trees,
his eyes as troubled and miserable as hers. Suddenly,
standing so close to him and seeing that he suffered, too,
she could not bring herself to repeat Ramla's base accusations. If Joseph had become Sagira's lover, surely he would
be with the mistress now instead of pacing in the garden!
Unless his conscience troubled him . . .

"Tell me," Tuya said, giving him a wobbly smile. "Did
you miss me?"

"Very much," he said, stepping closer. She thought he
would draw her into his arms, but he merely lifted her
hands and held them upon his own. He kept his eyes lowered—was he afraid to look at her?

Somehow she swallowed her fears and found her voice.
"Did you spend much time with Sagira?"

"Yes," he answered, returning her level glance. "Because you told me to. She thinks of me as a friend."

"Then why—" Tuya tried to keep her voice light and casual, "—why was your face stained with ochre when you
returned tonight? Have you taken to painting your lips?"

She could not tell if he blushed in the moonlight. "She

kissed me," he said simply. "A kiss of affection."

"She kissed you," Tuya repeated, lowering her hands from his. Suspicion rose again and snarled, blocking the voices of calm and reason from her mind. "When was the last time a mistress kissed her slave?" she asked, wincing at the edge of desperation in her voice.

"How am I to know?" Joseph answered, folding his arms in a pose of weary dignity. "She kissed me in affection. And you told me to be her friend."

"Her friend, not her lover," Tuya whispered.

Even in the darkness she could see defiance pouring hotly from his dark eyes.

"She kissed you, Joseph, so tell me the truth. Did she not long for more?"

Her question brought a hard frown and a glint of temper to his face. "Do you not trust me?"

She brushed his question aside. "Tell me, Joseph. Did she ask for more?"

"Yes! But so did you, remember?" His words cut through the night, lacerating her. Tuya backed away, pressing her hand to her mouth.

"Women!" Joseph turned and knocked a fist against his forehead. "If I would not lie with you, why do you think I would lie with a woman I do not love?" Keeping his back to her, he placed his hands on his hips and breathed deeply, and Tuya knew he was trying to control his temper and his thoughts.

"I am sorry, Tuya, that was not fair. The situations are not the same," he finally whispered, his voice husky in the darkness. "Sometimes I wish that God had not gifted me with a form pleasing to women. I walk in the marketplace and they call out to me; I walk in the threshing rooms and feel their eyes upon my back; I sit behind my master at dinner and my mistress smiles at me. . . ."

He walked to a tree and leaned upon it, crossing his arms as he faced her. "The same beauty that bound Rachel to Jacob now enslaves me. You should understand, Tuya, for God has gifted you with beauty, too."

"I understand this," she said, moving toward him as though being closer would make him understand. "I understand that you want to be free, Joseph, and that you have dreams of greatness. You are proud; you are ambitious; you dream of things in the future and yearn to prosper in everything you undertake. You are a fire-eater; you will do anything to keep faith in your dreams. I wonder if you will do anything to be free—"

He did not answer, but slouched before her, bleary-eyed and weary.

"There is no advantage or profit in loving me," she whispered, avoiding his gaze. "But there is much to be gained in pleasing a mistress. I love you, Joseph, and I know about your dreams. I will not stand in the way of their fulfillment. I cannot."

Before her heart could change her mind, she turned on her heel and left the garden.

The pleasant sounds of people at dinner drifted through the house as Tuya approached the main hall the next afternoon. Sagira, Potiphar, and Ramla sat upon chairs placed in a circle for conversation and ate from bowls that had been placed on stands near them. Between Potiphar and his wife, Joseph lingered like an obedient shadow, ready to do their bidding.

He caught Tuya's eye as she approached, and for the first time in her memory his eyes did not light with excitement when she entered the room. His smile was strained, his eyes wary. She glanced at him with no more outward interest than she would have given a wall painting, then prostrated herself on the floor before Potiphar's feet.

"What is this?" he asked, looking down at her over the deep crescents of flesh under his eyes. "I did not send for you, Tuya."

"If it please my master," she said, lifting her head from the floor. "I have a request."

"Should a slave beg for favors?" Sagira asked, but Potiphar smiled and leaned forward in his chair.

"Speak, Tuya. I will listen."

"Some time ago I displeased my mistress, and she wanted to send me away," Tuya said, knowing she had stepped onto a path from which there could be no return. "You, kind master, would not allow me to go. But if my lady still finds me displeasing, I am willing to go." She steeled herself to continue, "I have no place here."

"What is this?" Potiphar asked, turning to Sagira in surprise. "Have you quarreled with this girl?"

"How could I, my lord?" Sagira asked, lifting her shoulder in an elegant shrug. "She has been with Ramla for two months. This favor, I assure you, is a surprise to me."

"The captain of Pharaoh's guard would do well to consider her request," Ramla said, speaking in the low voice she reserved for dreaded things. "An unhappy slave can incite rebellion and mutiny among the others. Even you, Potiphar, may have trouble on your hands if the girl is forced to remain here."

"She cannot go," Potiphar said, slapping his knee. "She was a gift from Pharaoh. One does not cast off a presentation from the royal and divine hand." He glanced toward Sagira, another of his favors from Pharaoh, and lifted her hand to his lips. "Not that I would want to rid myself of any of our king's gifts."

"Still, Tuya is an old friend, and I do not want her to be unhappy," Sagira said, resting her hand on Potiphar's arm. "Perhaps you might approach the king or one of his counselors about the situation. I am sure you can find a solution, my husband."

Potiphar gave her an approving glance. "I shall try, my little wife," he promised, rising to his feet. He kissed her hand again in farewell, then turned toward Tuya. "I would hate to see you go, but if you are sure you cannot be happy here—"

"I am certain," she said, bowing before him again. She did not allow her eyes to lift toward Joseph's face.

Joseph fought against the maddening tedium of the after-dinner ritual. Potiphar left the house, Tuya slipped away, and Joseph attended Ramla and Sagira until they finished a lengthy, rambling conversation and moved to the women's quarters. When they had gone, he clapped his hands explosively to bring slaves from the kitchen to clear the room, then he hurried from the hall.

He found Tuya in the room where the lowliest of all slaves worked to grind corn into flour. On her hands and knees, she was bent over a slab with a heavy grindstone in her hand. The toothless old slave who usually ground the corn sat on the floor, watching with wide, amused eyes.

"What are you doing in here?" he demanded, pulling the grindstone out of Tuya's hand. "This is not your work!"

"I thought I may as well learn how to do everything," she said, not looking at him. "If a family can afford only one slave, they will purchase a woman for grinding, and so I thought I should learn—"

"You are not going anywhere." His hand closed around her upper arm and he pulled her from the room, oblivious to the old woman's curious stare. In the corridor, he stood Tuya against the wall and leaned over her, his arms blocking her escape. "What foolish, jealous notion was that today?" he asked, taking pains to keep his voice level. "You have harmed your reputation with Potiphar. I may be able to dissuade him from approaching Pharaoh, but now the master and mistress both know you are not happy. The damage is done."

"I am leaving, even if I have to run away and am beaten for it," Tuya answered, her eyes large and fierce with pain. "I cannot stay here, Joseph. I love you too much, I cannot bear to watch Sagira trap you—"

"I love you, and I will not be trapped," he said, pressing against the walls as if he would knock them down. What would it take to make her believe him? "Sagira may be infatuated," he said, lowering his voice, "but I am only her friend. My heart belongs to you, Tuya, and soon she will grow tired of me."

"She will not stop until she wins. She has the power to command you."

"Some things cannot be commanded."

"Then consider this—she has the power to take my life, and she hates me. If I stay, and if you refuse her, she will hurt me somehow, she has already hurt me—"

"So you would leave this house and go where I cannot protect you? What if you are sold to a cruel master? What if you find yourself commanded by a man who would ask more of you than Sagira asks of me? You are not thinking, Tuya! You would leave this comfortable house for a nest of vipers—"

"I do not know where I will go," she whimpered, sliding down against the wall. "I only know the gods have not smiled on us. Montu's strong arm has not been able to save you from Sagira, and your god is silent—"

He knelt in front of her and reached for her hands, his heart breaking at the sight of tears upon those lovely cheeks. "You must trust in the true God," he said, gentling his voice. "Please, Tuya, stay with me. Our time of waiting is nearly done, and then we shall be married and have a house of our own. I can handle Sagira even as I have handled Potiphar all these years. I need you here—"

"You think too highly of your own abilities, Joseph. You cannot hold Sagira off and yet cling to me. Such dreams are impossible; she will never allow us to be married."

"Faith is believing in the impossible, Tuya. Why can you not put aside your everlasting fear and trust me? You have no faith in me, no, not even in yourself, or you would see that you are as precious to me as life itself. Please, dear one, let me tell Potiphar that you have changed your mind about leaving."

"No," she said, pulling herself free from his grasp. She stood and stumbled as she moved away. "I love you too much, Joseph, and I know Sagira. Whether she wins or loses, you will suffer, and I cannot bear the exquisite torture of watching. I cannot stay."

~~Nineteen~~

"MY HUSBAND."

Potiphar was just about to oversee the changing of the guard at his prison, but Sagira's voice interrupted his thoughts. He turned in surprise; she did not usually venture into the courtyard in the heat of the day. Something serious must have brought her out. "Do you need me?" he asked, hurrying to her side.

"I would have a word with you, at your leisure," she said, giving his men a regal nod.

The little girl had become a polished woman of substance and discretion, and Potiphar's spirits lifted at the sight of her small form. "My friends," he said, flashing a smile toward his guards. "The lady has need of me."

They laughed and let him go, and Sagira gestured toward the pathway leading to the garden. He fell into step beside her, and she linked her arm through his as they walked. "I have been giving the matter of my unhappy slave a great deal of thought," she said, tilting her dark eyes toward him. "Pharaoh has an eye for beauty, and I am sure there are none to equal Tuya in the royal harem."

"She was destined for the harem when Pharaoh presented her to me," Potiphar said, musing upon the risks of this venture. "If he did not want her then, how do we know he will want her now?"

"She was a child then," Sagira answered lightly. "Now she has matured into a vividly beautiful woman. Pharaoh will be honored to have her."

The muscles of Potiphar's jaw worked silently as he considered her words. "I still cannot imagine why she wants to leave," he said. "I thought she and Paneah loved each other. I had promised to let them marry in two more years—"

"Childish infatuations vanish like dew under the sun's hot breath," Sagira said, sighing. "Now Tuya and Paneah argue whenever they catch sight of each other. I believe Tuya wishes to leave us because she cannot bear to be around Paneah. I overheard her telling him something like that only a short while ago."

"I suppose I can understand," Potiphar said, nodding, "and I am a reasonable man. So be it. I will take Tuya with me when I go to the palace tomorrow." He stopped and patted her hand. "I have to see to things in the prison, my dear. Is there anything else you need from me?"

"You have given me everything I need," she said, lowering her eyes demurely. "Thank you, Potiphar."

The early morning shadows in Sagira's chamber looked like stalking gray cats, but Tuya said nothing as she entered the room to face Sagira and the priestess. They had sent for her before daybreak, and Tuya obeyed with wooden resignation. This summons would be her last from the poisonous little Sagira. And yet this morning would also bring her last glimpse of Joseph's beloved form.

In order to make Tuya pleasing to Pharaoh, Sagira and Ramla were taking no chances. "We will personally oversee your toilet," Ramla remarked, eyeing Tuya with a critical eye. With the quiet air of one who has been chosen to be sacrificed, Tuya stood perfectly still as Ramla muttered incantations and anointed the slave's skin with perfumed oil. Sagira chose a fitted garment of white linen from her own wardrobe, and two slaves expertly sewed Tuya into it while Ramla lengthened the straps so that the dress revealed more of her beauty. Humming quietly, Sagira motioned for Tuya to sit, then picked up strands of her dark hair and began to braid them into delicately thin ribbons. As Sagira's nimble fingers flew, Tuya's eyes filled with bitter tears of remembering. Sagira had often braided Tuya's hair in just this way when they were children.

While Sagira braided and twined pearls and white beads into Tuya's hair, another slave deftly lined the girl's eyes with kohl and colored her lids with green shadows the color of the Nile waters. An hour later, when all was done, Sagira stood back and admired her handiwork. "Perfect," she said finally, flashing a white smile at Ramla. "Take her now to Potiphar. He waits in the courtyard."

Like a sheep led to the meatcutter, Tuya followed Ramla in tiny, mincing steps, all she could manage in the skintight dress. Every room of the house held a memory of Joseph, vivid images that closed around her and filled her with a longing to turn back. Desperately, she began to recite an ancient spell of forgetting, to block the recollections. She did not want to see Joseph or think about him, but the image of his haunted, pleading face remained uppermost in her mind.

The sun had risen by the time she reached the courtyard; the walls of the villa seemed to dance before her swimming eyes. Potiphar gave her a frankly admiring glance, then motioned for her to climb onto the litter that would carry her to Pharaoh's palace.

The litter bearers held the conveyance steady as she sat on the edge and swung her legs up. One more moment and she would be away. In one more hour she could forget that Potiphar's house had ever existed. After all, Joseph must not have cared for her too deeply, for he had not come to say goodbye. . . .

A voice from the portico made her cringe in sudden guilt. "Potiphar!"

Joseph's voice.

She did not turn around.

"What, Paneah?" Potiphar said, shading his eyes as he looked toward the house.

Joseph's light, quick footsteps crunched the gravel. "I

wanted to be sure, master, that you will not reconsider this action. Tuya is a valuable slave—"

Potiphar held up an interrupting hand, then turned toward Tuya. "Do you want to remain, my dear?" he asked, his voice oddly gentle.

"No," she said, keeping her eyes fixed on the gate. She braced her arms upon the sides of the litter. "I am ready to leave."

"She wants to go," Potiphar said, waving in farewell.

"One moment, sir," Joseph called, and then he stood beside her, looking as though he would pull her from the litter by force. Love and pain struggled in his eyes. "Believe in me," he whispered. "I need you to have faith. When I am free, and a great man, I will find you. I will rescue you from slavery."

She did not dare to steal one last look at him. "I thought you were a great man when I first met you," she whispered.

Potiphar gave the command, and the litter bearers stepped forward.

Arriving at the palace, Potiphar left Tuya with Kratas, the eunuch in charge of the harem, and then hastened to see that his guards were in place. Pharaoh's daily ritual, much like the daily routine of the temples' stone gods, had already begun. The divine king had been roused by priests singing a hymn of praise; then the priests had performed his morning toilet, perfuming his skin with oil and decking him with royal robes and Egypt's red-and-white double crown. The great king was presently at breakfast, and would soon be brought into the throne room to transact business and receive offerings.

Potiphar paced in the hallway. In the revealing dress and full makeup, Tuya looked like a different woman, and Potiphar was more than a little surprised by his wife's generosity. His child-bride had matured in the past year. The last traces of girlishness, uncertainty, and puppy fat had evaporated from her features and body; she had become a woman of distinction and charm. Since they had come to understand each other, she no longer wasted her energy on silly songs and suggestive dances. She behaved as a modest and mature woman should and even knew as much as Paneah about running the estate.

The sounds of music and singing alerted him that Pharaoh's entourage was about to enter the throne room. Automatically Potiphar straightened, adjusted the waistband of his kilt, and patted the heavy Gold of Praise about his neck. Any other man would have whispered a prayer to his patron god at the thought of what he was about to do, but Potiphar hoped only that he would find Pharaoh in a forgiving and generous mood.

———

"A gift for me?" The royal voice rumbled through the hall. The king's pet lion opened his mouth in a noisy yawn, and several of the queen's handmaids twittered. The queen, the court, and even Pharaoh's sons leaned forward in curiosity to see what gift Pharaoh's captain might have brought.

"Yes, divine Pharaoh," Potiphar said, straightening his shoulders. "Several years ago you gave me a beautiful child who has now blossomed into a flower of surpassing loveliness. She has remained untouched and sheltered in my house, and today I bring her to you as a gift. You have given me a house, a bride, the Gold of Praise. I honor you today with a gift worthy of a king's notice."

Pharaoh frowned for a moment, and the knuckles that grasped the crook and flail whitened as he considered his response. "It is like a man who loans silver to another," he said finally, leaning forward. "You bring me today the principal amount, plus interest."

Potiphar bowed his head. "In a manner of speaking, yes."

"Well then," Pharaoh said, relaxing upon his chair. He

cast a sidelong smile to Narmer, who remained as close to Pharaoh as a thorn to a rose. "I suppose, Potiphar, I shall be pleased according to how much interest the principal has earned."

"Bring forth the gift from Potiphar, Captain of the Guard!" Narmer called, his eyes dancing with mischievous delight. Potiphar clasped his hands behind his back and bowed as the tall double doors at the back of the throne room swung open.

You would love to see me fail in this, Potiphar thought, watching the younger man. *But you are not the only man who wears the Gold of Pharaoh's Praise.*

An audible gasp filled the throne room as Tuya stepped forward. She stood alone in the huge cavern created by the opening of the doors, and the white linen dress seemed to glow with an unearthly light. Her braided hair flowed down onto her shoulders in a soft dark tide that shone in the reflected sunlight filling Pharaoh's throne room, and above an expanse of white skin, her graceful neck curved upward like the sacred ibis taking wing. Her face was as pale as parchment, but her black eyes glowed with inner fire.

Narmer gaped like the fool he was, and even Pharaoh seemed stunned speechless by the sight of Tuya in her glory. The silence was broken by Amenhotep's second son, nine-year-old Abayomi. "Father," his treble voice rang through the chamber, "I want her!"

After a careful glance at the jealous gleam in Queen Merit-Amon's eye, Pharaoh nodded slowly. He extended his hand to Potiphar while releasing his eyes to feast upon the sight of Tuya. "I shall accept your gift in my son's name," he said, his voice tinged with regret. "You have more than doubled my gift, and today you may kiss my hand. This girl shall become the bride of Pharaoh's second son, a royal princess in the land that has given her birth."

The crowd of court observers buzzed as Potiphar bent to press his lips against the jeweled hand.

In the weeks following Tuya's departure, Sagira was careful not to push or press Paneah. The date for which she lived and breathed still lay many months in the future, and she wanted Paneah to come to her willingly, not out of fear or obedience. She watched his moods carefully, taking pains to cheer him up when he seemed lonely or to praise him when he grew quiet or depressed. Most of all, she kept him busy, knowing he would have neither the time nor the energy to mourn Tuya's loss if his mind was occupied by ambitious projects and plans.

With Potiphar's blessing, she called Paneah into the women's reception hall and described her plans to enlarge the villa and rebuild the walls. It would be a difficult project, she declared, but Paneah was the only man she knew who could bring the various aspects of planning and building together. When all was finished, Potiphar would own a grand house second only to Pharaoh's palace in elegance. And he, Paneah, would be in charge of every detail, from the crops planted in the fields to the sheets spread on the beds.

"I must have a special room," she said, spreading a papyrus roll in front of him. "See this drawing? I want my furniture gilded with the purest gold and lotus blossoms engraved around the legs and armrests of the chairs. I want a bed of gold with a canopy of gossamer hangings and lamps placed in every corner of the room."

He smiled at her words, but kept his eyes glued to the parchment.

"Do I seem to want too much?" she asked, tilting her head toward him. "I want the world, Paneah. I want everything life has to offer, and something in me thinks you want these things, too."

"I want only to fulfill my destiny," he said, turning the page of the plans. "If that means remaining a slave, then I am pleased to serve you."

"You will not remain a slave, Paneah," she said, daring to speak the truth. "I have asked Ramla to divine the future, and she sees great things for you."

Though he tried to hide it, a flicker of interest gleamed in his eye. Some of the depression which had seemed to weigh upon him lifted as he contemplated her plans. "It will take some work," he said, tapping a well-groomed finger upon the scroll. "But I have met an architect in the city who has done work on Pharaoh's tomb. If he could spare his trained slaves—"

"Do whatever is necessary, Paneah," she said, grinning out of an overflow of expectation. "Go wherever you have to go. No chains shall bind you, no purse restrain you. You are Potiphar's steward, and he has complete faith in you." She lowered her voice to a more intimate tone. "You shall soon be known as the greatest man in Thebes, the master designer of Potiphar's house. And after that, Paneah, who knows what the future will bring?"

Suddenly he laughed. It was a deep, honest laugh, good-natured and sincere, and it caught her off guard.

"Have I said something amusing?"

"No," he said, his smile melting the sudden frostiness of her heart. "It is just that—well, I have dreamed of greatness. And if this is to be how I gain it—"

"Be not afraid of greatness," she whispered, leaning toward him. She placed her hand on his and smiled inwardly when he did not pull away. "Obey its summons. Do your best, Paneah, as I know you will. And then you may reach for the stars, and Pharaoh himself will not be able to stop you."

———

Two weeks later, Tuya felt as if she were sleepwalking as the young boy stood on tiptoe to place the ceremonial crust of bread between her lips. In a moment, this child, a royal prince, would be her husband, but this reality was easier to face than the truth that she had walked away from the greatest love she had ever known.

Abayomi smashed the ceremonial jug of wine with a sword he could barely swing, and the spectators broke into perfunctory shouts of approval. No one cared, really, who the boy-prince married. Tuya knew she ought to be grateful. In this hour she had exchanged her slavery for royalty; she would be comfortable and protected for as long as her husband favored her. And if Abayomi decided next month that he no longer cared for her, she would be no worse off than she had been a month ago.

Last month, passion had burned while reason slumbered. Today, reason comforted her while she buried her passion.

The boy looked up at her with a singularly sweet smile and offered his hand. Taking a deep breath, Tuya adjusted the expression of her face and stepped out from beneath the bridal canopy with her husband, a boy eleven years her junior.

Sagira and Paneah were busy working on their plans for the villa when Potiphar passed through the main hall looking more flustered and frustrated than usual. "What is wrong, my lord?" Sagira called, glancing up from the scroll over which she and Paneah were hovering.

"The royal wedding," he said, shaking his head. "It is done, but Pharaoh was particularly concerned that nothing spoil it. He has heard rumors of a conspiracy to take his life, and his paranoia has reached the point of foolishness."

"A wedding?" Sagira murmured, making notes about the marble flooring to be installed in her bedchamber. "Did the king take another wife?"

"No. Pharaoh's second son married Tuya today."

A sudden shock rippled through her system. "Tuya? Our Tuya married a prince?"

Potiphar nodded and sank into a chair. "The same. The boy saw her and asked for her. And when the slave is beautiful and the queen is jealous, a prince may command even his father."

Silently Sagira turned to gauge Paneah's reaction. His eyes blazed for a moment, then dulled as his countenance fell.

She choked back an hysterical sob. A nine-year-old prince! Tuya may have married into the royal family, but she would be nothing but a nursemaid to her husband for years to come.

"A mere boy!" she said, smiling back at Potiphar. "Our Tuya has married a baby!"

"Do not be concerned," Potiphar said, resting his head upon his hand. "Boys do grow into men."

The days without Tuya melted into weeks, the weeks into months, the months into years. Two full years passed in Potiphar's house, and the estate which had been one of the most prosperous in Thebes now eclipsed all but the king's on a grand scale. Potiphar's nearest neighbors, afraid of appearing shabby next to his affluence, sold their lands to Paneah at bargain prices and moved far away from the burgeoning estate. Potiphar's cattle outgrew the stockyard until new pens were built; his fields outproduced others' three- and four-fold.

For every noble who feared competition with Potiphar, another sought the secret of his success. "I leave everything to Paneah," he often boasted. "I take care of Pharaoh, and Paneah takes care of me."

Extravagant offers poured in from every quarter of Egypt, but Potiphar refused to sell his slave. When it became clear that no amount of silver or gold could wrest Paneah from Potiphar's house, other stewards from noble estates came to consult with him, usually bearing gifts of silver, linen, or expensive oils and perfumes. They came expecting a miracle worker, and left with volumes of practical advice that did increase the productivity of their homes and fields. But no other estate came close to matching the success and bounty of Potiphar's enterprises.

Sagira watched in silent approval as the praise of nobles and merchants buoyed Paneah's pride. Their flattering words were like a soothing oil on his wounded heart, and within a few months the sureness was back in his step, his eye as quick and confident as it had ever been. He commanded the other slaves with authority, treated the visiting nobles with a dignified deference, and communicated more with an arrogant lift of his brow than Potiphar did in a hundred halting words.

At twenty-four, he was magnificently male, tall and lean, and immensely muscular from his labors. Though Sagira felt herself largely responsible for his confidence and success, she was a little in awe of the man he had become. And though she had planned to use him to father her son, now and then she wondered if he were using her. Like everyone who met him, she had fallen under his charming spell. In the afternoons when he dismounted from his chariot, she had to stop her eyes from feasting on his honey-colored skin lest she cry out to the world that she adored him.

She had never intended to love him, but in choosing to make herself pleasing to him, he had become unbearably precious to her. His attention was the only solid reality in her shifting, meaningless world. When he was away, her mind curled lovingly around thoughts of him. Her passion was a flower that flourished in the secret places of her heart, and she often confessed to Ramla that she had become caught in a web of her own weaving. Though her plan to seduce Paneah had been conceived in revenge and ambition, love had erased the dark, angry thoughts that first propelled her toward him.

She spent her days dreaming. Potiphar was fifty-one years old and would not live much longer. Her son, sired by Paneah, would also be fathered by him, for she would marry the love of her heart as soon as Potiphar departed this

life for the eternal one. Paneah would be rich beyond measure, the most powerful noble in Thebes, and when the royal
throne fell into her hands, Paneah would be Pharaoh, and
their son the next king. Two prophecies, his and hers,
would yet be fulfilled.

Sometimes Sagira thought her tremendous passion for
Paneah would force her to reveal the depths of her hunger
and would drive her to command Paneah into her chamber.
But the date had been foreordained by the goddess, and Sagira would not risk divine anger by disobeying. As she
waited, she fed her starving heart with fantasies and the
rich expectation of the moment that must finally come.

On the occasions when she could arrange to be alone
with Paneah, she baited him as she always had, lightly running her fingers over his muscled back. He did not acknowledge her touch, but neither did he shy away from her as he
studied evolving plans for the house and she coaxed the
tenseness from his neck. Once she planted a kiss upon his
ear, delighting in the blush that rose from his neck, and
more than once she gently needled him by saying that if he
grew any more handsome she would have to command him
into her chamber.

He always shook his head and laughed at her jests, saying, "No more tests, Sagira," and she answered with a
smile, pretending she had meant nothing even though her
arms ached to hold him. He was her god in slave's form, a
constant joy and torment, a contradiction in the flesh. In
conversation, whenever Paneah happened to say "we must
do this" or "we ought to do that," a thrill shivered through
her senses because he had mingled himself with her in the
simple word "we."

And so she counted the months and weeks of the last
year, looking forward to the day of the Nile's full fertility.
On that night she would command Paneah to come to her
bed—and mean it.

The eighteenth day of the second month arrived, the first day of the Feast of Opet. The festival began with the carrying of the god Amon from the dark shrine in his temple to visit his harem at the Temple of Southern Opet, and Sagira could hear the blast of the priests' trumpets from her bedchamber. Soon the entire city would pour into the streets of Thebes to gawk at the gilded shrine of the god as it traveled by barge down the Nile, and the house of Potiphar would empty of its slaves as well. Sagira had sent a note to Paneah the night before, asking him to remain behind but insisting that he grant liberty to all the slaves so that no one might be left out on this happy occasion. Potiphar, of course, would be a fixture by Pharaoh's side until the festival had ended.

Ramla arose from her bed and murmured incantations as she helped Sagira bathe; then she moved to scent the room with sweet incense while Sagira massaged perfumed oil into her skin from the base of her neck to the soles of her feet. A new wig waited on a wooden stand, a simple, short creation that made Sagira look as carefree and innocent as a young girl. Sagira had ordered a special white linen dress for this day, a simple garment of the uncluttered design that Paneah seemed to prefer. Wiping the excess oil from her hands, Sagira padded across the room and ran her hand over the sheer fabric. It was as soft as a kitten's ear and about as subtle as the parade of Opet. When she stood before Paneah in this revealing tunic, he would know what her full intentions were.

She slipped on the tunic and twisted to study the effect. The garment clung to her like a second skin. "Careful," Ramla cautioned from the bathroom as she emptied the wash basin. "He is not yet won."

Like a protective mother, the priestess entered the room and slipped Sagira's red cloak over the sheer tunic. The crimson color heightened the hue in Sagira's cheeks and matched the dainty leather slippers upon her feet. All was in readiness. The house was quiet beyond her chamber; no one stirred in the hall or the courtyard beyond.

"I am ready; you may leave me," Sagira finally said, eyeing herself in the new full-length bronze mirror installed in her bedchamber. "The curtains are hung on my bed, the incense burns on the brazier, and lotus blossoms cover the floor."

"All is ready," Ramla echoed, as intent as a soldier. She bowed slowly toward Sagira, then turned and disappeared as quickly as a shadow at noonday.

⟶ Twenty ⟵

ALONE AT LAST, SAGIRA PACED IN HER CHAMBER, every nerve strung in perfect tune. She had waited so long for this moment! So many nights she had lain awake imagining how it would be. Paneah, her Paneah, would certainly realize she had taken great pains to insure their privacy. For him she had designed Thebes' most beautiful bedchamber; for him alone she wore the most exquisite garment imaginable; for him she had perfumed her skin and softened her heart. She had incanted the proper petitions and given the proper offerings. Not one detail had been overlooked or neglected. They had until late in the evening when the servants would return. If they were discreet, Paneah might remain with her until nearly sunrise. . . .

She discovered she was walking on tiptoe and forced herself to take a deep breath and calm down. A strange knocking sound filled her chamber, and for a moment she froze in horror, then expelled a relieved laugh when she realized what she heard was the terrified pounding of her own heart. Far away, the wind's breath stirred the trees along the garden path; a horse whinnied and another responded; then all was quiet and still.

Now! Deftly, carefully, she lifted the bell which would summon Paneah and rang it with hope in her heart. The sound pealed through the corridor and echoed in the empty halls, and for a moment she feared he had not received her message. What if he had gone with the others to enjoy the festival?

But faint footsteps sounded on the marble in the great hall, and she turned from the doorway, suddenly afraid to face him. After a moment woven of eternity, she heard the creaking of the cedar door that led into her chamber.

"Mistress, you summoned me?"

Every nerve in her leaped and shuddered at the rich timbre of his voice. "Yes, Paneah, I did," she said, turning slowly toward him. "And it is Sagira, now, remember? We are quite alone."

He was wearing his best linen kilt, a pleated one of her own design, and the narrow waistline accented both his trim waist and his broad shoulders. Handsome leather sandals adorned his feet, and a single golden band lay upon his upper arm. His hair hung lush and lovely about his noble face, and his eyes waited her request. How godlike he was! And he had dressed in his best for this day!

"What did you have planned for today, Sagira?" he asked, pausing at the threshold of her chamber. "Do you want me to drive you to the river for the festivities?"

"I do not wish to be in a crowd today," she said, smiling at him through tilted eyes. "I want to enjoy this place that we have built—you and I." He still did not stir from the doorway, and she rolled her eyes, amused at his constant reticence. "Come here, Paneah, do not loiter like a child at the door."

"I am not quite the child you are," he said, obeying. "I am older than you by far."

"I am nineteen," she said, tipping her head back to look up at him. "Old enough to know what I want."

"I think you have always known," he answered, planting his feet firmly on the floor in front of her. "And you have yet to tell me what you want of me now. Do you have plans for another room? Another garden? Perhaps a pool to put even Pharaoh's to shame?"

"No." She formed what she hoped was a captivating pout. "I am in the mood for poetry, Paneah. Read to me from the scroll you will find on my bed."

He gave her a faintly reproachful glance, then crossed to the bed. Lifting the scroll, he began to unroll it. "Sit while you read, Paneah," she ordered, lying across the bed, her head propped on her hand. "You make me uncomfortable standing over me like that."

Sighing, he sat on the edge of her bed, his back to her. "Is there anything sweeter than this hour?" he read, the sound of music in his voice. Sagira turned onto her back and folded her arms, hoping the words came from his heart and not just his lips.

> For I am with you, and you lift up my heart—
> for is there not embracing and fondling when you
>   visit me
> and we give ourselves up to delights?
> If you wish to caress my thigh,
> then I will offer you my lips also—they won't thrust
>   you away!
> Will you leave because you are hungry?
> I can satisfy your hunger!
> Will you leave because you need something to wear?
> I have a chestful of fine linen!
> Glorious is the day of our embracings;
> I treasure it a hundred thousand millions!

"Thank you," she whispered, her voice breaking.

"What is wrong?" he asked, his voice alarmed. He turned to her, but Sagira would not allow herself to face him.

"Ah, my Paneah," she said, staring at the ceiling as if she would cry. "I do not expect you to understand."

"Have I not understood your hurts in the past?" he asked, his voice low and cautious.

"You have been the only one who understood—but now, dear Paneah, my heart breaks because I am a young woman and will never bear a son."

He turned away as if afraid to broach this very personal topic, but she rose and reached her hand toward him. He could not escape her now.

"Potiphar is old and more feeble than you think," she

went on, hurrying so that he could not question her. "I am young and yearn to suckle a baby." She was speaking the honest truth now, and the sensation gave her a feeling of reckless power. Why not be honest with him? The star of ambition burned bright in his character and the prophecy of his future; perhaps he would seize upon her dream as his.

"The royal blood of the pharaohs flows through my veins, and the child I *could* have," she said, "could someday be Pharaoh of all Egypt." She knelt at his feet and looked up at him, her hands outstretched. "If the gods decide to destroy Amenhotep's house, I will be the heiress, the embodiment of Horus, the Lady of Heaven. My husband will be Pharaoh, and our child will be the greatest king in the world."

"Potiphar would not accept the double crown, Sagira," he said, smiling in jest. "Has Ramla filled your head with these visions?"

"No," she said, grasping his hands. "The gods themselves have spoken. I will have a child, Joseph, born of the man I love."

"Potiphar will be pleased."

"Not Potiphar." His eyes were as indecipherable as water, and she yearned to look into his soul and see what thoughts stirred there. A simple smile rested upon his lips, and his hands held her firmly at arms' distance even though she leaned toward him, drawn irresistibly by the magnetic pull of his masculinity. "Not Potiphar, Paneah," she said, swaying slightly. "My son will spring from the loins of the man who has stolen my heart from its rightful owner."

He looked down at her in stunned disbelief. "Sagira," he began, trying to rise. "You do not know what you are saying."

"I know *exactly* what I am saying," she said, leaping to her feet. "Today, Paneah, you and I will share all that we should have been sharing for these many months we have known each other. Have you not seen how I adore you? I admire the curve of your mouth, the gentleness in your eye, the graceful strength of your hands."

"No, this is not right," he stammered. "I cannot—"

"Have you never had dreams of greatness, Paneah?" she pressed. "Ramla has read your future for me, and she has foretold that one day every knee of Egypt will bow to you." As if she had struck a chord, his resistance suddenly ceased.

Sagira clutched at the first appearance of victory. "Have you dared to dream as high as Pharaoh's throne?" she whispered. "The way to your destiny lies in my arms. How sweet this path is, my love! How gentle the gods are with us! Imagine it, my god in flesh, kings and queens from the world over will come and bow before your throne, Paneah! As the divine son of Osiris, even the sun and moon will bow before you!"

Inexplicably, he drew in a sharp breath, and Sagira smiled in triumph. Pride had paved the way to his heart, and ambition would propel him into her arms. He had never considered the possibilities that she might lay before him! She had already made him the most respected man in Thebes, slave or free, but she had so much more to offer!

In one deft movement, she stood and slid her fingers to the catch of the concealing robe that covered her shoulders. The heavy garment slipped to the floor like a pool of blood at Paneah's feet, and she stood before him in her sheer gown as exposed and vulnerable as a newborn baby. He gasped and closed his eyes.

"Lie with me, Paneah," she said, extending her hand in invitation. "Give me a son! The day is ours alone, and the night as well."

Desire, primitive and potent, poured through her veins, and the fires within her shot upward and outward as she pressed him toward her bed.

"No!" Joseph's shouted response was instant and complete. He lunged away from Sagira, unceremoniously thrusting her aside. Retreating, he moved back to the wall and pressed his hands to his head, struggling to regain his perspective. His senses throbbed with the scent and closeness of her, but what she was suggesting, no, *demanding*, was wrong! He was man enough to admit that his common sense skittered into the shadows every time she drew near him in that tantalizing way of hers. But she should not have worn that revealing gown before anyone except her husband, Potiphar.

For an instant he had believed her, had almost followed her into the lunatic fantasy of ambition that extended to the throne of Egypt. When she mentioned the sun and moon bowing before him, for a moment he had wondered if God had sent her as the fulfillment of his old dream.

But this devilish swirling heat inside his veins was not part of God's plan. She was another man's wife, and something dark and hidden shadowed her every move and motive. Even though she could make him forget who and what he was . . .

She had not given up. "I can fulfill your dreams," she said, rising from the floor like a determined tigress. Sagira was eying him with a look of scorching intent. "You cannot escape me, Paneah," she said, moving slowly, seductively toward him, "the house is empty. I know some silly shred of honor makes you regard your duty to Potiphar, but he has never been a husband to me. He cannot be, he was wounded in a battle long ago—"

"Stop," he said, putting out a hand to ward her off. "I will not do this thing, Sagira," he said, injecting a note of authority into his voice. "It would be a sin against God and against Potiphar. You cannot command me—I would suffer a whipping first."

"I would not mar this golden skin with a whip," she said, her voice low and promising as she reached for him again.

"Sagira—"

"Do not struggle, beloved."

"God, help me!"

Joseph frantically pulled away as Sagira laughed exultantly and seized hold of his garment. A loud ripping sound rent the air as he wrenched free and fled from her chamber.

Reaching the corridor, he turned toward his room to find a covering for himself, then realized she would go there first, seeking him. He knew she would hunt him down until she found him, for he had never seen such fierce determination in the eyes of any man or woman.

Where could he go? She was wearing too sheer a garment for the outdoors unless she donned her cloak. Then she could look for him in the garden, or even in the kitchen, but she was too fastidious to accost him in the stockyard.

Without thinking further, Joseph turned and sprinted for the cattle pens.

"Paneah!" Sagira called, holding up his kilt. "I have something belonging to you! Come out, wherever you are!"

She moved through the bedchambers and the great hall, but no sign of him could she see. He was being coy, she thought, playing a game. Men liked to be the hunters, not the hunted, and perhaps she had surprised him with her sudden declaration. But the day was yet early, and if she let him find her . . .

She walked slowly through the kitchens, idly running her hand over the bowls and pottery, hoping that he would rise up out of the shadows and claim her. She walked more briskly through the servants' quarters, wondering if he had found the courage to replace his kilt, but there was no sign of him there. He was not in the garden among the trees; he was not on the portico, nor was he hiding in her women's quarters. He had run away!

She fell onto her couch, exhausted and humiliated. With each passing hour of the water clock she waited, anxious that he appear, and several times she rang her bell to summon him.

But he did not answer.

Angry beyond words and furious at her vulnerability to a mere slave, she tore her dress and ripped handfuls of hair from her wig. She threw things, broke vases, upset the furniture in her bedchamber. In her fit of temper, she tore even his kilt in her hands, and then watered it with tears in a wave of regret.

She would have no child. No throne. No love. The prophecy, the day, her expectations, were all part of an elaborate jest Ramla had arranged to play upon her.

By the time the earliest servants returned to the villa, Sagira was sick with weeping. A young slave girl found her lying across her mussed bed, her eyes red-rimmed and swollen. "My lady!" the girl exclaimed, stepping over the broken furniture as she hurried to Sagira's side. "Who has done this to you?"

Sagira lifted her head from the mattress and weakly whispered: "Paneah."

———

"Where is she?" Potiphar snapped, tossing the reins of his chariot to the boy in the stockyard. "I came as quickly as I could."

The wide-eyed boy pointed to the house, and Potiphar took the steps of the portico in three long strides. A host of silent slaves stood outside Sagira's bedchamber, white-faced and somber, and he pushed the door open. Ramla sat in a corner of the room, as pale as the dead, and Sagira lay upon her back, her arms folded as if she had already departed this life.

"What happened here?" Potiphar said, glancing at the destruction in the room.

"Ask her," Ramla said, nodding toward the bed.

The form on the bed moved and a voice called weakly, "Potiphar?"

He strode forward and sat on the bed, lifting Sagira into his arms. "What happened, little one? Why did you remain here alone, without a guard?"

"I thought Paneah would take care of me," she murmured drowsily, like a sleepy child.

"I have given her a potion to calm her nerves," Ramla explained. "She was hysterical when I arrived."

"Where is Paneah?" Potiphar asked, brushing damp strands of dark hair from Sagira's eyes. A faint blue bruise marred her cheek, and he traced it with his finger. "How did this happen, Sagira?"

She groaned softly at his touch. "Paneah threw me down. He came into my room and—" She lifted an arm and pointed to a dress thrown over a chair. Even from where he sat, Potiphar could see that it was ripped and torn.

"Surely you are mistaken," Potiphar said, smoothing her brow. "Paneah would give his life to protect you—"

"I defended myself and saved my own life," she said. "See this—" Reaching forward with some effort, she pulled a man's kilt from under a linen sheet on the floor. "I threw a vase at him, and he ran away. But he forgot his kilt. Do you not recognize it?"

Potiphar looked at the garment in her hand. Without a doubt, it was the fine pleated kilt Sagira had recently ordered for Paneah.

"He is a Hebrew," she said, her eyes widening. "Whatever he tells you, do not believe it. The Hebrews lie, my husband. On their account Egypt has suffered before. And this Hebrew, this slave whom you bought, came in to make sport of me. And as I raised my voice and screamed, he left his garment beside me and fled outside—"

She broke into honest weeping, and Potiphar absently patted her head as his thoughts raced. "Break into groups of two," he instructed one of the guards who stood outside the door. "Search the grounds, the fields, the riverbank. No one will sleep tonight until Paneah is found."

"There is no need to search, Potiphar," a voice called

from the crowd. The assembled slaves parted as Paneah himself approached, a torn strip of linen tied around his waist.

Like an awakening giant, rage rose within him, and Potiphar stood to face his trusted steward. "Should I repeat what my wife has told me?" he asked, his face burning in the heat of his fury. Paneah did not answer but lowered his eyes to the ground. Potiphar could feel Sagira's eyes boring into his back. Outside the chamber, more than a dozen slaves waited to see how justice would be meted out to the greatest man in Potiphar's house.

"Is that your kilt?" Potiphar roared, pointing to the garment still in Sagira's hand.

"Yes," Paneah answered, meeting Potiphar's eyes without hesitation.

"Did you come in here to lie with my wife?"

For the flutter of a moment, Paneah's eyes drifted toward the woman on the bed, then he locked his gaze on Potiphar's. "No, master, I did not."

"Did you—" Potiphar pointed toward the torn dress, "—do that?"

"No, master."

"Then who did?"

Paneah pressed his lips together as if waiting for someone else to confess, then his eyes narrowed in pain.

"I suppose there is no one else who could have done this," Potiphar said. "You were the only one here, Paneah. If you will not speak in your defense, I can only assume you are guilty."

At these last words Sagira began to wail afresh, and the sound grated on Potiphar's nerves. Something had come up behind Paneah's eyes; he was defending someone or something, but Potiphar had no time for guessing games. Too many eyes were watching; too many tongues would carry the tale from this place.

"You have never lied to me," he said, an unchecked emotion suddenly clotting his throat. "You have been like a son. So instead of ordering your execution, I order you to prison. Go from this house, Paneah, and do not return again."

The proud head bowed before the sentence, and Potiphar watched the servant he had come to trust as a friend turn and walk away between two guards.

As Sagira whimpered behind him, Potiphar wondered if he would not be better served by ridding himself of his faithful wife and keeping his unfaithful servant.

JOSEPH

So Joseph's master took him and put him into the jail, the place where the king's prisoners were confined . . . in the house of the captain of the bodyguard.

Genesis 39:20; 40:3b

⟶ Twenty-one ⟵

WITH A SHOW OF FIERCE PROTECTIVENESS, RAMLA urged Potiphar to leave Sagira's chamber. The whispering crowd of servants and guards quickly dispersed, and the priestess closed the door. Turning to Sagira, she stroked her chin in a thoughtful gesture with her malformed hand. "Was he not all you thought he would be?"

The priestess's snide voice cut through the veil of gloom surrounding Sagira, and she scowled. "Have you no respect? I was attacked, injured so badly that I cannot rise from my bed—"

"Tell the truth, Sagira. Your handsome Hebrew would not have you, would he? He was a cobra, delightful in form, cool beneath your hands, but decidedly deadly in an embrace."

Sagira defiantly lifted her chin, but there was no reason to deny the truth. Ramla knew her far too well. "He had the gall to deny me," she whispered, the terrible sense of humiliation assaulting her anew. "On the appointed day, after years of preparation, he who swore undying obedience and love refused me and all that I offered him!" Tears burned her eyes as her cheeks grew hot. "He was ready, Ramla, he belonged to me, and then he cried out to his god and ran as if I had sprouted horns!"

"His god?" Ramla asked, lifting an eyebrow. "The Hebrew god who sees and knows all?"

Sagira shrugged. "What does it matter which god he called? In that moment I saw that my precious, priceless love meant nothing to him. I loved him truly, Ramla, I did! He awakened feelings within me that I never knew existed, but in one instant he spurned not only my body, but my heart and soul."

She shuddered and lowered her voice. "And my love, as limitless as the Nile, has turned into an abhorrence I shall carry to my grave. I hoped Potiphar would slay him before me so that I might steal the kisses I crave from his dying body, and yet my husband ordered him to the prison." She laughed drearily. "And so I lie here upon my bed while my much loved and hated Paneah will rot in a prison cell a moment's walk from my chamber. My nerves are on edge; I cannot sleep. I will lie here and listen for his cry in the night. I tremble to think that he might escape and try to kill me in the darkness. For I know that any feelings he ever had for me have become a hate as strong as mine. The love that might have blessed us both has become an enmity that will destroy one or the other of us."

"Or both of you," Ramla said, her eyes as hard as the stone gaze of the goddess.

Sagira sat up from her bed and crossed her arms, ready for the fight she had been eager to begin. "Enough about Paneah. I want to talk now about you, Ramla. You have lied to me, you and your divining bowl. You said this night was the ordained time for my child's conception, and there will be no child. You said I would live forever in the memories of men; you said Paneah would walk before all Egypt and every knee would bow."

Her eyes locked upon Ramla's in open warfare. "You lied, Ramla, but now I see things clearly. A foreign slave cannot become king! Paneah will die in prison. I do not know how you convinced me to believe you. You have never spoken a true word to me; your powers are a hoax used to prey upon wealthy and powerful women. I demand to know why you have manipulated my life!"

"You are pitiful," Ramla said, stalking toward Sagira with her mouth drawn into a disapproving knot. "I have spoken the truth to you, Sagira. What I read in the future *will* come to pass! And as for missing the chosen night, the fault is completely yours. You have had more opportunities than any woman in Egypt, and yet you fail the goddess at every occasion of grace."

"I did not fail!" Sagira said, violence bubbling in her blood. "I did everything in my power! Paneah failed me! *He* failed the appointed time! But regardless of your prophecy, I shall yet be remembered, I can still have a child! I will find another man, Ramla, a man of strength and glory, a man in whose frame dwells the brightness of the sun and the beauty of the lotus. I will find such a man, and I will prove that I am capable of bearing the first in a new line of pharaohs—"

"No," Ramla said, thrusting her head up in a stiff gesture. "I told you not to attempt this liaison with a slave, but you would not listen. I waited for years as you set your plan into motion. And now you have failed. The goddess does not give second chances." Her face was pale, almost bloodless as she stepped closer. "I am leaving you. I had hoped to follow you to glory and power. I will not follow you into failure and self-pity."

"You are leaving me?" The statement left Sagira shocked and breathless. "I am casting you out!"

"Good." Ramla turned to leave.

"Wait!" Sagira cried, suddenly overcome by a misty doubt. Ramla turned, one brow raised, and Sagira lowered her voice to a childlike whisper. "If you go, who will I have?"

A corner of the priestess's mouth rose in a half-smile. "You have the finest house in Egypt, a gaggle of slaves to wait on you hand and foot, and a husband who spoils you more than you deserve. Take pleasure in that—if you can."

Joseph smiled in grim irony as he approached the tall wall dividing Potiphar's house from Pharaoh's prison. He had never given the prison more than a disdainful glance, but according to Potiphar's verdict, he would spend the rest of his life amid the squalid, sun-bleached stone buildings that had been so effectively disguised by the wall Joseph had heightened and thickened. He knew he ought to be grateful for the sentence, for Potiphar could just as easily have ordered his execution, but Joseph's spine stiffened when he thought of the situation that had brought him to this place. Sagira, the woman he had believed his friend, had lifted the veil of pretense and revealed herself as an indulgent, sinful, bloodless creature with no heart and no remorse. Far worse than Sagira's defection was the knowledge that Potiphar no longer trusted him.

The guards wasted no time securing their prisoner, for night had swooped over the walls and no guard wanted to tarry in Pharaoh's prison after dark. The chief jailer assigned Joseph to one of the deep, ancient pits he had chosen to hide rather than improve. As the star-filled sky wheeled about its axis, he sat with his back against the warm stone and crossed his arms, swallowing against an unfamiliar constriction in his throat.

Joseph did not believe his turbulent thoughts would allow him to sleep, but he awoke suddenly, surprised for an instant that he was not in his room. Then memories of the previous day edged his teeth. Because he had chosen honor over ambition, he was a prisoner for life. What had God done to him now?

The hot sun bathed his prison cell in dazzling light. Stark, somber stone walls rose from four sides of the rectangular cell, and the dry air made Joseph gasp in the heat. Thin streams of blazing light poured through narrow cracks in the thatched covering above his head, and Joseph could see that the orange-tinted walls of sun-dried brick extended straight up at least twice his height. He pressed upon them, testing the strength of possible handholds, and the dry mud crumbled slightly beneath his hands.

The cell was empty but for two leather buckets, one

holding dusty water and the other obviously intended to serve as a toilet. Last night he had been given a kilt of rough hemp that scratched and tore at his skin. Joseph knew from studying the prison accounts that he would receive one daily meal, a bit of rough bread and greens, which would be lowered in a basket each morning. He would be allowed no visitors, no companions, no comrades, for he was a slave, a nonperson, the lowliest of the prisoners.

He shifted his weight and crossed his arms. He did not deserve to be in prison; he had done nothing wrong.

For the first few days he waited for news of Sagira's confession, but apparently that hardhearted girl would not recant her story. The second week he expected Potiphar to appear and announce that he had experienced a change of heart and needed Paneah to assume control of the foundering household. But Potiphar did not come. As Joseph paced in his cell, straining to hear the sounds of normal life in Potiphar's household, the days melted one into the other, periods of suffocating heat followed by cool darkness that chilled his bones and brought fever to his body.

The fever worsened until Joseph lay upon the sand in his cell and shivered like a dog even in the ovenlike heat of the day. His dreams were lost, the lights of life fading. His mind wandered in the twilight world of the half-alive and conjured up the faces of people God had taken from his life: Tuya, his father, his mother, his eleven brothers.

He had been in a pit once before. This darkness was like that one, this pain akin to the other, these prayers like the petitions he had lifted to heaven after his brothers had turned against him. What hostility drove his enemies? How could his brothers and his mistress profess to love him in one hour and devise to take his life in the next? What harm had he done? What quality in his personality drove them to such evil?

After a string of days, the fever broke, but the unanswered questions hounded Joseph's sleep and his waking hours. He had only done what he thought he ought to do.

He had overseen his brothers' affairs because he was a capable manager; he told his father about their mistakes because correction would benefit the entire family. He had managed Potiphar's affairs because he wanted Potiphar to succeed and do well; he had humored Sagira because she was his mistress and could not be completely scorned.

Why, then, had his brothers risen against him? Why had Sagira betrayed him after calling him her best and only friend?

At home he had been the favored son, the one for whom a highly colored and expensive coat had been designed. In Potiphar's house he had been the trusted steward, the de facto ruler of the mightiest house in Thebes. Now he sat in a prison pit, alone but for the occasional sag-bellied rat that fell into the darkness while searching for scraps of food.

Why, God? he asked, lifting his face to the sliver of black heaven he could see through the thatched covering ventilating the mouth of his cell. *Was I blinded by my dreams of power and authority? But You sent me those dreams; I have sought only Your will for my life. Sagira offered to fulfill those same dreams and I chose to honor You; yet You repay me by leaving me to rot in this pit. Why, God? Why don't You answer me in this darkness? This cold pit lies only a few paces from the rich chamber where I once lived as master of Potiphar's house, and yet it may as well be a world away. No one will hear my cries, God, unless You listen. Sagira will not come, nor Potiphar, nor Tuya, nor my father, nor my brothers. All I have is You, and yet You are silent. . . .*

His thoughts rambled in an incoherent jumble over and over the same stale ground. Two years before, he recalled, Tuya had seen Sagira's intentions and warned Joseph, but he had not listened. Many years before that, his father Jacob had admonished him against boasting that the sun and moon and stars would one day bow before him. Again, he had not listened. Pride had blinded him to his brothers' intentions, just as it had led him to deny Sagira's lust-laced infatuation.

You knew how she felt, an inner voice chided him. *Tuya warned you; Sagira herself demonstrated her feelings again and again. But you found secret satisfaction in her attentions. You avoided her presence, yet took pleasure each time she demanded that you appear by her side. You pulled away from her touch, yet you hurried to her chambers each time she called for you to work on another of her projects. She made you the greatest steward in Thebes, and you allowed her to do it. You were proud of being her pet.*

Pride. The seismic fault of his life. The very word stung like the bite of a scorpion. He had craved the rich possessions of Egypt, furnishing Potiphar's house with every treasure that struck his fancy. He had looked upon Sagira and wondered "what if?"; he had listened to and *believed* the vain flattery of the visiting nobles.

Joseph huddled over the ashes of his dreams and bowed his head to his knees in despair. He had been proud to wear the many-colored coat like a royal ensign before his brothers, flaunting his position as the most-beloved son among twelve. He had been proud of Potiphar's trust in him, placing his regard for his position even before Tuya's unselfish love. He had even been proud of Sagira's inappropriate interest in him and confident of his ability to keep the tigress at bay. Pride had enticed him into her den; only prayer had gotten him out.

And haughty eyes and a proud heart were loathsome to the Almighty God.

The endless monotony of confinement forced him to look at himself, and for the first time he saw Potiphar's Paneah through eyes blessed with humility. God had gifted him with Rachel's beauty, Jacob's keen intellect, his brothers' strength, and the Hebrews' divine covenant of blessing. But Joseph had accepted these qualities as his own, not recognizing that the gifts of God had been channeled to him through others.

"Would that I had been born ugly, dull, and weak," he murmured, coughing slightly as a cloud of dry dust entered his mouth. "Then I would not have cause to lift up my heart against God."

Still bent into a position of submission, he extended his hands and curled the palms upward toward heaven in mute supplication. "Speak to me, God, as you have spoken before," he whispered, his face resting upon the ground. "Speak to me though I have not spoken to you in many months. Do not forget me as I have forgotten you."

An hour passed. Joseph's eyes grew sandy and his bones ached. Grief throbbed dully in his soul. God had not spoken. Perhaps God would not forgive. Certainly the dreams would never be fulfilled, for he would remain in this pit forever, a victim of his own pride and foolishness.

He wanted to die, to lie under the desiccating orb the Egyptians called Re until nothing remained but a hollow shell of the promise he used to be.

Woe unto those who go down to Egypt.

He had not heard the voice in years, but he recognized it instantly. His eyes flew open; the hairs lifted on his arms.

Woe unto those who go down to Egypt and do not look to the Holy One of Israel. When pride comes, then comes dishonor, but with the humble is wisdom. Return to Him from whom you have deeply defected, O son of Israel, and like a hovering bird the Lord of hosts will protect you. He will protect and deliver you; He will pass over and rescue you.

El Shaddai had not forsaken him. Joseph covered his face with his hands. Tears of relief came in a rush so strong it shook his entire body.

"Potiphar!"

Khamat, warden of Potiphar's prison, waved from the prison gate, and the captain of the guard unwillingly slowed his step. Since Paneah's imprisonment he had avoided the jail, not wanting to consider again the question of his steward's disloyalty. The memory of Paneah's haunted face still troubled his sleep.

"What is it?" he said, turning around to face Khamat. "I have business in the house." Indeed he did, for problems had erupted like troublesome weeds ever since Paneah's departure.

"Surely you would like to visit the prison, Captain. It has been nearly a month since your last inspection and I wondered—"

"I trust you, Khamat. Things cannot have changed so much."

He turned to leave, but the warden's next words made him halt in mid-step. "If the steward troubles you, you do not have to look at him. He remains in his cell, far away from the others."

Thrusting his hands behind his back, Potiphar set his jaw and bit down an urge to slap the man for making such a presumptuous remark. But it was true, and everyone knew it. The entire household still buzzed with gossip about Paneah's arrest, and the once-unified team of slaves had divided into warring factions. Most of the men thought Paneah guilty, for they understood the urges of a virile youth and had often seen and remarked upon the close friendship between the steward and his mistress. Potiphar had seen it, too. He had encouraged the relationship because he knew Sagira was often lonely, but he believed his wife regarded Paneah with a sisterly sort of feeling akin to the paternal affection he felt toward the young man.

The female slaves, including Sagira's own handmaids, took Paneah's part in the debate. He was too beautiful, they insisted, to take by force what any woman on the estate, including the mistress, would have willingly given him. Sagira, the rumors said, had yearned for the handsome steward like a child for a forbidden and dangerous toy, loving him with a queer mixture of contempt and desire.

But rumors could not change Paneah's fate. A noblewoman's word was sufficient to convict a slave of anything. Even if Potiphar had found just cause to doubt his wife, the tear-stained kilt in her hand had sealed the slave's sentence.

What was he thinking? Potiphar wondered, clenching his teeth as he considered Paneah's blunder for the thousandth time. *Sagira is charming; she is lovely in her way; she has a way of making a man feel important—*

But Paneah should have known better than to fall into her trap. And now Potiphar must publicly support his wife, for to do otherwise would be tantamount to publicly admitting that he had driven her to seek pleasure in the arms of a slave.

Khamat diplomatically cleared his throat, bringing Potiphar back to reality. "The steward does not disturb me," he said, tossing the words over his shoulder. "He is no longer my property, but the king's prisoner. If anyone must worry about him, let it be Amenhotep."

⌒ Twenty-two ⌒

"TAKE YOUR TURN, MY WIFE."

Eleven-year-old Prince Abayomi shifted impatiently on his chair, and Tuya forced her attention back to the game board. Her small hound figurines stood in imminent danger of being devoured by her husband's ivory jackals, so she rolled the painted wands upon the wooden board. "Three squares, my husband," she said, choosing to move one hound out of the pack and around the circular path. "In a moment my hound will be chasing *yours*."

The royal mouth frowned, but the boy picked up the wands and rattled them enthusiastically. The young prince had inherited his father's long and straight limbs, but his mother's pale beauty had softened the dark eyes that glared so proudly from Pharaoh's visage. Abayomi's quick smile was set in the midst of a durably boyish face that either twinkled with mischievousness or glowed in the mystic contemplation of a daydreamer. Like his elder brother's, Abayomi's head had been shaved but for the princely lock of long dark hair that grew from his right temple.

That lock now quivered like a snake as he rattled the wands. "By the powers of Osiris and Amon-Re, I command double sixes!" he cried, throwing the wooden sticks.

One of the carved wands skittered across the board and landed in Tuya's lap. Amused, she tossed it back. "A five," she said. "You may catch one or two of my hounds, but I shall escape you yet."

Abayomi frowned and fingered his game pieces, trying to decide how best to move his jackals, while Tuya smiled at him with tolerant affection. The all-consuming grief that had covered her like a mantle in the first year of her marriage had eased somewhat. Though a weight of sadness lay upon her thin face, few things these days touched the secret pool of sorrow within her.

For two years the boy-prince had been her husband. Soon after their marriage Tuya realized Abayomi had asked to marry her because he considered her a pretty possession, a beautiful companion to sit by his side, listen to his dreams, and play his board games. He was yet too simple and immature to realize that dashed dreams and disillusionment had left her heart a mere shell of what it should have been. But he was kind and good-natured. He must have sensed her sorrow, for he took great pains to make her smile. At first his frantic efforts to please left her bewildered; in time the mere sight of him gaping up at her was enough to make her laugh. He fancied himself a good husband, often bringing her gifts: a golden necklace, a kitten, a bowl of candied dates.

As the wife of a royal son, Tuya had her own apartment in the palace, a bevy of handmaids to do her bidding, the use of a chariot whenever she wished, and a wardrobe box filled with the most lovely garments she could have ever imagined. Her husband, the prince, filled his days with training and warrior games, then usually called for her in the early evening. She dined with him in his chamber, nodding at his stories, laughing at his jokes, and smiling at his compliments. Often they played a board game, or Abayomi would entertain her with a demonstration of his skills in sword fighting or archery. And every once in a great while, when especially tired or weary, he would invite her to remain with him through the night.

He was yet a child, and these invitations to join him in the royal bed were, in effect, cries for companionship. Tuya often thought there was never a life as lonely as the one to which a royal prince was born; for though he was surrounded by tutors, warriors, servants, and counselors, Abayomi had no true friends or confidants. His secrets were too exalted to be shared with common, less divine folk, and his dreams too sacred to be entrusted to anyone but a wife.

And so, in a vague imitation of his father and his elder brother, Abayomi wrapped his arms about his wife's neck, then emptied his soul of its burdens, secrets, and joys. And Tuya, her heart stirred with compassion and maternal tenderness, brushed away the young prince's tears and resolved that though she might never be truly happy, she would always be grateful. The strong arm of Montu had not been able to bring her to Joseph, but it had kept her from Pharaoh's harem.

"Aha!" Abayomi exclaimed, jolting her from her thoughts. "My jackals have killed all but one of your hounds, Tuya!"

"Yes, my lord," she replied, quickly scanning the game board. "As always, you have won the game. My single hound cannot escape a pack of jackals."

"Shall we play again?" Already he was resetting the game pieces into their positions.

"I am tired, my husband."

"Please, Tuya? If you will play, I will tell you news of the court."

She shook her head. "I have no interest in people who do not concern me."

"But this is news you will want to hear. It concerns Potiphar—the man who brought you to my father."

"I see the captain of the guard every day in your father's audience chamber. He cares nothing for me, nor I for him."

"But this news—" Abayomi leaned forward and glanced left and right as if telling a very great secret, "concerns the man's wife. Lady Sagira has accused Potiphar's steward, the chief slave in the house, of attacking her."

"She lies!" The words fell from Tuya's mouth without conscious thought.

Abayomi shook his head. "There was evidence. The slave's garment was in her hand, I hear. And yet the man was foolish enough to come forward and contradict her!"

In a rush of bitter remembrance, Tuya saw Joseph smiling. *I can handle Sagira even as I have handled Potiphar all these years. . . .* He had not been able to handle either of them.

"Is it possible," she whispered, barely finding her voice, "that the steward spoke the truth?"

Abayomi leaned back in his chair, smirking. "They say he came forward with only a scrap of a feed bag to cover himself," he said. "Obviously, his guilt drove him to run from his crime, but he had no clothing and could not go into the streets, for they were crowded with people during the festival of Opet. Potiphar heard the evidence and sentenced the slave on the spot."

Tuya felt a rock fall through her heart as she listened, and her hand involuntarily rose to her throat. Ramla's prediction had come true, after all. Sagira had seduced her handsome slave. Perhaps even now her womb stirred with Joseph's child. And after accomplishing her victory, she had thrown Joseph out of the house and accused him of an act for which the penalty was death.

Tuya's hands, her feet, even her lips felt as cold as the tomb. "The slave is—dead?" she whispered.

"No," Abayomi answered, propping his gangly brown legs upon a footstool. "Potiphar sentenced him to prison. Apparently he had great affection for this steward and did not wish to see him die."

"The prison," Tuya murmured. A mingling of relief and dread rushed over her. Joseph's unseen God had spared his life, for any other husband would have killed an accused slave on the spot. But prison! She lowered her eyes, tasting her recollection of Potiphar's jail with a shudder. The place had lain behind the wall of the house, a desolate strip of red stone buildings and reed-covered pits from which she often heard the agonized screams of Pharaoh's prisoners. . . .

"My husband," she said, feeling suddenly limp with weariness, "the night waxes old and I am tired." *I want to weep. I want to close my eyes and cry for the noble Joseph I once knew, the man who would not betray his god or his father, the one who loved purely and honestly . . . that man is gone forever, and a cheapened Paneah resides in his flesh. I will mourn for Joseph. I will water my bed with tears for what might have been. Please, Montu, please let my husband dismiss me. . . .*

"One more game, Tuya, please," Abayomi said, leaning forward. "One more, and then we shall sleep."

Obediently, Tuya nodded and picked up the painted wands.

Potiphar's garden was dense with trees and leaves and blue shadows, and Tuya moved through it as if she had wings. Floods of cornflowers lined the tiled walkway, a blurred and heady bushing of color from potted and earth-sown plants. She felt happy and relaxed and invincible, for she had escaped the walls of the palace if only for this hour when she could meet alone with Joseph. A huge gnarled root at the bottom of one of the trees showed its dark power as it pushed up the earth, and she laughed at it, the poor earthbound thing.

Lowering herself to the ground under the tree, she gazed up through the sun-shot leaves, waiting for Joseph. The turquoise sky was filled with gold radiance, but nothing could match the beauty of the man she loved, the strength of his character.

"Tuya."

Suddenly he stood before her, awash in the sun's golden light, his dark eyes snapping with confident joy. With sure, bold steps he crossed the garden and knelt at her side, his hand lifting her chin, his arm encircling her. Tremors of rapture caught in her throat as he whispered her name, and she closed her eyes and gasped in a weak attempt to still the wild pounding of her heart. She trembled in his arms, fire racing through every nerve in her body, and then his lips touched the moist hollow of her throat.

"Joseph," she whispered, reaching out for him, but her hand closed upon empty air.

Stunned, she opened her eyes. She was alone in a leafless, dreary garden where a hot, whining wind hooted her name. Somewhere far away, a woman laughed in derision.

She woke herself with weeping and shuddered in the darkness, terrified by the reality and persistence of her dreams of Potiphar's garden.

———

Khamat let the rope slide slowly through his fingers and into the pit. He had placed an extra slice of brown bread and a dainty shat cake from Potiphar's kitchen into the steward's bucket. The prisoner had not eaten in seven days, and death would soon claim him if his appetite could not be tempted and awakened.

"If it please you, my lord, hear me." The slave's voice was surprisingly strong. Khamat leaned forward to peer into the pit, wondering for an instant if he had approached the wrong cell.

The Hebrew slave was emaciated, but alive. He sat on the ground with his legs crossed and his arms resting upon his knees. Through the glistening skin Khamat could count the man's ribs. "Speak."

The bearded face lifted, and dark, gleaming eyes flitted over Khamat's face. "If it please you—" The slave paused as if gathering his strength. "Would you ask the captain of Pharaoh's bodyguard to grant me an audience? I would like to speak to my master Potiphar."

"Potiphar says you are no longer his concern," Khamat answered, steadily eyeing his prisoner. The slave's mouth was slack with submission, but his eyes glittered with resolve. Khamat had heard that this Paneah possessed a keen intelligence; cunning and desperation were a dangerous brew. If this humble pose was not sincere, those eyes might flash with murder and rebellion when the warden's back was turned. . . .

"If he will not see me, perhaps you will relay my message," the slave called. "I would speak to Potiphar not as his favored steward, but as the king's prisoner, and one worthy of death. I will not ask for pardon. Even though I am innocent of the charge for which I am kept here, I am nevertheless guilty of a grave error—very grave."

His voice, without rising at all, took on a subtle urgency, and Khamat leaned forward in order to hear better. "I would ask Potiphar not for release or pardon, but for a duty. I served in his house and would like permission to work in his prison. Let me wait on these who have sinned against Pharaoh so I may learn the humility I have sorely lacked."

Khamat felt surprise blossom on his face. Serve the prisoners? No man with even a smattering of intelligence wanted to serve prisoners! The men in this place were the scum of the earth, beneath idiots, beneath slaves, even beneath prisoners of war. No, this request could not be sincere; the man had to have a hidden motive. Perhaps the cramped closeness of the pit had touched a claustrophobic nerve. Perhaps he looked for an opportunity to escape, or even to slip into the house to fulfill his beastly intentions for Lady Sagira.

"If you were to do what you propose," Khamat hedged, testing the waters, "you would not be transferred from this pit. After your work, when you had cleaned the cells of the others, you would find yourself back here again."

"It matters not where you confine me," the prisoner called, crossing his arms. "Do with me as you will."

"I would watch you like a hawk watches the rabbit, with a whip and sword in my hand. The gates and doors would be locked; there will be no opportunity for escape."

Paneah lifted a dark eyebrow. "Was it not I who ordered that the wall be made higher?" Looking away, he smiled as if he had been suddenly reminded of something, then lowered his head. "Use your whip, warden, even your sword, if you see a single sign of pride or rebellion cross my face."

Khamat paused. He had never thought to employ one of the prisoners as a servant, but the idea was delightful. Potiphar usually assigned the prison's cleaning detail to members of his guard whose misdeeds warranted disciplinary action. When there were no rebels, Khamat found himself emptying slop buckets, bandaging festering wounds, and carrying the dead from the cells in which they breathed their last. Why not use a slave to do a slave's work? The idea was certainly logical, and as long as the man could be trusted . . .

"I will speak to the captain," Khamat promised, withdrawing.

———

Two days later, pressed by his warden, Potiphar stood at the lip of Joseph's cell and barked out a greeting. Dazed by the familiar sound, Joseph scrambled to his feet. "Master!"

"I am your master no more," Potiphar said, his face lined with a scowl that did not quite reach his eyes. "Speak, slave, for my patience is limited."

"Thank you for coming," Joseph called up, wiping his hands upon his kilt. Now that his master stood before him, the eloquent words he had prepared slipped from his mind like water through his fingers.

"This is not a social meeting," Potiphar called down. Behind him, Khamat peered nervously over the captain's shoulder, and Joseph knew the warden must have had difficulty convincing Potiphar to agree to come.

"Master Potiphar," Joseph called up, finding his tongue at last. "I wanted permission to serve your warden in this prison."

"Indeed," Potiphar drawled, his dark eyes raking Joseph's face as if he would read his heart. "My warden says that you have admitted your guilt in this crime."

"Guilt, no," Joseph answered, slowly feeling his way.

The urge to reveal Sagira's role in the situation gnawed at his heart, but Joseph knew that temptation sprang from pride. His task was to align his own soul with God's purposes, no one else's.

"I admit," he said, fixing his eyes on Potiphar's, "that I was encouraged by the voice of ambition to lift my head above my station. I listened to those who praised my efforts in your household and took those voices too seriously. I was nothing but a slave, a reflection of God's wisdom, the instrument of His will. A slave has no right to claim honor and praise for himself as I did. My God has pronounced His judgment upon me, and He has brought me to admit the error of my ways. My faults are mine alone. My successes have sprung from the hand of God."

"Your pious babbling means nothing to me, Paneah. You know I judge men only by common sense and loyalty. If you will not admit your guilt, why have you called for me?"

"Idleness chafes at my soul, master. Let me restore my soul to humility by serving the warden of this prison. In this way I can serve you still."

He had hoped that his words would speak to Potiphar's heart, but the master's granite face was as expressionless as it had been on the night of Joseph's disgrace. "Do what you will with him," he said finally, jerking his gaze toward Khamat. "I care not what he does."

And so Paneah, chief steward and virtual master of the mightiest house in Thebes, became the only slave of Khamat, chief jailer of the king's prison. Each morning Khamat lowered a rope into the Hebrew's cell, and Paneah climbed forth to do his bidding. The unruly warriors from Potiphar's guard were excused from emptying buckets of human refuse from the prison cells, for Paneah cleaned them. He also carried fresh water and food from the prison gate to each individual cell. There were two distinct types of cells in

Pharaoh's prison: prison pits for the lowest criminals, and stone buildings where noblemen's servants and ordinary citizens were housed. Paneah served the inmates of both, and when his prison duties were done, he worked in Khamat's stone lodge, scrubbing floors, grinding corn, or cleaning the stall that housed the jailer's donkey. On slow afternoons when the sky glared hot and blue, Khamat ordered the slave to stand behind him and fan away pesky flies as the jailer napped in the sun. When the sun-god's Boat-of-Millions-of-Years finally finished its journey across the sky, Khamat escorted the prisoner back to his cell and pulled up the rope lest he escape.

The other prisoners, accustomed to giving Khamat a measure of surly respect, took immediate pleasure in belittling the new personality that entered their small world. This bearded and bedraggled scarecrow, obviously a slave and apparently deserving of his mean fate, accepted the bitterness they spewed upon him without comment. When he knelt to slide baskets of food beneath the iron bars, the prisoners in the walled cells spat upon him and cursed him for the food's poor quality and limited supply. Even the criminals in the pits scorned him, routinely calling him vulgar names and deriding his manhood because he meekly served them.

"Surely you are the son of a scared rabbit!" one man called as Paneah pulled up his bucket. "Why else would you haul filth for the men who hold you captive? What sort of woman gave birth to you?"

"One who wears bells on her skirt and sells her favors to the highest bidder," the man in the next pit called. He made an obscene gesture in Paneah's direction. "I enjoyed her company myself the week before I was brought to this place."

No matter how crude or lewd the comments, Khamat noticed that Paneah did not respond in word or deed. He moved through a hailstorm of indignities and insults as though his mind were attuned to another world, one in which men did not fall prey to the vilest inclinations of their natures. And while he worked, the slave neither glanced toward nor made reference to the barred door leading to Potiphar's house—and to freedom.

Paneah never offered his opinions unless asked, but once Khamat began to ask for them, he discovered that the slave possessed the organizational genius of a military officer and the nimble wit of a royal courtier. A source of incredible energy lay behind the skills which were now wasted on menial labor, but Paneah did not once hint that his personal situation should be reevaluated or improved. Khamat could find no trace of ambition or ulterior motive in the slave's conversation; nor did the man's words ever contain less than total truth.

In time, Khamat neglected to carry his sword while Paneah worked, and soon he also put aside his whip. The slave's silent endurance won the respect of the other prisoners; the ribald taunting ceased. Within a year, Khamat stopped supervising Paneah altogether, and within two years, he had made it a common practice to leave the long rope dangling in Paneah's cell. "Why should I get up early every morning just to drop a rope to you?" he asked his servant. "You would tell me if you were planning to escape, would you not?"

Paneah looked up from the sandy floor of his cell and regarded the chief jailer with a wistful smile. "God has a purpose for me here," he said, rubbing his hand over the crumbling stone walls as if he truly felt some affection for the place. "And I will not leave until He opens the door for me."

———

After his interview with Paneah in the pit, Potiphar did not venture into the prison again. The slave's words rankled in his brain for months as if urging him to *do something*, but Potiphar had no idea what he should do. Paneah had talked of his God, but Potiphar had no use for gods, visible or invisible.

Paneah and peace had departed from Potiphar's home on the same night. The house which had once brought him joy was now a shell of loneliness. Sagira, her charm and cultivated good looks destroyed by an overindulgence in wine, flirted brazenly with every man who crossed the threshold. More than once Potiphar had seen sheepish-looking suitors, both slaves and noblemen, departing from her bedchamber in the dark of night, but he turned a stony face from the sight and silently wished that Pharaoh had ordered him to lose an arm rather than receive a bride. Ramla, the iron-willed priestess whom Potiphar had endured for Sagira's sake, had not returned to the villa since Paneah's departure. Sagira now whined incessantly, sending handmaid after handmaid back to the slave market, unable to find a single girl capable of serving as her companion.

Potiphar possessed all he had ever wanted: a fine house, treasure in his coffers, a sterling reputation as a warrior and friend of Pharaoh. The Gold of Praise hung about his neck, prompting all who met him to kneel in reverent respect for one who had been admired and honored by the king.

But his house, which had once been a haven of rest, hummed with tension and distrust. After Paneah's departure, Sagira flatly refused to have anything to do with running the household. Potiphar extracted stern but capable taskmasters from his army and set them over his household. Even so, the house limped along, barely making a profit, the backs of its slaves bruised and broken by the whip.

No longer was singing heard in his house. The only laughter was drunken and coarse and usually spilled from Sagira's bedchamber in the heaviness of the evening.

In his weariness, Potiphar retreated to the palace, preferring to spend his time with the king. But Pharaoh had tired of military conquests and spent his days overseeing the craftsmen who were building his tomb in the Valley of the Kings. Thoughts of eternity pressed upon the royal mind, and Amenhotep's concern did not lie with his armies, but with the stone cutters and artisans who were fashioning the tools and treasures he would take with him into the next world.

And yet Pharaoh was but forty-two, while the captain of his guard was fifty-three. Potiphar thought he was much nearer to eternity than the king, but he was not at all eager to prepare for it. How could the future hold anything for the individual who had no faith in it?

~~~> Twenty-three <~~~

TWO YEARS LATER, IN THE GRAND CENTRAL HALL OF Pharaoh's palace at Thebes, the entire royal family gathered to celebrate the gifts bestowed by a group of visiting foreigners. Tuya sat on a chair beside Abayomi, her hand resting protectively upon the gentle swell of her belly. The priestess of Montu had declared that she would bear a son, and Tuya was frantic that the proper offerings be made every day to insure the child's safety. She had lost one love because she neglected to strengthen the gods with the proper sacrifices. She would not lose another.

Abayomi, caught up in the music, clapped in rhythm and occasionally glanced in her direction. She smiled in maternal approval, and he turned again to the musicians, his confidence bolstered. At thirteen, her husband was still much a boy. He had matured enough in the passing years to earn her respect and to father a son, though one had little to do with the other. She had come to respect him because the prince was a student of life. Anxious to understand the world around him, his insights into natural, divine, and human law were curiously creative. Not a good communicator, he often had difficulty explaining his ideas to others, but Tuya, who had been mother, sister, and wife for four years, gave voice to his insights and feelings.

His elder brother, the crown prince Webensennu, and his father, the king, did not understand Abayomi, for their thoughts were predicated upon military ideas of right and might; but Tuya was quietly glad that Abayomi would rather ponder the way of an ibis in the air than plunder an Asiatic village. Instead of collecting swords and shields, her husband filled his chamber with scrolls, art, and animals, both living and mummified. His name meant "he brings joy," and after the grief of her former life, Tuya had to admit that her husband-child had brought a fair measure of sunlight into her dark heart. She still dreamed of Joseph and Potiphar's garden, but not as often as she once had.

Pharaoh and Queen Merit-Amon sat across from a dark-robed quartet of Syrian dignitaries, and Tuya found herself studying the strangers' faces intently. They wore short, pointed beards, heavy robes, and no jewelry. For a moment she thought she gazed into a magical transforming mirror, for they were complete opposites of the clean-shaven, bejeweled, lightly clothed Egyptians. Awed by the ostentation of Pharaoh's palace, the visitors spoke little and looked much, their dark eyes darting quickly up, down, right, and left. Of course, they were impressed. Tuya had heard enough to know that no palace in the world could rival the beauty and opulence of Pharaoh's court. The center of the world was Thebes, and the center of Thebes was this room. From it Pharaoh's divine glory shone like radiant sunlight.

The Crown Prince sat at Pharaoh's right hand with two of his wives. Three years older than Abayomi, the Prince behaved as though he were Pharaoh already, nodding with grave dignity at a pair of wrestlers who competed for his attention, while acrobatic dancers whirled before the royal chairs in sheer veils. Though he still wore the prince's single lock of hair upon his right temple, Webensennu gripped an ivory-handled flywhisk as though it were the flail or the crook, the symbols of Pharaoh's office.

The Master of the Banquet clapped his hands; the dancers stopped, and the wrestlers prostrated themselves before Pharaoh. Without warning, a bevy of slaves spun into the room, each bearing a bowl of roasted meat or honey-glazed fruits. The delicious aromas of goose, duck, teal, and pigeon rose from the steaming bowls, and Tuya thanked the gods that the nausea of early pregnancy had passed. She had the appetite of a field slave at harvest time, and she intended to enjoy this meal to the fullest.

As Pharaoh's family, his noble guests, and the visiting Syrians plucked food from the bowls, a group of women musicians rose and danced to their own playing of the harp, lute, and flute. A white-robed priestess of Amon-Re strummed the sacred sistrum, and Tuya leaned forward to inquire if her husband found the meal pleasing.

The words never left her lips. A sudden shriek interrupted the music, and the women scattered as one of the king's food tasters knocked a bowl to the floor and staggered forward clutching his throat. As the crowd gasped in horror, the terrified slave tottered toward his god and king, Pharaoh, and then collapsed as blood ran from his nose and mouth.

In an instant, Abayomi's arm was about Tuya's waist. "To your chamber," he said, the pressure of his arm pulling her from her chair even as his eyes swept the room. "Wait there. You will be safe, I swear it."

An hour later, alone in her chamber, Tuya knelt before the stone statue of Montu and numbly gazed at it. What power would such a statue have against one who wanted to poison her husband or her soon-coming son? Montu's strong arm had done nothing to aid Joseph, and only blind luck had saved Pharaoh's life tonight. If the poison that struck the innocent slave had worked more slowly, Pharaoh would be well on his way to the underworld, and yet thousands of priests throughout Egypt offered daily sacrifices to protect their king, the Divine One.

Which of the gods of Egypt could help her? She despised Bastet, Sagira's goddess, and Montu had failed her in the past. Amon-Re was Pharaoh's divine father, and though she would not admit it aloud, she felt nothing but contempt for a god who would allow death to come so close to the anointed king.

Joseph had spoken of, and prayed to El Shaddai, the invisible god in whom the world lived and moved and breathed, and yet Joseph now passed his days in Pharaoh's prison. But in the year following his arrest, there had been no announcement of a child born to Potiphar's wife, so perhaps Joseph had managed to escape the trap Sagira had laid for him. Perhaps, Tuya mused in her reflective heart, prison had proved to be a place of refuge for Joseph, a way out of Sagira's reach. Tuya did not know whether this god could be trusted, but she had believed in His existence from the first time she heard Joseph speak of the Almighty One. He was real, for Joseph would not lie, and El Shaddai had manifested His power by saving Joseph's life. Because this god was so different from the gods of Egypt, omnipresent and yet invisible, perhaps He worked in different and unexpected ways.

Shyly, she turned from the statue of Montu and stared instead at the painted images of Pharaoh on the chamber walls. Distracted, she closed her eyes. "If You are there, Almighty One," she whispered, "hear the words of Tuya, a friend of Your servant Joseph. Protect my unborn child, and protect Your servant Joseph. If You do not do these things . . ."

She paused. Many Egyptians threatened the gods with the desecration of their temples or the withholding of offerings if petitions were not answered, but Tuya felt that threats might offend an all-powerful god. And how did one punish a god who had no temple and no priests?

"Please do these things," she whispered. "Please hear me, Almighty One. Today I have prayed only to You."

Potiphar strode into Pharaoh's chamber in the quiet of the afternoon, a time when the king usually rested or enjoyed entertainment by his dancing girls. Today, though, Amenhotep sat in his chair, pensive and quiet.

Potiphar cleared his throat, hoping the sound would spare him the agony of bending his arthritic knees to the floor. Fortunately, Pharaoh heard and gestured in Potiphar's direction.

The captain of the guard moved confidently into the royal presence. "O Pharaoh, live forever! I have important news, my king. We have investigated thoroughly and have determined that the shame of yesterday's attempt upon your life was made with the help of either the palace butler or the chief baker. The surgeons were unable to tell if the poison was ingested as a liquid or in the food, so we have arrested both men. They await your divine judgment."

"I will give it—later," Pharaoh said, inclining his head upon his palm. His thoughts seemed far away, and Potiphar shifted uncomfortably upon his feet. "Have you thought much about my reign, my captain?" the king asked suddenly, his eyes shifting to Potiphar's face. "You knew my father well—how would you compare my leadership to his?"

Potiphar hesitated, wavering between truth and diplomacy. "You are much the same, and yet different," he said, tightening his hand around the hilt of the sword in his belt. "Your father was a warrior, and you have the same fierce heart. Your father, Tuthmosis, fought until he died. But you, my king, have lately thought much of other things."

"The otherworld," Pharaoh murmured, taking his thoughts off again. "Do you know, Potiphar, that I can boast with the greatest of Pharaohs that no man has gone hungry during my reign? The Nile has brought forth her abundance every year; therefore I know the gods are pleased with me. No priest has dared think of bringing death to my door."

Aghast that the king would speak of the age-old rite by which a Pharaoh gave his life for his country, Potiphar's breathing slowed. In past dynasties, whenever the Nile did not flood sufficiently, famine smote the land so harshly the people cried out in grief. According to Egyptian religious belief, because Pharaoh was the giver of fertility and the preserver of all, he was also the Divine Victim who might be put to death to ensure the fertility of the land. In the an-

cient pyramid texts, the sages wrote that if the people had
not "eaten the eye of Horus" or bread, both the people and
the gods would demand the king's death so that the fields
might be watered and fertilized with his blood. Since the
kings were gods and immortal, this sacrificial death was
never declined, or at least Potiphar had never heard of any
king who refused his role in the ritual.

In a time of famine, when the priests decided that the
land had suffered enough, the high priest of Anubis would
present himself to Pharaoh wearing the jackal mask of his
god. In his arms he would carry the means of Pharaoh's
death: a basket containing a cobra. Knowing that the time
had come, the king would raise the lid from the basket and
lift the cobra to his breast.

Death by cobra poison came swiftly and easily. After the
king's death, his internal organs were removed during the
mummification process, and his heart and lungs ceremo-
nially buried in the soil to give breath and life to the earth.
A new king, his heir, would rise and confirm his right to
succession by installing his predecessor in the tomb, thus
insuring the dead king's place in the otherworld.

The kings of Egypt's eighteenth dynasty had died in various ways, but Potiphar could not name one who had sacrificed himself for the land. Did Amenhotep's new apprehension spring from a fear of famine? Did he suppose the
jackal-headed priest of Anubis to be lurking outside in a
corridor?

"Do you fear a famine, my king?" Potiphar asked, his
voice a subtle whisper in the room.

The king's head jerked toward Potiphar in surprise.
"Fear? Not I, Potiphar, surely you know better. I fear nothing in this world or the next, and yet sometimes . . . I wonder. As god I am the giver of all to my people. I worship
myself as god in living form, for I am the physical son of
Re." Amenhotep pulled back his shoulders and lifted his
granite jaw. At that moment, his dark, worried face seemed
never to have known a smile. "And yet I am as mortal as

other men. If I eat poison, I will die. I do not feel like a god, and I am sobered by the frightening possibility that I may not be a god." He threw Potiphar a look of half-startled wariness. "An entire life is a great treasure to risk upon a lie, don't you think?"

For some shapeless reason Potiphar thought of Paneah. "My king, I cannot say. I am not a priest," he answered, suddenly eager to leave the conversation. "And if you will excuse me, sire, the royal baker and cupbearer await me. We will take great pains to stall your journey to the next world for as long as possible."

The hot wind of the sirocco blew sand into Abayomi's eyes, and Pharaoh's second son signaled for the company to halt. His servants sighed in relief. "We will pause from our hunt, for the air is hot and the sun nearly overhead," the young prince called out, deepening his awkward voice to command the authority due a royal son. He stepped from his chariot and felt the heat of the desert sand through his sandals. "Lead the horses to shelter behind the Great Sphinx of Harmakhis and prepare a resting place."

His servants scurried away to do his bidding, removing the royal chariot to safe shelter from the desert winds. Their dark, bare feet skimmed over the blistering sand as if over live coals, but Abayomi placed his hands on his narrow hips and ignored them, choosing to study the half-buried Sphinx before him. His tutors had told him that Khafra, a king long before his father, had modeled this monument after his own likeness, in honor of the sun-god who ruled these vast deserts.

A smile played around the corners of the prince's thin lips. Where was the sun-god now, and did he care that the lion's body of his Great Sphinx lay buried beneath the desert? Only the wind-scarred head of Khafra was now visible, his chin resting on the blanket of sand like a creature resigned to inevitable suffocation.

"Prepare my tent here, before the Sphinx," the prince commanded the servants who fluttered nearby in anticipation of his wishes. "We will rest, and then continue our hunt."

A canopy appeared as if from nowhere. Four poles held its striped linen high above the earth. Another piece of linen, tightly woven to keep out irritating grains of sand, was spread on the ground, and on this the prince reclined in the shade of the canopy.

The sun threw the shadow of his distinctive profile onto the ground beneath him. He knew he was handsome, this second son of the king, and though his face still retained the softness of youth, the concentrated stare of his piercing brown eyes never failed to make a maiden blush or a servant grow pale. Taller than his mother, and nearly as tall as his elder brother, he possessed strong limbs and a broad chest, set off by the pleated kilt of fine white linen and the wide collar of gold about his neck. In typical princely manner, one magnificent tress of black hair grew like an exclamation from his right temple, the seat of deep thought and wisdom.

His eyes closed in the heavy heat of the afternoon; the Great Sphinx sheltered him from the hot winds of the sirocco. Sleep, when it came, was welcome.

The Sphinx spoke to him. "Behold me, gaze on me, O my son Abayomi," the creature said, the wide eyes of stone unblinking and yet seeing all. "For I, your father Harmakhis-Khopri-Tumu, grant you sovereignty over the Two Lands, in the South and in the North, and you shall wear both the white and the red crowns of the throne of Sibu, the sovereign possessing the earth in its length and breadth."

The prince blinked and sat upright, but nothing else moved in the hot afternoon. Was this a dream? Or had he dared disturb the mighty sun-god with his irreverent thoughts?

"These are words of blessing, my son," the Sphinx continued, his voice a roar that reverberated through the desert. "You shall be called Tuthmosis, and the flashing eye of the lord of all shall cause to rain on you the possessions of Egypt. Vast tribute from all foreign countries and a long life will be given you, as one chosen by the Sun. For my countenance is yours; my heart is yours; no other than you is mine."

"I am yours," the prince whispered, falling to his knees before the solid stone image. He lowered his head to the earth and felt the heat of the desert burn his forehead. "But I am a second son only. How can these things be?"

The massive stone head turned, the grating of stone upon stone caused the canopy poles to quiver. The prince raised his eyes slowly. Beyond the Sphinx, sand dunes rippled and flowed like water toward the mighty monument, and the mouth of the half-buried stone creature opened in an inhuman cry. "The firstborn of Egypt shall die," the monstrous voice shrieked. "You shall become king, my son, Tuthmosis."

The prince closed his eyes and moistened his lips as the horrible prophecy rang in his ears. "What would you have me do?" the prince whispered.

As if by command, the sand stopped flowing, the wind ceased. The Sphinx's mighty head returned to its habitual resting place and the mouth closed. But the voice still spoke. "Now I am covered by the sand of the mountain on which I rest and have given you this prize that you may do for me what my heart desires. For I know you are my son, my defender; draw nigh. I am with you; I am your well-beloved father. Release me from this mountain, and I shall give you what your heart desires."

"I will release you from the sand, I swear it," the prince answered, the scent of scorched linen filling his nostrils.

"Then this and more will I give to you, Tuthmosis, if you release me!" The mighty voice roared through the stillness of the desert, growing louder and stronger until the boy's hands covered his ears, and he too screamed, his cry lost in the buried god's awful wail.

The sirocco blew from behind the Sphinx in a miserable, commanding howl, and the prince jerked into wakefulness as an anxious servant timidly touched his shoulder. "May the gods grant you life, my prince," the servant said, bowing on the hot sand. "But you have slept for two hours. We feared you were not well."

"I am well," the prince answered, rising upon his elbow. He moved slowly, afraid a sudden flurry of sound or action would tear apart the fabric of sanctity surrounding the half-buried Sphinx. The fearsome sounds and images echoed in his brain as if they had occurred in reality, not in a dream. His father would insist he had imagined the episode, for Amenhotep believed the gods spoke only to him. But the prince recalled the devastating power of the Sphinx's voice and shivered, despite the heat.

"Mark this well, all who hear," he called in his most authoritative voice. "If the gods will that I be king, on that very day the sand of this mountain is to be cleared from the form of Harmakhis-Khopri-Tumu, the sun-god, that he may reign in beauty over the Two Lands, in the South and the North. It shall be recorded that I have done this in covenant between the god my father, and me."

The company of servants bowed in honor of the royal proclamation, and Abayomi ascended into his chariot and led the procession back to Thebes, too shaken to continue the hunt.

⤳ Twenty-four ⤳

THE TIME OF HER TRAVAIL FELL UPON TUYA quickly. She barely had time to send for the priestess of Taweret, the patroness of childbirth, before her son dropped into the world. As the grotesque priestess paraded throughout Tuya's chamber striking at invisible enemies with her ceremonial daggers, Tuya drew her mewling infant son to her breast and tenderly wiped the birth fluids from his skin. How perfect he was, and how unique! He was the only thing in the world that had ever belonged to her, and she would never surrender him to anyone. She had been born a slave, but this child would forever be a free man.

"What will you call him?" one of her maids asked, her hands folded reverently in front of her. "He is Pharaoh's grandson and should have a fine name."

Tuya pressed her finger to the child's cheek and smiled as the boy turned toward it, seeking a life-giving breast. She was about to answer when the door slammed open. Abayomi stood there, his eyes wide, his face stiff with fear. "I came as quickly as I could," he said, struggling to catch his breath.

"Would you like to see your son?" she asked, inclining her head toward the baby in her arms. "He has just been born. I think he would like to meet his father."

Abayomi panted his way through the knot of maids and knelt at Tuya's side. He studied the baby for a long moment, and then his worried face rearranged itself into a grin. "He is beautiful, Tuya," he said, giving her a smile that reached all the way to his eyes. "What baby name will you give him?"

"I think," she said, lifting the baby nearer to his father, "I shall call him Yusef."

Abayomi did not protest the strange-sounding name, but she knew he would not. He had a taste for the unusual. "Yusef," he murmured, offering the baby his smallest finger. "He is a fine son, Tuya."

"Thank you," she murmured, running her hand over the baby's damp hair.

The prince looked at her with something very fragile in his eyes, then suddenly indicated the door with a jerk of his head. "I should go."

"Why should you go?" she asked, looking up in surprise. "You are the child's father. You have a right to be here."

"But you have done *this*," he stammered, lifting his hands in a suddenly helpless gesture. "You have done a great thing! I want to get you something."

"Abayomi," she said, reaching for the hand of the boy who was, in a way, as much her son as the baby in her arms, "you have given me a child, the greatest gift a man can give a woman. I ask for nothing more."

"I wish you would," he whispered, but she laughed off his suggestion and turned again to the baby, dimly aware that Abayomi watched her as if she were some unparalleled work of art.

———

The hot wind blew clouds of yellow dust from the stone structures where the more noble inmates were housed, and Joseph paused outside the walled cell where Pharaoh's two newest prisoners had been incarcerated. His hands, calloused from carrying water buckets to and from these cells, tingled with exhaustion after a long, hot day in the blinding Egyptian sun. He set the buckets down for a moment and wiped the sweat from his brow with his forearm. He had hoped to fall asleep as soon as he returned to his cell, but a riotous clamor had broken out beyond the tall prison

LEGACIES OF THE ANCIENT RIVER

walls bordering the streets of Thebes.

"What is the cause for this noise?" a prisoner called through the iron bars of the door. The prisoners in this cell, both servants from Pharaoh's palace, had been imprisoned for nearly five months without an opportunity to stand trial before the king. The one who had spoken brushed his strong black hair from his face to better glare at Joseph. "It is not a feast day, nor a festival, nor Pharaoh's birthday. Why does pandemonium rise from the streets?"

"Let me talk to him," another voice muttered, and the second inmate pushed his way to the small opening in the door. He was a dusty man, with an aging yellow face and deep violet rings under his eyes, but his smile was quick and genuine. His gaze flickered over Joseph for a moment, then he smiled and bowed his head slightly. "Do you know why Thebes celebrates tonight?" he asked, his refined manner unusual for one who had been confined so long in Pharaoh's prison.

"I do not know," Joseph murmured, lifting the bolt on the door. The two prisoners stepped back, and Joseph moved inside to exchange the full water bucket for their empty one.

"I may know the reason," the second said, snapping his fingers. "The time is right for the lovely princess to deliver her child."

"Another royal brat," the other man groused, plopping down onto the reed mat that served as his bed. "Another mouth to feed! I am beginning to think I do not want to go back to Pharaoh's kitchen!"

"The lovely Tuya could not produce a brat if she were wed to Anubis himself," the other man replied, wagging a scolding finger at his companion.

Joseph's blood rose in a jet at the mention of Tuya's name. "You know Tuya?" he whispered to the gentler man.

"Know her?" The man laughed, leaning back with expressive nonchalance. "I have known her since she was a mere child. I was the butler for Donkor, you see, and she was a maid for Donkor's daughter. No one was more astounded than I to find she had grown up into a bride lovely enough for Pharaoh's own son."

Joseph stepped back in absolute astonishment. He had not dared to speak Tuya's name in five years, but suddenly her image rose up before him, vivid and close, opening the door on hundreds of memories he had tried to bury. The impulse to ask a thousand questions was a tangible urge, for the man who stood before him had talked to her, worked with her, perhaps his work-worn hands had even gripped Tuya's slender ones. . . .

Unthinking, he reached out for the ghost of her memory, and the man threw up his hands in a defensive posture, warning Joseph off. "Gather your wits, my friend! I am not that lovely lady!"

"I am sorry," Joseph answered, feeling the burn of a blush upon his cheek.

The prisoner dropped his hands and relaxed, then nodded in understanding. "I take it that you also have known Tuya. Calm yourself and let us talk."

"Please," Joseph said, overturning the empty bucket. "There is much I would like to know." He perched on the bucket's edge and rested his elbows on his knees, intent upon the prisoner's words.

"I am called Taharka," the man said, watching Joseph steadily through eyes that had paled with age. "I was summoned to work in Pharaoh's vineyard many months after Tuya had left Donkor's house. Later she told me that she had served in the house of the captain of Pharaoh's bodyguard."

"Potiphar," Joseph said, a bubbling furious excitement rising in his chest. In a moment Taharka would mention his own name, for surely Tuya had told her old friend about the love she shared with Joseph. . . .

But Taharka only scratched his head. "Yes. And Potiphar later returned her to Pharaoh. The kitchen slaves are fond of telling the story about our young prince falling in love the moment he saw her. So she was married to Abay-omi, and when I left the palace a royal child grew in her womb. The time is right for her baby to be born."

A child! Joseph felt his smile twist. He could not picture Tuya with another man by her side, and he could certainly not imagine her with a child in her arms. He had known that Tuya married a boy-prince, but in the void of prison life he had forgotten that time did not stand still outside the stone walls. If Tuya's prince was mature enough to father children, she was married now to a man. . . .

"I think we ought to discover," the dark-haired prisoner interrupted, smirking, "why the mention of our princess's name excites this slave. He reeks of enthusiasm for the lady."

Joseph turned, about to stammer out a truthful reply, but Taharka's wary eyes flashed a warning. Joseph closed his eyes, calming himself, then shook his head. "Who has not heard of the lady's beauty?" he finished, shrugging lamely. "Every man in Thebes has heard songs to praise her. I never thought to speak with a man"—his eyes met Taharka's—"who had actually met her." An understanding was reached and returned in that glance, and Joseph realized that Tuya's life at the palace was no more secure than it had been in Potiphar's house.

He left the two prisoners and made his way back to his own dark cell, haunted by dreams of what might have been.

———

Terrorized by nightmares, three prisoners stirred in their sleep and awoke with clear and unsettling memories of the night they had passed.

Joseph awoke slowly, burdened by the rueful accep-tance of a terrible knowledge. The meaning of his dream was all too clear. He'd seen Tuya standing on the opposite bank of the mighty Nile in the flood's ominous gray ex-panse. Upon her pale face she wore an expression of in-credible sadness, but she carried a baby in her arms while a young boy clung to her skirt. As Joseph watched, a wide crocodile rose from the engorged Nile and advanced steadily toward her, its golden eyes shining upon the babe in her arms. Suddenly the wavelets that had flecked the surface of the river flattened out, and a second crocodile began to crawl toward the unsuspecting Tuya.

She did not see, for her eyes were fastened upon the child in her arms.

From the opposite bank, Joseph struggled to reach her, but his arms were held by iron bonds. He threw back his head and screamed a guttural cry of terror, but his voice would not carry across the river.

Understanding hit him like a punch in the stomach, and Joseph awakened fully aware of what God wanted him to know. Tuya and her child were in danger. And if the boy clinging to her skirt was intended to represent her husband, his life would be also threatened.

But Joseph could do nothing to warn her. Wearily, he climbed the rope from his pit and proceeded to move about his work. For the first time in years, the comments of the condemned prisoners did not even register in his brain, so intent was he upon recalling every detail of his dream. There had to be a way to reach her. God would not have warned him unless he could do something to help. "Show me," he whispered, turning from the pits to the stone cells. "O God of understanding, make the way clear."

Suddenly he thought of Taharka, Tuya's friend. If God would provide a way to release the cupbearer, Tuya could be warned. He quickened his steps down the path, eager to speak to Pharaoh's servant.

But Taharka was in no mood for conversation. A crown of gloom lay upon both Pharaoh's servants, and Joseph dared not ask for a favor while the cupbearer and baker were in such foul moods. "Why are you upset today?" he asked, tucking their empty food basket under his arm.

"I did not sleep well," the butler confessed. "The baker

and I both had disturbing dreams, and there is no one here to explain their meaning."

"Why speak of it at all?" the baker groused, lying back upon his mat. He shaded his eyes with his hand and frowned at Joseph. "What can a lowly slave tell you?"

"Interpretations belong to God," Joseph answered. He knelt on the ground beside Taharka's mat. "Tell me, please."

Taharka's worried expression softened into one of fond reminiscence. "I dreamed I walked again in my vineyard. A vine sprouted in front of me, and three branches grew on the vine. As it was budding, its blossoms came forth, and its clusters produced ripe grapes, the finest I have ever seen. Suddenly Pharaoh's cup appeared in my hand, so I took the grapes and squeezed them into Pharaoh's cup, and then put the cup into Pharaoh's hand."

Joseph smiled as the meaning of the dream became clear. "God, the Almighty One, does not want you to be confused. This is the interpretation of your dream: the three branches are three days. Within three days Pharaoh will forgive you and restore you to your place, and you will once again put Pharaoh's cup into his hand as you used to do when you were his cupbearer."

As a smile of relief spread across the old man's features, Joseph put out a hand and touched his arm: "Please, Taharka," he whispered, taking pains to keep his voice under control, "keep me in mind when it goes well with you. Do me a kindness by mentioning me to Pharaoh, and get me out of this prison. You will not be circumventing justice, for I was kidnapped from the land of the Hebrews, and even here I have done nothing to deserve being put into a dungeon."

He did not dare mention Tuya, for he knew nothing of court life and did not know if even this man could be trusted. But Pharaoh could pardon any slave convicted by his master, and if Joseph were free, he could keep a watchful eye on the situation at court. From a distance, he could spy danger that might threaten Tuya or her child. . . .

"That was fascinating," the baker said, suddenly interested. "If I promise to speak to Pharaoh, will you give me a favorable interpretation of my dream, too?"

Impatient to continue his conversation with Taharka, Joseph nodded.

"In my dream I saw three baskets of white bread on my head," the baker began, sitting cross-legged upon his mat. "In the top basket there were all sorts of baked foods for Pharaoh, and the birds were eating them out of the basket on my head." He grinned. "In three days I will be serving Pharaoh again, correct?"

No. He will die. The silent voice spoke, and Joseph lowered his head as he sought the right words. "The three baskets are three days," he whispered, a pang of regret striking his heart. "Within three days Pharaoh will lift you from this place and will hang you on a tree. The birds will eat your flesh from your bones."

The baker's smile flattened out, and he trembled slightly as though a chill wind had blown over him. A full moment passed before he began to sputter helplessly. "That is not right," he said, smacking his fist into his palm. "You gave him a good interpretation! How do I know you are telling the truth?"

Joseph closed his eyes a moment, listening for the inner voice, and then he met Taharka's steady gaze. "Pharaoh's eldest son will die before today's sun sets," he said, stunned by the awfulness of the revelation that had come to him. "You will know that I speak truly when you hear of this thing."

At dinner that day, Prince Webensennu plucked a poisoned piece of fruit from Pharaoh's bowl and died within the hour. Potiphar and his guards quickly surrounded the royal kitchens, where a junior baker confessed to the crime. Two days later, under torture, the condemned man exposed a year-old conspiracy that had been orchestrated by Pharaoh's chief baker and funded by a group of rebel Syrians. The poisoning of Pharaoh's taster many months before had been the first attempt to steal the breath of life from the divine king.

Satisfied with the answers he had received, Potiphar left his guards with the nearly dead traitor and stalked to the great hall where the king was attempting to observe his birthday. He did not bother to bow as he entered the hall. Amenhotep sat upon his throne, untouched bowls of rich food spread before him, his royal visage cloaked in gloom and grief. The queen and other family members ate with little enthusiasm, their eyes occasionally darting toward the place where Webensennu usually sat with his wives.

Pharaoh's brow lifted when Potiphar stopped before him. "The murderers have been found," he announced, lifting his hand in a prideful flourish. "Two bakers in your kitchens are guilty, urged to commit this crime by the chief baker now in my prison. They were paid in silver by the Syrian dignitaries who sat at meat with Pharaoh some months ago."

Taking satisfaction in this somber birthday gift, Pharaoh stood and held a quivering hand over the banqueting assembly. "Let the chief baker be immediately removed from the prison and hanged high upon a tree outside the city walls. Let those who conspired with him be killed with the sword. And let all their bodies remain in place for the wild animals, for they do not deserve to enter immortality."

Potiphar bowed his head. "It shall be done. But there still remains the matter of Taharka, your cupbearer." He looked up, gently reminding the grief-stricken king of unfinished business. "We could not tell whether the first attempt involved food or wine, and Taharka has awaited your judgment in prison."

Pharaoh nodded, then took a deep breath and barreled his chest. "Let the cupbearer Taharka be restored to his former position and cleared of all suspicion." The king's eyes turned to meet those of his queen. "I have lost a son. Let no more innocent blood be shed."

———

When the seventy days of mourning for Prince Weben-sennu had passed, Pharaoh proclaimed that his fourteen-year-old second son, Abayomi, was henceforth to be known as Menkheprure, Beloved of Osiris, Tuthmosis, Crown Prince of Egypt. Tuya watched her husband's young face lengthen with responsibility as his thoughts grew more weighty during the months of mourning. Though he had told her of his strange vision before the Sphinx, she had not truly expected him to become Crown Prince. But as soon as he was proclaimed heir, her husband, the fourth to be named Tuthmosis, began to consider plans by which the great Sphinx might be evacuated from the sand which had all but smothered it.

And Tuya, who had steadily and quietly prayed for her friend Taharka's safety, thanked the Almighty God for the slave's release.

———

Driven by curiosity, Tuya left her baby with a wet nurse and slipped from her chamber to seek Taharka in the palace kitchens. Several startled servants, unaccustomed to the sight of a royal princess in the workrooms, dropped bowls and trays and hurried to prostrate themselves as she approached. "Do not trouble yourselves," she whispered, glancing around. "Where is Taharka?"

One of the slaves pointed shyly toward a back room, and Tuya startled even the balding butler when she stepped through the doorway. "By Seth's eyeballs, I did not expect you to come," Taharka blustered, struggling to lower himself to his knees.

"Rise, Taharka, I came to congratulate you, not to accept homage," Tuya said, injecting a teasing note into her voice. "I was distressed when you were arrested. I have prayed that you would be safely returned to us."

"Thanks to the gods, I am safe," the slave answered, wiping his hands upon the wine-stained apron over his kilt. "And thanks to the divine Pharaoh, of course. And to you, naturally. And to Horus—"

"You need not pretend with me, old friend," Tuya whispered fondly. She paused, wondering how she might ask the question pestering her heart. "You were a long time in the prison."

"Six months," Taharka boasted. "But I would do it again if Pharaoh demanded it. I will not be having it said that I am disloyal or bitter about it—"

"Be assured that I will say nothing of this conversation," Tuya said, wishing the cupbearer could forget that she was married to a royal prince. She wanted to ask a very specific question, but did not know how. Taharka knew nothing of her love for Joseph, and to tell him about it would be the worst kind of disloyalty to her own husband. And Pharaoh could not abide disloyalty from anyone.

"Did you meet many people in prison?" she asked casually, pretending to study a bowl of grapes fresh from the vineyard.

"By the gods, no," Taharka went on, expansive in his desire to talk. "We were kept in a dark cell no bigger than this workroom. Much smaller, in fact. The baker, may the gods condemn his soul for all eternity, and I saw no one but the warden and his slave. The baker—and you may pass this on to whomever you like—behaved as a guilty man from the first day we were thrust in together. He complained and uttered treasonous statements, he even called your son a brat, yes, that was his exact word—"

"Did you ever hear," she asked, unable to keep silent any longer, "of a prisoner called Joseph?"

Taharka blinked. "No. We were kept alone, I tell you, that cursed baker and I. A most foul and disagreeable sort he was, a loathsome toad—"

He knew nothing. "Thank you, Taharka," Tuya murmured, backing out of the room. "I wish you well."

———

Two years passed. The Nile rose and fell, blessing the land with bounty each time.

Prince Menkheprure left his wife and son at the palace and began his military training. His valiant efforts in battle earned him the title "Conqueror of Syria," and Tuya watched her dreaming husband become as fierce a warrior as his father. After his engagement in Syria, the prince led a campaign in Nubia and before thousands of Egyptians proved himself courageous and worthy to assume his father's throne. She saw little of him during those years, for when he was at home in Thebes, Menkheprure spent hours being tutored by the high priests of Osiris for the role that would one day be his. A godling, it seemed, had much to learn.

As Tuya's husband equipped himself for the throne, the priests prepared the people for the eventuality of his rise to power. They began to tell the story of how Amon consulted with the other gods to see who should bear his divine child. Thoth suggested Queen Teo, one of Amenhotep's many wives, and Amon visited her in the physical form of Pharaoh so that a divine child could be conceived. "Not once, but twice Amon visited a wife of Pharaoh," the priests explained to the people. "Pharaoh's second son is as divine as his first son was."

The afterbirth which had followed Menkheprure's body into the world was brought from its place of preservation. Wrapped as a mummy painted with a child's face, the deified placenta was known as the *Khonsu*. Just as Pharaoh's royal *Khonsu* was carried on a standard before the king on all state occasions, so Menkheprure's preserved placenta was paraded before the people whenever he appeared in the royal court. Soon just the appearance of the young prince's *Khonsu* elicited rapturous applause and cheering from curious crowds of well-wishers.

As Menkheprure evolved from secondary prince to heir apparent, Tuya noticed that Pharaoh's approving smile seemed to widen in gratitude and relief. Shortly after celebrating his forty-fifth birthday, Amenhotep II retired to his chamber and surrendered to an illness which had sapped his strength for many months.

"My father's death is the beginning of his journey to resurrection," the Crown Prince proclaimed to the assembled court in the palace throne room. "And as the gods once lived on earth, begat children, and died, yet they still live and have needs. My father has passed from one state of life to another, and we will help him prepare for the needs of the other world." With a graceful toss of his head, the new king faced his subjects, but as always, his eyes sought Tuya's for an instant of reassurance. She gave him a smile of encouragement, and he cleared his throat and went on. "We will mourn for seventy days while the king's body is prepared for immortality."

During the seventy days of mourning, Tuya kept her three-year-old son by her side as much as possible. The stubby-legged toddler seemed to be the only person in the world she could love without risk, for just as Abayomi had become Prince Menkheprure, the prince became Pharaoh Tuthmosis IV on the day of his father's death, and Pharaoh belonged to his people and to the gods. Now that her husband would wear the red-and-white double crown, Tuya knew that his priests, counselors, and diplomats would hold more power and influence over him than she could ever hope to have again. Tuthmosis would no longer need her motherly approval, for a host of courtiers yearned to assure him of his strength, wisdom, and authority. And now that he was king, he no longer needed her as a wife. An entire harem of the kingdom's most beautiful women awaited his pleasure and attention.

But in those early days Tuthmosis's devotion and adoration were reserved almost exclusively for the god who had spoken from the Sphinx. As he prepared for his coronation, he ordered slave crews to clear the sand from around the mammoth statute. Workmen labored in the blinding sun to repair the sacred figure, and between the monument's outstretched paws, Tuthmosis himself mounted a special stela engraved with the notice that he had restored the Sphinx in order to honor the god's promise to him. Tuthmosis believed that the Sphinx had brought his kingship to pass, and the impressionable and grateful young man was determined to honor the god who could work such a miracle.

As Tuthmosis worked on the Sphinx, the priests worked on the earthly remains of Amenhotep II. Tuya had often looked upon the face of death, but her fellow slaves had counted for nothing in the afterlife, so their bodies were tossed into the Nile as food for the crocodiles. But Amenhotep had spent the latter part of his life preparing for Paradise, and his divinity demanded that he be mummified with all ceremony and propriety.

Every morning the high priest of Osiris reported to Tuthmosis's throne room to explain the progress of the many rituals and funeral rites. Careful not to intrude, Tuya listened quietly from a corner. After the king's viscera were removed and placed in canopic jars, the priests split his body open with a flint. After seventy days of wrapping and encoffining, the royal cadaver, dried out, resewn, and reshaped, would be carried to the tomb to enact the entry of the king into the underworld. Tuthmosis would be required to preside over this elaborate ritual, for as the dead king had abdicated his earthly powers in favor of his son, the new king would establish the dead Pharaoh as a god in the other world.

The Nile had just begun to recede when the seventy days were completed. Tuya clutched her tiny son's hand as she joined the funeral procession and left the Nile's east bank, the land of the living. Hundreds of mourners, all dressed in white, crossed the swollen river on ferry boats and walked deep into the western valleys where jagged cliffs rose like armed warriors, safeguarding this place against the world beyond. Here, in the Valley of the Tombs, the eternal dwellings of the dead waited for yet another king.

An ox-drawn hearse, symbolizing the sun-god's blazing boat, led the procession with Amenhotep's mummified remains, and behind it followed a sledge, bearing the four canopic jars which contained the king's liver, lungs, stomach, and intestines. Behind Pharaoh's body marched a host of slaves carrying the furniture and other equipment Amenhotep would require in the life to come.

A freshly painted portico had been erected before the tomb, and at the left end of the shelter a pair of mummers performed a funeral dance. The special mortuary priests, the *hemu-ka*, slid the coffin from its sledge and stood it upright at the door of the tomb. One priest, his face hidden by the jackal mask of Anubis, supported the immense coffin while the chief mortuary priest symbolically restored speech to the dead king by touching the king's painted lips with an adze-shaped instrument. The ceremony was called *wep-ro*, the Opening of the Mouth, and the priests believed the rite would give speech to the king in his new life.

Tuthmosis, looking very young and frail in his heavy white headcovering, stood with the other male mourners at the right of the portico. Tuya and the other women sat behind him while Queen Merit-Amon wept and wailed in anguish at the side of the coffin.

The time had come for the dead to depart. The jackal-masked priest tenderly lifted the queen from the coffin, and a score of attendants placed the gilded box inside the granite sarcophagus. Before the heavy lid was put into place, Amenhotep's wives came forward in a final farewell, draping flowers upon his painted coffin. When each of the wives had passed, a score of shaven-headed priests heaved the lid into position, lifted the sarcophagus onto rollers, and proceeded to push this most intimate of the king's chambers through the tomb's tunnels. In the somber rhythm of their dismal chant, they trudged past the painted gaze of the gods and goddesses lining the walls.

Amenhotep's burial chamber was an immense hall entirely decorated with paintings that told the story of the king's life. The ceiling was supported by two rows of three pillars adorned with life-sized images of the king in the presence of the gods. Beyond the last two pillars, steps led down into a crypt where the great king's sarcophagus was laid to rest upon a granite slab.

When the sarcophagus and the canopic jars had been set in their places, the priests and relatives helped fill the rooms of the tomb with supplies for the king's life in the Other World: furniture, baskets of food, pottery, glass, garlands of fresh flowers, jewels, treasures, small funerary statues of servants, slaves, and wives. Several chambers bulged already with things Amenhotep had accumulated in his lifetime.

Tuya walked past a king's ransom in gold and riches as she carried her contribution for the king's eternal life: a small alabaster vase upon which she had painted the likeness of her baby, Pharaoh's grandson. Wading through an assortment of earthly treasures, she crept to the innermost burial chamber and knelt before the remains of the man who had been her sovereign and her father-in-law. After pressing her lips to the cold stone of the sarcophagus, she tenderly placed the vase within a wreath of lotus blossoms.

Queen Merit-Amon stood as if in a daze near the entrance to the burial chamber, and Tuya slipped her arm about the woman's waist as the priests installed the magic amulets which would guard against evil tomb robbers. As others lit the golden torches that would illuminate the chamber after they had gone, Tuya whispered in the queen's ear and coaxed her from the room. Carefully sweeping their footsteps from the sand as they backed out, the priests left the tomb, shutting and sealing the inner passageways one by one.

By the time Re's sun boat had sailed to the west, Egypt had a new king.

~~ Twenty-five ~~

ONE ASPECT OF HER HUSBAND'S CORONATION caught Tuya by surprise. Even before the dead Pharaoh was entombed in his grave, rebellion stirred in the northern nomes. To insure that the Mitanni empire would enforce the peace and maintain Egyptian interests in the northernmost lands, the royal counselors remembered an old treaty between Amenhotep and the king of the Mitanni tribe. Amenhotep had promised that one of the Mitanni king's daughters would marry the next king of Egypt, so a hasty union between Tuthmosis and Mutemwiya, a Mitanni princess, was arranged. Narmer, Amenhotep's faithful courtier, was dispatched to escort the bride to Thebes with a copy of the marriage contract. The agreement stipulated that the princess be designated as the Great Wife, Queen Mutemwiya. Since Tuthmosis had no royal sisters to vie for the title, the princess was readily accepted.

And so, on her husband's coronation day, Tuya found herself standing with her son among the other members of the royal family as her husband and his new wife were crowned King and Queen of the Two Kingdoms. Tuya told herself that the new marriage did not matter. The emotion she felt for her husband vacillated between affection and pity, and Mutemwiya would certainly face a struggle as she adapted to a new country and a new king. Born a slave, Tuya had never dreamed of wearing a crown. Even though she was technically a queen because she had borne the king's son, she had never believed that she might actually reign over the land of her birth. No, Mutemwiya was a royal heiress, and the people would give her their allegiance.

Tuya refused to allow anger or jealousy to prick her heart.

The queen was lovely, Tuya had to admit. Older than Tuya and probably twice the age of Tuthmosis, the woman moved through the great hall with a subtle and sensuous bearing, her golden face marked by crimson lips and mirror-brilliant black eyes. Her hair, which she had not yet cut in order to adopt the Egyptian wig, hung to her waist in a plume of black gold. Rumor had it that she had already buried one husband, and she looked more like Tuthmosis's mother than his bride.

But the eyes of every man in the room followed her as she moved toward her throne at Tuthmosis's side. She walked with the hard grace of one who has total control of herself, and her boldly confident eyes rebuffed every man who dared look at her, except one. Tuya noticed that Narmer met the woman's flinty gaze head on. Even now, as Mutemwiya stepped up to the dais and slipped her hand into that of Tuthmosis, Narmer's bold brown eyes raked his new queen with a fiercely possessive look. What, Tuya wondered, had transpired between these two on the journey from Mitanni?

The high priest's voice droned in the stillness, filling the room with blessings of prosperity and promises of fealty, and Tuya allowed her eyes to wander. Potiphar, watchful and paternal, stood nervously at the head of the guard, his hooded eyes searching the gathering as though assassins waited behind every pillar. Beneath the Gold of Praise, the brown skin of his neck sagged with age and weariness. He was an old, tired man, ready to meet his gods—if he had any.

Sighing, Tuya turned her attention back to the wedding canopy as the gathering cheered her husband and his new queen.

———

Pharaoh Tuthmosis sat bolt upright in bed and stared into the darkness, trying to see whatever it was that had slashed his sleep like a knife. A new kind of fear shook his body from toe to hair and twisted his face into an expression he was glad no one could see. He was alone, completely and totally alone with this nameless terror, and suddenly he yearned for Tuya.

"Abasi!" He yelled for the eunuch who attended him. His grasping fingers found the silken cord which hung by his bed, and he yanked it sharply. "Bomani! Chike!"

His servant, his guard, and his priest appeared in the doorway, their figures backlit by the torches that burned in the hallway. The servant and guard immediately prostrated themselves on the floor of his chamber, but the old priest took his time about it.

"Rise, all of you," Tuthmosis said, his nerves at full stretch. "Abasi, light the torches and then bring me the royal wife Tuya! Bomani—guard the door, and let no one in except Tuya. I fear for my life. Chike, high priest of Osiris—"

Light flooded the chamber from the torches, and the aging priest inclined his bald head. "Yes, my king?"

"Say prayers for me. Offer sacrifices of blood, of fruit, of incense. Make sure the gods are pleased with my kingship."

The old man's face was as inscrutable as stone, but he bowed and nodded. "It shall be done."

"Do it now," Tuthmosis said, gripping the sheet that covered him with white knuckles. "Abasi, why do you wait? Fetch Tuya, now!"

The eunuch sprinted out of the chamber as fast as his bare feet could carry him, and Bomani moved toward the door. The priest prepared to follow, but Tuthmosis did not want to be alone. "Wait—my priest," he said, searching for words that would not reveal the frozen, frightened thing in his heart. "Have any of the astrologers seen an ill omen in the skies?"

"None, my king," Chike answered, lifting an eyebrow.

"And the river—it flows according to schedule?"

"The goddess waters our land as always. You have won her favor, Divine One."

"The cattle—I have not heard of any plagues upon the cattle—"

"There are none, my king. All is well in the land."

The door opened. Tuya spilled into the room, clad only in a straight gown and a night shawl. She had risen in such a hurry that she forgot even to don her wig, and the sight of her short, rumpled hair brought a smile to the king's face despite his terror. None of the other wives would have come so quickly and in such a disheveled state.

"O Pharaoh, live forever," Tuya whispered, falling to her knees.

"Chike, you may go," Tuthmosis commanded. When the aged priest had closed the door behind him, Tuthmosis crawled to the end of his bed and peered down at his wife. "I am frightened, Tuya," he whispered, his voice sounding strangely weak in his own ears. "I need you."

Her soft, understanding eyes met his, and she rose and climbed into the royal bed. "There, my king," she whispered, slipping her arms around him. "Tell me what has upset you."

"I do not know what it is," he murmured, allowing her to draw his head onto her shoulder. "For two nights now I have been awakened in the darkness by something. An evil premonition holds me in its grip, and I cannot break free of this fear."

"Have you told anyone of this?" she whispered.

"No," he said, lifting his eyes to meet hers. "I do not want them to see that I am afraid. And I do not know why I am. I was not afraid to meet the Syrians, or to lead chariots into battle with the fierce Nubians. I am not afraid to die, and yet this terror sends my blood sliding through my veins like cold needles. A god should not be afraid."

She lowered her forehead to his in silent understanding, and he gratefully reached for her and lightly pressed his lips to hers. The gulf of age which had once separated them had lessened considerably, and he considered Tuya his favorite wife even though Mutemwiya sat on the throne next to him. Tuya was the only one who understood him, the only one in whom he could confide his dreams and his fears, and yet she asked nothing of him. Sometimes he wished that she would . . .

"Sleep, my husband," she whispered, pulling him down to lie upon perfumed sheets, "and I will watch over you. If the terror comes again, wake and tell me of it, and together we shall decide what is to be done."

She tenderly wrapped her arms around him in a warm embrace and kissed his cheek. Tuthmosis took one look around the chamber to make sure the torches still burned, then lowered his head to the softness of Tuya's shoulder and murmured his thanks through the embracing folds of sleep.

Tuya stifled a yawn as her husband slept. She had promised to stay awake, but their son had kept her up late the previous night. The irresistible warmth and delicious weight of sleep bore down upon her, and she struggled to keep her eyes open.

"Horus, help me!"

She was instantly awake as her husband sat up, his eyes like black holes in his pale face. When those horror-filled eyes turned to her, a look of intense, clear light poured through them.

"I know," he said, his voice resonating with fearful wonder and awe. "I have dreamed, Tuya, twice! I see clearly now in the light, for the demons of darkness have not stolen the visions away!"

"Dreams?"

"As real as the dream when the Sphinx spoke to me." He brought his knees to his chest and rested his elbows upon them. "But the dreams are not clear. I see the visions, I recall every detail, but there is no voice to explain it. Since

Horus has spoken to me before, why does he not speak to me now?"

"I do not know, my husband." Tuya pressed her lips together, thinking. "Perhaps it is not Horus who speaks to you."

"Another god? But my priests speak for the others. Every day I hear a score of messages from all the local deities. Why would one of them come to me in a dream?"

"Perhaps it is a god we do not know." A memory ruffled through her mind like wind on water. "Long ago, my husband, I knew a man who said an invisible god spoke to him in dreams. He called this god the Almighty One."

"An invisible god?" For a brief moment his face seemed to open. Tuya saw bewilderment there, a quick flicker of fear, then denial. "I am a god; I would know if this invisible god existed," he said finally, shaking his head. "Tomorrow I will call the priests from every temple in Thebes and set the details of my dreams before them. One of them will know the meaning."

He shot her a questioning look, waiting for reassurance, and Tuya pressed her hand upon his back. "I am sure you are right, my husband," she whispered.

The proclamation went out with the rising of the sun, and by midday a priest from each of Thebes' various temples had made an appearance before Pharaoh and heard the details of the royal vision. The priests consulted their scrolls, the ancient Pyramid Texts, the most gifted seers, and the oracles, but no one could agree upon the details of Pharaoh's dream. "If a man dreams of a cow," one of the priests offered, "it means a happy day in his house."

"No," another priest countered, "it means nothing of the kind. The seven cows are seven children who will be born to Pharaoh." The second priest turned from his colleagues and nodded to the king. "It matters not what a man dreams, my king, because we can provide magic spells for the exorcism of bad dreams. If a man's face is smeared with pesen bread, together with a few fresh herbs moistened with beer and myrrh, all evil dreams which he has seen will be driven away."

"Dreams do matter," Tuthmosis declared, iron in his voice. He stood to his feet and extended the crook and flail over the assembled crowd. "Dreams do matter, you foolish priests! Horus appeared to me in a dream and promised me this throne when I was a mere boy! The gods speak in dreams, and I would know which god speaks, and what he is saying to me!"

"Pharaoh must decide which god speaks," the high priest of Osiris called, his voice ringing across the throne room. "Pharaoh has heard from every priest in Thebes, and each has his own interpretation. Which god, O Divine One, speaks to you?"

Tuthmosis slowly lifted his head, hearing the veiled threat in the words. *If you are our divine king*, the priest was saying, *you should be able to tell us these things yourself.*

Abruptly, Pharaoh dismissed the lot of them.

Tuya uttered an indrawn gasp when she opened the door of her chamber and saw Tuthmosis standing outside, but she smiled without comment and gestured for him to enter and take a seat near the place where their son played on the floor. Never could she recall Amenhotep visiting the chamber of any of his wives; a king was supposed to command his wives to appear before him in his own chambers. But Tuthmosis stepped inside as he always had, as comfortable with her as he would have been with a sister. In a way, she supposed, they had grown up together.

"Shall I send for wine, my husband?" she asked.

He wordlessly signaled his approval with a wave of his hand, and Tuya sent her maid scurrying for the king's cupbearer. As the maid left, Tuya adjusted her wig and knelt on the floor at her husband's feet. Tuthmosis's handsome face was lined with exhaustion, his eyes puffy from lack of sleep. A worried crease divided his forehead, and his hands fluttered fretfully in his lap. The child, oblivious to the king's concern, toddled over to his royal parent and tried to climb into Tuthmosis's lap.

"Not now, Yusef," Tuya scolded the child gently, catching him under his arms.

"Let him be," Tuthmosis answered, reaching out for the boy. "Perhaps the god who speaks to me can speak through the lips of a child."

A knock rapped on the door, and after a moment Taharka entered with his slave. "I have brought wine," he said, carefully pouring the red liquid into one of Pharaoh's golden goblets. The slave tasted the juice while Tuya and the king watched, and after a moment Taharka poured another cup and handed it to the king.

"Thank you, Taharka," Tuya said, giving him the smile of an old friend.

The cupbearer tried smiling at Pharaoh but seemed immediately to sense that it was a bad idea. "I have heard of the commotion at court today," he whispered, more to Tuya than to the king who sat absorbed in his thoughts. "And find that I must now confess one of my own offenses."

"I'm sure your offenses are not very grievous," Tuya said, trying to dismiss him. "Pharaoh has much on his mind."

"I know," Taharka said, stepping closer to the king. He handed the pitcher of wine to his servant and clasped his hands in an attitude of humility. "If it please you, Pharaoh, hear me now. Two years ago Pharaoh was furious with his servants and put me in confinement in the house of the captain of the bodyguard, both me and the chief baker. And we had a dream on the same night, the baker and I; each of us a different dream."

"This is ancient history," Tuthmosis said, lifting his

eyes to the cupbearer in a piercing glance. "Why do you speak of things in the past?"

Taharka nervously shuffled his feet. "Because they might give aid to the present. A Hebrew slave was with us in the prison, a servant of the captain of the bodyguard, and we related our dreams to him, and he interpreted them for us. And it came to pass that everything happened according to his interpretation. Pharaoh restored me to my office but hanged the baker."

"A Hebrew?" Tuya said, her blood running cold. "One who served Potiphar, the captain of the guard?"

"Do you know this Hebrew?" Tuthmosis said, suddenly animated. He sat upright in his chair and leaned toward Tuya. "You know someone who can interpret dreams?"

A sudden sense of foreboding fell over her; she knew she walked the knife-edge of danger, but she had to speak. "I told you last night, my husband, of one who told me that his unseen God has often spoken in dreams. This Hebrew is the man I spoke of. He is called Joseph."

"This is not the same Hebrew," Taharka answered, shaking his head. "My dreams were interpreted by Potiphar's slave Paneah."

"He is Joseph," Tuya whispered, pressing her hand to her son's dark head. Would her eyes reveal her feelings? "Joseph and Paneah are one and the same."

"It matters not what he is called, let him be brought at once," Tuthmosis said, clapping his hands for his guards. "Send a messenger and escort to Potiphar's house, and have the captain of the guard bring this Hebrew to me. He is to be brought safely, and at once."

The servants outside the door heard the royal command and hastened to do their king's bidding.

MENKHEPRURE, PHARAOH TUTHMOSIS IV

Then Pharaoh sent and called for Joseph, and they hurriedly brought him out of the dungeon; and when he had shaved himself and changed his clothes, he came to Pharaoh.

Genesis 41:14

⸻ Twenty-six ⸺

"POTIPHAR! PHARAOH SUMMONS YOU!"

The sound of frantic shouting woke Potiphar from a deep sleep. He sat up in bed, fully awake, even as servants pounded on his door. "I am coming," he barked, thrusting his legs over the side of the bed. Dressing quickly, he snatched up his kilt and sword and cocked his ear to listen to the noises that stirred in the corridor beyond his chamber. Amid a few smothered laughs he heard the clink of weapons. This was no whimsical social summons.

"Master Potiphar!" his servant's voice came again. "Pharaoh's men await you on a matter of urgency."

"Have I not said I am coming? Take them to the courtyard, and I will join them there." He might be nearly sixty, but he was still captain of the king's guards and capable at a moment's notice to perform his duties. As he stalked through his chamber, his hand reached automatically for the sword and dagger resting on a stand near the door.

The crowd of callers, whoever they were, had left the corridor. Potiphar swept forward, his eyes intent upon the courtyard beyond, but a sudden movement in the dimly lit hall startled him.

"By the gods, what is this?" a male voice slurred. Potiphar snapped a torch from its bracket in the wall and stepped toward the intruder. There, in the gleam of torchlight, he saw Sagira spread unconscious upon the couch, her mouth open to the ceiling, her breath punctuated by drunken snoring. Her latest lover knelt on the floor, blinking rapidly in the light as he struggled to rise to his feet.

"This is the master of the house," Potiphar said, bridling his anger for the moment. "And you, sir, had best be gone when I return."

He turned with a quick snap of his thick shoulders and moved to the portico where a contingent of fully armed palace guards waited. "What is the trouble, Bomani?" Potiphar asked, recognizing Pharaoh's personal bodyguard. "For what possible reason would you leave the king unguarded?"

"Pharaoh sent me away," Bomani answered, flushing to the roots of his dark hair. "The king demands to see the Hebrew imprisoned in your house."

For a moment Potiphar's mind obeyed the force of long habit and blocked the name from his consciousness. For six years he had shied away from the tormenting thoughts of the Hebrew. Why should he be forced to think of the man now?

"Paneah?" Potiphar stammered, surprised by the erratic rhythm of his heart. "Why would Pharaoh want to see one of my slaves?"

Bomani pressed his lips together as a silent reminder that it was not Potiphar's place to question Pharaoh. Potiphar nodded rapidly, acknowledging his blunder, and moved through the squadron toward the barred gate that led to the prison. *Tuya*, he thought, fumbling with the keys at his belt. *At last the girl has exerted some influence and acted to free the man she loves. Though I do not know how she did it without arousing Pharaoh's jealousy . . .*

"If you must know," Bomani whispered, falling into step beside his captain, "Pharaoh has heard that this Hebrew possesses the power of interpretation. Our king has been unable to sleep on account of strange and troubling dreams. I myself have seen him wearing the look of a man who wakes to find himself at the edge of a precipice."

"Dreams?" Potiphar laughed as he fitted his key into the lock of the gate. "Dreams are but shadows of the mind, Bomani, surely our king knows this."

"Pharaoh is convinced that a god speaks to him," the

guard answered, lifting his chin as if Potiphar's answer had offended him. "And he believes this Hebrew can interpret the god's voice."

Potiphar shook his head as he swung the prison gate open. "Our king can have the Hebrew," he said, stepping aside so Bomani could enter. "I surrendered Paneah long ago."

Khamat blinked in surprise when the captain of the guard appeared at his door in the dead of night. "Master," he said, falling to his knees in fear that a prisoner had escaped. Unconsciously, his eyes darted to the sword in Potiphar's belt. "What brings you to me?"

"Do not fear, Khamat, we come only to relieve you of a prisoner," Potiphar answered, gesturing to the men behind him. "Pharaoh wants to see my servant Paneah."

"Tonight?" Khamat widened his eyes. "Surely not tonight! He stinks, he has fleas—"

"Clean him up," Potiphar said, pushing past the chief jailer and moving into the lodge. "We will wait."

"Paneah will not want to be bothered tonight," Khamat said, wrapping his kilt about him. "He prays at night, sometimes the entire night through. He doesn't know that I can hear him, but I have stood outside his cell and listened—"

"Since when does my chief jailer heed the wishes of his prisoners?" Potiphar snapped, taking a seat on a wooden stool in the room. "Bring him now. He can pray while we shave that foul beard from his face."

Khamat nodded rapidly, then took a torch from one of the guards and hurried toward the prison pits.

Joseph usually finished his duties as the sun set, then lowered himself back into his pit where he enjoyed the bit of food in his bucket. After eating, he lay back upon the sand and prayed as he watched night draw down like a black cowl. Khamat trusted him so completely that for four years he had been allowed to come and go within the prison as he pleased. The weathered rope hung permanently into Joseph's cell, and no one bothered to cover the opening of his pit.

Night after night, as he watched the stars spin across his small circle of sky, he thought of God's covenant and promise that Abraham's children would someday be more numerous than the stars, as countless as the sand of the sea. And though Joseph could only see a small section of the night sky, he *knew* the heavens were a broad expanse far deeper than the pit in which he lay.

He had learned many things during his six years of imprisonment. He had come to understand that humility was more precious to God than success, and that a man's reactions to life were more important than his actions. He had questioned whether his old visions of the sun and stars and sheaves of wheat bowing down to him were inspired by God or implanted by the Evil One, and finally he had realized that his visions did not matter. He had sought to fulfill them himself, and the quest had brought him nothing but despair and disgrace. Better to be a happy, simple shepherd than dream of changing the world and stumble over pride.

Each night he ended his colloquy with a fervent request that God protect Tuya and her son from whatever dangers surrounded her. When he had first dreamed of her two years before, the vision had left him feeling frustrated and helpless. Why had God warned him of Tuya's situation when Joseph could do nothing for her but pray?

In that question he found his answer. And as he prayed, his once passionate love for her faded to a warm memory, but his prayers nurtured a strong concern for her well-being and happiness.

He sighed deeply and closed his eyes, surrendering to the exhaustion that claimed him after a long day's work. He had nearly willed himself to sleep when noises from above brought him back to consciousness.

"Paneah! Rise at once!"

Joseph recognized Khamat's nasal whine. He was not in the mood to clean up after another drunken soldier who could not hold his beer.

"Can it not wait?" he murmured, not opening his eyes.

"Paneah! Pharaoh calls for you!"

That statement brought Joseph bolt upright, as wide awake as if he had just drunk a cup of strong tea. He lifted his eyes to the rim of the pit where Khamat stood with a torch. The jailer nudged the rope with his sandal. "Come up, my hairy one, and ready yourself for a bath and a shave. You look more like a monkey than a man, and if you wish to impress the royal eye, you had best hurry."

"Pharaoh wishes to see me?" Joseph murmured, standing. He grasped the rope and looked up at Khamat again. "This is not a jest?"

"No," Khamat answered, glancing over his shoulder. He squatted and gestured for Joseph to hurry. "Master Potiphar waits in my lodge at this moment to escort you to the palace. So hurry, Paneah, before I land in the pit with you!"

It is time. God's time. Whatever is to be done about my dreams, my past, my future, my love for Tuya, will begin in the next hour. Thanks be to you, El Shaddai, that I am ready for whatever you have planned. And strengthen me, Almighty God, so I will not fall prey again to my pride and ambition.

Lifting his eyes to the black heaven above, Joseph braced his feet against the mud walls and began to climb.

⎯⎯◦ Twenty-seven ◦⎯⎯

TUTHMOSIS PACED FOR OVER AN HOUR IN TUYA'S chamber, and nothing she could say or do would calm him. "Please, my husband," she said finally, gesturing to the child who slept with his head in her lap. "You will wake Yusef with that loud stomping of yours. Sit, calm yourself, and have another cup of wine. Bomani will bring this Hebrew as soon as possible."

"I must know the meaning of the dream before I sleep tonight," Pharaoh said, clenching his hands behind his back. "I cannot sleep again, Tuya, if the vision comes to me! The dream's implications grew more frightening throughout the day as priest after priest failed to explain it! When I think of it my blood roars in my ears like the howling of the Sphinx, and I cannot be calm."

Tuya leaned back in her chair. With every step, her husband's jaw became firmer, his muscles tighter, his heart more eager for a solution to the puzzle that had upset him. He was hungry for an answer, and if Joseph failed to provide it after her assurance that he would, Pharaoh would not be happy with either of them. With every moment that passed, the king became more certain of the slave's ability to provide a conclusion to his dilemma, and Tuya prayed silently that Joseph's unseen God would not fail him.

Finally she heard the steady sound of approaching soldiers; then someone rapped on the door. Pharaoh stopped his pacing and turned toward the doorway, his eyes lit with expectation. Bomani pushed the door open without a word.

With the hesitancy of one whose eyes have been burned by the sun and is afraid to gaze upon it again, Tuya turned toward the doorway. The guards' faces, even Potiphar's, blurred into irrelevance as Joseph stepped into the room, his wrists and ankles bound in shackles.

A thunderbolt jagged through her. Joseph had been attractive and handsomely built when she last saw him, but the man who stood before her now had the manner and appearance of a god.

He was thirty years old and in the full prime of manhood. His skin glowed over tightly defined muscles in the golden torchlight of her chamber. He stood tall and impressive beside those who thought themselves his captors, and rough black hair fell past his shoulders in a wild tangle. His face, cleanly shaved and sculpted with angular lines, shone with a powerful charisma and an aloof strength. Tuya steeled herself as she looked up at his eyes. The dark eyes that had always made her heart beat faster were now blazing brighter than the light from the torches burning upon her walls.

She hid a thick swallow in her throat and turned away, suddenly wishing that Pharaoh had chosen to spend the evening in Queen Mutemwiya's chamber instead of her own. Only sorrow could come from this night, and she would rather not know the outcome of this meeting. If Joseph failed Pharaoh at this point, he would surely die, and her heart could never erase the memory of him standing in her own chamber. If he succeeded this test, he would be rewarded, and she would have to look upon him, offer her congratulations, and pretend that her heart did not knock in anticipation with every breath that he drew. An odd coldness settled upon her, a darkly textured fear that chilled her to the marrow.

Pharaoh saw nothing of her reaction. He gazed in delight upon his visitor, and for a moment Tuya thought he would prostrate himself before the slave, so wide were the eyes and smile he turned upon the Hebrew. "Thanks be to Horus, you have arrived!" Tuthmosis exclaimed, clapping his hands.

Carefully maneuvering around the length of chain that bound his ankles, Joseph bowed and pressed his forehead to the floor. "May the king live forever," he said, his rich voice resonating throughout the room. "How may I serve you?"

———

Tuthmosis heard the voice through a daze of wonder. Surely the gods had fashioned and created this man for this moment! In all the temples of Egypt, there was not a priest like this, with tangled hair, a broad chest, and skin as golden as ripe wheat! The priests who stood before him were bald, reedy, flour-faced creatures who spoke in hoarse rasps and bedecked themselves with gold chains while proclaiming their poverty of spirit. Those weak-minded fools had been helpless before the complexity of his dream, but surely this man could unravel the enigma!

"Rise, Hebrew," Tuthmosis said, jerking his hand in Potiphar's direction. "Help him to his feet and remove those bonds." Slowly, stiffly the captain of the guard knelt at the prisoner's feet and pried loose the chains holding the man's ankles.

Tuthmosis lifted his eyes to those of the stranger. "And your name is—?" he asked, his brows slanting the question.

"Paneah," the slave said, nodding in simple dignity.

"He lives," Tuthmosis interpreted. It was a fitting name for this one, a triumphant name and a good omen. But a king could not declare victory prematurely or appear overeager.

"Paneah," he said, turning smoothly toward the chair at Tuya's side. "Last night my sleep was broken by disturbing dreams. No one here can interpret them, but I have heard that you can explain any dream you are told." The prisoner's gaze remained fixed upon him, and Tuthmosis hoped his excitement did not burn as bright in his eyes as it did in his heart.

"It is not in me to interpret dreams, mighty Pharaoh,"

Paneah said, inclining his head slightly. "God will give Pharaoh a favorable answer."

Tuthmosis nodded and perched on the edge of his chair. After studying the prisoner for another moment, he rested his chin upon two fingers and began to recount his nightmare: "My dream was this: I stood on the bank of the Nile, and behold, seven cows, fat and sleek, came up out of the water and grazed in the marsh grass. And then seven other cows came up after them, poor and very ugly and gaunt, such as I have never seen for ugliness in all the land of Egypt. And the lean and ugly cows ate up the first seven fat cows. And yet when they had devoured them, I could not tell that they had eaten, for they were just as ugly and gaunt as before."

A shudder shook him at the haunting memory, and he paused to look away. "Then I awoke," he whispered, his eyes meeting Tuya's. "I remembered nothing but my fear, and my wife bid me sleep again. But I dreamed again and saw seven ears of corn, full and good, come up on a single stalk. But then seven other ears, withered, thin, and scorched by the east wind, sprouted up after them. And the thin ears swallowed the seven good ears. And I awoke, and remembered all, and told these things to the magicians, but no one could explain these things to me."

Every man in the room held his breath while Tuthmosis looked up at the prisoner before him. Pharaoh realized that Potiphar, the guards, and even the servants leaned forward in anticipation of the Hebrew's answer. What would it be?

Paneah bowed his head for a moment as if searching inside himself for words; then he lifted his chin and stared at Pharaoh with blank eyes which gave nothing away. "Pharaoh's dreams are one and the same," he said. "God has told Pharaoh what He is about to do."

"I do not understand," Tuthmosis interrupted. "Which god speaks to me?"

"El Shaddai, the Almighty," Paneah answered. The name rang a distant bell in Tuthmosis's memory. Tuya had said something of this invisible god, which the Hebrews worshiped.

"The seven good cows are seven years," Paneah said, patiently explaining. "And the seven good ears are seven years, the dreams are one and the same. And the seven lean and ugly cows that came up after the others are seven years, and the seven thin ears scorched by the east wind are seven years of famine."

"Famine?" Tuthmosis snapped, the fist of fear tightening in his belly. The old rituals rankled in his memory. The Divine Victim must feed the earth if the people did not eat. . . .

"God has shown you what you must do," Paneah repeated. "Seven years of great abundance are coming in all the land of Egypt. After seven years, famine will come, famine so severe that the abundance will be forgotten, and scarcity will ravage the land. Now as for the repeating of the dream to Pharaoh twice, it means that the matter is determined by God, and He will quickly bring it to pass."

"Famine," Tuthmosis repeated, his mind reeling. "Of what use are seven good years if famine will destroy us in the seven bad years that will follow?"

"God is merciful," Paneah whispered softly. "Let Pharaoh look for a man discerning and wise, and set him over the land of Egypt. Let Pharaoh take action to appoint overseers in charge of the land, and let them exact a fifth of Egypt's produce in the seven years of abundance. Then let them store up the grain for food in the cities under Pharaoh's authority, and let them guard it. And let the food become a reserve for the seven years of famine, so the land of Egypt may not perish during the time of hunger."

Tuthmosis leaned upon the arm of his chair, thinking. This Paneah had no ulterior motive, for he had not asked for an audience with the king. He had no contact with other nations who might wish to rape Egypt and rob it of its produce, for he had been a prisoner for many years and cut off from the world. There was no apparent reason for him to lie.

"And this El Shaddai has revealed this to you?" Tuthmosis asked, lifting his head.

Paneah bowed slightly. "Yes. He is the Almighty One, the God above all others, the Unseen God who cannot be represented by the works of men's hands."

"I will think on these things," Tuthmosis said, nodding abruptly. "You, Paneah, will sleep here in the palace tonight as my guest, not as a prisoner. See to his comfort, Potiphar. You may all leave me now."

The knot of servants and guards at the door bowed and slipped from the room, taking Paneah with them. When they had gone, Tuthmosis turned to the unusually silent Tuya. "Do you believe in him?" he asked, gesturing toward the empty space that still vibrated slightly with the effect of the Hebrew's presence.

"Yes," she whispered, her eyes watering as she stared across the empty room. "I do."

———

Tuthmosis left soon after Joseph had been led away. After placing Yusef in his bed, Tuya paced in her chamber. How could she sleep knowing that Joseph breathed under the same roof? In Potiphar's house she could not sleep until she had first gathered a good-night kiss from Joseph, but those kisses belonged to another lifetime. Surely she was foolish to think of them now.

How strange that Joseph's appearance could put her husband's mind at ease and leave her own in turmoil. Tonight Tuthmosis would sleep like a child, his worries wiped away by Joseph's assurance, but she would watch and wait and pray—for what?

There were so many things she wanted to tell him. She wanted to confess her anger at the news that he had been arrested for attacking Sagira and her wrong of believing him guilty. She wanted to explain the child in her arms, to define her love for the young man who was both her king and her husband. She wanted to tell him that she had prayed for his deliverance from death, and she had recognized El Shaddai's work of preserving Joseph in prison.

His eyes had not caught hers during the interview with Pharaoh. There had been a time when she and Joseph could read each other's thoughts—if she looked into his eyes now, would she understand all that had shaped him in the eight years since they parted? Would he understand her precarious position in the palace? Would he know that she still dreamed of meeting him in Potiphar's garden?

Sighing in frustration, she paced throughout her chamber until a warm air current brought the promise of dawn into the room.

———

Joseph found it hard to believe that he was not still dreaming when he awoke the next morning. The heady scent of lotus blossoms filled the room where he slept on a real mattress. Gauzy curtains blew about his bed as a pair of lovely slave girls tiptoed through the chamber. When he rose up on one elbow, one of the girls giggled and picked up her lute, and in a moment the sweet sounds of music filled the room. The other girl, smiling modestly behind a blush as bright as a desert flower, silently offered up a bowl of fruit for his choosing.

Joseph smiled and waved her away, sinking back upon the bed. In prison he had not once seen a woman, heard music, or tasted the sweetness of fruit, yet all three had been offered to him in one moment. He closed his eyes, overwhelmed by the dreamlike lunacy of it all. What had God done? And why?

After a few moments he sat up, ignoring the curious stares of the slave girls. A basin of water lay upon the floor next to a pair of finely worked leather sandals. A new linen kilt had been folded upon a chair, and he ran his hand over it, relishing its silkiness beneath his palm. Last night he had wanted to run his hand over the softness of Tuya's cheek, but he had disciplined himself not to even glance her way. Interpreting Pharaoh's dream had been far easier than avoiding the magnetic pull of her eyes.

He rose from the bed and slipped into the new kilt. Waiting, he sat in the chair and nibbled on the fruit, amazed at the simple sweetness of it. One of the girls came forward and rested her hand upon his shoulder in an attitude of suggestive submission.

"Dance," Joseph whispered hoarsely, understanding completely what she offered him. His skin burned beneath her touch. "Just dance. I must be ready when Pharaoh summons me."

And so, while one slave postured and the other played her lute, Joseph sat in silence and wondered what God was about to do.

———

A pair of servants, not guards, arrived shortly thereafter to escort Joseph to Pharaoh's throne room. He paused at the threshold of the great double doors leading into Pharaoh's presence, his breath momentarily stolen by the opulence of the dazzling sight beyond. He thought he had seen everything Egypt had to offer, but never had he imagined anything to rival the unabashed elegance and beauty of Pharaoh's royal chamber.

He walked upon shining tiles arranged into the delicate designs of lotus blossoms. The walls of the grand hall glimmered with colorful pictures of the king and queen offering sacrifices to their gods. Windows high above Joseph's head let in light, but not heat, and a gentle breeze swayed throughout the room, dispersing the sweet incense that burned to honor the god who lived within. Hundreds of people, it seemed to Joseph, moved in orderly rows on the left and right sides of the chamber, but the center aisle had been left open for anyone who wished to approach Pharaoh, the reigning king and god of all Egypt.

At the end of the vast aisle, upon a golden throne, Pharaoh waited, his eyes lit with expectation and hope. Next to him, on a similar throne, sat a lavishly decorated woman with eyes too hard for beauty and a chin set in determination. A gold tiara rested upon her massive wig, and on the floor by her sandaled feet a monkey scampered upon a leash. As Joseph approached, he could read the words engraved upon the lady's chair: "Follower of Horus, guide of the ruler, Favorite Lady." If this woman was Pharaoh's favorite lady, Joseph mused, carefully veiling his eyes from her penetrating gaze, then why had he found Tuthmosis in Tuya's chamber?

He could feel Tuya's presence shining from behind the queen's throne, and knew without looking directly at her that she stood with her small son by her side. He wanted to meet her eyes and assure her that he was well, but he did not dare acknowledge her before so many others. So he directed his gaze instead to Queen Mutemwiya, who glanced at him in an oddly keen, speculative look. A richly dressed courtier wearing the Gold of Praise stood at the queen's right hand, and as their eyes met, Joseph was frankly surprised at the strong emotion that flickered for a moment over the man's face—it was hatred distilled to its essence.

Even here, there are enemies. No wonder Tuya is in danger. Reaching the throne, Joseph bowed before Pharaoh who today wore his full regalia. His short linen garment was girdled at the waist by an elaborate beadwork belt, supporting a sporran of panther pelt. From the back of the king's belt hung the traditional jackal's tail, and a heavy golden chain gleamed upon his chest. He wore the tall white helmetlike crown on his noble head, and the artificial beard, yet another symbol of divine authority, extended from Pharaoh's chin and was held in place by two slender leather loops hanging from the king's ears.

Pharaoh stood, extending the crook and flail. "Rise, Paneah, my much beloved friend and servant," Tuthmosis said, his voice like a warm embrace in the formal atmo-

sphere. "Last night you visited me and gave me the interpretation of my dream. You were the light that shone upon
the truth God sought to reveal to me, and through your
voice I saw the path that lies ahead for all Egypt. Tell these
assembled here, Paneah, how you came to be my light in
darkness."

Joseph cleared his throat as his face tightened. "I am not
the light, mighty Pharaoh. God is the one who reveals all."

"And which god is this light?" Pharaoh asked, theatri-
cally spreading his hands toward the scowling priests who
had been unable to solve his dilemma.

"The unseen God of my fathers," Joseph answered.
"The Creator. The beginning of all that is, and all that ever
shall be."

Pharaoh nodded and crossed the crook and flail across
his chest. "Take down my words, scribes, and hearken unto
me, all you who listen. Two nights ago I did not sleep, for
I was troubled by the dream this God revealed to me. Last
night I did not sleep, for I spent the night devising a plan
to insure Egypt's salvation. Seven years of abundance are
coming to the Upper and Lower Kingdoms, then seven
years of dire famine. The God who declared this future has
also revealed how we are to prosper through it."

The room grew silent, as if the walls themselves paused
to listen to Pharaoh's words. Tuthmosis stood in the hush,
exulting in the moment, and then lifted his chin to speak.
"I have consulted with my counselors and the priests of my
house, and they have agreed with what I am about to do.
Can we find another man like this, in whom is a divine
spirit?" The king stretched his hand toward Joseph as he
glanced around the assembled company. "Can we find a
man better equipped to lead Egypt through the darkness
than this one who has shone the light today?"

The crowd stirred, but no one dared offer another name.
Pharaoh put aside the crook and flail, and a collective gasp
broke the silence as the king descended from the dais and
walked toward Joseph. Apparently, Joseph mused, the di-

vine Pharaoh did not often leave his throne to walk toward a mere man.

"Since God has informed you of these things which are to come," Pharaoh said, lifting his hand until it rested upon Joseph's shoulder, "there is no one so discerning and wise as you are. You shall be over my house, and according to your command all my people shall do homage; only in the throne will I be greater than you. I have set you today over all the land of Egypt, and to signify that you speak with my voice, I give you my ring."

Pharaoh dropped his hand and fumbled with the scarab ring upon his finger, and for a moment Joseph caught sight of the seventeen-year-old boy inside the king. The ring resisted stubbornly; the boy-king frowned; then the scarab slid from Pharaoh's finger. With a sigh of relief, Tuthmosis held the golden band between his thumb and forefinger and presented it to Joseph.

"Thank you, my king," Joseph said, lowering himself to his knees. He was not sure what behavior was appropriate, but he took the ring and slid it on his own finger while Tuthmosis smiled in approval. "You shall have garments of fine linen," Pharaoh went on, clapping his hands. Instantly a group of slaves appeared from a room behind the throne, each carrying a box of the most exquisitely woven kilts and cloaks that Joseph had ever seen.

"And then, there is this," Pharaoh said, lifting the chain of gold from his neck. "My father bestowed the Gold of Praise only twice in his lifetime: once to Potiphar, captain of his guard, and once to Narmer, who has also served me well."

The courtier standing beside Queen Mutemwiya nodded gravely in acknowledgment of the king's praise.

"But to you, Paneah, I give the Gold of Praise and every honor I can imagine. This very day you will ride in the chariot behind me throughout Thebes. When my warriors cry out, 'Bow the Knee' in reference to me, every knee in Egypt shall bow in honor of you, also." Tuthmosis slipped the Gold of Praise about Joseph's neck, then stepped back as if to regard his handiwork. "Though I am Pharaoh," he called, his voice echoing off the walls, "yet without your permission no one shall raise his hand or foot in all the land of Egypt."

The order was unprecedented. Every face in the room bore the stamp of complete astonishment.

"May Pharaoh live forever," Joseph replied, lowering his head to the floor. It was a formal and automatic response, for his mind swam with disconcerting thoughts, and he could think of no other reply. He had traveled a great distance in less than a day, from a pit to the throne of the mightiest kingdom on earth.

"And there is this in conclusion," Pharaoh said, stepping back to the dais. His pronounced cheekbones and youthful, clear skin gleamed in the light of morning. "You have been called Paneah, *he lives*, and today I decree that you shall henceforth be called Zaphenath-paneah, *God speaks, he lives*. For today I have learned that the unknown god of whom I have heard much truly lives and speaks through His servants. And so that your seed may be forever established upon the earth, Zaphenath-paneah, I give you Asenath, the daughter of Potiphera, priest of On, to be your wife."

A murmur of pleasant surprise rippled through the crowd, a pair of silver trumpets shrilled, and the double doors at the far end of the room opened. Joseph turned as four priests entered with solemn steps, each carrying a pole to support a wedding canopy. Under the canopy walked a slender maiden in a dark Egyptian wig. For some shapeless reason, Joseph found that his eyes blurred with tears; he could not even distinguish the face of his bride.

Pharaoh had passed a sleepless night in order to honor him. Joseph knew he could not insult the royal benevolence by refusing any part of this tribute.

A tangible whispering floated through the air as Joseph woodenly walked toward his bride. Frankly jealous smiles and nodding faces wrapped around him like water around a rock. He stood beneath the wedding canopy as much a prisoner of fortune as Potiphar had been years before.

At the thought of Potiphar and Sagira, Joseph turned suddenly to the girl at his side. He scanned her countenance with cautiously appraising eyes, but upon that lovely face he saw only youth and freshness, submission, and a trace of anxiety. It was a quiet, oval face, dark and rather delicate, with not a trace of Sagira evident in either its composition or expression.

Turning to the priest in relief, Joseph accepted the hand of his bride.

⟶ Twenty-eight ⟵

THE SMILE ON TUYA'S FACE CHILLED AS JOSEPH'S new wife accepted the traditional crust of bread he offered. Everything had been set in readiness for a wedding—the canopy, the flowers, the incense. Why had she not recognized the signs? She should have known what Tuthmosis would do. She should have prepared herself for this eventuality.

Of course Joseph should be married; what man did not want children and a wife of his own? It would be unfair for her to expect Joseph to remain celibate while she enjoyed a husband, and unreasonable to think that Joseph's God would set him apart from other men. Though he had been able to withstand the temptation Sagira flaunted, Tuya had heard his heart pound and felt the heat in his kiss. More than any other woman, she knew that Joseph ought to be married. He had waited long enough for love.

But why could I not be the woman he loves? Why, Almighty God, would You not work this miracle? You freed Taharka from prison; You kept Joseph safe from Sagira; You have lifted my love to the position of leadership and authority that he deserves. I know that You are powerful. I agree with Your purposes. So why could You not bring Joseph into my arms?

Perhaps the Almighty God concerned himself with matters of life and death but not with matters of the heart. And yet Joseph had told her that his God loved His people with a jealous love. If this God felt human emotion, could He not see that her heart was breaking? If He loved her as He loved Joseph, why would He not do something about her pain?

One of the priests lifted the stone jar, another handed Joseph the sword. With one powerful, swift movement Joseph swung the blade in a clear arc, destroying the fragile pottery just as surely as his marriage had shattered Tuya's heart.

The crowd roared in jubilant approval. Tuthmosis beamed from his throne, then stepped from the dais for the ceremonial chariot ride through the streets of Thebes. The crowd swept forward, emptying the throne room in an enthusiastic rush, but Tuya hung back along the fringes of the crowd, keeping Yusef's hand tightly clenched in her own.

"Mama sad?" Yusef asked, raising his chubby face to hers.

"No, dear, Mama is happy," she said, smiling through the tears that jeweled her lashes.

————————

Pharaoh ordered his stonemasons to begin building a house for his new vizier, Zaphenath-paneah. From her chamber in the palace, Tuya could hear the sounds of chisel and cudgel, of axe and saw. The laborers worked from the rising of the sun till the setting of it, and as his house rose from a hilltop near the palace, Zaphenath-paneah conducted his affairs from Pharaoh's own throne room.

Egypt had known viziers before, but never one with this scope of power. With Pharaoh's full authority, Zaphenath-paneah divided the entire kingdom into tracts of land and classified them according to their fertility. There were three categories: those lands that regularly received the Nile's fertile flood, those that sometimes did, and those that seldom or never did. For the next seven years, Zaphenath-paneah proclaimed, taxes would be calculated according to the flood state at various locations along the river beginning at the isle of Elephantine near the first cataract. Based upon this measurement, crop quotas would be assigned. Four-fifths of the land's expected bounty would belong to the people who worked it, but one-fifth would belong to

Pharaoh and must be returned for storage in Pharaoh's granaries.

Tuya wondered privately how well Asenath had come to know her new husband, for almost immediately after his appointment, Joseph set off upon a tour of Egypt to determine if the present nomarchs were capable of gathering in the harvest from the coming years of plenty. A corps of scribes, accountants, and engineers accompanied him on his travels, and Pharaoh received daily reports that his vizier was busily collecting records of all the houses and estates in Egypt. While the scribes questioned the nervous nomarchs about their past administration and collection of taxes, engineers surveyed the land to best determine where the huge, cone-shaped granaries should be built for storage of grain. In cities where the vizier found the nomarchs resentful, unscrupulous, or inept, new local officials were appointed to oversee the gathering in of the earth's bounty.

Tuthmosis had been wise, Tuya realized, to appoint a vizier to handle the complicated details of taxation, for now the young king was free to concentrate on the work that he loved. Already he had restored the ancient Sphinx to its former grandeur; now he concentrated on raising the fallen obelisk of Tuthmosis III at Karnak. Many ancient temples and monuments had fallen into disrepair, and Tuthmosis, the dreamer, was far happier restoring the glory of the past than working out the details of a complicated present.

Not only did Joseph have to contend with the coming famine, but to him also fell the traditional duties of a vizier. The viziers of Egypt's past bore a host of titles and had filled at least thirty major functions, including: Manager of the King's Palace, Guardian of the Public Works, General of the King's Army, Commander of the King's Peace-Keepers, Patron of the Royal Artisans, Dispenser of Justice and Keeper of the Law, Judge over the High Court of the Land, Overseer of the Royal Farms and Granaries, Hand to Distribute Food to Laborers and the King's Officials, and He Who Gathers in the King's Taxes.

Perhaps, Tuya thought with a wry smile as she listened to the various reports Joseph sent daily to Tuthmosis, *the Almighty God prevented me from marrying Joseph because Egypt's new vizier has no time for a wife.* But still her heart leapt with joy when she heard that Zaphenath-paneah had finally returned to Thebes. Curbing her eagerness, she waited two full ten-day weeks before joining the others who assembled at the palace each morning in the hope that they would gain an audience with the king's vizier.

"Dress me carefully, please," she told her handmaid, but she dared not speak the reason for her concern: *for this morning I have decided to face Joseph.* Knowing Joseph's preference for simple things, from her wardrobe chest she selected a simple gown of cream-colored linen and a narrow band of gold for her throat. Modest leather slippers completed her outfit, and in her hand she carried a single lotus blossom, a symbol of their hours together in Potiphar's garden. Quietly leaving Yusef in the care of his nurse, Tuya slipped out of her chamber and down to the hall that had been designated a temporary reception room for the vizier.

A throng of dignitaries and nobles waited outside the chamber's closed doors, yet the crowd parted like the petals of a flower as Tuya approached. No one dared question her presence, for anyone might approach the vizier and offer a word of advice or congratulation, but Tuya spied more than one lifted eyebrow. Intuitively, she knew it would not be wise to speak with Joseph alone. The more witnesses to her audience with him, the safer they both would be.

Every morning the vizier went first to Pharaoh's private chamber for an intimate council, and the esteemed Zaphenath-paneah had not yet arrived to face his visitors. Tuya waited, hoping he would not leave her long with the men who cast furtive glances her way, and within the space of a few moments she heard the steady tramping of an approaching entourage. Joseph swept past her, surrounded by a host of scribes and supercilious nobles, but his eye caught hers through the crowd and his lips mouthed her name: *Tuya!* She caught a glimpse of fondness in his eyes as his guardians pulled him away, and her heart fluttered at the thought that he *remembered.*

For an hour, she waited. Those who had previous appointments came and went, and finally a servant dipped his knee before her. "Queen Tuya, the vizier bids me call for you," he said, motioning toward the reception chamber. Her heart pounding, Tuya rose and followed the vizier's servant.

Joseph sat on a gilded chair not unlike Pharaoh's throne. A thick carpet lay under his feet, the baton of state across his hands. The books of Egypt's laws—forty-two volumes containing all the wisdom of the world—were open on stands behind his chair, and an assortment of Pharaoh's officials and ministers stood around the vizier, intensely curious expressions on their faces as Tuya approached.

She smiled at her husband's ministers, then turned to Joseph. On the night of his release from prison he had appeared as wild as an unbroken horse; today he seemed no less powerful, but Zaphenath-paneah was as Egyptian as any man born along the Nile. He wore a fine pleated kilt and a mantle of leopard skin, the traditional garb of a prince. A handsome, clean-cut wig covered his head, and his paint-lengthened eyes smiled at the sight of her. "I am honored, Queen Tuya," he said, his voice reaching her as if from worlds away.

If not for the memories that came crowding back at the sound of his voice, she would have thought Joseph the Hebrew a figment of her imagination. She could see little of him in the king's vizier. Gone was the thick, unruly hair, the faltering accent, the boyish laugh. This stranger was an exquisite man, but he was not the youth she had known and loved.

"What brings Pharaoh's wife to me?" he asked, giving her a careful smile.

"One of Pharaoh's many wives," she said, searching for the meaning behind his greeting. Had he chosen those words as casually as his tone implied? Or was he trying to gently remind her that they were not the people they once had been?

"I come, my lord vizier, to welcome you to the palace." She bowed her head in a gesture of respect, grateful for the opportunity to lower her eyes as she forced her next words: "And, of course, to congratulate you on your marriage."

"Thank you." He hesitated as though he were feeling his way through a treacherous maze. "I had hoped we would have a chance to speak, gracious lady."

"Truly?" She lifted her head quickly. His dark eyes snapped with some urgent message, and she tightened her hand around the flower she carried, frustrated by the casually indifferent ministers who listened to every word. Joseph wanted to speak freely—what would he say?

Suddenly he stood with a graceful economy of movement and clapped his hands. "Clear the room of all who await business with the vizier," he ordered. "Queen Tuya should not have to speak before the common crowd."

"Let your servants remain, my lord," she whispered urgently, catching his eye. Rash actions would arouse suspicion, and as much as Tuya wanted to speak with him privately, she knew she did not dare. Pharaoh's court was quicksand; she had seen firsthand how petty jealousies and ambitions could flare to injure the innocent. Amenhotep's court had been rife with strife, and Tuthmosis was young enough to be easily misled.

"Of course. My servants shall remain, but my scribes"— Joseph gave the three men who sat at his right hand a blazing smile—"wait in the anteroom, please. The words of Pharaoh's wife do not need to be recorded."

Disgruntled, the men gathered their pens, parchments, and books and left the room, casting curious glances over their shoulders as they exited. When everyone had gone but the two servants who lingered at the door, Joseph stepped from the dais and the stiff, formal guise of the Egyptian vizier fell away. The expression in his eyes brought color rushing into Tuya's cheeks. For a dizzying moment the room whirled madly around her.

"Steady," Joseph murmured in a low voice. "You must remember where you are. There are many eyes about."

"I am all right," she said, pressing her hand to her throat. She breathed deeply, calming her heightened nerves, aware that the servants watched from the far side of the room. No doubt other faces were pressed to the slit of light between the doors.

"I have wanted to thank you, Zaphenath-paneah," she said, strengthening her voice so the eavesdroppers could hear. "You have done my husband and the kingdom a very great service."

"God has brought us to this place," Joseph answered, his voice ringing through the hall. "But I am enjoying the work. Egypt is a fascinating land."

"I have prayed to your God," she confessed in a whisper, suddenly as embarrassed as a child caught in a misdeed. "I prayed for Taharka's release, and when I saw that your God could deliver him, I prayed for you, too."

"And I thought my prayers did all the work," Joseph answered, his voice brimming with warmth. He thrust his hands behind his back and regarded her with honest affection. "It is comforting to know that I was in your thoughts."

A feeling of glorious happiness sprang up in her heart. "I nearly gave up," she said, looking away from his bold, black eyes. "But when I heard that Potiphar had spared your life, I knew your God would preserve you. Even though I thought you guilty at first—"

"Speak no more of the past," Joseph interrupted, lowering his voice. "I have prayed for you these many years, and I have begged God for an opportunity to speak to you."

His words made her breath leave her body. Was he about

to confess that he loved her still? Would he suggest a rendezvous? For what purpose? If they were to meet, even as friends, suspicious questions would be asked. A score of alluring and hideous thoughts flashed through her mind, and she stared at him, her mouth slightly open.

"I have dreamed again." His eyes darted toward the doors at the rear of the room; his voice was a thin whisper in the empty space between them. "The dream was another warning from God, Tuya. You and your son are in danger."

"Yusef?" she cried, momentarily forgetting everything else.

A corner of Joseph's mouth lifted in a half-smile. "Your son is called Yusef?"

"It is only his baby name," she answered, feeling the color rise in her face. "Pharaoh does not know what it means. I thought that if I could not have you, at least I could love my Yusef—"

"You must take care, Tuya," he whispered, a dark warning in his voice. "I do not know where the danger lies, but this evil would not hesitate to destroy Pharaoh as well."

Tuya shook her head, shrugging off his concern. "Like Tuthmosis, you are always dreaming," she said, giving him a rueful smile. "Is there danger in the court? Certainly, for even the suggestion of impropriety could spell exile for me and my son. But I am no threat to anyone. I hold no ambitions, I do not take much of Pharaoh's time. And Tuthmosis is a good king; he wants to do right, and he has surrounded himself with wise counselors." She lifted an eyebrow. "As you should know, Zaphenath-paneah."

Joseph ignored the compliment. "Even so, you must be careful. When I first had the dream, prison walls hindered me from warning you. And now," he tightened the arms he held behind his back, "I am hindered in another way."

"I know," she answered, cutting him off. Again the conversation threatened to pick up the strings of time, and a wave of emotion swept over her, choking off the words she wanted to say. She started to move toward him, hoping he could read her heart, but he backed up a hasty half-step and lifted his hands in warning.

Tears of shame stung her eyes. "Joseph," she said, staring at the floor as she strained to push her embarrassment aside, "you need not fear me. I will not bait you as Sagira did. I will not touch you. I will not linger in the hall for a glimpse of you. I will not give anyone cause to say that I am unfaithful to my husband or you to your wife."

She paused, struggling to gain control over her unsteady voice. Outside the room she could hear the murmur of voices, sudden laughter, and shushing sounds as waiting nobles remembered that a queen and the vizier held a conference nearby.

After a long moment, she met his eyes. "Perhaps the danger you dreamt of lies in Zaphenath-paneah. I am safe as long as I guard my heart from you."

"And they say I am the one who is wise," he murmured, his eyes darkening with a shadow of the love she remembered.

Tuya felt her heart turn over the way it always had when he looked at her, and the nostalgic memory made her smile. "Your God has surprised me yet again," she whispered, "and I cannot fight against the Almighty."

"My God," Joseph answered, giving her a quick smile, "has our good in mind. We must trust Him."

"Trust?" She could not keep a shade of bitterness from her laugh. "I do not know how. I know your God is powerful; I have seen Him preserve life." She wanted to add, *But since He has kept us apart, my heart wonders if He can truly be good!* She bit back those words and finished in a level voice: "You can trust in this, my Joseph—I have never loved another man the way I loved you."

Like the ripple of an underground spring, compassion stirred in his eyes. "Do not be sad, Tuya. God will not leave you alone. You must trust Him to provide for your needs—"

Suddenly she wanted to slap him. "You keep using that word!" she hissed. "I want to trust, Joseph. Throughout my entire life I have searched for one person who would remain with me no matter what. But there is no constancy in this world! I thought I could rely on you, but you would not believe my warning about Sagira, and look what happened! And now, through some miracle, we face each other again and my head tells me one thing while my heart screams something else. I know we cannot be together, but what am I to do with the unspent love in my heart?"

"Faith is the heart of the mind," he answered, his dark eyes moving away from hers. "Despite the feelings of your heart and the reflections of your mind, trust God to work for your good."

"I see. I should trust El Shaddai to take care of me, so you will no longer be bothered by dreams." She jerked her chin upward. "So be it. Fret not for me or my son, Zaphenath-paneah. I will not be unfaithful to Pharaoh in thought or deed. I will not tug on the loyalty you wish to give your wife."

She nodded abruptly and pivoted on the ball of her foot, then stopped as a sudden thought whipped into her mind. "The ancient gods of Egypt offer us spells to destroy our enemies," she said, tossing the words over her shoulder. "Has the Almighty God a ritual to destroy this enemy love? Perhaps He will have mercy on me and rid my heart of this troublesome emotion."

"The Lord God does not engage in magic," Joseph said, shaking his head as he walked slowly back to his chair. "But He often works in ways we cannot understand. My father, for instance, used to tell the story of my great-grandfather Abraham and his much-beloved son, Isaac." He spoke slowly, as if he dictated to scribes who were recording every word. "Isaac was the son of Abraham's old age, but El Shaddai commanded Abraham to offer the boy as a sacrifice unto the Lord."

Despite her own turmoil, Tuya felt a whisper of terrified sympathy run through her. "Your God would command such a thing?"

"You asked if He would destroy love," Joseph said, sinking into his chair. He looked out at her with a level gaze. "Judge for yourself. Abraham obeyed, placing his total trust in God. He risked everything he held dear, certain that God would not kill the one he loved. He was convinced that God would raise the boy from the dead, if necessary."

"Did the child die?"

Joseph tented his fingers and leaned forward. "Abraham climbed to the chosen mountain, gathered stones for an altar, and embraced his son before binding the boy's hands and feet. He placed Isaac upon the wood for a burnt offering, then lifted his dagger to strike his son."

His voice softened as he sat there, gazing into private space. "But the angel of the Lord stopped Abraham's hand. A ram, caught in the thicket, was offered as the sacrifice instead of the boy."

Tuya frowned, unable to understand the point of the story. "If your God is almighty and all-knowing," she asked, frowning, "why did He have to test this Abraham?"

"Abraham was not the only one put to the test," Joseph answered, looking up at her with an invitation in the dark depths of his eyes. "God was, also. Abraham tested the strength and goodness of God. He learned that no one can live in doubt when he has prayed in faith."

Tuya paused, considering the story. If El Shaddai asked her to sacrifice her son, she would retreat, refuse, run away. Yusef was the only person in the world who belonged only to her, and she would not surrender him even for the Almighty.

As anxious as a child who has stumbled on something she does not understand, Tuya bid Joseph a hasty farewell and swept from the reception hall.

Two days later, Pharaoh came to Tuya's chambers by night. He played for a few moments with Yusef, then motioned for the child's nurse to take the boy away. When they had gone, he sank onto the small couch in the front room of Tuya's quarters and patted the empty space next to him. "So, my wife," he said, waiting for her to sit, "we have not spent much time together in the last few months. And it occurs to me that I have not lately told you how beautiful you are."

"Dear Pharaoh," she murmured, sinking onto the couch but ducking his embrace as she bent to pick up one of Yusef's paddle dolls. "There has been no time available for me. You spend more time with your new vizier than with me or your son—"

"He is a marvel, is he not, Tuya?" Tuthmosis said, settling into the gentle curve of the couch.

"Our son? I have always thought so."

"I meant the vizier. He is so wise! For months the priests of Ptah in Memphis have badgered me about a territorial conflict, but Zaphenath-paneah heard their complaint and settled their dispute in an hour! The plan for storing the harvest is well begun, and the Nile-readers from Elephantine have predicted that the flood will be high this year. The land will be green with life this spring, and the abundance will be great—"

"Hush," Tuya said, turning to face him. She tucked one leg under her body and leaned toward him, playfully pressing her finger over his lips. "I have heard too much already about the bountiful crop we will have. The entire palace is abuzz with talk of Zaphenath-paneah."

"He is a wonder."

"Of course, my husband. Would you chose anyone less than wonderful for your vizier? Now, let us talk about your temple or the work at Karnak, anything but Zaphenath-Paneah." She dropped her hands and folded them in her lap, aware that Tuthmosis's eyes had narrowed. He pinned her with a long, silent scrutiny.

"Is something wrong, my husband?"

For a moment he squinted, as if in embarrassment. "Did you know him, Tuya, when you lived in Potiphar's house?"

Sudden fear spurred her heart to beat unevenly. He had merely asked a question, this was not an interrogation, and yet she felt her face stiffen in fear. What had he heard? Someone had told him of her visit to the vizier, of the whispered conversation, of the dismay on her face when she fled from Joseph's presence. She must sort out her thoughts, arrange them, impose order before she could answer, but there was no time for anything but simple honesty.

"Yes, my husband," she answered, meeting his eyes. "I knew him."

"Did you love him?"

By all the gods, who had put these ideas into his head? Tuya closed her eyes, searching for a way to tell the truth without wounding this young man who was as vulnerable as he was powerful. He had been a child during the time she loved Joseph, and even though she still carried the memory of that love in her heart, the passion did not burn with the intensity it once had. . . .

"My husband," she said, turning to lace her arms about his neck. "Do you love me?"

"Yes," he said, drawing back slightly as the question offended him. "You know I do."

"And do you love Queen Mutemwiya?"

He gave her an impenitent grin. "Tuya, you know you should not ask such things."

"I have known you forever, I can ask anything. So, do you love Queen Mut?"

His mouth tipped in a grudging smile. "A little."

Tuya lightly traced his brow with her finger. "And the girls from the harem, my husband, do you love them?"

"Tuya, that is not fair. A king should not show partiality."

"Then the answer is yes. You love all of us, my husband, but in different ways."

The king suddenly unsmiled. "What has this to do with my question? I am waiting for an answer."

She sighed and feathered her hands over his strong

chest. "Yes, my husband, I knew Zaphenath-paneah when he served in Potiphar's house. I loved him. And then I entered the palace and married you. I love you in a far different way, for you are my king, my husband, and the father of my son, who is dearer than life to me. And so, though I once loved Zaphenath-paneah, my love for you gives breath and purpose to my life."

She pressed her cheek to the flesh over his heart, hoping her words would assuage his doubts. He remained silent, thinking about her answer, and after a moment she felt his lips brush her hair.

———

He rose from her bed early the next morning. "As soon as Zaphenath-paneah's trial is settled, we shall go down to Memphis and visit the temples there," he said, stretching lazily in the dim light of the room. "Would you like to come?"

"A trial?" Tuya echoed, trying to throw off lingering wisps of sleep. "What trial?"

"The high priest has suggested that my vizier would be more respected if his name were cleared," Tuthmosis answered, adjusting the striped linen headpiece he wore while within the palace. "Today we shall summon those who had him imprisoned. I shall render my judgment and the gods shall acquit the innocent and condemn the guilty."

"Sagira and Potiphar?" Tuya sat up, suddenly wide awake. "You will call Sagira and Potiphar as witnesses?"

"I will call Potiphar as the judge and his wife as the accuser. And since the captain of my guard must report to my vizier, I am certain Potiphar will be relieved when Zaphenath-paneah's name is cleared." A sympathetic chuckle escaped him. "Surely he has felt awkward accepting orders from the man he sentenced to prison."

Tuthmosis moved casually out of the room as if this day were the same as any other, but Tuya sprang out of bed and hastily slipped into a morning dress, then clapped her hands to summon her maids. This day would bring high drama to Pharaoh's court, and Tuya wanted to look her best. Once the news spread, everyone who was anyone in Thebes would fly to Pharaoh's court like wasps shaken from their winter sleep.

The royal summons came before the Boat-of-Millions-of-Years had reached its zenith in the sky. Potiphar read the message with a quick glance, then let the scroll fall from his hands onto the dusty marble floor of his once-elegant villa.

So it had come to this. For two months he had sneeringly dismissed the knowledge that his men snickered behind his back, but now the rumors would be publicly confirmed. Pharaoh's gallant Potiphar, who wore the Gold of Praise and commanded Tens of Thousands, had been duped by his wife. His tongue had condemned an innocent man to a lifetime of imprisonment. Worst of all, Pharaoh had openly declared that a divine spirit rested in the innocent man who was now the vizier of all Egypt.

"How was I to know, Paneah?" Potiphar mumbled, looking around at the hall which had been one of the loveliest rooms in Thebes. The furniture lay broken and soiled now, the gardens and fields outside were withered and burned by the sun. There were no servants to tend to the villa, for most had been sold to satisfy Sagira's gambling debts. The breath of blessing that had arrived with Paneah departed with him, also.

At first Potiphar blamed his troubles on Sagira's drinking and the excesses of her lovers, but now the truth would be whispered in every villa and dwelling of Thebes. "My neglect drove my wife to attempt the seduction of a god," he whispered brokenly, gripping the hilt of his sword until his knuckles whitened. "And now, Sagira, we will both pay for our crimes."

Today he had been commanded to stand before Tuthmosis IV as he had stood before Amenhotep and Tuthmosis III. But instead of praise and honor, he would hear condemnation from the lips of his king: "You, Captain of the Guard, Appointed One of Pharaoh, have grievously erred. You have stolen six years of an innocent man's life. . . ."

This young king would not consider the injustice done to Sagira. Whatever her faults, she had married Pharaoh's choice, expecting a full measure of a husband's love and attention. She hadn't even received the full measure of a man.

Horses' hooves drummed against the dry earth of the courtyard; the voices of messengers rang out to command him to the king's court. Potiphar stood at attention and pulled his sword from its belt. "Hail to thee, Zaphenath-paneah," he said, bringing the golden hilt of his sword to his scarred face. "*God speaks, he lives!* Live in peace, my son Paneah, for I cannot!"

With a defiant flourish, he swung the blade through the air in a wide slash, then he knelt, his knees cracking against the tile floor. Placing the sharpened point of the blade in an open space between his ribs, he saluted his king in a mocking whisper. "Farewell, Pharaoh, my only god."

Bracing the hilt of the sword against the floor, Potiphar thrust himself forward upon the blade.

Twenty-nine

NEWS OF POTIPHAR'S SUICIDE REACHED THE COURT just ahead of Sagira. When one of the guards told her the news, her only reaction was a subtle increase in wariness. She had long dropped any values or dedications beyond her own body, and Potiphar's death did not rend the veil of drunken bitterness that enclosed her.

Walking into the throne room, she sensed the tide of public opinion had altered. An hour ago she had been considered a pitiful, foolish woman, hardly worthy of notice. But the crowd in Pharaoh's court room thirsted to right the wrong done to Zaphenath-paneah. Potiphar, who might have borne more than his share of the scorn and disgrace, had deserted her. She alone would stand and face the society that had embraced her former slave. The painted faces that turned toward her seemed to whisper *outcast, she-devil.*

But she would not take Potiphar's cowardly way out. Through the years since Paneah's rejection she had learned to distance herself from humiliation and pain. Nothing would ever hurt her again. And she was still Pharaoh's cousin. Royal blood would always flow in her veins.

The revenge-hungry crowd in the judgment hall parted and silenced as she walked forward, her mind thumbing through names and faces along the wall. She knew all these people, had drunk at their parties, danced for their entertainment. They had laughed at her, teased her, praised her for her jewelry, her fine clothes, her handsome servants.

She smiled with remembered pleasure. Paneah had

liked her, too, despite his resolve to keep her at arms' length. He had been flattered by her interest, pleased at her attentiveness, honored by her desire to be with him. The memory of that final night shuddered through her mind like an unwelcome chill, but Sagira passed over it and let her mind run backward. The memories were hazy, no longer in focus, but she remembered Paneah's laugh, his awkward attempts to retreat from her embraces, his embarrassed fumbling with papers and pens whenever she happened to run her hand over his honey-colored skin. She had done everything for him because she loved him, and because of the prophecy, the child she had never borne . . .

She stopped before the golden throne. Pharaoh sat in front of her, looking very much like a teenager, and beside him sat the stern-faced queen. Sagira gave her kingly cousin a brief smile and searched the royal family for Tuya. There! She stood behind a pair of guards, one arm across her chest, the other hanging limply, the pose of an insecure schoolgirl. But her features were lovely still, as handsomely sculpted as the statues of Isis in the temple.

A trumpet blared behind her and Sagira jumped, not used to the sound.

"O Pharaoh, live forever," someone called at her right hand, and Sagira hugged herself and trembled. Though she had not heard it in years, she knew that voice.

She turned slowly. *He* stood there, dressed in the robe of a king, with a golden crown on his head and the Gold of Praise about his neck. A great exultation filled Sagira's chest until she thought it would burst. Paneah, her Paneah, was more beautiful than ever, and today she would tell the world how badly he wanted her!

Paneah spoke to Pharaoh, and the king replied; but Sagira hardly heard a word, so dazed was she by the simple fact that Paneah stood beside her. More magnificent than any mortal man, his very words made the pillars in the hall sway and rumble.

Without warning, the vision turned to her and spoke. She blinked several times, then staggered upon her feet. "What?" she asked, gazing up at him from beneath the heavy fringe of her wig. "Did you speak, my beautiful one?"

The faces around her tumbled into laughter, but Sagira ignored them. Let them laugh. At last, finally, Paneah stood by her side!

He looked at her with a tinge of sadness in his eyes. "I will repeat the question. Do you still say that I, your slave, attacked you?" he asked, speaking slowly and carefully.

Sagira smiled at him with white teeth, white lips, and white rage. How long she had waited for this moment! "Of course you attacked me," she said, clenching her hands as she leaned toward him. "You were in love with me. You wanted me to bear your son."

The laughter in the room abruptly ceased. Sagira stood in the silence, goading herself with her memories the same way a desert lion lashes up his temper with the bony spike in the end of his tail before he charges at the hunter. He had wanted her! He had sought her arms for comfort; she had wiped his tears with her hands! She was not so foolish as to throw her pride after a slave, a man who could bring her nothing but heartache!

Paneah turned away and said something to Pharaoh, who replied again while Sagira played her blazing smile upon the assembled crowd. Suddenly the doors behind her opened with a sound like the clap of thunder, and Sagira whirled around to face another ghost from the past.

"Ramla!"

The priestess nodded as she walked forward, a cynical, amused resentment evident in the slight curl of her upper lip. Tall and formidable, she approached and saluted Pharaoh with a stiff bow.

"Tell us what you know about this situation," the vizier commanded, and then Ramla's voice, high-pitched and reedy, echoed in the hall. The words poured over Sagira like water over a rock, an endless stream that had no meaning. Sagira heard Ramla's voice as it had spoken years before, when the optimism of youth had colored their lives: *You will be remembered through all time . . . as long as men walk upon the earth, they will speak of you. Your memory will be immortal . . . you will leave an imprint upon the sands of time that cannot be erased.*

With a sudden intake of breath, Sagira returned to the present. "She thought the prophecy meant she would have a baby to replace the present line of Pharaohs," Ramla was saying.

Treason!

"She wanted to conceive a child with a slave to punish her husband. And she was certain that this child would rise to replace Amenhotep's own son."

Conspiracy! I shall die for this!

Pharaoh's face flushed crimson. "I need to hear no more," he said, his knuckles tightening around the crook and flail in his hands "I find you, Sagira, wife of Potiphar, guilty of treason, of conspiracy, of giving false witness against an innocent man!"

The rage in him was a living thing; the assembly quaked before it.

With a visible effort, Pharaoh reined in his temper and turned to his vizier. "I have rendered judgment in your place because you were personally involved in this situation," he said, his anger lingering like an invisible dagger that must soon find its way into Sagira's breast. "But you are the Dispenser of Justice, Zaphenath-paneah. You shall decide what this woman's fate will be."

"Pharaoh gives me complete freedom?"

"I do." The king's long nose was pinched and white with resentful rage, but Sagira kept her eyes fixed on him, not daring to look at Paneah. Undoubtedly a deep-buried fire of anger had kept him alive in prison, and now those flames would consume her.

Her beloved Paneah! How could he hurt her?

"I grant Lady Sagira freedom to return to her house," the vizier said, his voice soft and eminently reasonable. "Furthermore, I shall appoint a manager to oversee her affairs so that Potiphar's estate may once again rise to its position of glory. From my own estate I grant her two handmaids who will care for her health and see that she does not harm herself."

Sagira stared at the king in total incredulity. Her mind had surely snapped. He had ordered her death, and her brain had mistranslated the sentence. Send her home? What a jest!

But Pharaoh seemed as surprised as she. "This is a most unusual judgment, Zaphenath-paneah," he said, his brows lifting in astonishment. "Are you certain this is what you wish to do?"

"For as long as the lady lives, she shall remain under my guardianship," the vizier answered. "I shall appoint honest and fair men to see that Lady Sagira will not want for anything. I believe she has suffered enough, my king."

The line of Pharaoh's mouth curved; then he nodded. "Thus shall it be," he said, his voice ringing through the judgment hall. "Let it be known throughout the kingdom that Zaphenath-paneah was unjustly accused and imprisoned, and that the Lady Sagira has this day been found guilty and shown mercy."

For the first time since hearing his judgment, Sagira turned to look at Paneah. If he had ordered her thrown to the crocodiles, she would have spat in his face and then wrapped the rags of her dignity about her and marched down to the Nile. She did not know how to cope with kindness.

The double doors of the hall slammed open. After bowing to Pharaoh, the vizier turned and left the hall, his business done. No one else moved. Sagira stared after him, knowing the assembly waited for her response.

Finally, after a long moment, she lifted her chin and stepped carefully toward the doors, walking in the wake of the looks of awe and reverence directed at Zaphenath-paneah.

~~~⌃ Thirty ⌃~~~

JUST AS JOSEPH FORETOLD, DURING THE SEVEN
years of plenty the land brought forth abundantly. Zaphenath-paneah's overseers gathered grain and corn and placed
the food in cities, thus the Egyptians stored up grain in
abundance like the sand of the sea. The vizier finally
stopped measuring it, for it was beyond measure.

Before the year of famine came, two sons were born to
Joseph and his wife, Asenath. Joseph named the firstborn
Manasseh, *making to forget*, "for," he told his wife, "God
has made me forget all my trouble and all my father's
household." And he named the second Ephraim, *fruitful-
ness*, explaining, "God has made me fruitful in the land of
my affliction."

As the land brought forth its bounty, Zaphenath-paneah
defined and redefined all that a vizier should be. So wide
and broad were his duties that in the years to come Egypt
would find it necessary to have two viziers, one for the
northern kingdom and another for the southern kingdom.

After taking private council with Pharaoh each morning, Zaphenath-paneah stepped outside in full public view
and reported to the king's chief treasurer that all was well
with the kingdom. The vizier then unsealed the doors of the
royal estate so the day's business could begin. Every person
and item of property entering through the palace doors was
reported to the vizier, and it was said that Pharaoh did not
cough without Zaphenath-paneah knowing about it.

The local authorities of each nome reported to the vizier
in writing on the first day of each season: inundation, emergence, and drought. Often the vizier was required to su-

pervise disputes in local governments, so he traveled up and down the Nile on Pharaoh's official barge. Pharaoh's vizier also detailed the king's bodyguard, as well as the garrison of whatever city Pharaoh happened to abide in. Army orders proceeded from the vizier, the forts of the south were under his control, and the officials of Pharaoh's navy reported directly to him. The vizier was the official minister of war, but whenever Pharaoh traveled abroad with the army, Zaphenath-paneah remained behind at Thebes and conducted the administration of domestic affairs. Because timber was precious and scarce in Egypt, no tree could be cut without his permission, and no buildings begun.

All things were regulated under Zaphenath-paneah's watchful eye, and God blessed Egypt under Joseph's rule just as He had blessed Potiphar's house. In time, the Hebrew who had entered the land as a half-dead slave came to be regarded as the people's great protector.

Ambitious men throughout the kingdom sought positions in Zaphenath-paneah's service. These men were carefully screened, and after they had passed a series of tests, the vizier's assistants were presented to Pharaoh and charged in a formal ceremony. Tuya often joined the royal court for these rituals. She thought it important to honor her husband by understanding the affairs of the kingdom, and she yearned for opportunities to watch Joseph from a careful distance.

"Let not your heart be puffed up because of your knowledge," the vizier's voice rang out from the pillars of Pharaoh's throne room in a commissioning service one afternoon. "Be not confident because you are a learned man. Take counsel with the ignorant as well as with the wise. The full limits of skill cannot be attained, and there is no skilled man equipped to his full advantage. Good speech is more hidden than the emerald, but it may be found with maidservants at the most humble grindstone."

Tuya smiled. Only a man who had spent time in slavery could have gleaned that insight. "If you are a leader commanding the affairs of the multitude," he further encouraged his assistants, "seek out for yourself every beneficial deed, until your own affairs are completely without wrong. Justice is great, and its appropriateness is lasting. It has not been disturbed since the time of him who made it, whereas there is punishment for him who passes over its laws. Wrongdoing has never brought its undertaking into port. It may be that fraud gains riches, but the strength of justice is everlasting."

Tuya listened carefully to Joseph's words about justice and punishment. He had proved to be a firm disciplinarian with those who broke Pharaoh's laws, and she wondered for the hundredth time why he had been so merciful to Sagira. That woman's great folly had forever marred at least three lives, but now she lived in a restored and prosperous villa.

Perhaps, Tuya mused, Sagira paid for her crime in other ways. Tuya knew for certain that Sagira had no friends among the nobility, for she had been cast far from Pharaoh's favor. Court gossip reported that Sagira suffered from a wasting disease which would surely take her life unless the gods proved to be as merciful as Zaphenath-paneah.

A blaze of trumpet fanfare ended the ceremony; the flushed and happy civil servants bowed their knees to Joseph, then prostrated themselves before Pharaoh. Tuya sat silently in the cheering crowd, grateful for the anonymity of the assembly. In a gathering like this she could watch Joseph without worrying that her eyes gave her heart away.

He had been Egypt's vizier for six years, and since their first interview she had not spoken to him except in the most ceremonial of greetings when they chanced to pass in the palace hallways. With a lovely wife and two fine sons, Joseph had probably forgotten all about her.

But still she dreamed of Potiphar's garden.

⟿ Thirty-one ⟿

NARMER SLIPPED OUT OF THE CROWD AND HURRIED through the halls, slinking through shadows until he reached the private corridor that led to Queen Mutemwiya's elegant chambers. Ducking through the doorway and the outer room, he insinuated himself between a pair of draperies on the queen's bed and waited until he heard footsteps approaching. "Thank you, ladies, but I shall not need you tonight," he heard her call, then Mutemwiya closed the door behind her. "Narmer?" she whispered.

"Here," he said, stepping out of the curtains. He pressed his lips together as a sign of pique. "I thought you would never come."

"That silly ceremony," she fussed, slipping the heavy wig from her head. Carelessly, she tossed it onto the floor, then took a seat on her couch, curling her legs beneath her. "Well," she purred, smiling in her controlled, unmirthful way, "come and sit. Tell me what you think of our grand vizier's new faces."

"They are like the old ones," Narmer groused, sinking into the chair opposite her. "The same enthusiasm, the same impartial glances, the very same glow of righteousness lies about all of them. What I would give for one single covetous soul!"

"There will be no bribing the vizier's men," Mutemwiya said, gesturing with her finger. "He has chosen well. Do not attempt it, for they will tell Pharaoh what you have done and then where will you be, my ambitious love?"

"In the underworld with you," Narmer answered, accustomed to her sharp tongue. He sat next to her, allowing her to drape an arm over his shoulders. "In any case, I will not bribe the vizier's men. He has surrounded himself with souls who are faithful and true—even his wife cannot be swayed from his side. Believe me, I have tried to gain the lovely Asenath's attention"—he grinned at the anger in Mutemwiya's eyes—"and failed."

"She would not have an old goat like you," Mutemwiya snapped, pushing the words across to him. "Why should she? The one they call the Pride of Egypt is hers."

"And the treasure of the kingdom is his," Narmer answered. "And Pharaoh, your young fool, is a puppet in the vizier's hands."

"As I am a puppet in yours," Mutemwiya replied. She looked up quickly, an alluring smile crinkling the corners of her eyes, and for a moment Narmer was distracted. Mutemwiya's exotic beauty had always held more fascination for him than the tender fragility of the young Egyptian maidens. Mutemwiya, his luxury-loving lioness, had been bred in the wild lands of the north country, and her temperament was as unpredictable as the weather in that changeable land. She moved with animal assurance and spoke with the confidence of a woman who knows the potency of her charm. Narmer had been thoroughly in her power since the day he negotiated Pharaoh's marriage contract, and she had immediately recognized his political talent, natural charisma, and gifts of persuasion. He owed her a great deal, for she alone had convinced Pharaoh that Narmer would be the natural choice to replace Potiphar as captain of the king's guard.

The strength of her gaze pulled him toward her now. Pleased at her open delight, he forgot what he had meant to say. His hand swept to the back of her neck.

"The time is coming, my dear Narmer," she purred, leaning toward him, "when the people will tire of giving their abundance to Pharaoh. They will groan under the weight of this senseless hoarding."

"According to Zaphenath-paneah and his Almighty

God," he answered, caressing her with his eyes, "the Nile will not flood next year. The famine is coming."

"I forgot." She pulled away, yawning, and tapped her crimson lips with her hand.

"You do not believe him?" he murmured, slipping from the couch. He fell onto his knees before her, his hands spanning her waist.

"No," she answered, resting her hands upon his shoulders. Her touch triggered primitive yearnings, and Narmer steeled himself to be patient. "I have not heard the voice of this god, and neither have any of my priests. Only Zaphenath-paneah hears the unseen god, and only Zaphenath-paneah profits from Egypt's abundance."

"There may be something in what you say," he said, catching her hand and pressing it to his heart. "If the Nile floods next year, the people may well rise up and rebel against this vizier. But what if a famine does come? How can we argue against one who has been proven right?"

"I have been studying you Egyptians," she said, leaning closer to him. "If famine comes, your people will resent having to buy what they themselves have put into the granaries for storage. Grain will be precious. A loaf of bread will sell for a bag of silver, and the poor will starve. When they carry complaints instead of offerings to the temples, the priests will demand the life of Pharaoh. The Divine King will give his life to feed the earth, and since there is no royal heir, whomever I take as my husband will ascend to the throne."

"You are sure of this plan?" he whispered, knowing with pulse-pounding certainty that she would not have spoken unless she would stake her life on this venture. "But what of Tuya's child? A son of Pharaoh lives."

Mutemwiya sniffed. "Tuya is a lesser wife, an ignorant former slave, and the life of the child is nothing. Trust me, Narmer, no one will dare stand in our way. If the land brings forth her abundance next year, you shall overthrow this vizier."

"And if famine comes, as the vizier has said it will—"

"Then we will wait until his precious food supply runs out." She tucked her hand around his neck with easy familiarity. "Zaphenath-paneah has been busy running the palace and training assistants, dear Narmer. Do you truly believe his granaries and storehouses contain enough to feed the entire land of Egypt?"

"We can lead a revolt only if the priests approve," he murmured, covering her hand with his own. "It would be difficult to lead the people without the priests' sanction."

"The priests will be eager to lead the people back to the ancient gods," Mutemwiya answered. "They have grown jealous of the vizier's Almighty God, for even Pharaoh has grown less fervent in his worship of Horus and Osiris. So we will begin to make generous offerings now, Narmer, and win the loyalty of the priests. If famine comes, in time the people will cry out against the harsh god who would dare smite the land of Egypt, and we shall rise like the phoenix from the ashes of a burnt and starving kingdom."

Overcome by her clever logic, he pressed his lips to her palm in a fervent rush, and she lowered her forehead to his. "Yes, my Narmer, think of it! You and I as husband and wife, rulers of the Two Kingdoms and more! For my Mitanni tribe will ally itself with us, and we can unite the world under our thrones!"

Tuya felt a curious, tingling shock when her young servant told her the king's vizier stood outside her door. "Zaphenath-paneah?" she asked, suddenly nervous. "The vizier wishes to see me?"

The frightened girl nodded wordlessly, and Tuya waved her away. "Give me a moment. Seat the vizier in the front room. I will be out in a moment."

The girl padded quickly away, and Tuya hurried to her dressing table to check her makeup and wig. This wig was a short one, well above her shoulders, and very fashionable among the ladies of Thebes. She hoped it made her look younger, for she had not had a private conversation with Joseph in years, and she was now thirty-four and the mother of a ten-year-old son. Under her wig, she had already sprouted more than a few gray hairs.

She adjusted her eyeliner and finger-smudged the lines of dark kohl to disguise the crinkles at the corners of her eyes. After tossing the bronze hand mirror to her dressing table, she straightened her dress and took a deep breath. Why should facing Joseph make her feel so nervous? He was an old friend. But he must have news of some importance, or he would have sent a messenger instead of coming to see her himself.

His back was to her when she entered the room, for he was watching Yusef play the lute. "Excellent, my boy," she heard him say. "I hope my own sons show half as much talent as you do."

Yusef blushed and smiled when he saw Tuya. "Zaphenath-paneah likes my playing!" he said, rising eagerly.

"So do I," Tuya answered. "Now go and show your nurse how well you are playing." Yusef hurried away, and Tuya turned to face her guest. With numb astonishment she realized that Joseph had aged more than she. Contentment and joy shone in his eyes, but stress and responsibility had etched lines in the forehead that had been smooth six years before.

"Tuya!" The sound of joy in his voice brought a maidenly blush to her cheek.

"Zaphenath-paneah." She kept her voice low and gave him a properly formal smile, aware that there were servants about. "What brings our king's vizier to me?"

"Must we be so stilted with each other?" he asked pleasantly, gesturing toward a couch. "You have never called me anything but Joseph."

She shrugged, not knowing what else to say. "All right. What brings you to me, Joseph?" He smiled, and some of the starch went out of her knees.

"I have come with something important to discuss, but thought I might at least ask about your health."

"My health is fine." Stepping awkwardly to the couch, she perched on the edge while he sank beside her. She put her hands in her lap and pressed them together. "Please, Joseph, tell me why you have come."

"All right." He sighed and frowned. "This is not an easy request to make, but I feel it is important."

"Then speak."

"Do you remember the story I told you about Abraham?"

She stared at him, puzzled. Every word Joseph had ever uttered in her presence was a precious memory, and she recalled the story very well. But what could it mean to her now?

She pretended to think, then nodded slowly. "The man who took his son to the mountain for a sacrifice."

"And God preserved them both."

"Yes. I remember."

"Tuya." He pressed his hands together, unconsciously imitating her. "I have dreamed again of you and your son, and the danger is nearer than it was years ago. I believe that you can save your son, but there is only one way."

"Save my son from what?"

"I am not sure."

"Well, Joseph, you can't ask me to do something unless I know why." She swiveled her eyes toward him and lifted a brow. "And what, exactly, are you asking me to do?"

"One thing: offer your son to Pharaoh, and let him be betrothed to Queen Mutemwiya. It must be done if he is to be declared the Royal Heir. You must do it now, Tuya."

"Why?" she sputtered helplessly. "Yusef *is* Pharaoh's heir. None of the other wives have given birth to a son, so he is the heir, without question—"

"No." Joseph's voice was suddenly firm, the voice of Justice and Egyptian Law. "If Pharaoh were to die today,

Egypt would have no king until Queen Mutemwiya marries."

Unable to follow his reasoning, her thoughts whirred and lagged. "But Yusef is Pharaoh's son," she protested, lifting her hand.

"Pharaoh intends for Yusef to be king," Joseph went on, his eyes compassionate and still. "He means at some future date to declare the boy Crown Prince, but we dare not wait. Yusef must immediately be named Crown Prince, he must be recognized as the betrothed husband of the heiress. Thus he will be king upon Pharaoh's death."

"My baby? The queen's *husband*?" Tuya's voice rose in an undignified shriek.

"Her ceremonial husband," Joseph answered, closing his eyes as if he could not bear to bring her further pain. "Remember Abraham, Tuya. He trusted God to spare the life of his child, yet he was willing to surrender that life."

"I cannot give my son to that witch," Tuya said, standing and backing away. "Not now, not ever. Yusef will not understand; he will think I care more for ambition than I do for him. I do not care if he is king, I just want him by my side—" She glanced wildly about as if she could somehow recapture the words of Joseph's suggestion and return them to his dark dream.

"If you do not do this thing," Joseph warned, "and Pharaoh dies, the Queen who ascends will not allow Tuthmosis's son to live. He will have an accident, or a mysterious illness." He leaned forward. "I will explain matters to Yusef. He will understand that it is for his sake that you do this."

Tuya shook her head, still unwilling to consider the possibility. Tuthmosis was not about to die! He was twenty-three, young and healthy, strong and sure. . . .

"Please, Tuya," Joseph said, standing. In three long strides he crossed the room and gripped her arms. She flinched, resenting his familiarity and the way her heart turned over when he looked into her eyes. "Tuya, you must trust the Almighty. He has warned me, and I have warned you. Do not be afraid."

"I cannot," she cried, her voice breaking. Tears flew down her cheeks like rain.

"You must," Joseph said, releasing her.

The sound of hurried footsteps broke the silence, and Joseph pulled away and slipped from the room as Tuya's maids entered from another doorway. "Mistress! What's wrong?"

She threw herself upon the couch and sobbed, too broken for words.

For a week she spent her days debating Joseph's words and her nights praying by the small stone altar in her bedchamber. She had trusted the unseen God to aid Joseph and Taharka. She had seen His hand of blessing upon both Potiphar's and Pharaoh's houses. But she had never asked El Shaddai to help her.

It is one thing to support a god with offerings and prayers, she told herself as she paced in the torchlight of her chamber. *It is still another to place one's son in His hands. For now that I have surrendered Joseph's life to Pharaoh and his heart to Asenath, all I have left is my own Yusef, the one who has received the love I would have given Joseph. And yet Joseph's God would have me place Yusef in the hands of the woman who may be my enemy.*

She paced until she was blind with fatigue, then fell onto her bed and slept. Even then, her sleep was cruel, and she drifted through clouds and temples and over mountaintops until she stood upon a place of stone. A pile of timber had been gathered there, and a dagger lay in her hand. Upon the wood, curled up like a puppy, Yusef slept.

The hard fist of fear clutched at her stomach. "I know where I am," she whispered, the sharp stones cutting her bare feet. "Abraham's altar! But, God, I cannot do this thing!"

A stentorian voice rumbled down from a mass of boiling clouds and echoed around the mountain.

"I called for a famine upon the land," the voice said,
"I broke the whole staff of bread.
I sent a man before Israel,
Joseph, who was sold as a slave.
They afflicted his feet with fetters,
He himself was laid in irons;
Until the time that his word came to pass,
The word of the Lord refined him.
The king sent and released him,
The rulers of peoples, and set him free.
He made him lord of his house,
And ruler over all his possessions,
To imprison his princes at will,
That he might teach his elders wisdom."

Odd wind-borne sounds came to her, and then, with the wind, the voice spoke again:

"Tremble, and do not sin;
Meditate in your heart upon your bed, and be still.
Offer the sacrifices of righteousness,
And trust in the Lord."

Tuya stepped forward, clutching the dagger in her hand, and the form on the altar shifted. "I will trust Yusef to You," she cried, her voice mingling with the wind and the sharp crack of the weathered wood on the altar. "I have no other choice!" She lifted the blade and felt her heart break, then thrust the dagger down into the blanket that covered her son.

There was no resistance. Pressing her hands to the scrap of wool, she found that Yusef had been removed. Had he been spared—or taken to the otherworld? Collapsing upon the altar, she spread her hands upon the empty blanket and wept.

The morning after her dream, Tuya slipped into her best dress and wig, adorned herself in Pharaoh's favorite jewelry, and set out for the throne room. Involved in other things, Tuthmosis had not come to see her in many days. It would be difficult to offer her suggestion before a formal audience and perhaps dangerous, when she had not seen the king in many days and had no way to gauge the royal temperament. If the king was ill-disposed or in a bad mood . . . but El Shaddai would know these things, and her son's fate rested in His hands.

Pharaoh sat upon his throne in the full bloom of youthful power, an assortment of maps and scrolls spread before him. Queen Mutemwiya sat beside him on her chair, an expression of utter boredom on her face, and beside her, the captain of the king's guard lounged with a critical eye upon the open maps. Several military generals stood before Tuthmosis; perhaps they were planning a military expedition of some sort. *Well, today I go to battle, too,* Tuya thought, squaring her shoulders as she approached the throne.

Tuthmosis saw her coming and held out a hand in greeting. "My lovely Tuya," he said, giving her a disarmingly generous smile. "What brings you out of your bower?"

Tuya fell to her knees and bowed her head. "Only one thing, my husband and king. I have a boon to ask of you."

"What is it?" Tuthmosis asked, obviously feeling expansive before his generals. Honest pleasure shone from his eyes, and he leaned forward eagerly. "You shall have it, even if it requires that I sell half the furnishings in my royal tomb."

"It is this." She lifted her eyes to meet his, ever mindful of Mutemwiya's cold glare. "Take our son, my husband, and declare him to be the Crown Prince and your heir. He is the only son of Pharaoh, and I surrender him to you this day."

Tuthmosis's eyes flickered in surprise. "You would surrender your son?" he asked, astonishment ringing in his voice.

"So there will be no doubt of his right to reign, I surrender him to be betrothed to Queen Mutemwiya," Tuya said, looking at the older woman. The queen's eyes were expressionless, shrewd little chips of bright quartz in a dark face.

For a moment Pharaoh seemed speechless, then he lowered his voice. "In truth, I had thought to do this thing later," he said, his words for her ears alone. "I wanted our son to remain by your side for as long as possible."

"He is ten and nearly grown," she answered, carefully choosing her words so that she would not reveal Joseph's warning. "It is time he began his princely training. Take him, my husband, with my love . . . and my unfaltering trust."

Pharaoh turned a frankly admiring smile upon her and declared that it would be done immediately. Tuya bowed in gratitude, and as she turned to leave she caught a glimpse of Mutemwiya's face. The queen's beaked and suddenly surly features reminded Tuya of a watchful, hungry vulture.

The ceremony took place one week later in the temple of Horus. Pharaoh and Queen Mutemwiya walked through the tall pillars of the temple with the young prince between them. As the child knelt before the altar, a temple priest proclaimed that the boy was the rightful heir of Pharaoh and the future husband of the Great Wife, Queen Mutemwiya.

"From this day forward," the priest intoned, "let him be called Amenhotep, the third of that name, in the tradition of the Pharaohs of the Two Kingdoms."

From her place in the crowd, Sagira covered her lips with her hand and hiccuped, the sour taste of wine filling her mouth. Tuya's child, the Crown Prince! It was too much to believe. Tuya was nothing but a slave whom the gods had indifferently blessed with beauty, and that beauty alone had put her in Pharaoh's bed and begot her a child.

She laughed in derision. Pharaoh was doubly a fool. Not only had he embraced a slave, but he had been foolish enough to marry an aging queen who would never give him a lawful son. "By the crust between Seth's toenails," Sagira snorted, not caring who heard her, "that is no prince. I have more royal blood in my big toe than that child!"

Several people retreated from the area as if she were dispensing poison, but Sagira only shrugged. "Cannot bear the truth, can you?" she called after them, staggering slightly on her feet. "There is more I could tell you, but you will not get a word from me!"

The crowd rippled away and pretended to ignore her, but one richly dressed man stepped from the group and bowed respectfully. "Lady Sagira, is it not?" he asked, a smile upon his darkly handsome face. "You may remember me. I helped arrange your marriage when your parents were alive. I am Narmer, the captain of the king's guard."

Sagira tilted her head back and narrowed her eyes. The man did look familiar, and he was handsome, with a strong, dauntless air about him. "I am pleased to see you, Narmer," she said, nodding with what she hoped was regal grace. "And because you have been so gracious today, I will forgive you for marrying me to Potiphar."

He laughed softly, then glanced up at the temple altar as if he did not approve of the ceremony. "Foolishness, is it not?" he asked, lowering his voice. "I heard your comment. I was surprised to see that many people did not agree with you."

"They ought to agree with me, for I know about these things," she answered, arching an eyebrow. "The one they call Queen Tuya was my slave, you know, both in Potiphar's house and in the house of my mother. And my mother was Amenhotep's sister."

"Ah," Narmer bowed more deeply. "I am more honored than ever, my lady. Mistress of a queen and Pharaoh's cousin! Now if you only knew our king's vizier—"

"Bah, I know him, too," she said, spitting the words as

if she found the subject distasteful. "Of course, you know about the attack."

"Of course, how could I have forgotten? My sympathies are with you, dear lady."

"They are?" She was honestly surprised, and her heart warmed to the man beside her.

"Yes, they are," he said, smiling suggestively. "And I would love to hear the entire story from your perspective. Tell me all about this vizier, and how he came to harm you."

Sagira felt her heart skip. It had been so long since a sober man noticed her! Fuddled by longing, she allowed him to take her arm and lead her from the temple. "Well," she said, feeling herself flow toward him as they walked, "Paneah was difficult to handle from the beginning. In fact, Potiphar had to return Tuya to Pharaoh's harem because she and the steward were lovers. Many a night in my garden I found them in each other's arms. . . ."

Tuthmosis allowed the priests and singers to finish their ceremonial hymns as they sent him off to bed, but when they had gone, he sat up and stared at the wall. His mind was too full for sleep, the day had been too eventful. What wisdom had inspired Tuya to surrender their son? He had seen her grief-stricken face peering from a portal of the temple, and his heart swelled with such tender love for her that he nearly paused in his walk down the aisle. But she had not looked his way, she had eyes only for their son. . . .

She was right, of course, as always. He should have begun to train his son months ago, for a prince had much to learn. Had he not been so caught up in his work with Zaphenath-paneah, he might have found the time for the boy, but sometimes he still thought of himself as a prince. Twenty-four was not so vast an age, and yet he often felt like a schoolboy pretending to play at being a king.

He lay down again and folded his arms beneath his

head. He could send for one of the harem girls, but he wanted to talk and Tuya was the one he wanted to talk to. But she would be upset, for tonight Yusef slept for the first time in his own chambers. Tuthmosis could not find the courage to face her red-rimmed eyes.

How he loved her! He loved the loose wisps of hair that made dark commas on her slender neck and the lovely sleepy-cat smile with which she greeted the morning. With every passing day she grew more precious and unique, and yet before her he often felt as awkward as an adolescent. She had mothered him, befriended him, and borne him a son, and now he yearned to make her love him.

None of the others loved him, and he did not particularly care. They were his wives for political or pleasurable reasons, and they understood their roles. Spoiled and selfish, they were born and bred to be pampered. Mutemwiya would never have surrendered a child to another wife. The harem girls would have demanded to be made queens themselves before they would have given up a living soul that had sprung from their womb.

But though it had obviously caused her a great deal of pain, Tuya had selflessly given her child into his care. She was always giving, never asking for anything, even when he begged her to name a gift that he might find for her. He wanted to give her everything, and yet all she had ever wanted was the son she surrendered today.

Tuthmosis stared at the ceiling, filled with remembering. *You have given me a child, the greatest gift a man can give a woman,* she had told him on the day of Yusef's birth. *I ask for nothing more.*

And yet his heart yearned for her to ask for more, to ask for *him*. She liked him, she petted him, she showed him affection. But she never spoke to him in the same adoring tone she used with their son, and she never looked at him in the dreamy way she watched Zaphenath-paneah from across the room.

The divine Pharaoh of the Two Kingdoms curled into a

ball, protecting the place in his heart only Tuya had ever reached.

———

Narmer hurried to Mutemwiya's chamber and was filling two golden goblets with wine when she finally entered. "To life," he said in greeting, lifting the cup as she came toward him. "To our success."

"How can you drink to that," she said, frowning, "when Tuthmosis has just set a roadblock before us in the form of this child?"

"Because when the time has come for our divine Pharaoh to be sacrificed to satisfy his starving people, this child and the vizier can be removed in one swipe of the tongue." Narmer pressed a goblet into her hand. "I have had a most interesting conversation with Potiphar's drunken widow. It seems that Zaphenath-paneah and our favorite wife Tuya were lovers when they lived together in Potiphar's house."

"No," Mutemwiya drawled, her mouth curving with the faint beginnings of a smile.

"There is more," Narmer said, tapping the side of his goblet to hers. "I think we can convince all Egypt that the child Tuthmosis proclaimed Crown Prince is not his son at all."

Mutemwiya frowned. "How? Tuya is doggedly, boringly faithful. Anyone who knows her—"

"The people do not know her," Narmer replied, already tasting success. "And they will want to believe that love found a way to unite our handsome vizier and our ravishing Tuya. And when the populace is convinced, the priests will never allow the son of slaves to assume the throne of a divine Pharaoh."

Mutemwiya swirled the wine in her cup. "But I am betrothed to the boy. When Tuthmosis dies, the throne will be his."

"A ceremonial marriage that has never been consummated can easily be annulled," Narmer answered, shrugging. "And children are frail things, easy to be rid of."

A look of mad happiness gleamed in Mutemwiya's eyes. "My Narmer," she said, her smile as hard as marble. "Your battle ethics never cease to surprise me."

"Enjoy your princely husband while you can," he whispered, eying her over the rim of his cup. "For one day soon he will be nothing but the son of slaves."

AMENHOTEP III

Now, therefore, it was not you who sent me here, but God; and He has made me a father to Pharaoh and lord of all his household and ruler over all the land of Egypt.

Genesis 45:8

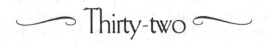

Thirty-two

AS WAS HIS CUSTOM, PHARAOH PAUSED IN HIS morning prayers and murmured a decidedly untraditional phrase under his breath: "And unto you, El Shaddai, I give praise, honor, and obedience in gratitude for sending Zaphenath-paneah to Egypt."

Through the first seven years of Zaphenath-paneah's authority over the land of Egypt, the eternal cycle of inundation and irrigation, emergence and planting, drought and reaping did not vary. After the seventh year's harvest, the emerald grass grayed in the heat of the desert sun and finally withered. As the year ended, the astronomer-priests searched the skies for Sirius, the brightest of all stars, whose appearance just ahead of the rising sun would signal the coming flood. When at last Sirius rose through a hint of thinner darkness in the east, the priests sent the traditional messengers to Pharaoh. The new year had begun, and the Nile would flood within forty-eight hours.

On this new year's day, the Nile-watchers at Elephantine checked and rechecked their measurements. The Nile rolled steadily northward, bright as a spill of molten metal from a furnace, but the creeping floodwaters were at a record low, barely above the level of the emergence. Hasty offerings were made at the temple of Hapi. Had the god fallen asleep? Had the limitless bounty of the river god's pitchers finally come to an end?

The glassy surface of the heaving river scarcely rose at all. Lands that had lain fallow during the arid days of summer received only a trace of moisture when the river dams were cut open. As the winter passed, the ground lay as hard as stone beneath the planters' feet, every sign of green burnt away. Dust whirlwinds swept across dreary flats, and Egypt's fabled black earth blew as dry and barren as the gray deserts to the east and west. Unable to find hay, wealthy landowners released their grass-greedy cattle into the desert. The hunting of wild rabbits and waterfowl, once a sport, became a serious endeavor.

By the time of spring and the emergence, the river had thinned like a starving child, and only an occasional heavy dew watered the thirsty earth. Summer arrived with bone-dry, desiccating sirocco winds that often obscured the sun and cloaked every exposed object in heavy dust. The wind sucked the moisture from animals and men alike, drying skin until it cracked and bled, parching mouths and nostrils until every living thing gasped for breath.

While heat, drought, and famine came at the world like a mortal enemy, the people of Thebes retreated behind the walls of their homes and gave thanks to Zaphenath-paneah's Almighty God, for news of the prophecy had filtered down to even the lowest estate. And as windblown sand scoured the fields of other cities, Zaphenath-paneah's assistants opened the granaries throughout Egypt. Even those who had heard and ignored the rumors of the coming famine were able to buy enough grain and corn to feed themselves and their families.

In the palace at Thebes, Pharaoh watched the sun he had once worshiped burn the land to dust. Egypt had once been a land of severe contrasts: the verdure of the Nile valley implanted against the sterility of the desert, the dark gray waters of the inundation feeding the fertile green fields, the teeming life of the Nile abutting the desolate wasteland. Now, however, the kingdom stretched before Pharaoh like a single curling sheet of dingy parchment. Even though he knew the time of famine would last only for seven years, often it was difficult to believe that the earth of Egypt would not forever be mottled yellow-brown and stained with death.

But the people would not starve. Tuthmosis shook his head, his mind swimming in grim thoughts of what could have been. If not for the unseen God who spoke to Zaphenath-paneah, the priests of Anubis would have come to his chamber with the cobra. How wise Zaphenath-paneah was! And how honorable, for praise fell from his shoulders like water from a duck's wing. "It is God who works," Zaphenath-paneah always protested whenever Pharaoh attempted to commend his vizier. "The Almighty has seen fit to save us for His pleasure."

As the first year of famine passed and the earth became harder and drier beneath the sun's scorching rays, Pharaoh urged his vizier to tutor eleven-year-old Amenhotep. In recent months Tuthmosis had come to realize how important was the agriculture he had always taken for granted, and Zaphenath-paneah certainly understood more about cultivation and husbandry than Tuthmosis could ever hope to know. "The vizier fills the room with light and wisdom," the king told Tuya one afternoon, explaining why he had asked Zaphenath-paneah to spend time with the boy. "From him Amenhotep will receive straight talk and simple answers."

She nodded in response, her eyes brightening for the fraction of an instant, but she said nothing. They sat together on a narrow couch beside his private garden as the sun boat dipped toward the west. Though his head lay in her lap, she would not look down at him.

Tuthmosis scratched his chin in contemplation. Of late Tuya had often been slumped into morose musings and none of his gifts or jokes could lift her sad countenance. Though she was as beautiful and kind as ever, somehow she seemed shadowed even when an aura of sunlight surrounded her. Her wistfulness was like an on-again-off-again pain, and despite his desire to please her, Tuthmosis often had the feeling he held a wilting flower in his arms.

At first he thought the change in Tuya's mood was related to the dim character of the landscape. She had always loved the gardens and groves, so he assumed the withering aspect of the countryside accounted for her dampened spirits. But always at the mention of Amenhotep's name, Tuya's demeanor altered as swiftly as a chameleon changes colors. Sunshine broke across her face for the fleetest of moments, then she reined in her emotions with a visible effort and pretended an offhanded indifference.

He marveled that he had not linked cause and effect together before. Was this melancholy only the result of a mother missing her beloved son?

"Tuya," he asked, grateful that they were in the privacy of his quarters, "what occupies your mind?"

She seemed lost in another time and place, but she managed a weak smile and murmured, "Nothing, my husband."

"Tuya," he insisted, slipping his hand around her neck as if he could pull her soul to him. "Talk to me. We are alone, and I speak now not as your king, but as your husband and friend. You have not been yourself in these past few months."

Tears jeweled her lashes as she smiled down at him. "I am sorry, Tuthmosis. I should work harder to please you."

"You have always pleased me," he whispered, feeling the chasm between them like an open wound. "Have I done something to drive you away? I know I have been busy with my work on the monuments, and Zaphenath-paneah requires a great deal of my time—"

"You have done nothing," she said, her hands coming lightly to rest upon his shoulders. Her eyes clouded with hazy sadness as she studied the acacia trees bordering the garden. "I miss the lotus blossoms. Have you noticed that they have not grown up along the river's edge? I used to enjoy them when I was a girl, especially the sweet-smelling blue ones."

"There are lotus blossoms in the palace water gardens. Walk there, and you can enjoy your fill of them."

"They are white, they are not the same," she whispered absently. "The blue ones bloom in the daytime, the white ones do not like the sun." Presently her face cleared and she gave Tuthmosis an incomplete smile. "Do not fret about me, my husband. You are a good king and a wise father. I have seen how you encourage Yusef—"

She suddenly bit her lip as if she had said too much, and Tuthmosis blew out his cheeks. "By all the gods, Tuya, why did you not say something sooner?" he snapped, sitting up. "I thought you missed the boy! Why did you not speak to me? Are you too proud to admit that you need to see your son?"

"Not proud, my lord," she whispered, her eyes wide. "Afraid."

"Afraid of what?" He shifted, staring at her in bewilderment.

She shook her head quickly, unable to speak in the face of his anger, and he took a deliberate breath to calm himself. He ought to be more gentle with her. Though she had never voluntarily spoken of her past, he knew that she had been a slave, and no slave had an easy life.

"Speak freely," he said, taking pains to soften his voice. "Of what are you afraid? Has someone threatened you?"

She shook her head again and sniffed. "I did not think it would be right for me to be with the prince," she said, looking away. "He is no longer my son; he is Mutemwiya's future husband and the kingdom's future Pharaoh. The women of the harem are so jealous! Your other wives would cause trouble if I, a former slave, became overly familiar with the Crown Prince—"

"And yet even the lioness who drives her cub out of the den still watches for his safety," Tuthmosis said. He ran his hand over the softness of her shoulder and felt her gentle breath as she sighed. "Our Amenhotep should thank the gods that you are his mother. Do not fret about Mutemwiya; she does not even think of him. When he is Pharaoh, he shall marry whomever else he pleases. But to ease your mind, tomorrow I shall ask Zaphenath-paneah to hold the prince's lessons in the garden where you may walk without worrying about gossiping tongues. Watch Amenhotep as often as you wish, talk to him, be with him."

Her eyes filled with a tenderness he had never seen in them before. "You are very kind, my husband," she murmured, lowering her cheek to rest upon his chest. "You are too good to me."

"No," he said, slipping his fingers through the silkiness of her hair while a lace of confused, pleasant thoughts fuddled his mind. "I am often not good enough. I should have recognized the source of your sorrow long before this."

She did not answer, but sighed contentedly, the whisper of her breath warm on his skin. "Tuya," he whispered, squeezing her shoulder, "I am king. No one will hurt you, and no one will harm our son. This I swear to you upon my own life."

She rested in the crook of his arm like a lion cub that nestles between its father's protective paws, and Tuthmosis relaxed in the satisfying victory. "You have missed our son," he said, grateful that the gathering darkness cloaked the schoolboy blush that burned his face and neck. "Did you not think that I would miss you? I did, you know."

Lifting her head, she gasped slightly in surprise, and Tuthmosis steeled himself for either laughter or sarcasm. One of his life's guiding principles was *never reveal your true feelings to any of your wives lest they compare notes and torment you.* But love compelled him to be honest and urged him to risk opening his heart.

"How could you miss me?" she asked, a gentle teasing note in her voice. "You sent for me often."

"And your mortal shell came to my bed," Tuthmosis answered, relaxing as he responded to the tender touch of her arms about his neck. "But *you*, dear Tuya, were far away."

"I am here now," she whispered, tilting her head back. Her dark eyes glowed with black fire in the rising moon's light, and Tuthmosis abandoned all reserve as he drew his arms about her and surrendered to the crush of feeling that drew them together.

Tuthmosis will never know what a gift he has given me, Tuya thought, dressing the next morning. *Though he lodges in his own chambers away from me, my son is mine again. I will talk with him and walk with him, and Joseph will share in our happiness.*

Her dress was of bleached linen as crisp and white as an egret's wing, and she knew she made a pretty picture as she dabbed her fingers in her makeup pot and colored her eyes and lips. Tuthmosis had been more understanding and sympathetic than she had ever dreamed he could be. In the years since he had learned of Joseph's El Shaddai, the king had been increasingly open to new ideas and less apt to adhere to the traditional, formal ways of living. The gods of Egypt had failed to predict or prevent the famine that presently swept the world, and Tuthmosis knew only a greater God could have sent Zaphenath-paneah to lead them through the catastrophe of worldwide drought.

Tuya spent the morning listening to the idle chatter and gossip of her maids, then she slipped out into the gardens where she knew she would find the Crown Prince and his tutor. The sky above was pure blue from north to south, without even a slight suggestion of cloudiness to come. Already a living warmth emanated from the sun, and a delicious sense of anticipation spread through Tuya's limbs as she walked among the flowers and waited for her loved ones to appear.

There. Ahead of her on the path, the prince walked with the vizier. Her son's head came to Joseph's shoulder, and Tuya noticed with a tinge of pride that Amenhotep's shoulders had begun to broaden. The result of the pair's time together was already evident, for they moved in unison down the path as if they were reflections of a single soul. Both walked with their heads held high, their hands clasped behind their backs, their shoulders squared.

Tuya hurried forward and called a greeting. "Oh

Zaphenath-paneah, live forever! And, Amenhotep, Crown Prince, may the gods grant you a hundred and ten years of prosperity!"

The two turned, still alike in their posture, and regarded her with pleased surprise. "Pharaoh said you might be joining us," Joseph said, warming her with his smile. "We are honored to walk with you, Queen Tuya."

Her son did not answer, and Tuya saw from the confusion in his eyes that he did not know how to respond. Tuya reached out and drew him to her side. "It is all right, my lord and prince," she said, allowing herself to cling to him only for a moment. "Though you have a new name and a new position, I am still your mother and you may tell me anything you wish. I can keep a confidence as well as the vizier." She felt herself dimpling. "And I am nearly as wise."

A sharp retort of laughter escaped from Joseph, and the prince met Tuya's eyes with a smile that reached all the way to her heart. "It is good to see you, Royal Mother," Amenhotep said, his voice deeper than Tuya remembered it. "I have missed you."

"And I you," Tuya whispered. She draped her arm over the boy's shoulder and turned to Joseph. "Now, what were you two discussing? Perhaps it would be helpful to have a woman's viewpoint."

"Indeed it might," Joseph answered, thrusting his hands behind his back again. And on they walked, discussing the plight of the farmers far south of Thebes. It was not until Tuya returned to her chamber that she realized that during the time with Joseph she had not once thought of the garden at Potiphar's house that used to haunt her dreams.

After closing the door to the queen's private chamber, Narmer leaned against it and regarded Mutemwiya with a lurking smile. "What?" she snapped from her bed, her anger resonating in the quiet room. "Why do you stand there grinning like a fool? I told you not to come to me again unless you had good news."

"Perhaps I do," he said, slinking across the room. He sat in a chair and crossed his legs, confident of his ability to please her. "What sort of news do you want to hear?"

"I want to hear something I do not already know." Mutemwiya swung her legs from the bed and leaned toward him, her spine curved like a curious, confident cat's. "Do not tell me that the Nile has failed to flood a second time. Do not mention that the earth bakes beneath our feet and yet still there is food enough for all of Egypt. And do not remind me that Pharaoh is healthy, young, and strong while you grow older with every passing day—"

"You grow older too, my dear Mut," Narmer answered, his eyes narrowing as he watched her. "How many years have you waited for this ultimate rebellion? Forty? Forty-five? Or are you ageless like the Sphinx our beloved Pharaoh honors?"

"Be quiet," the queen snapped, turning her head from him. She crossed her arms in defiance. "Two years ago you told me it would be simple to destroy the vizier and the brat foisted upon me, yet the boy is almost of age, Narmer! When Pharaoh dies, Amenhotep will not need me to be his regent. And if he suspects that you are less than absolutely devoted, he will be old enough to replace you as captain of his guard and send you to the gallows!"

"That will not happen," Narmer said, lifting a brow. "Egypt will starve soon—"

"Egypt will not starve! That cursed vizier has enough provisions stored for ten years!"

"But he has not made provision for everything." Narmer uncrossed his legs and leaned forward, eager to share the plan he had been formulating for weeks. "You are right, dear Mut, about the king's health and power. And I suspect that you are right about the stored provisions, but none of Zaphenath-paneah's men will discuss the matter with me.

Apparently he has warned them about attempted sabotage, and he does not trust even the captain of the king's guards."

"The vizier is a clever man," she said, glaring at him. "No wonder Pharaoh adores him."

Narmer tilted his head and shrugged. "The time has come, dear Mut, to take action of our own. We can no longer wait on the gods to open a path for us. We must send Tuthmosis into the underworld by the strength of our own hands."

She did not grow pale, faint, or scream at his suggestion of murder, but merely stared at him as if measuring the determination behind his words. "So," she said after a long moment, "how can this be done without leaving blood on our hands?"

A flicker of an admiring smile rose at the edge of his mouth, then died out as Narmer leaned forward and lowered his voice. "I have thought on it for days. Tell me, dear Mut—what does your husband, our Pharaoh, dearly love to do?"

Mutemwiya frowned and tossed her hair over her shoulder. "Refurbish the ancient temples?"

"No," Narmer said, leaning back. "A hunt! Do you not see? The other day while I was visiting his tomb in the Valley of the Kings, I studied the pictures painted upon the tomb walls. The artists have depicted him in his glory, riding in his chariot and pulling back his golden bow with all his celebrated skill! Before his painted chariot the artists have drawn the many lions, tigers, antelopes, and gazelles the king has slain—"

"What," the queen interrupted, looking bored "has this to do with us?"

"Do you not see?" Narmer asked, his voice rising in his excitement. "The king hunts! He is young, he is powerful but hunting is a dangerous sport."

Mutemwiya did not speak, but her eyes widened

Narmer lifted a brow and gave her a calculating look " shall take him hunting," he explained, tenting his fingers

"I shall take our Pharaoh to hunt the most vicious, most powerful animals in the earth. And he shall not come back alive."

Mutemwiya sprang toward him, her hand clenching his arm like an eagle's talon. "Are you certain this will work?" she whispered, her face frozen in speculation. "Quite sure?"

"Do not worry, my dear, you will risk nothing," Narmer whispered, leaning close. "No one will know but you and me, and if the gods take my life instead of the king's, this conversation will perish with me. I assume all the risk, and as my right, I expect all the glory when I return."

She sniffed with satisfaction at this arrangement, then promised him the world in a white-hot kiss.

For ten days Tuya did not see Tuthmosis; then she heard from one of the king's servants that Pharaoh was planning a hunting expedition in the lands south of the first cataract. He would be gone for some time explained the slave who brought her the news, and so he was busy arranging matters with his vizier and giving gifts to all his wives and concubines.

She rolled her eyes at the news of yet another of his adventures, then retreated to her chambers. For some reason the knowledge that he had visited the other wives sparked a jealous fire in her soul, and she wondered that she *could* feel jealous after sixteen years of marriage to a man with a multitude of wives. But Tuthmosis had been more than kind to her, allowing her to visit daily with Amenhotep and Joseph in the garden. She knew he could have easily forbidden her this special favor, particularly because now Amenhotep was practically Mutemwiya's husband, and legally no longer Tuya's son. By allowing her to continue her relationship with her child, he risked causing great turmoil among the petty royal women. Fortunately, Mutemwiya did not seem to care what Amenhotep did.

Tuya had everything she had ever dreamed of wanting, and yet still she wished Tuthmosis would come or send for her. He had always been able to make her laugh, and lately his strength had been a great comfort. After missing him for so many days, she felt as if whole sections of her body were missing, somehow torn away. Surely this was not love—or was it? The emotion was not the same rush she had experienced in Potiphar's garden with Joseph, and yet sparks of unexpected excitement shot through her whenever she heard the steady tramp of footsteps outside her door.

Tuthmosis finally appeared at her chamber door two weeks later. The priests sang their hymns and symbolically put him to bed; their servants removed the double crown and the traditional elements of regalia. When everyone had gone and finally left Tuya alone with her husband, Pharaoh opened his arms to her, but Tuya turned and walked away.

"What is this?" he asked, concern edging his voice. "Do not tell me you are angry because I am going away."

"You have been gone already," Tuya said, pretending to pout. "You have kept yourself away from me for nearly a month as you said goodbye to all your other wives. Your servants told me what you were up to. You were so busy taking the others their presents—"

"I had to give them something," he said, tossing the ceremonial bedcovers away. He stood and walked up behind her. She felt his breath on her neck, but he did not touch her. "They are my wives, Tuya. I must honor them."

She casually opened her hand and lifted it over her shoulder. "All right. Where's my gift? I suppose I can toss this gold necklace into the treasure box with the others."

"No." A smile rippled through his voice, and Tuya turned around in surprise. With an arrogant grin, Tuthmosis thrust his hands behind his back. "No gold necklace for you, oh, bride of my youth. I married you because you were beautiful, you know, and I keep you because you are honest."

"Honest?" His teasing smile brought a warm tingle to

the depths of her soul. "Wives can be too honest, my husband. Now give me my present so I can wear it tomorrow as we wives watch you depart our palace. I do not want to be the only royal wife without whatever it is you are offering."

"I offer you my heart and soul," he said, his eyes steady upon her.

"I accept," she said, nodding. "Now give me my token trinket so you can be on your way with a clear conscience."

She walked toward him, trying to reach whatever he had hidden behind his back, but he dodged her with athletic grace, grinning the entire time. Finally, breathless and smiling, she stood before him with her hands on her hips. "Tuthmosis," she said, trying to keep laughter from her voice, "give me the cursed necklace!"

"I did not bring you a necklace," he said, suddenly sheepish. "I hope you will not mind being the only wife without one tomorrow."

"What, then?"

"Put out your hand and close your eyes."

Tuya did so, a little reluctantly, and gasped when a featherlight object brushed her palm. Opening her eyes, she saw that her husband had given her a blue lotus blossom.

"Oh," she whispered in wonder, breathing in the heady scent. "Where did you find it, Tuthmosis?"

"I have had my most trusted men searching for blue lotus plants ever since you told me you loved them," he answered, his eyes fastened to her face. "We found some growing far south of here, and we will plant them in the pools of the garden where you walk every day. And Zaphenath-paneah is to bring you a bowlful of blossoms every morning as long as we are apart. They are my offering to you, Tuya."

"It is beautiful," she said quietly, running her finger over the flower's delicate petals.

"Do you truly want a golden necklace?" Tuthmosis

asked, a doubtful look crossing his face. "I could get one for you—"

"—with no trouble at all," Tuya finished, lifting her eyes to meet his. "And the gift would not mean nearly as much as this simple flower. I do not want gold, my husband. All that I want," she extended her hand to him, "is right here."

He opened his arms and she came into them, resting her head on his shoulder. Tuthmosis was more comforting than challenging, but he had invested more of himself in this simple gift than in a thousand chains of gold. Though she had never realized it, she knew at that moment that Tuthmosis loved her with his life, she was his heart's companion and soul mate. Though Mutemwiya wore the crown, and though other wives were younger and more vivacious than she, she knew her husband best, and his heart had come to trust in her.

"Did you mean it when you offered me your heart and soul?" she whispered.

"Yes," he answered, his hand brushing her hair. "And my love, Tuya, is yours if you will accept it. Now that I am a man, I know what love is, and I know that I love you more than the others, more than life itself. That is why I waited to come to you. I saved the best for last."

She looked up at him and knew in an instant that her heart, vain and wishful organ that it was, had spent too much time yearning for the past. Joseph had been the love of her youth, the boy who taught her to lift her eyes above slavery and captivity, the man who taught her to dream. But love, genuine love, existed in this man who had given her a son, the king who brought her lotus blossoms and called her friend.

His hand traveled tenderly up and down her back, and Tuya tilted her head to study his handsome face. Had her infatuation for Joseph caused Tuthmosis much grief? She suspected that he knew far more than he revealed, yet his was a trusting soul. Even knowing that she and Joseph shared a past, he was brave enough to trust Joseph as vizier and loving enough to allow Tuya to spend time with Joseph and Amenhotep.

"My beloved husband," she said, wrapping her arms about his slender waist. "I accept your love with gratitude and freely give mine in return. You are a truly good king and a wise man." She flushed as a wave of warmth swept over her. "God was good to me when He brought me to you. I pray He will preserve you while we are apart."

"Love of my heart," Tuthmosis answered, his lips moving over her cheek with exquisite tenderness, "I'm half-returned even before I go."

~~~⌒ Thirty-three ⌒~~~

THE SUN SANK TOWARD A LIVID PURPLE CLOUD bank piled deep on the western horizon as Narmer and the royal company reclined in the shadow of their tents and recounted the day's adventures. They had been gone from Thebes for a full month, and among their hunting trophies were scores of antelope, oryx, and gazelles. Pharaoh had, on this day, shot and killed a lion with his golden bow, and already the men were composing songs to praise their divine king's skill and talent. *"Even the lion of the land knows his god Pharaoh,"* they sang, their voices rising in the stillness of the wilderness. *"He stands and awaits the golden arrow of his king."*

But this hunt lacked the thrill of the chase, for the famine that had turned Egypt to dust had also wasted the African wilderness. Not a trace of green could be seen. Even the wiry bushes growing in the gorges were as desiccated and dried as the mummies of men dead a thousand years. The act of killing was a mercy, for there was no grass for the gazelle and antelope to graze upon. The lion had been sleek and fat, but in time even the king of beasts would be unable to find prey. Only the vultures, which fed on carrion, would thrive during the bitter famine.

Pharaoh sat by the fire, his eyes wide and fixed upon nothing, his thoughts a thousand miles away. Narmer pressed his lips together. The pensive look upon the king's face could only mean that he had grown weary of the hunt and would want to return to Thebes. Tuthmosis loved hunting, but found little joy in pursuing skeletal animals with barely enough strength to outrun the chariots. He had enjoyed pursuing the lion, but as much as Pharaoh loved the chase, he also revered wild creatures. He would not want to take another of those magnificent beasts.

It was time to present Pharaoh with the ultimate challenge. "They say," Narmer said, nodding casually in respect to his king, "that south of us is a place of great trees with timber enough to build a house for every man in the world."

"I have heard of this place," Pharaoh said, looking up. A definite gleam of interest flickered in his eye, for the land along the Nile was woefully bare. "But we have not left Thebes to hunt for timber, Narmer."

"No, but another animal lurks in these forests," Narmer went on, idly fingering the Gold of Praise about his neck. "Elephants. Thousands of them. And upon each bull's snout rests a king's ransom in ivory."

"I have seen pictures of these elephants," Pharaoh said, looking into the fire. "They are big and slow, lazy creatures."

"Indeed?" Narmer allowed his mouth to twist into an indulgent smile. "I have heard that they are the greatest challenge a man can face. They say manhood is proved or lost when a hunter faces an elephant bull."

As Narmer had hoped he would, Pharaoh took up the challenge. "I had thought to return to Thebes tomorrow," he said, looking about his tent at the trusted warriors who awaited his instruction. "But we have strength enough for one more journey, do we not? We shall find this grove of great timber, and ride without fear into a herd of these creatures. And I shall bring home twin tusks of an elephant bull—one I shall offer to Zaphenath-paneah's Almighty God, and the other to Queen Tuya, the mother of our Crown Prince."

A smile crawled to Narmer's lips and curved there like a snake. "As you wish, my king," he said.

⸻ Thirty-four ⸻

"NO!" TUYA SAT UP IN THE DARKNESS AND WINCED slightly as if her flesh had been nipped. A confusing rush of dread whirled inside her. A dream, a terrible, horrible nightmare had disturbed the peace of her sleep, and her skin crawled with the memory of it.

She lay back down and turned onto her stomach, clinging to the soft darkness as hard as she could, but sleep would not come. The specter of fear pushed away any thought of rest, and finally Tuya rose from the bed, wrapped herself in a light mantle, and padded out of the bedchamber. Going to the front hall of her quarters, she pulled a cord and rang for her servant.

Within moments the maid stood in the room, her eyes heavy-lidded from sleep. "Quietly and quickly," Tuya said, keeping her voice low, "run to the vizier's house and ask him if he will come here. Tell him Tuya summons him, and the matter is of great importance."

The girl nodded dully, then slipped out into the corridor. Tuya sat on her chair and rubbed her hands together, trying to ease the worries from her mind. Joseph would know the meaning of this dream. And, being Joseph, he would know how to prevent the disaster it foretold.

———

A quick footstep in the corridor sent Queen Mutemwiya dashing into the shadows as she left her quarters. She had grown lonely without Narmer's company and sought to invite sleep by walking through the palace's torchlit halls. On a perverse whim of fancy, she had turned into the hall that led to Tuya's modest chambers. Her feminine intuition had alerted her to the fact that Pharaoh had come to prefer the company of the younger wife, and though she cared nothing about losing Pharaoh's affection, she could not bear to think that the king of mighty Egypt preferred to spend his time with a former slave.

She breathed a sigh of relief when she recognized Tuya's servant in the hall, but then her curiosity was aroused. For what reason had Tuya summoned her handmaid in the darkest hour of the night? Had she taken ill? Or did she entertain a midnight guest in Pharaoh's absence?

Scarcely daring to hope, Mutemwiya slipped from her hiding place and padded quietly behind the slave girl. When the servant finally heard and turned, Mutemwiya gave her a brilliant smile. "Do not fear," she said, her voice echoing in the empty hall. "Is Queen Tuya well?"

The girl's eyes narrowed. "Yes."

Mutemwiya smiled. "Then she must have need of something. Is there something I can get for her from my rooms?"

"I think not," the girl hedged, twisting her hands. "I have an errand to run."

The queen lost her patience. "Speak, slave, and tell me truthfully what errand you are on." She gave the girl a brittle smile. "If you do not tell the truth, immediately, I will tell the guards I found you stealing from my room. You will spend the rest of your days in Pharaoh's prison—"

The maid looked nervously about for a moment, then lowered her voice to a whisper. "Lady Tuya has sent me for the vizier. She said it was urgent. That is all I know."

Stunned, Mutemwiya let the girl slip away. Why would the vizier be called at this hour? Was Tuya responding to some secret communication from the king? No, for if anyone brought word from the hunting party, she would have heard from Narmer. No, Queen Tuya wanted the vizier, and if she sent a lowly, inconspicuous handmaid for him now, under cover of darkness . . .

Smiling, Mutemwiya slipped back toward a hiding

place among the pillars in the corridor. Like the cobra who sits motionless and quiet until the mama bird hops away from its nest, she would wait and see what this night brought to pass. Better yet, she would summon a royal scribe to witness this midnight liaison—no! A priest! One of power and authority, a man whose honor might easily be offended . . .

Quickening her step, Mutemwiya pressed through the halls of the palace and hurried toward the temple of Osiris.

Tuya wrapped her mantle closer about her as she hurried to answer the gentle rap on the door. Joseph stood there with her slave, his wig askew, his face unpainted and strangely drawn in the dim light. He greeted her in a terse, vigorous voice: "Is Amenhotep well?"

"Yes—I mean, no. I don't know." She dismissed the slave with a distracted wave and pulled Joseph inside. When the door had closed behind him, she turned toward the single candle in the room so he might not see the fear in her eyes. "Forgive me for pulling you from your family, Joseph, but I have suffered much this night on account of a dream."

"A dream? I thought you did not believe in them." His words were faintly mocking, and she clenched her hands at the unsettling thought that Joseph remembered the past so clearly.

"How can I not believe?" she answered dully, wiping a tear from her rebellious eyes. "I saw Pharaoh's dream come to pass. Your dreams, as grandiose as they were, have been fulfilled. And now I stand before you half-blind with terror that the events of *my* dream might actually happen. . . ."

She heard him move to the chair; the wood creaked as he lowered his strong frame into it. "Tell me, Tuya," he urged in a night voice. "It is God who speaks through dreams. He is trying to speak to you."

Tuya wondered if her fragile soul could bear to relive

the black dream, but she took a deep breath and began. "I am walking along the banks of the Nile," she said, not daring to look at Joseph. "There are bundles of dry rushes burning on the watch-fires. It is dark, but then the flames leap up and push the darkness back so that I can see clearly."

"What is it you see?"

Tuya shook her head. "I do not understand why, but Amenhotep is a baby again, and in my arms. And Pharaoh walks beside me, his hand holding the edge of my skirt."

She paused, suddenly feeling foolish. "I suppose it is quite silly, actually. You must think me an awful coward."

"Never," Joseph answered loyally. "Go on, please."

Tuya shrugged and turned to face him. "There are crocodiles in the water, and they begin to advance toward me. One has his eyes fastened upon the baby, and the other snaps his fierce jaws toward Pharaoh."

Suddenly she broke off and sat on the edge of a chair, hanging her head. "I am sorry I brought you here, Joseph. It is probably nothing but a childish nightmare, brought on by the fact that Pharaoh is away from me. But something urged me to fetch you, and I never dreamed you would come. . . ."

"Go on, Tuya," Joseph said, his eyes wide and fixed upon the floor. "Please."

She pressed her lips together, struggling to maintain her composure. "The rest is too awful; I hesitate to speak it. The land grows dark, but the flames of the watchfires dance in the wind while streams of sparks whirl off into the terrible darkness. I scream and try to shield Yusef as best I can, and while I am struggling to run from the first crocodile, the second lunges toward Pharaoh and drags him into the Nile."

She shuddered at the memory. "That is when I awakened. . . ." Her voice trailed off as she waited for Joseph to assure her that the vision meant nothing. But he who had never been at a loss for words met her curious glance with astonished silence.

"I have had this same dream," he said, his voice filled with tremulous fear. "But not in some time. God has not spoken to me this time, Tuya, but to you!"

"What does it mean?" she asked, panic rising in her chest.

"You do not need me to tell you," he whispered, his eyes veiled with sorrow. "We both know."

She sat motionless for a long moment as the full meaning of his words sank into her mind; then she beat her hands upon her knees and bowed her head in despair. "Is there nothing we can do? Perhaps God seeks to urge me to do something! You saw the coming famine, and so you urged Pharaoh to prepare for it! I see my beloved Tuthmosis dying, but if I can stop him—"

"The famine came," Joseph said, lowering his head into his hands. "And God was merciful, for we were prepared. What you have seen will come to pass, Tuya. In His mercy, God urges you to prepare for it."

He lifted his eyes and looked at her with a kind of resigned weariness while Tuya sank into a devouring gulf of despair. "Why," she whispered, lifting tear-blurred eyes to his, "when I have just begun to love him as he ought to be loved—"

Joseph said nothing but stood and rested his hand on her head. "Take heart in God's mercy," he said, genuine remorse in his voice. "Take courage in God's love. He has shown you what is to come and urges you to be ready."

"For what? Loneliness and suffering? I have already walked miles with those two companions. I know them well enough to understand that the pain of losing someone never truly goes away."

"No, Tuya, it does not. But you must be ready for your son's sake. In the dream, the baby remained in your arms. Amenhotep will need you when Pharaoh is gone."

Suddenly her mind blew open. "Oh, my dear Yusef," she whispered, staring past the lamp at the elongated shadows on the walls. "You will be a young and vulnerable Pharaoh."

Mutemwiya waited until the vizier left Tuya's chamber and then turned the wide eyes of innocence upon Chike, the high priest of Osiris. "I thought to have you offer a blessing for Queen Tuya who cannot sleep," she said, pretending to be shocked. "But apparently our Tuya meets with our vizier this night."

"It is an odd time for a meeting," Chike said, his aged eyes peering through the darkness at the retreating vizier's dark form.

"Is it not," Mutemwiya murmured. "Well, I am sorry I have disturbed you, Chike, but I only wanted to be of service to our dear sister. Please forgive my error."

The old man bowed and shuffled off, grumbling under his breath. "Hold this inconvenience entirely against me," Mutemwiya called, her voice echoing down the hall, "but do not forget this night."

For three weeks Pharaoh's party traveled down the course of the Nile. A broad savannah of grassland stretched before their chariots, blown by the hot wind and browned by the scorching rays of the burning sun. The great trees Narmer had promised rose like a protective backdrop to the east and west. One afternoon, just after the sun boat had reached its zenith, living gray mountains appeared on the horizon. "There!" Narmer said, brimming with anticipatory adrenaline. He lifted his arm and pointed. "See there, my king! Elephants!"

Like solid rocks in the plain, the great gray forms moved along the fringes of forest at a slow and steady pace. Thousands of them, large and small, trudged alongside herds of antelope and gazelle with the superiority of a haughty race.

"Let us stop and make camp!" Pharaoh called, lifting his hand to signal the other charioteers. "We shall unload our supplies and ready our bows. Not a moment is to be wasted!"

In a state of controlled excitement, Narmer slapped his reins and turned his horse. From captured Nubian slaves he had heard bloodcurdling stories about the surprising might and power of the elephant. One man could never bring down a bull, the slaves said, nor even ten men. But Pharaoh, trusting in his divinity, might be tempted to risk everything.

And his and Mutemwiya's hands would remain free of blood and blame.

"Give the horses drink," he called to the warriors who were chattering like magpies. "Tighten and secure the traces. We ride in an hour."

Pharaoh had dismounted and stood as if in a delighted trance, his face turned toward the lumbering giants. Narmer called out to him. "May the gods be praised, Pharaoh, to have delivered such a goodly number of elephants into our hands. I know Queen Tuya will be pleased to have an ivory carving for her chambers."

"Yes, yes indeed," Pharaoh murmured, his eyes alight with expectation. He gestured behind him to his quiver-bearer. "Check my arrows and mark each with my motif. I will know which man's arrow kills one of these beasts."

"Which motif should I use, my king?" the servant asked.

Pharaoh's lips parted in a secret smile. "A lotus blossom," he answered.

———

After the provisions and tents had been unceremoniously dumped by the river's edge, Narmer, Pharaoh, and a handful of the best hunters mounted their chariots. As a matter of pride, Pharaoh rode with only his chariot driver beside him, choosing to handle his own bow and arrow like a true sportsman. Narmer dismissed both his charioteer and his quiver-bearer with a single harsh glance. "Get away, you fools," he said, adjusting his leather gloves as he prepared to assume the reins. "I will not hunt. I ride only to guard Pharaoh."

The slaves backed hastily away. Pharaoh's driver slapped his reins across his horses' backs and turned the royal chariot toward the herd of elephants in the distance. The great giants moved slowly, feeding themselves from the tender foliage they had ripped from towering trees. Stout branches lay broken and scattered over the ground, mute evidence of the animals' great strength.

Narmer smothered a smile. An older, wiser king would have pulled back and sent his men in to gather the trophy. But Tuthmosis possessed the stubborn courage of youth in full measure.

Pharaoh advanced to within a moment's ride of the animals and halted his chariot. The herd noticed his approach, for the females gathered the young into the midst of the herd, then turned outward in an expression of maternal guardianship. The mammoth bull, however, went on grazing as if nothing had happened, and not until Pharaoh's horse broke the silence with a nervous whinny did the bull lift his head and turn to face the divine ruler of the Two Kingdoms.

The creature's great, leathery ears spread slowly and seemed to block out the sky. His tusks, broad yellow shafts of ivory, stood out from his bewhiskered head like the pillars in Pharaoh's throne room.

"Look at that," Narmer called up to Pharaoh. "Imagine what the Crown Prince will say when he sees those tusks!"

Pharaoh did not answer, but gestured for his driver to wheel the chariot slowly to the left. As the horses moved forward in a gentle trot, the old bull turned slowly, keeping his eye upon the intruder, and Narmer held tight to his reins. The other hunters dispersed to stalk other prey, leaving this particular herd and its bull to the divine king.

The chariot slowly circled its quarry, leading the bull, then cut between the cows and the bull so that the male was effectively singled out of the herd. Pharaoh lifted his bow and notched a barbed arrow. He pulled and aimed, his muscles shining golden in the sun. As the elephant wheeled to turn again, Pharaoh let the arrow fly.

The missile lodged in the great bull's side, and the beast suddenly let out a blood-chilling squeal. Narmer's horses shied at the piercing sound and trembled in the traces, requiring all his strength to hold them steady. Pharaoh's team lurched forward at the noise. Quick as a gazelle and as nimble as a leopard, the bull snorted and charged with surprising speed. Narmer smiled in satisfaction when he saw Pharaoh's jaw drop in stupefaction. The chariot driver's face was frozen in fear as the vehicle turned and raced away from the raging anger following them.

Narmer tightened his hands upon the reins as Pharaoh drew the mad beast nearer. As the king's chariot bounced over the uneven ground in its headlong rush, Pharaoh lifted his bow and notched another arrow, but seemed to realize that he was leading the bull toward Narmer. He yelled an order to the driver and the chariot swerved, drawing the bull to the east, but not before passing close enough for Narmer to see a look of deadly concentration upon the king's face.

Pharaoh lifted his bow, took careful aim, and told his driver to swerve again. The slave did so, this time to the north, and in the instant that the bull's flank was exposed, the king released his arrow. The bronze-pointed barb went in behind the animal's shoulder and buried itself in the folds of gray skin.

The bull bellowed again in rage and pain, but he did not stop his charge or lessen his speed. As his vast leathery ears slapped against his shoulders, he pressed forward, quickly bridging the gap between the king's chariot and those swordlike tusks. "For the love of Osiris, run, you beast!"

Narmer whispered under his breath, willing the animal strength and power.

Unfazed and undaunted, the king kept shouting directions to his driver. At each turn of the chariot, Tuthmosis managed to sink another arrow into the great bull's ribs. Arrows now bristled from the beast's side, and blood streamed from his flank like great tears. With every trumpeting squeal, a red cloud spurted from the massive trunk, but still the creature reached out for the king in an agony of hatred and anger.

For a moment, Narmer thought Pharaoh would escape. His chariot began to pull away from the weakening beast, but the driver, frightened out of his wits by the bloody apparition off the chariot's footplate, veered too sharply at a turn. The chariot teetered on one wheel for a long moment, then fell upon its side. Screaming in their traces, the horses dragged the splintered contraption out of the mad bull's reach, but the human cargo was not spared.

Goaded by pain and the frenzy of fear, the elephant vented his anger upon the hapless driver, stomping the life out of him. Not far away, Pharaoh rose to his knees and crouched down to run. Narmer's hands gripped the rim of his chariot. Instinct prodded him to act. If he urged his horses forward, he could draw the rampaging monster away from his helpless king. But he had not come on this journey to save Tuthmosis.

Pharaoh broke into a sprint; distracted by the flurry of movement, the bull turned and charged. Narmer watched in sadistic horror as one of the huge tusks gored the king as easily as a knife slices butter.

The elephant trumpeted in triumph, lifting Pharaoh from the ground. Staring in silence, Narmer's fingers fluttered in fear as his heart raced. He had hoped for such an accident, but he had never thought to witness it. Despite the heat, cold air brushed across the back of his neck, and his scalp tingled beneath the heavy hair of his wig. *Oh, Mut,*

if you could see how the gods have answered our peti-
tions. . . .

The bull shook Pharaoh the way a puppy shakes a rag
toy. The body slid easily from the giant tusk and flew into
a scrubby patch of brush as if it had been made of nothing
but papyrus reeds. As Narmer continued to watch in horror,
the bull shivered and staggered. A bright flood of blood
rushed from his mouth, and the giant fell onto its side.

Like a statue, Narmer remained frozen in place for a
long moment. The alarmed cries of the other hunters finally
stirred him to action, and he slapped his reins and drove
toward Pharaoh's broken body. A strange, cold excitement
inside him threatened to explode into a fit of laughter, but
Narmer carefully arranged his face in lines of dismay and
despair. He was, after all, the captain of Pharaoh's guard,
and responsible for his life. He must feel regret, grief, and
unrelenting guilt.

He did not even glance at the granite corpse of the elephant, but hurried to the grassy place where Pharaoh's
body lay. Sweat and blood had soaked the royal chest and
stained the linen kilt; a dark pool of life seeped into the
ground beneath him.

Narmer knelt at the king's side and rested his hands
upon his knees, mindful of the others who were watching
from a respectful distance. "Poor Pharaoh," he murmured.

At the sound of his voice the king's eyes flew open.
Narmer jerked backward, nearly losing his balance.

"Narmer," Tuthmosis said, a death rattle in his throat.
The wounded king lifted a blood-streaked hand. "Take
word to the Queen that Amenhotep now reigns. It is the will
of the Almighty God."

"Yes, my king," Narmer replied automatically, staring
with horror as the king's eyes rolled back into his head.
Tuthmosis stiffened, shuddered, then explosively released
his last breath and surrendered his life.

Narmer remained by the king's side until the others forced him to move away. Later that night he noted with satisfaction that not one drop of the king's blood had stained his hands.

⟿ Thirty-five ⟿

TUYA PAUSED IN HER WALK TO INHALE THE DELI-
cious scent of the blue lotus blossoms now growing in the
pools of the palace garden. Joseph and Amenhotep, unaware that she lingered, kept walking, their hands lifting occasionally in emphasis as they debated the wisdom of the
ancient laws. Watching them, Tuya smiled. Joseph had appeared at her door each morning for over a month, offering
her a bowl of blue lotus blossoms in the name of the king.
And as pleasant as the gift was, Tuya longed far more for
the sight of Tuthmosis's royal barge upon the Nile. Only
when she had seen him safe again upon his throne could
she believe that her dream had been a meaningless premonition, a toothless lion stalking her in the dark.

A guard stepped into the path before Joseph and saluted
smartly. "I beg Zaphenath-paneah's and the prince's pardon," he said, bowing before the prince and the vizier. "But
a messenger has come from the river. He brings a message
from Narmer and Pharaoh's hunting party."

A message from Narmer? Any message should have
come from Pharaoh himself. A wave of grayness passed
over Tuya as Joseph nodded. "Bring the messenger to me at
once. Bid him make haste."

As the guard hurried away, Tuya put her hand to her
throat. "Joseph," she began, her voice trembling.

He turned and cast her a warning glance, his hand falling upon Amenhotep's shoulder. "We should meet the messenger in the throne room," he said, offering a careful smile
that said *remain calm, remember your son.*

"Yes," she whispered, lowering her hand. Despite the

tight place of anxiety in her heart, she smiled and placed her hands upon Amenhotep's shoulders. "Live, O Prince, and prosper forever," she murmured, lowering her head to rest upon his. "Know that your father and I love you dearly."

She might have held him forever, but Joseph cleared his throat and led the prince toward the throne room.

Everything went silent within her as Tuya heard the clear and forthright message: ten days before, while engaged in a brutal battle with an elephant, Pharaoh Tuthmosis IV died a glorious and victorious death. His body had been carefully wrapped and was on its way home with the two tusks of the great elephant that had set him on his way to Paradise.

The message had been witnessed and signed by Narmer, captain of the king's guard, who was traveling home with Pharaoh's body.

A thick silence fell upon the throne room as Joseph finished reading the scroll, then Queen Mutemwiya broke forth into loud, hiccuping sobs. Her ladies helped her from the room, and the priests hurried to make preparations and engage the professional mourners who would weep and wail for the departed king throughout the next seventy days. Amenhotep stood by the vizier's side with wide eyes and a dazed expression on his face. In an oddly detached manner, Tuya found herself thinking that twelve was too young to lose both a father and a king in one moment.

She looked at Joseph, waiting for soothing words. His hand, which had been resting upon the prince's shoulder, suddenly lifted. Zaphenath-paneah, beloved of Pharaoh, dropped to his knees before the child. "O King, live forever," the vizier said, lifting his eyes to meet the wide brown gaze of the frightened boy. "Now you are no longer Prince, but Pharaoh in word and deed. Your people will look to you for leadership and courage."

The boy's chin quivered, and for a moment Tuya feared he would cry. But the steel of the royal bloodline asserted itself and the prince squared his shoulders. "Rise, Zaphenath-paneah," he said, his voice a childish treble in the throne room, "and help me prepare my father's tomb."

Joseph rose and nodded respectfully, then followed the new king from the room into his private chamber.

A servant came for Tuya within the space of an hour. She dried her tears and washed her face, then hurried to the chamber that had been her husband's and was now her son's. The guards at the door stepped aside as she passed, and after her knock a servant admitted her to the royal presence.

Amenhotep lay on the bed, his eyes red and swollen with weeping. Joseph sat in a chair near him, his face strained with weariness, but he gave Tuya a helpless smile when she entered.

Pharaoh lifted his head. Tears had tangled his thick lashes and smeared the paint on his eyes. "Royal Mother," he whispered, his face locked with anxiety, "what am I to do?"

Tuya wanted to scream that she didn't know, that she was as bereft and grief-stricken as he, but in a flood of memory, Joseph's words of warning washed over her. The dream that had warned her of Pharaoh's death urged her to protect and shelter this other love of her life, her child.

"My dear son," she whispered, rushing to him. She sat next to him and slipped her arm about his shoulders. "My boy. You shall be a great king. You have your father's most trusted advisor at your side, and Egypt awaits your command. The Almighty God would not leave you unprepared at a time like this. You must trust me, my son, and you must trust God."

Joseph's strong gaze pulled her eyes to meet his, and she gave him a half-smile. "El Shaddai is great, my son, and you can trust Him with the kingdom as did your father."

One of Joseph's eyebrows lifted in a silent question, but he said nothing as he motioned for a slave to fetch the priests who would put Pharaoh to bed.

The ceremonial barge of Tuthmosis IV appeared upon the Nile three days later. Narmer had done his best to preserve the king's immortal body, emptying it of all organs but the heart, the organ of life and intelligence, and the kidneys, for they represented the sacred Nile. The body had been stuffed and sprinkled with salt, then wrapped tightly in linen and hurried to the river. Fortunately, the low waters of the Nile ran swiftly northward in the hot winds, and after taking the king's body aboard the barge at Elephantine, the royal party had made good time.

The royal party. Narmer liked the sound of those words, for Tuthmosis was no longer king. Narmer supposed that in actuality, he directed the affairs of the kingdom. The court at Thebes did not know this yet, but the men aboard the ship did not doubt that Narmer held the reins of power.

Tuya stood on a portico of the palace and lifted her eyes to the river. The priests, their bare heads gleaming in the bright light of the sun, lifted their arms in homage to their dead king, whose body was now being lifted and carried toward the temple of Horus for mummification. The dreadful ululations of mourning rose and fell like ghostly screams in the broad light of day, and Tuya shivered. For the first time she saw herself as a king's widow, a purposeless, useless object. Mutemwiya was queen, Amenhotep officially her husband and Pharaoh. Tuya had not felt so alone since the night she had been cruelly abandoned by Sagira.

The group of warriors who had accompanied the king walked at the side of the body, their swords lifted across their chests. Narmer walked at the fore, the Gold of Praise gleaming in the sunlight, his chin lifted high as if in defiance of death. Solemnly he sang a song of mourning, his high, nasal voice cutting through the wails of the mourners on the riverbank:

> Death is in my sight today
>> as the odor of myrrh,
>> as when sitting under sail on a breezy day.
>
> Death is in my sight today
>> as is the odor of lotus flowers,
>> as is the presence of hearts heavy with grief.
>
> Death is in my sight today
>> as a well-trodden path,
>> as when a man returns home to his house from war.
>
> Death is in my sight today
>> as a clearing of the sky,
>> as a man discerning what he knew not.
>
> Death is in my sight today
>> as when a man longs to see his home again
>> after he has spent many years in captivity.
>
> Nay, but he who is Yonder in the Otherworld
>> will be a living god,
>> inflicting punishment for evil upon him who does it.
>
> Nay, but he who is Yonder
>> will stand in the bark of the Sun-god
>> and will assign the choicest things therein to the temples.
>
> Nay, but he who is Yonder
>> will be a man of knowledge,
>> not hindered from petitioning Ra when he speaks.
>
> Nay, but my soul has set aside lamentation,
>> for when he is joined with the earth,
>> I will alight after he goes to rest.
>
> Then we shall make an abode together!

Tuya pressed her fingers to her lips, silently remembering Tuthmosis's energy and life, while from her portico,
Mutemwiya drew attention with much weeping and wailing. Amenhotep, who stood gravely by the queen's side
with the double crown of Egypt teetering on his head,
looked often to the vizier for comfort and encouragement.

Tuya's eyes followed the white-wrapped bundle until it
safely passed into the outer courtyard of the temple, then
she slipped from the portico and walked slowly to her
chambers. In that moment she felt as ancient as the pyramid
of Khufu. Surely she had outlived her usefulness, for she
had outlived her love. In previous dynasties, the slaves and
wives of great kings had been entombed with the deceased
Pharaohs, but since that practice had been ruled barbaric,
stone representations of a king's slaves and wives would be
placed in the king's tomb to follow him into the otherworld.
Would it not be better, Tuya wondered, to follow Tuthmosis
into death than to spend a lifetime mourning him? She had
wasted so many years yearning for a love that was not
meant to be . . . but at least she had discovered her love for
Tuthmosis before it was too late.

She pressed open the door of her chamber and slipped
off the scarf she had used to shield her eyes from the
scorching sun. On a stand in the middle of the room, a half-
dozen blue lotus blossoms floated in a silver bowl.

Joseph had not forgotten Pharaoh's last wish. He would
honor Tuthmosis and his son for as long as he lived.

Tuya pressed her face into flowers, then choked back a
sob as grief erupted anew.

The city mourned for its lost king that night. Scattered
watchfires along the Nile dotted the darkness; huge tongues
of flame leapt into the air, followed by boiling clouds of
dust and debris. Keening wails from the mourning populace echoed over the land, stretching across the city and filling the palace with a series of endless cries. The horrible

sound terrored Tuya's dreams, and she tossed on her bed of grief, unable to sleep.

In the darkest hour of the night, the doors of her chamber burst open. "What?" she screeched, half-afraid one of her dreams had suddenly materialized. "Who moves there?"

Two of Narmer's guards stalked into the room, spears in their hands and swords at their belts. A captain she did not recognize stepped into the dim rectangle of light cast from the lamp in the outer room. "Queen Tuya, you are summoned to appear in the throne room of the Two Kingdoms," he said, iron in his voice.

"Who summons me?" she snapped, anger rapidly overcoming her initial fear. "Surely not Pharaoh."

"Narmer, captain of the king's guard, and Chike, high priest of Osiris, await you," the captain answered, his eyes glinting toward her in masculine interest. "You are to dress and come with me immediately."

"I will dress before no man but my husband," Tuya answered, tossing her head back. "Leave my chamber and wait outside."

"I cannot."

Tuya snapped her fingers in annoyance. "You _will_. There is no escape from this room, and no reason for you to guard me. I will be with you in a moment, so leave now, or by the life of Pharaoh I will have you flogged!"

The captain grinned for a moment as if he would taunt her with a threat of his own, but at the last moment he turned and gestured for the two guards to follow. When they had gone, Tuya swung her legs out of the bed and dressed in a simple linen sheath. She was about to slip on her wig, then decided against it. They had roused her from her bed for some foolish reason, and she was not about to dress to impress such ruffians.

She ran her fingers through her short hair, smoothed her skirt, and opened the door. The two guards immediately stepped into position at her side as if she were some sort of dangerous prisoner. She looked up at them with sudden understanding. Tonight her dream would be fulfilled. The danger was real; the enemies waited in the throne room. They had taken Pharaoh, and they were about to threaten her son.

With the fierce and angry pride of a lioness whose cub is threatened, she lifted her chin and glared at the captain. "Lead me on," she said.

Thirty-six

POLISHED AND FULLY DRESSED, QUEEN MUTEMWIYA sat in her gilded chair, the double crown of Egypt upon her head. Amenhotep, who should have been upon the throne with the regal beard of Pharaoh strapped to his chin, sat on a low stool before the queen. The throne itself stood empty, but Narmer paraded before it with the air of a conquering hero.

Tuya's blood boiled when she realized who had authored the plan of destruction unfolding before her. Narmer and the queen, no doubt. For Mutemwiya had not been suddenly pulled from her bed to witness an inquisition; that lady was fairly purring with expectation as Tuya walked into the crowded throne room between two towering guards.

She felt Amenhotep's eyes fasten upon her, but she did not dare look at him lest her fear show in her face. "What is the meaning of this?" she said, pushing words across the room to Narmer. "Who has dared disturb the king's wife on her bed of grief?"

"Tuthmosis is king no longer," Narmer said, his eyes falling upon her with a look that made her shiver. "And you were once a slave. Perhaps you shall be a slave again."

Tuya felt herself trembling all over, and the heat in her chest and belly she recognized as pure rage. She wanted to scream, to stamp her feet and roar, but Narmer was right—she had no power now, and no authority except that which was granted her by Pharaoh. And Amenhotep did not wear the crown at this moment—Mutemwiya did.

The double doors of the throne room slammed open

again, and another bevy of guards approached. In the midst of them walked Joseph, his hands bound together.

Tuya's head snapped toward Narmer. "What is the meaning of this? What wrong has he done?"

Narmer's mouth curved into a predatory smile. "You and the vizier have been brought here to face a serious charge. Queen Mutemwiya will serve as a witness; Chike will hear the evidence and speak for the gods."

"What charge?" Joseph asked, his voice surprisingly calm.

Tuya swallowed an hysterical surge of angry laughter. This should not be happening, but it was. Someone had taken great pains to arrange this trial, for the walls of the royal throne room were lined with somber-faced, wide-eyed onlookers.

Narmer held up a hand and turned to address the gathering. Studying the crowd, Tuya saw that a varied host of people had been assembled: nobles, warriors, priests, and many of the hunters who had accompanied Tuthmosis on the fateful trip. Thrusting his chest forward like a bantam rooster, Narmer preened before them, confident in his approach and performance.

"I was favored by the gods to reach the dying king before he breathed his last," Narmer said, pausing a moment to cast a look of compassionate concern toward Mutemwiya. "Anyone in the hunting party can support my words. They saw the king speak to me; they saw me bow in grief at his words."

"What words did my beloved husband speak?" Queen Mutemwiya said, leaning forward in interest.

Narmer hung his head. "It grieves me, gentle queen, to repeat our divine king's last words before your ears. For he revealed a shameful thing, a sorrow he has borne since his ascent to Egypt's throne."

"What sorrow?" The queen shot him a half-frightened look.

Narmer paused. "The divine Tuthmosis, on his way to

the otherworld, told me that one of his wives was guilty of the worst kind of disloyalty. He said the greatest of his sorrows was that Queen Tuya had given her love to Zaphenath-paneah."

An audible gasp rose from the assembled crowd, and Tuya closed her eyes, recognizing the trap in which she would be caught. Joseph stepped forward. "I do not believe you," he said, his voice ringing through the crowd in the unmistakable tone of authority. Several of the nobles whispered among themselves. The priests raised their eyebrows and slanted questions at one another.

"You dare question the dying words of a divine king?" Narmer asked.

"I dare question you," Joseph answered, his words quick and raw and tempered with anger. "And any charge brought before this throne must have witnesses to prove it."

A murmur of voices, a palpable tenseness, washed through the room, and Tuya felt the attention and suspicion shift to the man parading before her.

"Very well," Narmer said, setting his face into determined lines. "I have made investigation into this matter. With the aid of the gods, the pieces have fallen into place, and the picture shall be revealed this night, before this company. Before the sun-god takes his bark to ride across the sky, all you who hear shall know that the child you knew yesterday as the Crown Prince"—his bony finger pointed at Amenhotep—"is the child of Tuya, a former slave. And Pharaoh, before he died, told me he would surrender his life rather than accept the child forced upon him by Queen Tuya and his own vizier. They thought to make their illegitimate son into a king of Egypt!"

The crowd buzzed like insects in the tall grasses alongside the Nile. Tuya felt the room spin around her. The claim was ridiculous, but over the years she had seen Narmer insinuate his way into honors and positions far above his rightful station. The dark gods had gifted him with intelligence and cunning.

Queen Mutemwiya rose from her throne, though her hands clung to the armrests as if she stood in danger of collapsing before the crowd. "Prove this charge," she cried hoarsely. "Prove this, Narmer, and if you preserve the throne of Egypt from defilement, I will reward you! The people shall praise your name, and you will be honored above all men!"

Narmer bowed as if he had already won his case. "O Queen, live forever," he said, wrapping his heavy cloak about him in a theatrical gesture. "I shall do my best to serve you."

The litany of accusation began. Quaking beneath Narmer's fierce gaze, Tuya's servants testified that they had seen her walk in the garden every morning with the vizier and the prince. One girl admitted fetching Zaphenath-paneah to Queen Tuya's chambers in the dark of night. The prince's aged nurse told the crowd that the baby name of the Crown Prince had been "Yusef," a variation of the Hebrew "Joseph," the name by which Lady Tuya addressed the vizier. Abu, the goatherd from Potiphar's house, recounted the many occasions he spied upon Joseph and Tuya in the garden and told the gathering that everyone in Potiphar's household knew that the steward called Paneah and Tuya were deeply in love.

As the testimony against her droned on, Tuya felt her anger dissolve into despair. It would not matter that she had not yearned for Joseph in months. The witnesses were honest, and in its essence, the charge against her was true enough. She had been married to Pharaoh while her disloyal heart dreamed of another. Guilt avalanched over her, pressing her down with its weight, and she would have collapsed before the company had Joseph not stepped forward.

"These charges have nothing to do with the truth " he said, his elegant voice commanding attention and respect. "You have impugned the right of a prince to his throne. The child was fathered by Pharaoh. During the time of his conception and birth, I was a prisoner in the house of the captain of the guard."

A smirk crossed Narmer's face. "I would like Khamat to speak," he said, opening his hand to the crowd. The assembly rippled as an aged man stepped forward. "Khamat was the chief jailer of Potiphar's prison at the time of our vizier's imprisonment," Narmer explained. "He will tell you how Tuya's son came to be born. Khamat, tell these nobles how you allowed the slave Paneah to come and go at will in your prison. Tell them how you left a rope dangling for him to climb in and out of his pit, how you trusted him completely and in all things."

The old man glared at Narmer. After gazing at the crowd in defiance, he purposely knelt at Joseph's feet. Again, the crowd buzzed in speculation, and Narmer gestured to two guards who roughly jerked Khamat upright. "Speak," Narmer growled, "and tell the truth. You allowed Paneah to come and go freely, did you not?"

"Paneah was righteous and altogether honest," Khamat whispered, his voice like gravel in the stillness of the room. "He wanted to minister to others in the jail. But he did not leave the walls of the prison and venture into the house or the city beyond."

"Do you know this for a fact?" Narmer said, scowling. "Were you awake at every hour to watch him? You kept a rope suspended in his cell; at any time he could have climbed forth. He knew the prison well; he knew the house beyond; he knew how to sneak out in the dead of night and return before daybreak. He wormed his way into your confidence, old man, and convinced you that he was a humble servant, but look how he stands before you now!"

The old man studied Joseph's royal clothing and the Gold of Praise, then he met Joseph's gaze. His eyes crinkled as he smiled. "I see a man whom the gods have elevated," he said, his smile like sunshine in the room. "I know him as a man in whom the spirit of God resides. He would not commit this sin."

"The gods will decide his guilt, not you," Narmer snapped, gesturing for the guards to carry Khamat away.

Chike leaned forward and interrupted. "If he was confined in the prison, how are you to prove these things, Narmer?"

The captain of the guard paused only for a moment, then pressed his hands together as if he pondered a weighty matter. "It is said, most high priest, that our kings are divine because the gods visit our queens and plant seed in their wombs," he said, total conviction in his voice. "And you will recall that our divine Pharaoh recognized the spirit of a god in this one called Paneah. Khamat, foolish old man that he is, has just said the same thing."

Narmer paused and waved his hands for emphasis. "How can we say that his spirit did not depart from the prison and visit Pharaoh's wife in her chamber? Look at the boy! He walks and talks like the vizier, he holds his head in the same angle as this foreigner who entered Egypt as a slave! If the act of disloyalty was not accomplished in the physical body, then it was accomplished in the spiritual, for the boy you see before you is the spirit child of the vizier, and not of Pharaoh! It is recorded in the annals that on separate occasions, both the vizier and Queen Tuya came to Pharaoh many months ago and asked that the child be betrothed to Queen Mutemwiya in order to secure the succession. But our dying Pharaoh decried this act! Restore justice, high priest and counselors, and keep the royal throne from this illegitimate son who has no part in Egypt!"

Chike leaned forward to confer with several priests, but Tuya could see that they were not convinced that Narmer spoke the truth. Joseph himself was a powerful testimony to righteousness, for his visage and posture were regal, and the Egyptians were not quick to criticize or question those whom the gods had placed over them. But Narmer's words had cast a strong shadow of doubt upon Joseph's intentions and Amenhotep's lineage.

"Noble captain, I have something to say regarding this

matter," Mutemwiya said, standing again from her chair. She cleared her throat as if hesitant to speak, then cast her eyes to the ground. "My husband Tuthmosis loved me dearly and confided in me one night as we lay together. He told me that the gods had told him that he would father no children in this life, but that his heirs would follow in the life to come. That is why my womb remained barren. But as for this boy—"

She gestured toward Amenhotep and shrugged as if to say she did not know from where he had come. Tuya felt her cheeks burn as Amenhotep cringed. By all the gods, this was not right! Her son had done nothing wrong, nor had Joseph sinned. Pharaoh would rise from his grave if he knew what mischief his queen and captain were working on this night—

But if Mutemwiya could speak, so could she. "Can a mother not defend her child?" Tuya called, her voice ringing through the room.

"Please, speak," Narmer said, lifting his brows. "You have said nothing; we thought you had nothing to say."

"I have much to say," Tuya replied, eyeing Mutemwiya with a stern glance. "Amenhotep, my child, is Pharaoh's son. I loved Tuthmosis and was faithful to him from the day of our marriage."

"Do you deny that you loved Paneah?"

"I did love him, once," Tuya said, her voice softening at the memory. "As a young girl loves a young man. But that love faded in the light of adulthood, and in the light of my love for the king."

"And yet you are friends with Zaphenath-paneah."

"Yes, we are friends. He was a close advisor to Pharaoh, and is a tutor to the prince."

"Then tell us," Narmer's brows lifted the question, "to this day, why does the vizier himself bring a bowl of blue lotus blossoms to your chamber? What sweet token of love is this?"

The question brought a hushed silence to the throne

room, and Tuya felt the darkness of grief press down on her. "It is my husband's token of love," she whispered. "He promised me blue lotus blossoms every morning that we were apart. He said the vizier would bring them until he returned."

A stunned silence followed her declaration, but Narmer broke the hush with a sharp laugh. "Has the king," he said, turning to Queen Mutemwiya, "ever brought you flowers?"

A scowl crossed Mutemwiya's lovely face. "Why would a king bring worthless flowers?" she asked. "The king presents his women with gifts of gold and jewels. Ask any one of Pharaoh's wives. This woman lies."

"Tell the truth, if you can," Narmer said, turning to Tuya with new fervor in his eyes. He had tasted victory and knew the end of the struggle was near. "Is the prince a child of the divine Pharaoh?"

"Yes."

"How, then, do you explain his resemblance to the vizier?"

"He looks nothing like Joseph. He is his father's—"

At the mention of the word *Joseph*, Narmer held up an interrupting hand. "You have just used a Hebrew name, the same name you gave your son as a baby." He turned toward the crowd and paced before them, his hands thrust behind his back. "I believe, Queen Tuya, that you loved the vizier and were unfaithful to Pharaoh. This child, called Amenhotep, was born to you and fathered by the Hebrew. While in Potiphar's house, you fell under the spell of the god which resides in this man, and together you plotted to usurp the authority of the gods of Egypt. You have conspired to take the throne from the rightful rulers."

"No!"

"Then why are there no statues of Horus or Hapi or Osiris in your chambers?" Narmer said, stopping suddenly before the priests. "Why do you not offer gifts to the gods of Egypt? Tell us, lady, which god you worship."

The trap had been carefully laid, and Tuya suddenly realized how completely she had been snared. *Treason.* Yet unspoken, the word hung over her head like a mist, cutting off her breath. A moment ago she had been about to hang for the crime of adultery, and now with one false word she would condemn herself, her friend, and her son to the gallows.

Merciful God. Why have You allowed this to happen?

Narmer's exultant face blurred before her eyes, and she turned to Joseph. He stood like an oak between his guards, reducing them in his steadfast confidence to misshapen stumps of manhood. *Have faith*, his eyes seemed to say. *You have trusted the unseen God for others. Now trust Him for yourself.*

Tuya stared past her accuser's mocking face into her own thoughts. All her life she had clung to those she could love: Sagira, Joseph, Amenhotep, and Tuthmosis. One by one, her loved ones had been removed from her life, and she was left shipwrecked by grief, marooned on an island of doubts and fears. And yet gently, persistently, the Almighty God had sheltered her, protected her, and brought her to this place where she had no one left to trust but Him.

An old memory opened before her as if a curtain had been ripped aside. "Belief is a truth held in the mind, Tuya, but faith is a fire in the heart," Tuthmosis had told her once, explaining why he believed Zaphenath-paneah's prediction of famine. "My heart burns to know the Almighty God who could speak to me in a dream."

Her heart burned, too. Suddenly, in a breathless instant of release, faith freed her from fear. "I will tell you which God I serve," she said, turning to Narmer with a note of triumph in her voice. "I worship El Shaddai, the Almighty God, the Creator of heaven and earth. In Him alone do I trust."

Narmer was aghast. "You would cast aside the gods of Egypt?"

"I did not intend to cast them aside," she answered truthfully. "But I have found them helpless. The Almighty

God is greater than all and wiser than all. Pharaoh realized this, and for this reason he lifted Zaphenath-paneah to the position of vizier. And God knew that Pharaoh hungered after the true God, therefore God has saved Egypt."

"Bah!" Narmer shouted, turning from her with a disdainful wave of his hand. He gestured toward the priests. "Listen to this one, disloyal to her husband, her king, and her kingdom! Look at this boy who would claim Egypt's throne! See how he favors the vizier, for he has the same beauty and clarity of features—"

"The beauty is his mother's, not mine," Joseph said, commanding attention with only a nod of his head. "As God lives, I have fathered only two sons, Ephraim and Manasseh."

"You are not capable of such restraint," Narmer snarled, scowling at the vizier. "There is yet another witness who will come forward to testify to your misdeeds. One more voice will prove my contentions and our Pharaoh's dying words."

In a voice as cold as his eyes, Narmer turned toward the double doors of the throne room. "I call Sagira, widow of Potiphar, to speak to us!"

———

From the outer hall, Sagira heard the summons and nervously ran her hands over her gown. The doors swung open to admit her, and she blinked rapidly, a little afraid she had forgotten some item of dress in her hurry to answer the midnight summons. Narmer's messenger had been most explicit—she must appear, she was very important, she would be highly rewarded for her cooperation.

Her knees quivered as she stepped into the room, but she held her head high. She had not been invited to appear at the royal palace since Paneah's trial, and the magnificent room seemed broader and taller and more colorful than she remembered it. Her eyes were involuntarily drawn to the square of inlaid tiles where she had stood under a wedding canopy and received Potiphar as her husband. But that day belonged to another lifetime, to another, younger girl.

The mood of the gathering was somber, the faces around her drawn and tense. In the open space before the throne, Tuya stood between a pair of royal guards like a frail lily between two watchdogs. Across from Tuya, Paneah stood surrounded by six of Pharaoh's bodyguards. Drawn like a moth to a flame, Sagira stared at her beautiful former slave. She thought he nodded toward her in recognition, and she was puzzled by the friendliness in his smile.

Between the prisoners and the thrones, Narmer paced with the vigilance of a dog marking his boundaries. Wisely, he said nothing as she approached, allowing her to make a suitably impressive entrance, and Sagira took advantage of the silence to run her eyes over the crowd. The gathering included half a dozen men and women wearing the shaved heads and spotless robes of the priesthood, a few nobles, Paneah's stricken wife and her maids, and a remnant of Pharaoh's loyal guard. A dozen scribes sat in one corner, scribbling furiously to record this event for posterity. Upon her gilded chair, Queen Mutemwiya sat as regal and composed as ever, while the Crown Prince cowered upon a stool at her feet, his face pale and streaked with tears.

Sagira paused at the end of the aisle, accustomed to bowing before the throne. To whom was she supposed to give respect? Narmer must have sensed her discomfiture, for he cocked his head and launched immediately into a long recitation of her history. Sagira listened halfheartedly as her eyes drank in her surroundings. Everything in sight might have been hers if Ramla had spoken a true prophecy. But the priestess had lied. Sagira would die alone and forgotten, and she would die soon. The disease that had left her barren and bleeding was slowly robbing her of life. At thirty-three, she was not so much past her prime as having missed it altogether.

But she was still of royal blood, and by all rights she should have been included in the family members seated behind the throne. This conviction sent her spirits soaring, and she smiled broadly at the assembled crowd as Narmer finished his speech: "So, this gentle lady, the widow of Potiphar, can attest to Zaphenath-paneah's crime. She will prove his words false, for he has never been able to restrain himself when faced with a beautiful woman. He once attempted to force even her, his master's wife."

Like a many-eyed organism, the company turned to her. She met their eyes boldly, determined to face down the rumors that had circulated in Thebes for years. The gossips had called her a drunkard, a harlot, a fool, but she was better these days now that fortune had smiled upon her. She was the daughter of a princess, a widow with money and authority, a woman not to be underestimated.

A pair of mirror-brilliant eyes in the crowd before her caught Sagira's attention. Ramla! The priestess of Bastet stood behind Chike, her clawed hand dutifully folded at her waist, her head inclined as if in mild interest. But from those dark eyes blazed blind ambition, hunger, and zeal. The priestess nodded slowly, acknowledging Sagira's gaze, and flashed her brows in a silent signal: *Tell them, Sagira, what they want to know, and you will be rewarded. Narmer will allow you to assume your rightful place in the palace, and I will again be your priestess. Can you think we have not heard of your lonely and silent house? Tell them, Sagira. We are waiting.*

The intensity of those black eyes left Sagira feeling shaken. With an effort, she wrested her attention from Ramla and struggled to find her voice.

"Well?" Narmer questioned, leaning closer. "We are waiting for you to confirm the vizier's character."

"Pharaoh has already ruled on a trial regarding these accusations," Chike interrupted. "The divine Pharaoh declared Zaphenath-paneah innocent of all charges."

"But Lady Sagira did not recant her accusation," Narmer pointed out, his finger wagging like a scolding schoolteacher's. "What if the vizier's magic was strong enough to dupe even a god?"

A murmur of wonder rippled through the crowd, and Narmer again turned to Sagira. "We are waiting, Lady."

"I will speak," she began, glancing around. Tuya stood straight and tall between her guards, surprisingly youthful without her heavy wig. How could they have been childhood friends? Sagira felt as though she had lived fifty miserable years.

Reluctantly, Sagira's eyes lifted again to meet Paneah's. She expected to see revulsion, hatred, even resignation on his face, for had she not once destroyed him? Like the glorious Phoenix, Paneah had arisen from the ashes, but now Narmer extended the power with which she could destroy him again. With a handful of words she could take Paneah's unfairly favored life, snuff the intelligence from his exquisite eyes, and send his soul to the otherworld. He had to know what she was thinking, that her soul yearned to find significance . . . for *this* she would be remembered as long as the Nile flowed.

She lifted her eyes to his. An odd mingling of compassion and curiosity stirred in his face, as though he did not care what she might say, but felt pity for her need to say it. Pity! For her? She had received no pity from the nobles of Thebes, from the women of Pharaoh's court, or even from her own servants. Only Paneah and Tuya, once upon a long ago time, had ever shown her the slightest bit of sincere compassion or concern. The two most caring people in her life had also been the most loved, the most hated, and the most beautiful. . . .

Her blood ran thick with guilt. In quiet serenity, Paneah and Tuya stood beside her even now. Sagira had been surrounded by beauty throughout her life, but until this moment she had never realized that the beauty of Tuya and Paneah was not so much a physical manifestation as it was an inner one. The accused man standing beside her bore the fine wrinkles of his age with elegance. Gray hair sprouted from his temples, yet there was not a more striking man in the room. And though grief had left Tuya's pale face haggard and tense, her eyes shone with a confident peace Sagira had never known. Behind the throne, the ugliness of Ramla's fevered ambition raised its horrid head, the same prideful zeal that had convinced Sagira to consider herself inferior and despise the only true friend she had ever known. . . .

Abruptly, she turned to Chike and lifted her chin. "I want the entire assembly to know the truth," she said, her clear voice ringing through the crowd. "I tried to seduce my own slave, but he would not submit, nor would he be disloyal to his master. I believe Zaphenath-paneah to be incapable of disloyalty. He would not be unfaithful to Potiphar; he could not be unfaithful to Pharaoh. This inquest, this charade, is a naked attempt to steal the throne from Pharaoh's only son. If you must seek an adulteress, look to the woman who sits upon the throne. She and this man, Narmer, have been plotting to take the throne for years. Queen Mutemwiya plans to discredit the rightful prince, then marry Narmer and make him Pharaoh."

"She lies!" Mutemwiya shrieked, rising from her chair with such force that it toppled from the dais and clattered to the floor.

"No," Sagira said, slowly shaking her head. "I have no reason to lie and nothing to gain by falseness. Illness has shortened my days, and only by the blessing of the Almighty God will I live to see the land green again. Upon my life, I have spoken the truth."

Narmer stuttered in astonishment while Sagira prostrated herself on the floor before Amenhotep. After a moment of whispered consultation with his fellow priests, Chike stepped forward. "May Thoth, who judges the hearts of men, judge yours with mercy," he told Sagira as she stood to her feet before him. "May the Almighty God bless you for what you have done here tonight. I speak for the gods of Egypt, who approve an honest heart, but never a deceitful one."

The priests murmured in agreement with Chike, and one by one, they approached Amenhotep, who stood while they knelt before him.

"This is an outrage," Narmer said, finally finding his tongue. He stamped his sandaled foot upon the marble floor. "Pharaoh's dying words—"

"Are known to the Almighty God, but not to us," the vizier said, holding up his bound arms to be unloosed.

Sagira shivered in happiness when Zaphenath-paneah smiled at her in gratitude.

⟶ Thirty-seven ⟵

TWO MONTHS LATER, AS THE SUN CONTINUED TO
toast the Egyptian landscape, Pharaoh Tuthmosis IV was
laid to rest in his extraordinary tomb. With the blessing of
Queen Tuya, the high priest Chike appointed Zaphenath-
paneah to act as Amenhotep's regent until he came to an
age where he would be capable of ruling the kingdom. The
vizier inherited another title: "Father to Pharaoh." The fate
of the two conspirators, Narmer and Mutemwiya, was left
to Zaphenath-paneah, who decreed that the two should be
exiled in the empire of the Mitannis, far from Egypt's borders.

The trade routes over which the Egyptian guards escorted the two evildoers had widened considerably in the
last year, for men throughout the world had heard that grain
flowed like water in Egypt. Famine and drought had
shrilled over the entire earth, and foreigners from throughout civilization journeyed southward to trade in Egypt.
While the young pharaoh studied his lessons and prepared
to lead his country, the treasure houses of Egypt steadily
filled as the princes of the world brought gold and jewels
and silver in exchange for grain, that they might live and
not die. And the people of Egypt blessed Zaphenath-
paneah and their new king, for despite the famine, the hand
of a protecting God had made provision for their lives.

Tuya still walked in the gardens with Joseph and her
son, and often she stopped by the pool where the blue lotus
flowers bloomed in abundance. After plucking a flowering
stem, she would wrap the long tendrils around her bare arm

and fondly remember the boy who had grown into a man and a truly great king.

"You miss him, don't you?" Joseph asked one afternoon as she savored the fragrance of a blossom. Amenhotep was walking ahead of them, well beyond the range of their voices.

"Yes, I do," Tuya whispered, fingering the gentle petals of the flower. "I am sometimes sorry that I did not appreciate him sooner. He was a noble king and a wise man. He hungered for God in a way that few men do."

"I know." Joseph thrust his hands behind his back as they walked. "Amenhotep, you know, has a fine mind, sensitivity, and courage. He could be the greatest king Egypt has ever known."

Tuya smiled. "We shall see."

They walked on in companionable silence for a moment; then Joseph's eyes flashed when her gaze crossed his. He cleared his throat. "I do not want you to be lonely," he began, setting his jaw in determination. "And at last the time is right. Will you marry me, Tuya? There is no reason why you should not."

When her amazement had abated, Tuya laughed softly. "I can think of a good reason," she said, wrapped in the warmth of contentment. "Years ago, you told me about your father and his two wives."

"Leah and Rachel?"

"Yes." She stopped upon the path and turned to face him. "Your father loved one, and was kind to the other. And yet because he did not love them both, you and your family have greatly suffered."

Very tenderly she lifted his hand and pressed it to her cheek. "Asenath is a lovely woman, and you have two fine sons. You will not be happy loving one wife and offering kindness to the other."

His hand curved around her cheek, and he pressed his lips together, then nodded. A moment later he was gone, following Amenhotep. But Tuya remained on the path, rel-

ishing the warmth from his hand upon her face.

"And I, having known love, could not live on mere kindness," she murmured.

The hot wind blew the lotus plants on the water, and Tuya breathed in the sweet scent of them and smiled.